Lorenzo Carcaterra is the author of the memoir *A Safe Place* and the *New York Times* bestsellers *Sleepers*, *Apaches* and *Gangster*. He has written scripts for movies and television and is currently at work on his next novel.

Praise for Lorenzo Carcaterra

'An extraordinary read, like crossing *The Shawshank Redemption, State of Grace* and *Goodfellas*' TIME OUT

'Reads like a treatment for a Martin Scorcese script' INDEPENDENT

'A courtroom drama as gripping as any by Grisham' THE TIMES

'A brilliant, multilayered novel that breathes and bleeds on every page. This book transcends the genre of 'crime fiction'. It is a full-blooded novel, and an epic read' ROBERT CRAIS

'A quick, brutal tale' INDEPENDENT ON SUNDAY

'[A] tough, two-fisted tale of New York street-life and the victory of rough justice over the law' FINANCIAL TIMES

'Horrific . . . violent . . . a compelling and intense tale' EXPRESS

'Riveting . . . gripping . . . unexpectedly poignant'
SUNDAY TELEGRAPH

'An incredible tale of cruelty, endurance and revenge . . . impossible to put down' MAXIM

'If you are a Sopranos fan, this is the book for you . . . these people are fascinating, in the way tarantulas seen from a distance are fascinating. But one wouldn't want to get too close' IRISH TIMES

D0057246

ALSO BY LORENZO CARCATERRA

A SAFE PLACE:
THE TRUE STORY OF A FATHER, A SON, A MURDER
SLEEPERS
APACHES
GANGSTER
STREET BOYS

PARADISE CITY

LORENZO CARCATERRA

POCKET
BOOKS

LONDON · NEW YORK · SYDNEY · TORONTO

First published in Great Britain by Simon & Schuster UK Ltd, 2004
This edition first published by Pocket Books, 2005
An imprint of Simon & Schuster UK Ltd
A Viacom company

1 3 5 7 9 10 8 6 4 2

Simon & Schuster UK Ltd
Africa House
64–78 Kingsway
London WC2B 6AH

www.simonsays.co.uk

Simon & Schuster Australia
Sydney

A CIP catalogue record for this book is available from the British Library

ISBN 0 7434 9574 8
EAN 9780 7434 9574 5

Typeset by SX Composing DTP, Rayligh, Essex
Printed and bound in Great Britain by
Cox & Wyman Ltd, Reading, Berkshire

For my mother,
Signora Raffaela Carcaterra

January 8, 1922–March 6, 2004

Revenge triumphs over death; love spites it;
honor aspireth to it; grief flieth to it.

—FRANCIS BACON

PARADISE CITY

Prologue

The boy stared at the open coffin. He sat on the edge of a metal chair, his hands resting flat across his legs, his thin neck chafing under the heavy starch of a tight white shirt and black clip-on tie. He wore a black blazer handed down to him from a cousin in New Jersey he had never met and dark slacks with half-inch cuffs that brushed the tops of Buster Brown loafers. His thick white socks were stretched as far up as they would go.

His eyes, dark as winter clouds, never strayed as they focused on the face of the man in the coffin. The boy was three weeks removed from his fifteenth birthday and had never seen a dead body until this day. He had been to several funerals with his parents, but had always managed to keep a safe distance from the front of the musty rooms, relieved to let others grieve over the cold corpse of someone they loved. But this was one body he couldn't avoid. With this one, he was required to be up in the first row, sitting alongside his mother and next to his Aunt Theresa, her gnarled left hand occasionally reaching over and patting him on the center of his back.

This time the body in the coffin wasn't a distant relative or a neighbor. It wasn't a family friend who was seldom seen or an individual whose local standing required that respect be paid. This time the body in the coffin belonged to his father.

The room was crowded; somber and sobbing faces filled seven rows of chairs spread out eight across, most of them women dressed in black, eyes shielded by veils. The walls were lined with men in uncomfortable clothes, heads bowed, their talking restricted to muffled hisses, eyes looking away from the man many had known since they were young and living in another part of the world. There were four tall lamps placed in each corner of the room, low-watt bulbs giving off dim glows. A series of white votive candles had been placed around the edges of the coffin, their flickering flames licking at the ceiling. The room had wall-to-wall thin-ply carpet with a dark blue pattern that was faded in the corners and at the center. There was no door leading into the chamber, which could be reached from the top of the second-floor landing. To the right of the coffin was the guest book, its pages held open with a black felt-tip pen jammed in the middle, ready to be signed by each mourner.

The boy would have preferred to be alone. To be allowed to spend time with his father in a private way, free of the cries and shrieks of family and strangers. To whisper words meant only for his ears. To say a final good-bye.

The boy paid little attention to those around him. Instead, his eyes were fixed on the waxy glaze of his father's handsome face, harsh makeup giving the cheeks an artificial glint. The heavy odor of the undertaker's fluids and powders made his nostrils burn, and the greasy gel spread through his father's thick hair gave off the aroma of rain on a humid night. An ill-fitting dark suit did little to hide his father's muscular chest, but it did cover the three bullet holes that had sapped the life from his body. Three bullets fired from a gun whose owner would never be arrested.

The boy, even at such a tender age, was aware of the closed world he lived in. He knew it was a sphere where secrets were kept for decades, where ancient customs and rituals of a faraway country overruled the laws of a new homeland. On the streets of his East Bronx neighborhood, those customs required residents to live under the thumb of the Camorra, the harsh and brutal wing of the Neapolitan mafia. While most of his neighbors had come to America in pursuit of a dream, like his father's desire for a better life in a sweeter part of the world, the Camorristas arrived to further spread their control.

It was the leaders of the Camorra who decided who would live and who would die. They chose the men who worked, offering them steady jobs in the businesses under their control—the West Side docks, the Fourteenth Street meat market, the midtown garment centers, and the three area airports—in return for kickbacks often as high as half their weekly wages. One nod from a Camorrista and a man would be frozen out, forced to go without table money to feed his family until well on the brink of starvation, until he agreed to do the criminal's bidding. The Camorra arranged and approved marriages, always for a fee and often choosing the best brides for their own members. They lived without fear, as dismissive of New York's power structure as they had been of the elected officials in Naples. "They line everyone's pockets, especially their own," an old man once told the boy, his voice filled with a lifetime of bitterness, "only they use our money to do it. It's been true since I was your age and it will be true when you are mine."

The boy's father had been one of the few men who balked at the daily demands the Camorra made on his life. He had paid the bounty they claimed on his butcher's wages, but kept his distance, avoiding any contact with the gangsters who ruled the streets of his neighborhood. "Your father was a proud man," his mother told the boy the night of the murder. "A good man. No matter what others may ever tell you, you must always believe he died a hero."

The boy never said a word. He lowered his head and stepped out onto the fire escape that faced a long wall of tenements, ignoring the stream of visitors bearing sympathy and food.

He knew his father's killer was somewhere in the mourning room. He didn't need to turn his head or glance in the man's direction to know where he was, standing in the back, shaking hands, receiving his due respect, as if he were the host of a festive function. The boy didn't know why his father had been targeted by the Camorra, what a man who hadn't missed a day of work in six years could have done to incur their wrath. But he knew that Don Nicola Rossi had the answers he sought. The boy had known Don Nicola all his life and had even been to the majestic three-tiered house the gangster lived in, just across the street from Woodlawn Cemetery. He knew that all the money the men of his neighborhood kicked back from wages and high-interest loans found its way into his pockets. He knew the ones who didn't or couldn't pay back the full price suffered whatever loss he deemed necessary. Don Nicola didn't control the neighborhood as much as own it, and the lives of those who lived on its streets. His word was the only law that mattered and his verdicts were always final. And the boy knew it had been Don Nicola's verdict for his father to be shot dead, his body left lying between two parked cars on a side street off White Plains Road.

The boy took a deep breath and stood, taking several steps toward his father's coffin. He could feel the room grow quieter behind him and then turn absolutely still as he knelt on a wooden slab, hands folded in prayer, his face inches from the only man he had ever loved.

Giancarlo Lo Manto said that final prayer to his father with tears falling down the sides of his face, his lower lip trembling, head bowed, eyes closed. He followed the brief prayer with a silent vow and a promise. He would seek vengeance for his death as well as for all the other innocent men who had died as he had, on the vicious whim of a career criminal. He didn't know when or how he would do it, only that he would. Lo Manto pulled a folded note from his shirt pocket and kept it hidden in the palm of his right hand. He leaned closer to his father and gently slid the note into the side pocket of his blue jacket. He patted it in place, glanced down at his father, and kissed him gently on the forehead.

Lo Manto then stood and walked out of the room as silently as he had entered.

As a prince must be able to act just like a beast, he should learn from the fox and the lion; because the lion does not defend himself against traps, and the fox does not defend himself against wolves. So one has to be a fox in order to recognize traps, and a lion to frighten off wolves.

—NICCOLÒ MACHIAVELLI, *The Prince*

1

Giancarlo Lo Manto had his back against a ragged stone wall, a nine-millimeter gun in his hands, one bullet slipped into the chamber. He lowered his head and closed his eyes, alert to any sounds in the vestibule closest to apartment 3E. He could smell burnt meat sizzling in oil and he heard Eros Ramazzotti singing "Dammi la Luna" on a dusty CD. He knew most of the other apartments were empty at this hour on a Sunday morning—husbands, wives, and children off to morning mass and a casual outdoor breakfast before spending the rest of the day with relatives. He also knew the four men who lived in the small apartment in the middle of the hallway on the third floor had no plans for their day other than to lay low and wait for the sun to set.

Lo Manto opened his eyes and looked at the two men standing across the hall. They were each about a decade younger than he, dressed in civilian clothes but with Kevlar vests strapped over their shirts, guns in their hands and police IDs pinned to their jackets. They were nervous, their faces coated with thin lines of sweat, their eyes fixed on the dead-bolted door in front of them. Lo Manto glanced at his watch, then looked back up at the two officers and nodded. They moved to either side of the door and waited, hands wrapped around their weapons, eyes on Lo Manto, backs jammed hard against the wall. Lo Manto leaned his body into the apartment door and banged on it three times with the butt end of his gun. He waited through several seconds of silence, then repeated the knocks. He moved his shoulders off the door as soon as he heard the dead bolt snap free. He could feel the door give against the weight from the other side. He looked down and saw the doorknob turn slowly and then stop. Lo Manto took three steps back, stretched out his arms, and pointed his gun at the middle of the door.

Then they all waited for the first move.

Lo Manto had experienced a lifetime of these situations during his seventeen years on the Naples police force, the last eight working perhaps the most dangerous beat in all of Europe, the homicide division. He had enough scars on his body and enough long stays in hospital wards to know that what would soon happen would be decided within the snap of a second—and that luck as much as skill determined who died and who walked. He glanced at the two young officers assigned as

14

his backup, both woefully inexperienced for a one-man street takedown, let alone a break-in bust of four Camorra shooters. He could see their fear. They prayed to avoid moments such as those that were about to happen. Lo Manto's prayers, however, pointed in a different direction. His life was designed around pursuits, shoot-outs, and captures. He loved every second of being a street cop. He relished the piecing together of clues and working the streets to gather information he needed to build a case. He would circle his prey and then, once a criminal's mistake was made or an informant's tip proved accurate, make the move that would lead to either cuffs slapped on a pair of unwilling wrists or a body bag zippered over a hard-eyed face. It was during those moments of high tension, with lives on the line and where any one decision could prove fatal, that Lo Manto was most in control and in command.

It was a place where he truly belonged.

Lo Manto saw the door open a crack and made his move. He lowered his shoulder and rushed the door, sending the man behind it reeling, knocking over a chair and a flowerpot as he fell. Lo Manto rolled onto his knees and came up staring at four men, one on the floor and three spread across a tiny dining area, each with a gun in hand, cocked and pointed down at him. The two officers outside the apartment held their position as he had previously instructed them to do. "Who do I talk to?" Lo Manto asked, speaking in a full, rich Neapolitan dialect, his eyes moving slowly from one face to the next.

The skinny man in the center of the room nodded and lowered his gun. "Me," he said. "I'm in charge."

"Okay if I stand?" Lo Manto asked, easing one leg off the floor. "Makes it easier to talk."

"Leave the gun on the floor," the skinny man said. "And your hands at your side."

Lo Manto put his gun on the hardwood surface and stood. He straightened the collar of his thin black leather jacket and walked toward the table in the center of the room. He looked into the kitchen and saw a large pot of coffee resting on the front burner of the stove. "Why don't you pour me a cup," he said to the skinny man, "and I'll tell you why I'm here. Three sugars, but only if you make it strong."

Lo Manto pulled a wooden chair away from the Formica table and sat down, his eyes on the skinny man, his back to the three others. The skinny man jammed his gun into his waistband and stepped into the kitchen, reaching out his left hand for an empty cup. With his right, he lifted the pot from the stove to pour out a thin line of coffee. He put the pot back, walked to the table, and slid the cup toward Lo Manto. "We're out of sugar," the skinny man said. "You have to drink it the way I made it."

Lo Manto lifted the cup to his lips and swallowed two quick gulps. "It's a good cup of coffee, but not great," he said. "Has that harsh prison taste to it. You let it cook too long. You're not used to working with a stove after all those years brewing coffee by candle flame."

The skinny man reached for his gun, raised it, and pointed it at Lo Manto's chest. "You know how much I can make for shooting you dead?" he asked. "You have any idea what the Rossis would pay to see your funeral?"

Lo Manto casually finished the coffee and rested the cup on the edge of the table. "Two hundred and fifty thousand euros, last I heard," he said. "But they don't plan on paying it. That's why it's so high. So, if you kill me, they would then simply kill you. Which now brings me to the reason I'm here."

"I'm listening," the skinny man said, nodding at the three men behind Lo Manto. "We're all listening."

"I have a warrant in my jacket pocket to arrest the four of you," Lo Manto said. "That explains the business with the door and the reason for such an early visit."

"What's the charge?" the skinny man asked.

"I didn't read it all the way through," Lo Manto said. "But from what I did see, it fits your usual pattern. Attempted murder, drug possession, conspiracy and— I'd have to look again to make sure—kidnapping. With your records, a conviction on any one of those charges would have you making coffee by candlelight the rest of your lives."

"You're not arresting anybody," the skinny man said with a crooked smile that showed off a row of darkened lower teeth. "Not today and not with four guns pointed at you."

"I don't want to arrest you," Lo Manto said. "And with your help and a little bit of luck, I won't have to."

"What do you want?"

"A name," Lo Manto said bluntly. "And a place where I can find that name."

"Whose?"

"The man who killed Peppino Alvatar," Lo Manto said. "I want him and you know who he is and where he is."

The skinny man shook his head, the smile fading from his face. "I let you arrest me, all I get is a prison sentence. I give you that information, I get a death sentence. And I'm not looking to die."

"Take a minute and try to think smart," Lo Manto said. "Sooner or later, the Rossis are going to look to lose baggage like you. For all the good you do, you also cause a lot of grief. With each arrest, that's only going to get worse. They know your kind breaks and talks and they won't ever let that happen. Before that day comes, I can have your sentence for these fresh charges kept to a minimum. *But* I need a name and a place."

The skinny man held Lo Manto's look for several seconds, his breathing coming heavier, fingers stroking the sides of his handgun. "Maybe that's all true," he said. "But maybe all that goes away if I bring the Rossis something they've always wanted."

Lo Manto smiled and sat back in his chair. "Me?" he asked.

"You," the skinny man said. "Dead on their doorway.

After all I heard this morning, that sounds like the best deal of all."

"Some deals are tougher than others to close," Lo Manto said.

"Not this one," the skinny man said, raising his gun and cocking the trigger. Behind him, Lo Manto could hear the other three men step in closer.

Lo Manto kept his eyes on the skinny man and then slid off his chair and lifted the Formica table by the two front legs and swung it around the room, using it as a shield. From outside the apartment, the two officers tossed in three hissing smoke grenades and followed them into the tight quarters, guns drawn and aimed at the three men firing at the table. Lo Manto grabbed his nine-millimeter and fired off three quick rounds in the direction of the shooters, the apartment now completely engulfed in smoke. He heard two drop and left the third man to the officers who would be positioned against the walls closest to the foyer closets, giving them both leverage on the shooter and protection from any wayward shots. That left only the skinny man. He had run through the kitchen and was climbing over the terrace railing, his hands gripping the black iron bars of the railing. Lo Manto kicked aside the table and walked into the kitchen. He stopped at the base of the terrace and saw the skinny man hanging on the edges of the curled bars with two hands, gun buried inside his waistband.

"We got two down and one in cuffs, Inspector," the youngest of the two officers shouted out to Lo Manto.

"Wounded or dead?" Lo Manto asked without turning his head, eyes on the skinny man.

"One's alive," the officer said. "At least for the moment."

"Call for an ambulance and the morgue truck," Lo Manto said. "Then take your prisoner in to be booked. I'm going to spend a few more minutes with my friend."

Lo Manto looked past the skinny man and down into the tight backyard three floors down. "It's a broken leg at the very least," he said. "But that's if you fall right. You get yourself hung up on one of those lines or brush against those trees, who knows what can happen?"

The skinny man turned to look down and then back at Lo Manto. "Help me up," he said.

Lo Manto put his gun back against his spine and rested his arms on top of the iron railing. "I was only kidding before," he said to the skinny man. "I really did like that coffee you made. I'm going to get myself a second cup. While I'm gone, try to remember that name and place I was asking about."

"Help me up first," the skinny man said, his fingers starting to tremble from the grip he held on the curved bars.

In the kitchen, Lo Manto found a clean cup and poured himself some coffee, the smoke from the grenades washing past him like clouds. He looked toward the skinny man and smiled. "Are you sure you don't have any sugar?" he asked.

2

Lo Manto walked alongside his mother, her arm resting on the fold of his elbow, down the path of her lush backyard garden. On all sides of them, plants and bushes were in full summer bloom. The orange and lemon trees she had planted twenty-three years ago, soon after their move from New York City to the two-story stone house off Via Toledo, were now in the early stages of adulthood. His mother, Angela, fretted over her garden, worked and toiled over it much like a dedicated nurse hovered over a sick patient. He knew it was her way of letting the past rest, allowing her to put distance between her life in Naples and the turbulent one she had endured in America. In all the years since, in their many walks and talks together, neither one had ever made mention of their time in New York. It was as if those years were as deeply buried as the roots of the trees lining the garden walk.

Angela Lo Manto had buried her husband in Woodlawn Cemetery on a rainy Tuesday morning. By that Friday, she had sold what few belongings she had, closed her bank account, and booked three coach tickets to Rome for herself, her son, Giancarlo, and her daughter, Victoria. They traveled by train to Naples and spent their first three months in the city living with her mother's uncle Mario, a tram conductor and lifelong bachelor. She took a job in a neighborhood bakery, putting her skills to good use and, in ample time and with the help of small loans from several relatives, scraped together the down payment for the house off Via Toledo.

Lo Manto and his sister, then seventeen, had a difficult period of adjustment, which their mother would brush away with the wave of a hand and a shrug of her shoulders. "These things take time," she would tell them. "And when you're young, time is something you have in abundance."

Lo Manto missed his friends in the Bronx. He longed for Yankees baseball in the summer, Knicks basketball in the fall, and Giants football when the cold winds of winter were strong enough to push a man down a side street. He found it hard to turn his back on the only life he had known. Most of all, he thought it would be all but impossible to avenge the death of his father living in a city so far removed from where the crime had occurred.

In time, Lo Manto grew accustomed to his surroundings. He excelled at school, helped by the fact that he already spoke Italian. The slower pace of Neapolitan public education also proved less demanding than the daily curriculum of the Marist Brothers of the Bronx. He learned to appreciate the ins and outs of a heated soccer match, visualizing it as a speeded-up version of a baseball game, with all the intricate plays and moves that both sports demanded. He found a core group of solid friends whose company he enjoyed and whom he valued as much as those he had left behind. He loved the food and the temperament of the people of Naples. He loved to listen to the sounds of the women singing old ballads as they hung fresh wash out to dry, and the heated political arguments of the men standing in front of cafés at the end of another long workday. The people were loud, funny, stubborn, and kind as they forged a life on the streets of the toughest and poorest city in Italy.

Lo Manto was one week shy of his sixteenth birthday when he first discovered that the power of the Camorra resided in Naples as much as it did in New York. He was walking home from school, enjoying the gentle late fall breeze coming off the bay, when he heard a window shatter. He looked across the cobblestone street and saw three men in dark suits circle the owner of the produce shop, two with hands in their pants pockets, one holding open a notebook. They pinned the owner, a small, rumpled man in a wool work shirt and cuffed dark jeans, against the edge of a wooden stall, its rows filled with eggplants, artichokes, tomatoes, and escarole. The man with the notebook spoke in a low voice, his lips pressed to the shop owner's right ear, each word measured and deliberate, each vowel tinged with venom and threat.

Lo Manto stood in the entryway of a nineteenth-century three-story walk-up, its foyer steps done in marble, its wooden door polished enough to see a reflection, and he watched the scene play out—one he had witnessed many times in the Bronx neighborhood where he was raised. Now he knew the evil he thought had been left behind not only lived on the streets of his new city, it thrived. He studied the moves of the three men, so familiar to him by now—gestures and head tilts and smiles all meant to inspire fear—and decided that if he was to make the Camorra his own personal enemy, he needed to know everything he could about them. He needed to absorb himself in their history, embrace their tactics until he knew them well enough to be unleashed as a lethal weapon against their own members.

He would turn the predator into the prey.

"I left the water on for pasta," his mother said to him. "I made a fish sauce earlier this morning, spicy the way you like it and the way the doctor says I can't have it. This way we'll both be happy."

"Do you ever miss it?" he asked her, his back to her, plucking out two fresh tomatoes from her row of vines. "Life back in America, I mean."

"I remember it," she said, uncomfortable with the topic. "And will never forget it. That doesn't mean I miss it. It was just a part of my life."

"A lot has changed," he said, turning to face her. "The city you left behind is not the city you would find."

"The faces are different, but their hands still control

the lives of others," his mother said. "That will never change. You saw it as a child and you've seen it as a detective. The power will always belong to the ones who live in the dark. In that country and in this city."

"You sound like my boss," Lo Manto said, offering her a quick smile. "He told me he's been fighting the Camorra in Naples for thirty years. Arrested hundreds of them, shot and killed dozens more. And now, they're twice as strong as they were when he first put on a badge."

"Pietro is a very lucky man," Angela said. "He made it to an old age. I pray every day you do, too. This fight against the Camorra is not made for you to win, no matter how hard your battle."

"I don't expect to beat them all, Mama," Lo Manto said, handing his mother the fresh tomatoes. "Just one family is all I want."

Angela held the tomatoes against her chest, lowered her head, and led the way out of the garden and into her kitchen. "It's time to sit and eat," she said. "Forget about the Camorra. At least for one meal."

3

Lo Manto sat on the stone steps leading to the vast church of San Paolo Maggiore, opening his fourth pack of chewing gum of the day, waiting for an informant who was fifteen minutes late. He watched the sun fade in the distance, freeing the early evening winds to come down off the bay and refresh the humid city. He loved Naples at this time of day, the locals emerging from all quarters, free of work and eager for their nightly stroll. The men were dressed in starched shirts, creased trousers, and shiny loafers, jackets hanging loose off their shoulders. The women wore fine cotton dresses and low-heeled pumps, their hair flowing past their faces, bags hanging off their shoulders, their children eagerly keeping pace with their steps. In those minutes before dusk, the city turned into an open-air market for conversation and gossip, brimming with life. It was part of what made Naples such a special place to call home. And it was only then, as he looked out at the faces that walked past him, at the sights and sounds that so easily turned it into a magical city, that Lo Manto was able to forget the demons at the controls.

"What is it with you and churches?" the voice behind him asked. "You thinking of saving souls instead of arresting criminals?"

"Not even St. Peter has enough clout to save your soul," Lo Manto said.

He watched as the man moved down a step to sit next to him, a cigarette hanging from his mouth, his brown cotton jacket so dirty it shined. He was in his late twenties, thin, with a scraggly three-day growth, and long brown hair bunched together at his neck with bobby pins. He had teeth the color of yellow chalk, hazel eyes with lids that fluttered, and a half-moon scar over the top half of his right cheek. He was a habitual heroin user and had been one of Lo Manto's street sources for three years. His information was reliable and despite his status as a junkie, he seemed to be trusted by the lower-level Camorristas who sold him drugs. Lo Manto had made dozens of attempts to get his informant into one of the city's rehab centers and off the street life. Each time he met with failure, wasting effort and losing out on valuable information that might lead to yet another arrest.

"Did Alberto tell you what you wanted to know?" the informant asked.

"That's between me and Alberto," Lo Manto said, his coal-colored eyes still gazing out at the passing street traffic, the informant inching closer, his body an oil spill of drug sweat and body odor.

"They give you any trouble?" the informant asked. "Or was it a clean bust? Arrests don't upset the bosses as much as shootings do. They figure they can always get their men out of jail. All you can do at a wake is send flowers."

"Buy a paper, Pepe," Lo Manto said. "That's where I look when I want news. But when I want information, I turn to you. So, tell me what you came here to tell me."

"How do you know I have anything?" Pepe asked.

Lo Manto turned and looked at the weary young man flashing him a wide grin, cigarette clenched between his teeth, two of which looked to be sharp enough to draw blood. "I'd bet your life on it," he said.

Pepe lost the smile and the cigarette, crushing what little was left of the hand-rolled tobacco with the heel of a worn boot. "City's running dry, every skinner I know is waiting for a dealer to fill his bag. It hasn't been this tough to score since the pope came to visit, and that lasted only a few days."

"What's being done about it?" Lo Manto asked.

"There's something big on the way," Pepe said. "My dealer told me to make do until the middle of the week. By then, he'd have enough smack to keep me going for a full month. And prime grade, he said, not the kind that's sliced thinner than skin."

"Any word on where or when?"

"Don't know the time but I know the place," Pepe said, lighting a fresh Lord cigarette, hands shaky, long fingernails lined with a coat of dirt and dried blood.

"You going to tell me," Lo Manto said, "or are you going up to the church and confess it all to a priest?"

"This isn't just giving you a tip on a name," Pepe said. "This gets back and they hear I talked, then I'm floating in the bay without a head."

"If you're so worried about dying, you wouldn't be a heroin addict," Lo Manto said. "A bad batch will kill you long before the Camorra."

Pepe took a long drag on the cigarette, the smoke filtering through his nostrils and open lips. "Ercolano," he said. "It's always filled with tourists, walking in and out of the ruins. Perfect place to leave one package and pick up another."

Lo Manto stood and glanced down at Pepe. He pulled a fifty-euro bill from his jacket and shoved it into the front pocket of the addict's soiled shirt. "Since there aren't any drugs around to buy, get a good meal instead," he told him. "Maybe a shave and a haircut, if there's anything left over. And stay out of sight until this is cleaned up."

"With the Camorra, there's no such thing as out of sight," Pepe said to him, shielding his eyes against a disappearing sun. "More than anybody, you should know that."

Lo Manto stared out at the Bay of Naples. He sat on a rusty iron mooring, his legs dangling over the edge toward the lapping waves, his back to the city he had lived in since he left New York. He had finished high school in Naples and then did his mandatory two years of military service in the Italian navy, spending most of it on a rusty destroyer cruising the African coast. He toyed with the notion of returning to New York and joining the police force there but felt his time abroad would serve more as deterrent than advantage. Those were awkward years as he tried to grasp his bearings, a determined young man without a city to call his own. He was a New Yorker by birth and, based on the comments he heard, in attitude as well. But he was a Neapolitan at heart, finding comfort in the center of a maligned city. In time, he had learned to blend the strengths of the two cities, traveling from one to the other as he hunted down the members of the Rossi crime family, a syndicate entrenched in both places.

Lo Manto had filled out the forms, taken the exam, and gained acceptance to the Naples Police Department before he mentioned his career choice to his mother. As it was, it came as no surprise to her when he finally did break the news. She had long suspected her son of harboring a desire to avenge his father's death, but chose to bury the matter and not deal with it until it surfaced. "You can arrest every member of the Camorra," she told him when that day finally arrived. "Both here and in New York. And it won't bring your father back."

"This is for me," Lo Manto said, "not for my father."

"You can do so much better for yourself," his mother said. "You can go to the university. Find a line of work you will enjoy, not one that can get you killed. The Camorra are too big for one man to fight, Giancarlo. Even one with as much hate for them as you."

"You start by stopping one," Lo Manto said. "That much one man can do."

"How can you say that and still not believe this isn't about your father?" she asked.

"It's not about him," Lo Manto said. "It's about the next boy whose father might be killed for no reason other than he stood in their way."

"I pray for your father's soul every day," his mother said, turning her back to Lo Manto. "Now I'll say a second to help keep his son alive."

Lo Manto joined the Naples police force one week past his twenty-first birthday and was initially assigned to a street patrol unit designed to keep the main tourist areas free of vagrants, hookers, and pickpockets. It was boring and routine work, but Lo Manto turned the weakness of the beat into a future strength. He seldom arrested any of the street thieves he came across, working instead to build up a valuable network of confidants and informants who would, over time, grow in number and supply him with a steady stream of leads as he moved up the police ranks. He never judged what the hustlers and con men did in order to survive and feed their families, understanding how impossible it was for them to land steady employment in an impoverished city and how easy a lure it would be to grasp for the outstretched hand of the Camorra.

Lo Manto sought help for as much of the street population as he could: reaching out to the mother superior of a nearby convent to get a prostitute's daughter into a good preschool; finding an apartment for a homeless pickpocket with too many cold children huddled in corners. With an unemployment rate always hovering near the 20 percent mark and with corruption as much a part of the city's landscape as its churches, crime was not merely a choice but often the only alternative for thousands of its residents.

Within a few short years, his methods and his solid-as-steel word helped make Lo Manto one of the most trusted cops in Naples, the one the street crowd always turned to for a favor or a break. Lo Manto, meanwhile, utilized their help as he focused his attentions on the higher-ups in the criminal landscape, putting numerous dents in the stranglehold of the Camorra, doing damage to all, including the Rossi crime family, the most powerful of the organization's many branches. He began small, breaking open a half-dozen illicit gambling operations, often working on his own clock, as he pieced together the street info he was fed on a regular basis and inched his way into the heart of a vast criminal network. It didn't take Lo Manto long to discover that the Camorra's reach did not end at the doors of the local precincts. He caught the knowing nods and glances that passed between a suspect he was bringing in for booking and the detectives who mingled in the squad room. Graft was an accepted practice in Naples and the poorly paid and overworked members of the police department were not immune to its immediate and gratifying spoils. "You will find you are your only friend, Lo Manto," a bought-and-paid-for police inspector once told him. "And that is no way to survive, especially for a cop."

In addition to a vast amount of skill, Lo Manto also grabbed a handful of luck. His tactics, honesty, and impressive arrest record soon caught the attention of Pietro Bartoni, the commander of the Naples homicide division. The newspapers often referred to Bartoni as the Italian Eliot Ness, a son of a slain cop and a brilliant detective with a clean reputation and a stellar record of arrests and convictions. Bartoni had stood up to the weight of the Camorra for more than two decades and dozens of shoot-outs that left bodies strewn on both sides. When the time came for him to be promoted into a supervisory position, he wanted his replacement to be a detective who would never be satisfied with just one bust, one arrest. He wanted a detective who wanted to bring the Camorra to its knees, weaken it to the point of surrender. And he wanted a cop who was not available at any price.

Bartoni found that detective in Giancarlo Lo Manto.

Lo Manto studied under the master detective's supervision for ten years, working homicide and narcotics cases, the older cop marveling at his young protégé's interrogation skills and crime-solving abilities. "You can never go into a case thinking you're smarter than the man you are trying to snare," Bartoni had told Lo

Manto late one night, both men sitting in a corner of a dark trattoria after another successful takedown. "That leaves you open for mistakes. You must always be the one with the questions looking only for that one answer —how did he commit the crime? All your thoughts, all your actions, your entire time spent on the case should be directed toward finding that one response. The drive to get to that answer, the refusal to accept the inability to close out a case, is what stamps a detective as great."

"Do you remember all the ones you've solved?" Lo Manto asked him.

"No," Bartoni said. "Only the ones I didn't. Those you can never forget."

"Have there been many?"

"One would be too many," Bartoni said.

"What do you do?" he asked. "When that happens?"

"You learn to carry it with you," Bartoni said. "It's branded onto you like a scar. It's not like other jobs where a mistake or an occasional failure can be corrected. When you slip on that gun and badge, you take on all the good and bad it brings."

Lo Manto sat back and looked past Bartoni, gazing at a middle-aged man gently holding a sleeping infant to his chest. Bartoni was quick to catch the look and stayed quiet for several moments, lighting a fresh cigarette and pouring out the remains of his Peroni beer. "My father died when I was young, too," Bartoni said. "It left me angry and resentful for many years. I always felt there was something I could have done, should have done to save him. There's no real reason to feel that way, but you do."

"I couldn't have saved my father," Lo Manto said. "If I had been with him that night, they would have killed me too."

"But still you're driven by revenge," Bartoni said. "You want the Camorra to pay the price for what you lost."

"Wouldn't you?" Lo Manto asked, defiant as well as a bit defensive.

"Anger and revenge will help make you a great cop, Giancarlo," Bartoni said. "But they always leave in their wake a bitter man."

Lo Manto stared back hard at Bartoni. The older detective was an elegant-looking man, always stylish in dress and modest in temperament. His hair was a thick patch of white, kept razor-cut and combed back, matching the neatly trimmed Vandyke that helped give his tanned and lined face a regal look. He was slight of weight and build, his designer suits bought not through corruption but at a steep discount through a brother-in-law in the trade. The older members of the force referred to Bartoni as "The Baron," and he did nothing to distance himself from the name.

"Or a dead one," Lo Manto said.

Lo Manto turned his back to the bay and walked down a side street, heading toward his second-floor, five-room apartment near the Piazza Dante. He felt bone-weary;

his workout-solid thirty-eight-year-old body seemed to be aging at warp speed. He hadn't taken more than a week's vacation since he joined the force and the only extended absences he had were spent recuperating from various battle wounds. At Bartoni's urging, he had put in for a month's vacation and booked a stay at a resort on the isle of Capri. He needed the time away and would take it as soon as this latest drug deal in Ercolano was cleaned up. He was tired of being alone, of having so few around him to trust or confide in, wondering if he would ever catch the criminals he so desperately sought. He had been putting dents in Camorra enterprises for most of his seventeen years on the force, and despite all that, all the arrests and the drug seizures, they had only grown stronger in power. Pete Rossi, who replaced Don Nicola as overlord of the Camorra, lived in a Manhattan brownstone and was married to a woman stunning enough to be a model, with three young sons who would one day be trained for a business the family excelled in. And all Lo Manto had to show for his efforts was a long string of arrests credited to his record and a wide array of scars decorating his body.

He had grown into a double for his father. They both had thick dark hair, which Lo Manto kept long and loose over his ears and neck, and hot-coal eyes that pierced the skin. He was slightly taller than his father, standing at a firm six feet, and had his walk and many of his mannerisms. But the smile was Lo Manto's alone. It was as expressive and open as a sunrise, instantly capturing the heart of its intended target. He turned many a woman's head when he put it to proper use, usually to elicit information, but was shy in using it around the many young ladies his mother was always forcing him to meet.

He crossed against a red light, ignoring the angry yells of a driver in a red Fiat, and stepped into Piazza Dante. He slipped a hand into his pants pocket and pulled out a fresh pack of gum. He unwrapped three pieces and jammed them into his mouth. In most cultures, the pressure to marry by a certain age is strong. In a city as ancient in its thinking as Naples, it was almost unbearable. But Lo Manto never gave the idea any thought, no matter how much family and peer weight was brought to bear. He had no intention of leaving behind a widow, and in his line of work, with the crew he was determined to go up against, he believed that would be the only possible result.

Giancarlo Lo Manto wanted no one to waste her love and her years crying over his grave.

4

New York City
Summer 2003

Pete Rossi sat behind a thick mahogany desk, his back to a glassed-in view of the New York waterfront. His fingers rested on the arms of an Italian leather chair, his nails shiny and manicured. He had on a dark blue Armani suit and a blue-striped Tripler shirt, a blood-red tie knotted tight at the neck. His gold cuff links, with his initials embossed in their center, matched the gold pin holding his tie in place. He was thirty-two years old and *GQ*-handsome, his face tanned and wrinkle-free, his eyes winter dark and his rich brown hair combed back, two thick curls flopping at the edge of his forehead.

Rossi had an economics degree from Boston University and an MBA from New York University, graduating at the top of his class at each school. He was the president of a multimillion-dollar import-export house and had financial interests in three Manhattan restaurants and a

Bronx catering hall. He steered clear of the stock market, investing his spare cash in municipal bonds, T-bills, and European cell phone enterprises. He was married and had maintained a hectic social schedule, his face gracing the gossip pages of the city's tabloids as often as it did the financial broadsheets. To those who followed the day-to-day activities of the business world, Pete Rossi was a young man on the rise.

In the criminal world, he was already there.

He was the youngest and most powerful of the Camorra dons, the poster child for the syndicate's new and intricate way of controlling their criminal base. Decades earlier, the Camorra rulers had decided to leave the headlines and the page-one arrests to their counterparts in Sicily, the Mafia. There was no profit in doing business in such a way and no gain to be had in advertising and flaunting their behavior. Instead, the Camorra chose quietly to raise their own members. They would recruit from impoverished families in Naples who were either in debt to them or eager to see a son set free into the world with the guarantee of a prime education and a chance to flee a life of despair and ruin. The elders studied each child and fit the schooling to match the boy's skills, covering every base from medicine to finance. Within the span of four decades, the Camorra had infiltrated every ring of life both in Naples and New York, their surface legitimate, their dirty and more profitable work done in silence and cloaked in darkness. Among thousands of recruits, there had been no better match for the Camorra than Pete Rossi, the son of a respected don.

Rossi took a deep breath and looked up from his ledger at the older man who sat across his desk, an unlit Cuban cigar in his right hand. "He's got somebody on the inside tipping him off," Rossi said, sitting back against the cool leather of the chair. "A street informant can only know or hear so much."

"Whoever it is, he can't be that high up the circle," the man said. "Otherwise, this cop be making bigger trouble for us."

"He interrupted a hundred-fifty million in business last year alone," Rossi said, a tinge of anger to his voice. "How much more trouble you looking to get from him, Frank?"

"He's one guy, is what I'm saying," Frank said. "We can handle one guy."

"I think it's time we did," Rossi said. "We can't even let one step on us in any way. It might start to encourage others."

Frank Silvestri stood up from his chair, placed a pair of thick, pudgy hands into the pockets of his tailored pants, and walked toward the large window. He stared down at the waterfront. Silvestri was in his early fifties and had been a member of the Camorra since he was an eight-year-old abandoned on the streets of Naples by a young mother too desperate and deranged to raise her only son. The Camorra had tried the restless boy in a number of schools, but none seemed to fit his volatile personality. A year spent with the monks in an academy near Monte Cassino, just outside Salerno, helped curb his temper and taught him the value of patience. In time, Silvestri, tall and muscular and with a boxer's stamina, matched his brawn to his brain and became an invaluable soldier to Pete Rossi's father, Don Nicola.

Silvestri knew when to attack and when to lay low. He learned early on that while it might be easier to exploit an enemy's weak spot, it would be much more effective as well as profitable in the long run to destroy him by going against his strength. This method would not only put him in control of someone he had defeated but would eliminate any attempt at retribution through the sheer power of fear. When it came time for the old don to name a right hand for his son to turn to for counsel and strategy, he knew he would find no one better suited for the position than Frank Silvestri.

"He's a fly hovering over shit," Frank said, his steel gray eyes following a garbage ship running down the center of the Hudson. "Let the locals handle him. There's no reason for us to get our hands in this. Not at this level, anyway."

"The locals have had a shot at him since he was on the force," Rossi said. "Hell, I was still in high school and you were still chasing guys behind on their loans when he first became a cop. They didn't stop him then, they're not stopping him now."

"I'll keep an eye on him, if that's what you want," Silvestri said. "Maybe put a tag on his head, give the locals a paycheck for their troubles. Other than that, I don't think he's worth us getting too involved."

"We *are* involved," Rossi said. His voice was low and ominous, his eyes, gazing up at Silvestri, hard and unwavering. "And we've *been* involved from the start. This isn't a cop looking to make captain before he retires. This is a guy out to stamp us. And he's doing it in his own way and in his own time."

Silvestri turned away from the window and walked closer to Rossi. "You know him?" he asked.

"We've never met," Rossi said. "But I know enough about him to know I want him out of our business."

"So, it's personal, then," Silvestri said.

"Anytime you touch our business, it's personal," Rossi said.

"I can put a team on him," Silvestri said. "Have them in place by the end of the week. Sooner than later, they'll paint the target."

"No," Rossi said, slowly shaking his head. "No farm jobs. I want to send a signal. It should be us that puts him flat."

Silvestri looked down at the polished wood floor, the shine clear enough to give off a reflection. He had been in the Camorra most of his life and had learned many lessons during those years. Those lessons had helped make him a rich man, owner of three homes, with several million dollars safely washed and stashed in a half-dozen offshore accounts. The most valuable of those lessons had been the easiest to learn—know your don even better than you know yourself. Anticipate his moves, learn to adjust to his mood swings, and, most important of all, quickly grasp when a decision is grounded not on sound business reasoning but on personal motivation. Silvestri's old boss, Don Nicola, was a hot-tempered man, making it often difficult to divide the business end of the ledger from the personal. He was an old-school don, in line with the modern way of running a crime family, but more suited to the knife and gun ways of the past. To Don Nicola, *every* decision was a personal one.

Pete Rossi was cut from a thicker cloth. He shielded his emotions and buried his motives, even from the tight circle of advisers he had known since he was a child. He didn't need to be taught not to trust too willingly; that seemed as much a part of his personality as his taste in expensive clothes, fine wine, and antique cars. He sought advice to reinforce a decision he had already made, not to help him decide which direction to go in. He was a model don, the brutal face of his business brilliantly shielded behind the mask of civility he presented to the outside world. So Silvestri understood without having to be told more than he already knew that this situation with the cop in Naples meant more to Pete Rossi than clearing away a dent in the family business.

"You want me there to handle it?" Silvestri said. "I can be in Naples by midweek."

"No," Rossi said, in a whisper of a voice. "Let's bring him to us. It's time for this cop to come home. He deserves to die in the city where he was born."

5

Ercolano, Italy
Summer 2003

Lo Manto stood in the center of the House of Telephus, staring at the first-century relief that narrated the tale of Achilles. He stood apart from the small throng of two dozen tourists, an odd mix of German, Italian, and British, all listening intently as a young tour guide explained in three languages the history of the myth that had lasted centuries. He stepped back into the cool shadows of the long hall, watching as the tourists took pictures and ran their hands across the wall of ruins. He rested his head against the cool stone, closed his eyes, and listened to the droning voice of the college-aged guide rattle off a speech he had already given to three other groups that morning.

Ercolano was home to Herculaneum, which, like everything else in Naples and the land that neighbored the city, had spent several centuries under Greek rule. It wasn't until 89 B.C. that the town fell into the hands of the Roman Empire and was turned into a residential municipality and resort. The eruption of Mount Vesuvius in A.D. 79 brought the tranquil period to an end, and the lava that had buried Pompeii left Herculaneum covered with a deep layer of mud. In the eighteenth century, a long period of excavations helped to uncover the Roman houses that had been structured in a rectangular order, including one such home, the Villa dei Papiri, that the tour guides claimed was the inspiration for the J. Paul Getty Museum in Malibu, California. It was a place rich in history and touched by the hands of honor. And now, it was less than fifteen minutes removed from being the location of a million-euro drug deal.

Lo Manto had walked the path of the ruins many times in his life, both as a teenager and as an adult. He found pleasure in each new ancient discovery, his trips feeding an insatiable curiosity in history, one of a hand-ful of hobbies that consumed him, each designed, in its own peculiar fashion, to make him a better detective. His firm belief, and one that had been reinforced many times by Bartoni, was that a wide and wealthy range of knowledge, in combination with a finely honed brand of street savvy, would be the deadliest combination for an enemy of the Camorra. So, Lo Manto made it his business to learn. He haunted the dark halls of museums and art galleries. He read the great works of literature as well as the latest bestsellers. He consumed a wide array of magazines and newspapers, keeping current with events of the day as well as those from past centuries. He loved the old movies of Vittorio De Sica and Roberto Rossellini and the modern brilliance of Martin Scorsese and Michael Mann. He was comfortable with the sweet sounds of Tony Bennett and the pounding beats of Italian and American hip-hop and rap. He was a fixture in the cavernous halls of the Naples Public Library, known by name and face to the librarians who worked in silence as he read books under the dim light, sipping iced espresso as he gently turned the pages of each new book.

He had helped chisel his own private world, removing himself mentally from the dangers of his job and the ghosts of his past. He cast a wide net with his choice of reading. He devoured books on organized crime, allowing him to see the apparent links and patterns among the Japanese Yakuza, Sicilian Mafia, Chinese Triads, Russian gangs, and the Camorra. He was current on forensics and the latest technology used by international police forces to snare criminals and by organized crime members to avoid detection. He read biographies of world leaders, celebrities, and military men, always eager to find what common thread they might have all shared to drive them to their goals. He was especially drawn to stories about fathers and sons, trying to find in those tales signs of the bonds he had longed for since the death of his father.

Lo Manto was a well-rounded man. That, in turn, helped make him an even better and much more dangerous cop. "The most experienced man on the force will tell you that in order to catch a criminal, you must think and act like one," Bartoni said to him during one of their many late-night stakeouts. "And anyone who believes that is a fool. The average criminal is an idiot and yet most of them spend their lives without ever once getting caught. That's what thinking like them gets you. If you truly want to trap the rat, then you must be smarter, better, more cunning, know everything they know, plus everything they can't even conceive of knowing. For a detective to be great, his brain must be as important a weapon to him as his gun."

Lo Manto stepped out into the glaring sun, walking past the House of the Gems, when he spotted the man with the backpack. He was tall, thin, wearing granny glasses, blue jeans, a polo shirt, and a Milano soccer cap. He stood near the group but only feigned listening to the tour guide, whose enthusiasm never wavered, eager to tell all the history lessons he had spent hours burning into memory. The man pulled a cigarette from the back of his jeans, lit it, and took a long drag, blowing a thin line of smoke toward a cloudless sky. The ocean blue backpack was full and weighed down on the thin man's shoulders, forcing him to move with a slight hunch. Lo Manto eased into the middle of the small crowd, scanning the faces, seeing nothing much beyond tourists out for a morning walk and talk. He figured there would be three for the drop and pick—one with the money, one with the dope, and a pistol to cover both. And they would know not to send the obvious, since a street hood would shine like a fog light in this group and this setting. Which meant he needed to seek out the least likely suspects.

He caught the glance at the gymnasium area, along the large pool, which centuries earlier had been used by Roman athletes preparing for their games. It was a quick eye exchange between the tour guide and an elderly woman in a blue dress and a straw hat, her arm resting gently under the folded elbow of a white-haired man in a loud print shirt. The man held a cooler in his free hand, its weight forcing his body to shift; occasionally, he rested it on the stone ground. Lo Manto checked his watch: fifteen minutes till the end of the tour. At which point everyone would be directed back to the waiting bus. But he had been on enough of these to know that there were always a few who stayed behind, squeezing in one more photo or one more question for the tour guide to answer.

Lo Manto pulled a disposable camera from his shirt pocket and clicked off several shots, capturing the regal bronze statue, with the thin man with the backpack in the foreground. He got a wide shot of the refectory, the elderly couple standing right in the middle of his photo. Then he walked over toward the tour guide, who was standing off to the side of the group, allowing them a few minutes to take in the scenery. Lo Manto held out his camera. "Would it be too much trouble?" he asked the guide. "It's really for my mother. She's too old to get around. So she likes to see the tours through my pictures."

The guide stared at Lo Manto for several seconds and then nodded. "I can't ever say no to my mother," he said. "How could I say no to someone else's?"

Lo Manto handed him the camera and caught the slight bulge on the right side of the guide's shirt. He figured it for a Luger, the perfect gun for an up-close shooting. "The only shame is that I'll be in the picture," Lo Manto said. "Ruining all the beauty that surrounds us both."

"I'm sure your mother won't notice," the tour guide said. He lifted the camera, waited for Lo Manto to get into position, brought it closer to his eye, and clicked off two shots. He then handed the camera back to an approaching Lo Manto. "The second one is in case I left you without a head on the first," the guide said. "It's a specialty of mine."

"My mother will be pleased, however the photos turn out," Lo Manto said, taking back the camera.

"I think we've seen enough of this room," the guide said, easing his way past Lo Manto. "And we still have two more stops left to go before we're at an end. And I always like to finish my tours on time."

"It's a good summer job for a student," Lo Manto said, walking with him back to the scattered group. "The salaries are low, but the tips from the tourists help make up for that. And it doesn't take up too much time, leaving you free to pursue any other interests."

"I'm majoring in ancient history at the university," the guide said. "And a job like this one looks great on a résumé."

"But drug dealing doesn't," Lo Manto said, watching as the tour guide slowed his movements, instinctively raising his right hand toward his gun.

"I have to get back to work," the guide said. "There isn't much time left."

"Then let's make the most of it," Lo Manto said, running a hand against the front flap of his sports shirt, giving the guide a glimpse of his badge. "You let the plan play out. Let the old couple and the one with the backpack go with the exchange at the end of the tour. Make sure the gun they gave you stays strapped where it is. And we all walk happily away."

"I don't know what you're talking about," the guide said, a thin line of sweat beads forming on his upper lip.

"I'm talking about fifteen years of your life," Lo Manto said. "That's how much prison time you'll be saving by doing what I tell you. And that's only if the deal goes down without a glitch. That happens and you reach for that gun, you've at least picked a beautiful place to die."

"I've never done something like this," the guide said.

"I don't care," Lo Manto said. "Just don't do it now."

"I have to," the guide said. "I don't have a choice."

"I'm giving you one," Lo Manto said. "I don't know how you got into this, but if you let me, I can get you out."

"They have my brother," the guide said, staring over at Lo Manto. "If I make this deal happen, I get him back. And they'll clear away all his debts."

Lo Manto looked back at the boy, gazing into a sad but determined set of dark eyes. "Finish the rest of your tour," he told him. "They're waiting."

They reached the gathered group and Lo Manto moved toward the rear of the circle, the thin man to his left and the elderly couple to his right. He looked at the tour guide and then followed the crowd out of the gymnasium toward the House of the Stags, one of the more elaborate homes left standing in Herculaneum. He stood over by the arbor that had a view of the Bay of Naples and watched the sun sparkle on the shiny waves, content to let the final minutes of the tour come to an uneventful end.

The crowd had dispersed, most of them heading for the air-conditioned bus, a few making their way to a stand selling fresh ices and fruit drinks. The elderly couple and the thin man with the backpack lingered behind, standing in front of the Trellis House, one of the few ancient multi-family dwellings remaining in Europe. The old man placed the cooler next to his right leg, while the thin man dropped the backpack alongside it. The tour guide stood with his back to them, his eyes fixed on Lo Manto, his hand resting on his hip, fingers touching the top of his gun.

Lo Manto slipped a slice of gum into his mouth and walked closer to them. He was calm, prepared for either a shoot-out or a settlement, having weighed that the likelihood of either one happening depended more on what he said than on what he did. Lo Manto was less than four feet away from the tour guide when he saw the old man reach down and pick up the backpack and with a great deal of effort toss it across his shoulders, his wife helping to steady it in its place. The thin man slowly straddled the cooler, hands in his pockets, a fresh cigarette between his lips.

"Let them have it," the guide said to Lo Manto. "If I don't help them make this deal today, someone else will tomorrow, so what difference does it all make?"

"Part of your job to let them know the deal is done?" Lo Manto asked.

"Yes," the guide said. "When I call in, that's when they let my brother loose."

"Then do two favors for me," Lo Manto said. "Call your contact now and tell him the exchange was made and everything's the way it's supposed to be, no problems."

Lo Manto walked past the guide and toward the elderly couple and the thin man. "What's the second one?" the tour guide asked.

Lo Manto turned back toward the guide. "Trust me," he said to him.

"I've been looking everywhere for those," Lo Manto said, standing between the old couple and the thin man. "A cooler and a backpack. Do you have any idea how hard it is to find them in Naples? It's almost impossible. You're better off looking for gold."

"Most department stores sell them," the old man said,

the front of his shirt tinged with sweat. Next to him, his wife nervously bit at her lower lip. "I'm sure you'll find one, if you keep looking."

"But who really has that kind of time?" Lo Manto said. "And the ones I'd buy in any store wouldn't have in them what I really want. So it would all be a wasted trip."

The thin man looked past Lo Manto at the guide, nodding his head, the cigarette smoke forcing one of his eyes shut.

"Right now you're just couriers," Lo Manto said, his eyes moving from one to the other. "Maybe doing what you're doing for reasons beyond your control. That shouldn't come with a lot of jail time, if any at all. And two of you are too old to die in prison and one of you is too young to go."

Tears ran down the sides of the old woman's face; her hand gripped her husband's arm. The thin man's shoulders sagged and the cigarette fell from his lips to the ground. The old man was the only one who remained defiant. "What will you do?" he asked Lo Manto. "Keep the money and sell them back the drugs? Is that how you earn your way?"

"No," Lo Manto said, shaking his head. "It isn't. But it's not a bad idea. Truth is, it's one of the best ideas I've heard in a long time."

Lo Manto reached down and picked up the cooler. He then waited as the old man slid the backpack off his shoulder and handed it to him. "Where were your drop points?" he asked.

"Halfway up the courthouse steps," the old man said. "I was told to leave the backpack there at six-fifteen and then walk away."

Lo Manto looked at the thin man, waiting for his answer, sensing a mixture of arrogance and mistrust in both attitude and manner. "And you?" he asked.

"A church," the thin man said.

Lo Manto smiled. "Any one in particular?" he said. "Or did they leave the heavy thinking to you?"

"San Lorenzo Maggiore," the thin man said in a low voice. "At seven o'clock."

Lo Manto turned to the tour guide standing just beyond his right shoulder. "Your call go through?"

"Yes," the guide said. "I told them the deal went and the packages were on their way."

Lo Manto put down the backpack and unzipped it. It was jammed with thick packets of one-hundred-euro bills, each one double-wrapped with rubber bands. He grabbed two and zipped the backpack. He walked over to the tour guide and handed him the two packets of cash.

"Find your brother," he told the guide. "Then the two of you pack what you can as fast as you can and leave Naples."

"And go where?" the guide asked.

"It's your choice," Lo Manto said. "Don't tell me. Don't tell anybody. Just go. Be on your way out of the city before the first drop is made."

"What if they come looking for us?" he asked,

apprehensive, his eyes darting past Lo Manto and toward the three standing at his back. "What if they come looking for all of us?"

"They won't," Lo Manto said. "You're not that important to them, and neither is your brother. None of you are. It's the drugs and money they need. And it's the one who took it they'll want. That brings it down to me."

The guide slid the money under the waistband of his beltless pants and then looked back up at Lo Manto. "I can't repay you," he said, nodding his thanks.

"Then it's a good thing it's not my money," Lo Manto said.

Lo Manto watched as the guide turned near the House of the Bicentenary and disappeared from sight. He walked over to the elderly couple and the thin man, offering each a piece of gum. The old woman reached for hers with a trembling hand.

"What about us?" the thin man asked, rejecting the gum, his diffidence not doing much to mask his concern. "How much you going to give us to go away?"

"He finished the job he was given," Lo Manto said. "You're only halfway through yours."

"We can't go back empty-handed," the old man said. "And we can't tell them what happened. We must hold up our end of the deal if we're to come out of this alive. If it were only my life at stake, I wouldn't care. But there are others involved, all of them innocent, my wife included."

"You'll keep to the deal," Lo Manto said. "The only new wrinkle is me, and the only one who knows about me is you."

"They'll kill us all if they even *see* us with you," the thin man said, his voice breaking. "Not that you even care what happens to us. All you want is an arrest."

Lo Manto looked at the old woman, her body shaking, her face wet with a cold sweat. "How about you save the see-Naples-and-die scenario for your next visit?" he said to the thin man. "For now, you just do exactly what I tell you. If that happens and you have any kind of luck, then the only people who might end up dead will be the ones who forced you into this mess."

"I hope you're good at what you do," the elderly woman said to Lo Manto, resting a rail thin hand on his arm.

"We'll know soon enough," he said.

Lo Manto wrapped the backpack around his shoulders, picked up the cooler, and led the way out of the ancient city of Herculaneum, heading for his car and the short journey back to the streets of Naples.

Lo Manto sat behind the wheel of a black Mercedes sedan, its window down, across the street from the main courthouse in Naples. He watched as a young man in a leather jacket and designer jeans walked up the stone steps and headed for the abandoned backpack, his eyes scanning the antlike army of lawyers, judges, defendants, and tourists making their way out of the building and onto the bustling boulevard. The thin man from the walking tour was next to him on the passenger side. Lo Manto had phoned ahead and ordered a police escort to the train station for the elderly couple, complete with two first-class rail tickets to Milan and enough pocket money to steer them clear of trouble for at least a week.

"That's the one who approached me," the thin man said, pointing a finger past Lo Manto and toward the courthouse steps.

"But he's not the one I want," Lo Manto said. "He gets paid to run errands. My guess is he'll drop the pack in the trunk of the dark blue sedan parked next to the restaurant and then call it a day."

"What happens then?"

"We'll follow the sedan to San Lorenzo Maggiore," Lo Manto said. "I'll get us there a few minutes before they do. Then, you get out, leave your cooler in the designated pew, and get on with the rest of your life."

"You gave the tour guide a bundle and set off the old couple just right," the thin man said. "What do I have coming toward my end?"

"Nothing," Lo Manto said, his eyes fixed on the man on the steps and the parked sedan.

"Why did they rate the special treatment?"

Lo Manto turned and looked at the thin man, his eyes hard, his voice controlled. "They're civilians," he said. "They got tossed into this because of family troubles and gambling debts. But you're Camorra. Or even worse, a wannabe Camorrista. So the only break you're catching

57

is that I'm not going to arrest you or shoot you. At least not today."

"And for that I'm supposed to thank you?" the thin man asked.

"No," Lo Manto said, turning his attention back to the street. "For that you're supposed to shut up and follow my plan. Remember, it's the cooler that's important, not the idiot they got to put it there."

"How do you know I won't make a phone call soon as I'm out of your sight?" the thin man asked. "Make points with the bosses. Tell them what happened and who it was that took them off?"

"Actually, I'm counting on you to do just that," Lo Manto said. "But before you do, keep in mind how poorly they react to bad news. And they're going to have a lot of questions and are going to expect you to have all the answers. A wannabe like you ready for the kind of heat that brings?"

"What's to tell?" the thin man said. "They got taken by a cop on the loose. They'll figure that out pretty much on their own when you arrest them all."

"I'm not going to arrest anybody," Lo Manto said. "The people in that car, the guy on those steps—none of them have broken any laws. None that matter to me, anyway."

"There's a million euros in that backpack," the thin man said. "And heroin worth more than twice that in this cooler. That's not enough for you?"

"There's no money in that backpack," Lo Manto

said. "Just a bunch of old rocks from Herculaneum. I don't know if they're worth anything, but I doubt it'll come anywhere close to a million euros. What cash was in there is in my trunk and will be on my boss's desk later tonight."

"What about the cooler?" the thin man said, checking to make sure it was still in the middle of the backseat.

"I bought a block of ice from the fruit vendor at the entrance to the ruins," Lo Manto said. "The drugs are near the money. I'll drop them off later, just as soon as I get rid of you."

The thin man stared at Lo Manto, his lower lip hanging open, his eyes cast wide in amazement. "So why are you even bothering to follow them?" he asked. "You know nothing's going to go down."

Lo Manto watched as the young man dropped the backpack into the open trunk of the waiting sedan, slammed it shut, and then hustled away around the closest corner. He turned the ignition key, letting the engine purr for a few seconds. He waited until the sedan pulled away from the restaurant, then shifted into gear and slowly eased the car out into the congested traffic. He then turned to the bewildered thin man by his side. "To see it through," Lo Manto said. "Make sure it happens right. Everything I do, I like to see through to the end."

6

The chief inspector put a match to the packed end of his thin cigar and sat back, his silver hair resting against the soft fold of a brown leather chair. On the carpeted floor, beside his black briefcase, rested a dozen wide stacks of euros and ten thick packs of heroin. Bartoni looked across at Lo Manto, sitting with his legs spread out, feet crossed one over the other, and smiled at his enterprising protégé. "There will be a great deal of tears shed over pasta bowls tonight," Bartoni said. "This haul was meant to fall like heavy rain over the drug addicts of Naples. Now, bodies will fall in its place. Camorra bodies."

"The deal was worked through a Camorra crew working out of Margellina," Lo Manto said. "A haul like this would have gone a long way toward showing the bosses that they were the real deal and could deliver the heavy goods."

"They are the Camorra's worry now," Bartoni said. "Not yours. It's always a blessing when we can get them

60

to do our work for us. The more of them who waste each other, the better it is for Naples."

"I'm catching the first hydrofoil out in the morning," Lo Manto said. "I'll stop by before I leave and hand over the paperwork."

"There's no rush," Bartoni said. "You can even mail it to me from Capri if you wish. I'm confident you did everything according to the rules."

"I followed the rules as I understand them," Lo Manto said.

"Which is all I can ask of any of my men," Bartoni said. "I'll keep an eye on your mother for you while you're away. Make sure she doesn't need for anything."

"The timing couldn't be better for you," Lo Manto said. "Her tomatoes are in bloom, and she has enough fresh basil in her garden to supply every restaurant in the city."

"It's going to be good for you to get away," Bartoni said. "Read a few books, swim every day, eat and drink to excess, and let the Camorra slip from your mind. At least for the month you're on Capri."

"Even the Camorra take vacations," Lo Manto said. "Who knows. If I'm lucky, I may run into some old friends."

"It'll be even luckier if you don't," Bartoni said. "I only want to see pretty postcards from you for the next thirty days. If I want to read about shootouts, I'll get them from the daily reports."

"If they decide to come at us because of this score we

took from them, I want to know about it," Lo Manto said. "It's still my case, whether I'm here or not."

"If you hear from me, you'll know there's trouble," Bartoni said. "Other than that, enjoy your stay in paradise. You'll be back working in hell soon enough."

"It's only hell if you hate it," Lo Manto said.

Lo Manto came out of the bathroom and walked into his large bedroom, glass windows looking out over the wide expanse of the Piazza Dante. He had a blue towel wrapped around his waist and another draped across his shoulders, his body still wet from the long, hot shower. There was a brown leather duffel bag on his bedspread and clothes strewn on all sides. In one corner of the room, next to an end table, was a tall stack of books, magazines, and newspapers he was eager to read. At the edge of the bed, next to a pair of black Puma sneakers, were his three guns—two nine-millimeters and a .38. On the CD player, Lorenzo Jovanotti was rapping his way through his latest hit, "Salvami."

Lo Manto paused in front of the bureau that dominated the center of the room, a gift from his mother when he first got the apartment. He stared at himself in the long, wide mirror that hung above it. His eyes were always drawn to the scars, etched on his body like lines on a mountain ridge. There was a long, curving slice running under his right breast, courtesy of a slashing he had received less than six months into his police career. The half-moon jagged scar along the side of his neck came from a bullet from a .38 that missed the kill mark by less than a centimeter. There was a six-inch scar just above his navel, where he had been stabbed with a shank of wood during a waterfront brawl on the night of his first big drug bust.

He gazed at the small creases caused by more than three dozen stitches he had received during his battles with the Camorra, cuts that ran from his shoulders down to his legs, some noticeable only to his eye, others as visible as the stone-hard muscles that filled out his frame. Lo Manto scanned the healed wounds and damaged torso and shook his head as he sat on the edge of the bed. He smiled and wondered what kind of an old man he would end up becoming, assuming he made it that far. Probably the kind who smoked harsh-tasting tobacco out of a chewed-down pipe, telling and retelling the same old police stories to uninterested faces and uncaring eyes. It was one of a police officer's biggest fears. Many lived with the quiet dread that a career devoted to keeping the bite of the wolf from the door of the innocent would skid to a silent end. Lo Manto wanted what he had accomplished to have some weight, to have an impact on the people he helped and on the criminals he put away. It mattered to him that his life would not be wasted, but one that served the greater good. He remembered his father telling him many times that a man could make such a life for himself in America. Lo Manto wanted to think that he could do the same in Italy.

He turned when he heard the front door bell. Stripping off the two towels, he reached for a pair of jeans, slid into them, and walked out of the bedroom, past the small dining room and down the length of the long foyer. *"Regina, bella,"* he said as he opened the door and saw his sister, Victoria, standing there. He reached out and gave her a tight hug and immediately knew something was wrong.

He walked her into the kitchen and sat her at the chair closest to the stove. "I'll make coffee," he said, "and you talk."

Two years older than Giancarlo, Victoria was a beautiful woman in the truest southern Italian tradition. She had long, thick brown hair, a shapely body she didn't need to exercise to keep toned, arms and legs naturally tanned and thin. Her oval face lit up when she smiled, and her olive eyes could raise a man's temperature, though today there was no smile to be found and her eyes bore the burden of sorrow. She had married young, too young according to their mother, and the wrong man, according to the whispers of friends and family. Her husband, Fabio, worked for a midsize bank, earned a good living, and, on the surface, all seemed well. They had one child, a daughter, Paula, who had just turned fifteen and was babied and doted on by relatives on both sides of the aisle. Victoria managed a floral shop in Lungomare and drove a bloodred 1998 Porsche she bought at a good price at a police auction, a car that may have suited her personality but certainly not her needs.

Lo Manto put the espresso pot on the stove and turned the burner on low. He glanced over at his sister, catching her nervous gestures and fearful glances. "Coffee will be ready in less than ten minutes," he said, "and you still haven't said a word."

"Paula's gone," Victoria said, her usually calm voice filled with anxiety and worry. "No one's heard a word from her in three days."

"When did you find out?" he asked.

"About an hour ago," Victoria said. "I got a call from the family she's living with in New York. They told me not to worry—she might just be visiting some friends. Maybe she thought she didn't have to let anyone know about it."

"They call the police?"

"The mother called them just before she called me," Victoria said. "They were on their way to the precinct to fill out a missing-person report."

"How well do you know this family?" he asked. He remembered checking them out with his friends in the NYPD the minute he first heard about his niece's plan for a one-month trip living as an exchange student with a husband, wife, and two children on Manhattan's East Side. By all accounts, they were an acceptable family.

"They have a great reputation, Gian," she said, waving away his mistrust. "You're not the only one who knows how to use a phone and ask hard questions. They've been taking a teenager in every summer for the last six years and nothing's ever happened. One of my neighbors, Constanza, sent her daughter Claudia to live with them last year."

"And with all that experience, they still waited three days before calling you and the police," Lo Manto said.

"It's happened to them before," Victoria said. "Three times in the last six years and always with the same result. Every other time, they called the cops and filled out forms and nothing was done. Eventually, the kid makes her way back to the apartment and thinks nothing of the worry he or she put everyone through. They're teenagers, Gian. They don't always do what's right."

"Paula knows better," Lo Manto said. "Besides, where would she go that she wouldn't want anyone to know? Who would she be with who would make her forget to call? Even if she didn't trust this family, she would have called you. And if she was in trouble, she would have reached out for me."

"I need your help," Victoria said. "I need you to find her."

"She have an international cell phone?" Lo Manto asked.

"No, just a local one," Victoria said. "She's been calling at least once a week."

"When's the last time you talked to her?"

"The day before she disappeared," Victoria said. "We spoke for about twenty minutes—fifteen or so with me, the rest with her father."

"How'd she sound?" Lo Manto asked. "Anything in her voice that didn't feel right, that made you think something was off?"

"She was a little homesick, but nothing more than that," Victoria said, reaching for a napkin and wiping at the tears forming in the corners of her eyes. "She had just come back from a day at an amusement park and planned to go to the movies with some friends. She even won a prize, a stuffed teddy bear. She was going to give it to Mama when she got back home."

"You know the names of any of her friends?" Lo Manto asked. He poured two cups of espresso and gave one to his sister, watching her reach for it with a trembling hand. "She ever mention them in her calls?"

"Only one time," Victoria said, resting the cup at the edge of the Formica table. "She met a girl at some party who spoke Italian. Turned out she lived nearby and had similar interests, so they started going to galleries and museums together."

"You get a name?"

"Clara," his sister said. "I never got her last name. But Paula did tell me that her friend's grandfather was born in Naples, which I thought gave them something else in common."

Lo Manto pulled out a chair and sat down facing his sister, his steady hands holding tight her shaking ones. "I'll make some calls to New York," he told her, "see what I can find out. I'll also need you to give me the name and number of the family Paula is staying with. After that, you go home and stay with your husband. I'll call as soon as I know something."

"She's been missing for three days, Gian," his sister said, the hard edge back in her voice. "People run away every day in New York; it's the easiest city in the world to disappear in. And they are *never* found. I won't allow that to happen to Paula. The New York police might look for her, but they won't find her. To them, she's just another name on a form, a stranger they know nothing about. She's more than that to you. She's your blood."

Lo Manto stared at his sister and stayed silent. Outwardly, he maintained a calm and reassuring presence, content to allay Victoria's fears, choosing his words carefully, weighing each question without making it sound accusatory. But he knew time and reality were against finding his niece if she'd been grabbed or simply didn't want to be found. Three days missing was a lifetime to a cop. Any clues left behind had to be treated as cold, any changes in pattern as too late to follow up. "I don't want Mama to know anything about this just yet," he said, his voice low and in control. "If you can't hide it from her, then avoid seeing her for a few days."

"Fabio was going to take me to Lake Como for a short vacation," Victoria said, holding her brother's hands tighter. "Mama doesn't need to know we're not going. I'll leave her my cell phone number in case she needs anything."

"She thinks I'm going to Capri for a month," Lo Manto said. "And that's what I want her to keep thinking."

"Find her, Gian," Victoria said, voice cracking from

the strain. "Promise me that. Promise me you'll bring my daughter back to me."

"She told me she wanted to be here for Mama's birthday party next month," Lo Manto said. "Help her blow out the candles. I'll make sure that's what she does."

"I'm sorry, Gian," Victoria said, overtaken by a sense of relief, tears once again flowing down the sides of her face. "This was the last thing you needed to find on your doorstep. I know how much you were looking forward to getting away. I never want to bring you any trouble. That job of yours gives you enough of that."

"Nothing's changed all that much, Victoria," Lo Manto said. "I was going to Capri, but I had nothing planned. Instead, now I'm going to Manhattan and I've got something to do while I'm there, something that's important to both of us. And as far as I can see, one island is just as good as the other."

7

Lo Manto looked out at the lush farmland that separated Naples and Rome. Bartoni was shifting gears effortlessly as they eased their police sedan out of the congested city traffic and made for the wide-open Altostrada and the two-hour drive to the Leonardo Da Vinci airport. He could have taken a twenty-minute puddle jumper from one city to the other, but once he informed Bartoni of the change in his plans and the reason behind it, the chief inspector insisted on personally driving him up to Rome.

He had packed in less than twenty minutes, leaving behind the books, newspapers, and magazines, but putting two of the guns in a corner of the duffel bag with as many extra clips as he could find and jamming a nine-millimeter into his hip holster. He placed two calls to New York, the first to his oldest friend on the force, Captain Frank Fernandez of the 47th precinct. He had known Fernandez since the captain was an undercover detective working buy-and-bust operations in the East

Bronx, Lo Manto's old neighborhood and still prime Camorra turf. Through the years, as each rose up the ranks of his respective department, the two worked on a dozen two-city task force operations, including a takedown of a $50 million drug smuggling ring. It was a bust that sent three high-ranking Camorristas to jail for double-digit sentences and put three others into early graves. They spoke frequently and e-mailed each other on a regular basis, sharing information and favors. As a visiting detective from a foreign country working on a case, Lo Manto would be thousands of miles beyond his jurisdiction and maintain no powers of search, seizure, or arrest. He would need to check in with a New York precinct, where the local commander would then team him with a shadow partner. Lo Manto could think of no one better suited to help find his niece than Frank Fernandez.

His second call was placed to a pay phone in the rear of a dusty old candy store on the north side of the elevated subway tracks on White Plains Road in the Bronx. Lo Manto waited through eight rings before he heard the irritated, smoke-clogged voice on the other end.

"This better be worth me getting off my ass," the voice barked into the phone.

Lo Manto smiled when he heard him. "It will be unless you screw it up," he said into the receiver.

"It's the wop cop," the voice on the other end said. "Is it Christmas already or you just feeling lonely and decided to call the one friend you *think* you got?"

71

Carmine DelGardo was the best set of eyes and ears Lo Manto had in New York City, which was all the more amazing since he very seldom ventured beyond the borders of his candy store. Lo Manto had known him since he was a boy, and even back then his store had been nothing more than a poorly disguised front for the neighborhood gamblers and loan sharks to use as a base. He was not a member of the Camorra, but he cut them in on a fair share of his action and in return was allowed to run his business as he pleased. He also passed around regular payments to the uniformed cops who patrolled the neighborhood, asking only that they turn their heads when it came to his end of the street. DelGardo had no cell phone, pager, or beeper. He used only a battered pay phone, which was both unlisted and unregistered with any area phone company, next to the closet-size bathroom in the store. Once a month he had an ex-con nephew from Brooklyn come in and sweep the store for bugs. He didn't smoke or drink anything heavier than a root beer packed in a large cup of chipped ice. He was as up-to-date on current events as he was on street rumors and the who's-in-and-who's-out carousel of crime life. He loved women, and his mood would always brighten whenever a young lady found her way to his store, looking to buy anything with a fresh expiration date.

And there was always music blaring from the back of his shop.

DelGardo was a Motown fanatic, collecting singles

and LPs from every group to ever find its way to Detroit. He knew every member's name and history and the title of every song they sang and recorded. He could rattle off within seconds how much money they *should* have made as opposed to how much they actually took in. "You want to steal and walk away clean," he once told Lo Manto, "find your way into the music business. In that world, you don't need a gun or a knife. All you need is to know somebody who knows somebody who works at a record label. After that, it all just takes care of itself."

Lo Manto knew that DelGardo had been a good friend to his father, though the two had never talked about it. His father had spent a lot of his free time in front of DelGardo's store, sitting on the ends of wooden crates, drinking cold beers wrapped in paper bags, talking sports and work, the sounds of the Temptations or the Four Tops drowning out half their words. Lo Manto also knew that Carmine DelGardo did all that he could to keep his father from confronting the men who would eventually kill him. He tried to calm him, tried to make him understand there was no other way to go, no other place to turn, but failed.

Lo Manto also knew there was a lot more that DelGardo knew about his father and his run-in with the Camorra than what he had heard from the gossips of the neighborhood. He just didn't know if that was a conversation that the two men would ever be destined to have.

*

Bartoni eased the sedan into fourth gear, riding the left lane of the superhighway, the sun at their back, the city of Salerno a dozen kilometers off to their right. "Take as much time as you need," he told Lo Manto, who sat next to him, gazing out at the passing farmland, quietly chewing two sticks of gum. "Even after it's over and you find Paula, take a few extra days and enjoy the city."

"You seem pretty confident I'll find her," Lo Manto said, turning to look at the chief inspector. "By the time I land in New York, she'll have been gone five days. You know better than anyone how low that makes the odds."

"The odds are insurmountable," Bartoni said with a knowing nod. "But that's only if Paula was the target. And I don't think that was the case."

"Then who?"

"The Camorra has grown in number and power in New York," Bartoni said. "They are as fully entrenched in that city as they are in ours. The two cities feed off one another, the strength of Naples reinforcing the muscle of New York. Any damage to one is seen as hurtful to both."

"We've put some dents in that," Lo Manto said. "Not enough to stop them flat, but enough to cost them time, money, and members."

"And they take such matters very personally," Bartoni said, his eyes shifting from the road to Lo Manto and then back. "And they look to rid themselves of anyone who brings harm to their business."

"What's all that have to do with Paula?" Lo Manto

asked. "They never lift kids. There's too much risk and too little profit in it."

"That's true," Bartoni said. "When I worked the streets and I got information about a chicken hawk looking to make money off innocent children, I wasted no time in spreading that word to the Camorra. The hawk would be off my street in a matter of hours."

"But still you see a connection between them and Paula," Lo Manto said, running a hand through his thick hair, his mind racing as he tried to recall any links between his niece and the criminals he fought.

"If she's not the target," Bartoni said, "she's the trap."

"You going with more than your gut on this?" Lo Manto asked.

"You're not the only one with friends in New York," Bartoni said. "And mine are older, which puts them higher up the command chain. And that means faster answers to my questions."

"I'm listening," Lo Manto said.

"The family Paula's staying with is as clean as a polished window," Bartoni said. "So there's no trouble there."

"That part I know," Lo Manto said. "Tell me the part I don't."

"Their daughter goes to a private school less than two blocks from their building," Bartoni said, his manner calm, his voice never hovering beyond its normal docile tone. "It's the same school where Pete Rossi sends his daughters, and she's in the same class as one of them."

"Is the Rossi daughter the one Paula went on an outing with?" Lo Manto asked. "The one she's become friendly with?"

"I couldn't find that out," Bartoni said. "I doubt it, though. Rossi wouldn't risk that close a link. But I'd bet my pension that she's from a family he knows or one he can get near."

Lo Manto turned away from Bartoni, rested his head and shoulder against the side panel of the door, and focused his attention on the road ahead. Up to now, he thought he had managed his police career in a way that kept his family outside the reach of harm. He had shielded them from all knowledge of his activities, leaving them little choice but to learn about his arrests and cases from the daily newspapers and weekly magazines that devoted as much space to the Camorra as they did to the latest celebrity scandals. He had also allowed the fact that the Camorra steered clear of civilians, unless they were in debt to them, to lull him into a state of comfort. Lo Manto was a man who devoted all his energy to avoiding mistakes. Now he might have made one that placed a girl he dearly loved in the center of a minefield.

"They can come after me in Naples just as easy as they can in New York," Lo Manto said. "It shouldn't make a difference to them what city I die in."

"It might to Pete Rossi," Bartoni said. "It's his crew that has felt the brunt of your hits, including your last little adventure in Herculaneum. And besides, as well as you may know New York, you don't know it the way you know Naples. You'll be a much weaker opponent fighting him on foreign ground."

"What if you're wrong?" Lo Manto asked, sitting up, his left hand resting on the leather door handle. "What if Rossi has nothing to do with Paula going missing? What if she was lifted off the street?"

Bartoni turned the wheel just a quarter inch, navigating a sharp curve at one hundred and ten, and then shifted into overdrive. They were now less than forty minutes from the Rome airport. He looked over at Lo Manto, a weary sadness filling his face. "The answer to that is something both of us already know," he said. "And neither wants to hear."

They drove the rest of the way in silence, the CD on low volume, the haunting voice of Andrea Bocelli the only company to their thoughts.

8

New York City
Summer 2003

Detective Jennifer Fabini spotted the man in the leather coat on the corner of Sixteenth Street and Irving Place. He was tall, reed-thin with a short-cropped Afro, and walked with a slight limp, just as the all-points bulletin had described. The dozen other men and women making their way up and down the steamy street were all dressed in as few clothes as possible, the oppressive August heat holding the city in a death grip. Yet the man in the leather coat didn't even seem to be breaking a sweat as he moved with decisive steps toward Third Avenue, Fabini keeping pace a few strides behind. The rule book call would be for her to radio for backup, since the man in the leather coat, Luther Slyke, was a predicate felon, known to be dangerous and more than likely heavily armed. He had no qualms about shooting a police officer and had done so twice in his thick yellow-sheet criminal career. He was listed as six-feet-two, 185 pounds after a heavy rain, with a set of false upper teeth and three puncture wounds in his chest from previous shoot-outs.

Fabini thought about making the call, but that didn't appeal to her as much as the idea of taking down Luther on her own. She was well aware of the danger inherent in the situation, but that only helped make it a more attractive possibility. Besides, she much preferred working alone, which was one of the factors she found most appealing in her multi-borough plainclothes unit. "Look up Jennifer's photo in her high school yearbook," her father, Sal, often said to his retired police buddies in the Queens bar where he spent most of his pension. "Under the photo, there's a caption that reads 'Does not play well with others.' She'll make a great cop but a shitty partner."

Sal Fabini was an NYPD legend, a gold-shield detective with more homicide arrests and convictions than any cop in the history of the department. He spent twenty-six years working the streets, banging heads, breaking down doors and rules, never giving in until he had a suspect in cuffs and a confession written out on a thick legal pad. He had shot and killed four men in the line of duty, wounded dozens of others, and was awarded enough citations and medals for his police work to fill two sides of his wood-paneled basement game room. In the months following his retirement, Fabini was offered several high-end and well-paying security jobs and passed on all of them. "That shit's not for me," he told Jennifer early one morning, the two sharing a cup of coffee. "Don't look for me to turn into some stoop-shouldered, white-haired loser standing guard over somebody else's money, wishing all along that I'd caught a bullet to the head while I was on the job. That's not gonna happen."

"It's not like that anymore," Jennifer said to him. "No one's asking you to stand in a bank lobby pointing people to the next teller. These are high-tech security firms, with offices all around the world. With the technology that's out there, you can do a lot of good in a job like that."

"Security's still security, and it's all for shit," Sal said with a dismissive wave. "I couldn't wait to get out of a uniform when I was a cop, and I'm not eager to get back into one now that I'm an old man."

"The job comes with a suit and an expense account," Jennifer said, trying to fight off the frustration she always felt when talking to her father. "The salary plus your pension can get you a nicer house or a better car. You shouldn't just blow it off the way you do everything else."

"I got all the house and car I'm ever gonna need," her father said. "So let's just close the case on this security talk. It's a dead issue as far as I'm concerned."

"I'm sorry for even bringing it up," Jennifer said, each word drenched in sarcasm. "You can do so much more with the last years of your life sitting by the wood at the

Three Aces, kicking back shooters, and making sure no one runs out of the bar without buying a round for the boys."

"Look," Sal said, his jaw clenched, his dark eyes hard and filled with menace. She could well imagine how many made men and career thugs had seen their bravado melt under the heat of that gaze. "I never missed a day in my twenty-six years—not one. Even when I was shot, I filled out my paperwork from the hospital bed. I've earned the right to spend my time how I want to spend it. And from you, I expect less lip and more respect. I raised you better than that."

"Mom raised me," Jennifer said, standing up and staring across the table at her father. They were in the kitchen of her parents' two-story wood-shingled Middle Village, Queens, colonial. The worn black and white tiles on the floor were the same ones that were there the morning she found her mother's body slumped over the sink, cold water tap still running. The carving knife had been jammed into the center of her stomach and the blood had oozed down the front of the cabinet and welled by her feet, turning her blue house slippers beet red. "Mom did everything that needed to be done. She cooked, cleaned, and made sure she was there when I needed her to be. But more than anything, what Mom did was waste her life waiting for you to come through that front door. Drunk or sober, it never mattered to her. Just so long as you were home."

"We both had a job to do and we both did it," her

father said, his lips barely moving. "And we both did it well or else you wouldn't be standing here, fancy college diploma hanging in your room upstairs."

"You can take credit for the collars," Jennifer said. "Those belong to you and your partners. It was Mama's work and Grandma's money that put me through college. Nothing came out of your end."

Sal stood up and walked to the wood cabinets lined up next to the one-door refrigerator. He swung a door open and pulled down a half-filled bottle of Dewar's, along with the old jelly jar he'd been using as a glass since she was in high school. He poured three fingers and downed it in one gulp. "Something must have come out," he said, his back to her. "You went and joined the police department, looking to fill my shoes. And I don't need to see you in uniform to tell you that is something you will never be able to do. Not in this lifetime and not on this planet."

"I joined the force in spite of you, not because of you," Jennifer said. "The papers treat you like a legend. The old-timers talk about you like you were one of the Apostles. But not everybody wearing blue thinks you walked on water. There are even some who think you should be in a yellow jumpsuit doing a stretch."

"A cop, and I'm talking about *any* cop, is only as good as the information they can get," Sal said, turning to face his daughter. "It's the one difference between getting a medal pinned to your chest and having a bullet land in your back. And from what you just told me, a floater running facedown in the river has a better bead on what went down than you do."

"That's right," Jennifer said, choking back the urge to cry as she flashed on the image of finding her mother's body slumped over the sink. She was fifteen years old, still dressed in her high school uniform, her legs trembling, her hands balled into tight fists. "I forgot I was talking to a Hall of Famer. You're the cop that solved all his cases. All except one. The *only* one that should have mattered."

"Your mother was a *suicide*," Sal said, slamming the jelly jar on the kitchen countertop. "You're the only one who ever thought it was anything more than that. You were wrong then and you're still wrong now."

"She wouldn't have done something like that," Jennifer said, "knowing I'd be the one to find her body. She wouldn't have left me with that as a memory. Hell, I don't think she would have even done that to you, as much as you deserved it."

"Let it rest, kid," Sal said, his tone starting to soften. "Leave it the way it is and make your peace with it. You start shaking the past, you'll only find trouble. Maybe the kind of trouble you don't want."

"I'm a cop, Dad," Jennifer said, heading out the back door. "And your daughter. I can handle trouble."

Luther Slyke stepped into the vestibule of a five-story brownstone just off the corner of East Twelfth Street. Jennifer stopped at the newsstand across the street, picked up a copy of the *New York Post* and dropped a quarter on the counter plate. She crossed against the light and walked up to the building, the stone façade just off a fresh water wash. She waited until she heard Luther get buzzed into the building, then scampered up the five steps to the double wood door, chrome handles polished and gleaming in the early morning sun. She scanned the names on the six mailboxes that were lined on one end of the concrete wall, looking for a name she could hook to Luther. She leaned over and glanced through the curtained door separating her from the first floor and caught a glimpse of Luther rounding the stairs at the top of the second landing. She turned back to the names on the mailboxes and pressed them all, then wedged her body against the door and waited to be let in. In less than thirty seconds all six residents responded and buzzed back, only one of them bothering to shout down into the intercom system, a male voice asking if it was a delivery.

Jennifer slipped into a dark corner of the first floor, her eyes on the walnut door closest to her, the dead bolt on the other side released from its slot. The door opened halfway and a young Hispanic man stepped into the hall. He was wearing clean jeans, flip-flops, and a cowboy hat. He was shirtless, the front of his Rikers Island chest adorned with a black and red serpent tattoo, its rattle tail starting down below his navel, its open mouth, fangs dripping blood and venom, jumping out from the center of his thick breastbone. He walked out of his apartment and toward Jennifer, a curved and weird smile on his face. She could hear Latin music coming out of the rooms behind him, dishes being moved, and a woman's voice asking him to hurry. She could also smell the acrid odor of marijuana mixed with burnt coke. "You forgot the pizza," the Hispanic man said to Jennifer. He was standing less than three feet from her, his breath harsh enough to wilt plants. "And I called for that shit more than an hour ago. I got hungry people in there."

Jennifer pushed aside the right flap of her blue jeans jacket and showed the man the shield pinned to her pants. He also caught a glimpse of the butt end of her nine-millimeter, jammed into a holster against her hip. "I can also forget about the possession charge I can lay on you and your girlfriend if I walk into your apartment," Jennifer said in a low voice. "For me to do that, all you have to do is turn around, go back inside, and shut up."

"What are we supposed to do for food?" he asked, taking several steps back toward his door.

"Have a salad," Jennifer said.

She eased her way past him and walked up the stairs to the second floor, her left hand braced against the hard, cool wall. Above her she heard two male voices, both agitated, each a few ticks removed from danger. She turned the tight corner on the landing, crouched down and stared up, the voices coming at her from the third floor, the long shadow of Luther's leather coat swaying in the light breeze coming through an open hall window. She pulled the nine-millimeter from her holster, checked the clip, and moved carefully up the stairs.

Luther Slyke was towering over a chubby man in a Knicks T-shirt, black running shorts, and bare feet. The man had a lit cigarette in his mouth and was holding the round end of a miniature pool cue. He stood with his legs apart, his bald head gleaming like a waxed ball and a set of steel-gray eyes staring up at the anxious felon. Jennifer watched the chubby man through the slits in the railing. She knew from both the sound of his voice echoing up and down the halls and the shifts in his body that this was not the first conversation he'd ever had that could end with the spilling of blood. He had a lion's head tattoo on the top of his right shoulder and a tiger's head on his left, both marking him as a gangbanger who had served some serious prison time. She had enough experience in these setups to realize she wouldn't have to wait very long to find out if Luther Slyke was really tough or only talked that way.

"You gotta have nuts big as wrecking balls to come walking up to my home like you been invited for lunch," the chubby man said, angry and ready to act on it. "All the heat that's resting on you, and you come *my* way. Up to this second I only *thought* you were a dumb ass. Now, you might as well have it spray-painted across the walls."

"Take a deep breath, you fat bastard," Luther said,

still with an edge to his voice, not yet ready to crumble under the verbal weight. "I ain't an easy man to follow. Least not as easy as you think. I slip and glide my way down the streets. Came in clean, nobody on my tail."

"Not easy to follow?" the chubby man said, laughing out the words. "In *that* coat? In *this* weather? Are you for sane? Man, that blind bitch from *Red Dragon* could find your ass in a Times Square crowd. I'd lay you five hundred of my dollars against one of yours that there's a whole gang of cops having a picnic lunch on my stoop waiting for your skinny little ass to come out this building."

"What I got couldn't wait," Luther said, sounding just shy of defensive, glancing briefly over the fat man's shoulders at the open door behind him, a scrawny orange cat resting across the welcome mat. "I need to move it fast and nobody better than you has that kind of speed."

"Move what?" the chubby man asked, curious, his anger simmering while he smoked out the details of a potential deal.

Luther looked to his left and right and then turned back to the fat man. He undid the four buttons on his leather coat and then, with the fingers of both hands, spread the jacket open. He broke into a gap-toothed grin when he saw the fat man's eyes shimmer as he looked down at the six small, clear Hefty bags taped to the furry inside of the coat, each one filled with cocaine. "You rip a player off?" the chubby man asked. "Or you come by that stash on the square?"

"I didn't find religion or a new way to have sex in the joint, Hector," Luther said, still holding on to the grin. "I found a dealer who can set me straight. This is my first heavy buy from him, made the score late yesterday."

"You ain't on CNN, loser," Hector said, glancing up both sides of the hall. "I don't need to know the details. All I care about is that the shit is yours, which means if I buy I can make it mine."

"You can sleep on that," Luther said. "And if you got fifteen thousand in spare change buried under all that food you keep in the fridge, then I can leave here a lot lighter and a lot richer."

"This connection of yours, he can supply you regular?" Hector asked. "Two-a-week drops, thirty going back to him?"

"He can fill you up floor to ceiling," Luther said. "Turn you into an honorary Colombian drug king overnight."

Hector scratched the gray stubble on his chin and gave the cocaine packs dangling off Luther's jacket a hard stare, gently tapping the thin end of the pool cue on the red painted cement floor. "Take a breath," he finally said. "And pull those bags off your coat, lay them out by my door. And if you get mugged while I'm gone, the deal's off."

"Make it a fast one, fat man," Luther said, peeling off one of the Hefty bags. "Don't stop to munch."

*

88

Jennifer was spread down across the cold ground, her legs dangling over the top steps of the stairwell, the cocked nine-millimeter in her right hand, her eyes, half hidden by the brim of a Yankees cap, on Luther and the fat man at the end of the hallway. There was an eerie silence to the building, few noises coming from behind any of the apartment doors, no cooking odors and no dogs barking and scrubbing their paws against the wood, anxious to hit the street. She watched as Hector walked back into his apartment and closed the door, leaving Luther alone to pile his coke stash on the welcome mat. She wasn't as trusting of the fat man's motives as was Luther in the leather. She figured there was little chance that a hard-time gangbanger would do business of any kind with a shaky street skel, especially one who was a step away from a bust and a sure bet to flip inside a locked interrogation room. The simple fact that the fat man was doing business in the hall instead of inside his apartment was another tip-off that this deal was destined to end not with a handshake but with bullets.

She slid her body along the ground, trying to get to her knees and into a better shooting position. She was giving up height and weight to both men, but was working with the advantage of surprise and the confidence that neither could take her down unless he had amazing luck or an extra set of eyes on her she hadn't caught. Jennifer figured Luther would take longer to get to his gun, buried somewhere in the back of his thick coat, well out of Hector's view. She was also betting that his pull would be slow and his aim off, his reflexes marred by the drugs in his body and the years spent in prison. That made Hector her primary. She slowly eased up to her knees, flipped her cap around, the bill now hanging flat against the thick strands of her rich blond hair, and aimed her gun into the shadows of the poorly lit hall.

Hector opened the door to his apartment, a D'Agostino paper bag in his right hand, and stared down at the pile of drugs next to his chubby feet. "At least you can follow directions," he said, nodding toward Luther. "That's more props than I was set to give you."

"When it comes to cash, you can put my name on any list," Luther said, starting to sweat for the first time that day, his eyes fast on the paper bag in Hector's hand. "It's the only reason to open your eyes in the morning."

"The world gets its gas tank fueled by greed," Hector said. "Lucky for my end of business that there's a lot more needle freaks breathing than money-grubbers. That's how I keep my end filled."

"Then we both walking away happy as pigs rolling in shit," Luther said. "That is, soon as you hand me over what's in that bag. You might wanna do that sooner than later, got to be getting close to your feed time."

"I can eat anytime," Hector said. "I always got an appetite. Ain't missed a meal since I was livin' off my mama's tit."

Hector stepped closer to Luther and reached a hand into the paper bag. His eyes stayed on the taller man in the leather coat, following his hands, watching as sweat bubbles formed on the sides of his face. "You okay, player?" he asked him. "I swear to heaven's Mary you starting to turn pale on me. This heat and that coat gotta be enough to melt any man's skin."

"Don't lose any worry over me, Hector," Luther said. "I'm good. And I'll be even better soon as I get my end of the score."

"Let's finish it then," Hector said, his hand buried inside the paper bag.

"Right there," Jennifer shouted from down the hall. She was walking toward them, her arms stretched out, the nine-millimeter and her eyes aimed straight at Hector. "Don't even twitch. And if you want to end the day without losing blood, slide your trigger finger off the gun."

Luther looked at Jennifer and then back to Hector, the chubby man relaxed, willing to wait for the good-looking lady with the tough eyes to make her way to him. "She right?" he asked, taking a hard look at the paper bag. "You were going to take me out? Drop me right in front of your door? What the hell you play me for, Hector?"

"Stay calm, Luther," Jennifer said, close enough now to take out one but unsure whether she would be fast enough to drop both if they moved at the same time. "This ends the right way and you'll both go to jail. You'll have plenty of time to square things with Hector once you get settled upstate."

"I tell you what," Hector said, throwing Jennifer a

casual smile. "Pretty little bird like you can't take us both, even if one of us is as dumb as a tree stump. You got Luther on more charges than you can type up. Possession alone should be good for a seven-year ride. All you got on me is that maybe I got a gun in this bag. With the lawyers I can dial, that's a long way to go for a short walk."

"So you give me Luther and the dope and I let you walk?" Jennifer said, holding her place, sneakers spread apart, gun steady, pointed just below Hector's neckline. "That what you'd like to see happen?"

"Makes the most sense," Hector said. "You get an easy collar and maybe a boost in pay. I lose a guy who could only lead me down troubled ways, and it can all be wrapped and set before lunch."

"You'd flip me that fast, you fat bastard?" Luther said, the sweat now pouring off him like a stream, shading the color on his torn brown T-shirt.

"Like a flapjack, loser," Hector said, the heat of his anger rising to match the weight of his words. "Guy like you don't play in the same town I do, never mind the same league. You been processed so many times, prison cops got your ID number burned to memory. I'm a *gatto grande*, that's big-time. We piss on nickel-and-dime dealers. Especially ones come in wearing leather coats in August looking to move shit packed in garbage bags. I made bigger scores than that before I had hair on my balls."

"Put the bag down, Hector," Jennifer said. Her voice

was calm, soothing and steady, not looking to add to the heat meter. "Then we can all start walking out of here."

"I got a better one for you, cop," Hector said. "Why don't you go away for five minutes. Grab a cold root beer at the bodega around the corner. Then come back. When you do, you'll find everything you need spread out on the floor—drugs on one side and Luther on the other. The only thing missing will be me. We can save our bounce for some other time."

"I'm not going to tell you again, Hector," Jennifer said, her voice still at the same level. "Put the bag and the gun down."

"That's a favor I gotta take a pass on," Hector said. "I'm taking Luther out, for bringing cops and drugs to my door and just because I don't like the fucker. If that means I have to put you down next to him, won't make me happy, but I'll make it happen."

"You're too smart to take a risk like that," Jennifer said. She could feel the sweat damp and cold on her neck, droplets running down the length of her back. "Not unless the *gattos* let any moron with a tattoo into their gang."

"What risk, baby?" Hector asked, brushing aside the insult. "Luther's packing, no doubt. But odds are heavy he shoots himself before he even gets one off near me. That leaves it down to the two of us. And as good as you *think* you are, that's how good I am."

Jennifer took a deep breath and shrugged her shoulders. "That's probably true," she said.

"Now you thinking right, baby," Hector said, tossing a quick glance over at Luther. Jennifer waited until Hector's eyes were back on her, the two holding the look, the hefty gangbanger biting down on his lower lip, standing fearless despite the one gun aimed his way and the other now wedged against the back of Luther's spine. "If I knew you a little bit better, I'd watch and let you do Luther here. Toss a favor to the blue team."

"I'll remember that when I type up your report," Jennifer said. "Might shave off a day or two on your sentence."

"It's your move, baby," Hector said, tilting his head toward Jennifer. "The pawns are out of the game. It's down to the king and queen. So, what's it gonna be?

"Checkmate," Jennifer said.

She fired off two quick rounds, one hitting Hector in the fat of his right shoulder, the other smashing bone on his elbow. The power of the blows knocked Hector to the ground, his head slamming against the concrete wall, the paper bag with the gun falling to the floor next to the pile of coke. Luther jolted when he heard the gun fire and backed up against the railing, his right hand reaching behind his leather coat. Jennifer kept her eyes on Hector and walked closer to the wounded man.

"Don't even go there," she said to Luther, kicking the paper bag farther down the hall, out of Hector's reach. "Remember, I came here for you. Hector's just an extra prize in the Cracker Jack box."

"He's the prize," Luther said. "A prime-time player.

Me, I'm just another number on a yellow rap sheet. Nobody cares about me."

"Don't get all sobby on me, Luther," Jennifer said. "I care about you. I carry your picture with me all the time. Now, take that coat off and let it drop to the floor. And do it as slow as you do everything else. Then, turn around and step toward me."

Luther moved away from the railing and let the coat fall off his shoulders. Then he put his hands out at his side and turned. Jennifer leaned forward and pulled out the snub-nose .38 that was jammed between his stained pants and torn shirt. She looked down at Hector, his eyes following her every move, his right arm drowning in blood, a thick puddle starting to form on the floor. Jennifer reached behind her jean jacket and pulled out her handcuffs. She grabbed a hand radio out of her back pocket and called for her second unit and an ambulance.

"I'm going to cuff you to Hector, toss the guns and the dope into the paper bag, and then we'll all sit here and wait for a few of my friends," she told Luther. "That sounds nice, doesn't it?"

"I'd rather you put one in my head than have you cuff me to this reeked-out loser," Hector said, through the pain of the wounds.

"Talk it all you want, you three-belly punk," Luther said to him. "Word gets out you got taken down by a little girl with a gun, you'll be doing your prison time wearing lipstick and heels."

Jennifer slapped one cuff against Luther's skinny wrist

and then jammed the other around Hector's much beefier one. She pushed Luther face forward against the wall, his leg brushing up against Hector's shoulder, blood oozing past his boots. She picked up the paper bag, hearing the screaming sirens outside, and tossed Luther's gun in next to Hector's Magnum. She piled the drug packs on top of the guns one at a time, shoved the bag up to the railing and then leaned next to it, her gun back in its hip holster.

"Hope the cops keep that leather coat safe for you," Hector said to Luther. "And giving it a tumble dry wouldn't be a bad way to go, either. My cat's ass is cleaner than that dishrag. And that's what I want you to be wearing when I set fire to your punk ass. Light you up like a dry tree and grill me a burger over your melted bones."

"The only thing you gonna be lightin' up is your husband's joints," Luther said. "Shape you're gonna be in, they might as well send you to do your time in a woman's prison. You gonna go from *gatto grande* to *gatto bitch*."

"You guys should have your own talk show," Jennifer said, glancing down the stairwell, watching as four uniform officers and two EMS workers ran up. "Put you against Howard Stern and see how you do."

"Who's Howard Stern?" Luther asked.

9

Lo Manto stood in the middle of the detectives' squad room, scanning the printouts that listed all the missing-person reports filed in the last week. "There's close to five hundred names here," he said to Frank Fernandez. "How many of them do you ever find?"

"It depends," Fernandez said. "First off, not everybody on that list is really missing, but they have family that thinks they might be. So, it'd be a safe bet to scratch off about one-quarter of the names. Then there's another group that *are* missing, but by their own choice. And if you're old enough and didn't do anything illegal and want to skip town, then that's your business, not police business."

"And the other fifty percent?" Lo Manto asked, handing the sheets back to the captain. "What happens to them?"

"Four out of ten are never seen again," the captain said. "Three end up on a slab in one of the morgues. And if we catch a little luck, we get to bring three of them back home to their families."

Lo Manto nodded and stared around the large room, filing cabinets, printers, and Xerox machines eating up huge chunks of space. Small desks, grouped together in packs of twos, filled the middle of the room, red lights on black phones running at a steady pace. "You promised me some coffee," he said to the captain. "Maybe even something to go with it."

"That I did," the captain said. "But while you're eating and drinking, keep it in the back of your mind, I never promised you it'd be any good."

"It wasn't any good the last time I was here," Lo Manto said. "I wasn't looking for it to change."

"Good," Fernandez said. "I always hate to disappoint a friend."

Frank Fernandez was one of the few precinct bosses who hadn't tested his way to get a captain's desk. Instead, he earned his stripes with hard-nail police work. He was the only son of a retired Bronx plumber and a mother who spent more than thirty years working for the phone company back in the days when there was only one in the entire New York area. His parents were hoping their only son would find his way to a top-tier medical or law school, wrapping a thick yellow bow around their American dream. He had the grades and wouldn't have flinched at the work, but lacked the desire to pursue either profession. All Frank Fernandez ever wanted, all he dreamed of since he was old enough to run and talk and be aware of what happened on the streets of his middle-class Queens neighborhood, was to be a cop with a badge, chasing the bad away from the good.

Fernandez moved from uniform to plainclothes to undercover narcotics in less than three years, earning a drawerful of medals and citations along the way, always quick to stamp his mark on whatever beat he was given, whatever gang he was expected to take down. Much like Lo Manto, he was not a stickler for rules and regulations, bending them to suit his needs whenever he could but always smart enough to give himself cover in an open court when called to testify. His impressive string of arrests and willingness to do whatever was required to get the job done caught the attention of the department chiefs, who were just shy of desperate in their search to find minority candidates worthy of promotion. But Fernandez never thought of himself as a quota boost, and neither did any of the hard-chargers he made sure were part of every detail he worked. He had earned each promotion, and anyone with a badge pinned to their waist or on their chest took it as gospel.

Fernandez was a demanding captain. He expected his sector to have a low crime rate and instructed his officers and detectives to do what was necessary to ensure that the people who lived on their precinct turf felt secure. He demanded that any arrest made be strong enough to hold to conviction in an open court and that a cop be as prepared as any lawyer who would question his motives and actions when he took the stand. And he went after dirty cops harder than he ever chased down a street thug, ensuring that the 47th precinct could withstand the heat of any internal affairs investigations that might come its way. He was golden copy to the crime reporters covering the police beat and a shining knight in a sea of blue to the bosses at One Police Plaza, all eagerly awaiting the day he would be announced as the next commissioner.

All this attention and reverence gave Frank Fernandez a lot of leeway in how he did his job, and he took full advantage of the opportunity to work without the brass constantly at his door, questioning his every move. So, while other precinct captains were grilled on a weekly basis about crime statistics and questionable shootings involving their men, Fernandez was allowed to float with casual ease under the radar. This allowed Fernandez to attempt what no other captain in the city would even dare try. He selected five of his best young officers, all raw in experience but each eager to make a lasting impression, and turned them into silent watchdogs working well beyond the borders of his own precinct. He assigned them the task of frisking out fresh street information on any gang or mob activity, any white-collar irregularities, any corruption connections to NYPD higher-ups, and any shakedowns that had gone unreported. With a wink and a nod from a deputy inspector who approved of his operation, Fernandez, within an eighteen-month period, had accumulated data on any criminal enterprise worth noting in the five-borough area. He also knew who, among the brass and the politicians and the lawyers and judges they mingled with, was tainted. It helped make Frank Fernandez one very good cop to have on your side of the table.

"I don't suppose you'd let me drive around the city on my own?" Lo Manto asked Fernandez, both of them sipping hot black coffee from a pair of *Law & Order* mugs. "You know, check out the sights, maybe even go to a Broadway show."

"You know me," Fernandez said. "I love to see my friends have themselves a good time. But I always find it's better to see this city with someone who knows it pretty well. Point things out you might miss on your own. At the same time, that person can also steer you clear of any trouble spots you might walk into by accident."

"Will my new friend have a badge and a gun?" Lo Manto asked. He rested the mug on the edge of the captain's desk, scanning the room, gazing at the vast collection of baseball memorabilia that crowded the shelves and cabinet tops.

"Yes," Fernandez said. "But you won't. You can leave both of those with me, just like I did with you when I came to Naples. I couldn't nail anybody there. You can't bust anybody here. We don't have to like all the rules, Gianni, but some we have to follow and this is one of them."

"How good?" Lo Manto asked. "If I have to have a shadow, I want one that can keep up with me and not get lost in a small crowd. I have to move my way and at my pace and I won't have the time to look over my shoulder to see if the ghost is still on me."

"She'll be there," Fernandez said, his voice filled with assurance and confidence. "This kid's got the chops to give even a hard-ass like you a fast turn. And if you do run into any kind of trouble, she's going to be the one you most want covering your back. Other than me."

"How much does she know?" Lo Manto asked. "About me and about why I'm here."

"I told her just the skeleton," Fernandez said. "You're a detective from Naples, and you're here for a few days trying to help us find your missing niece. She doesn't know anything about your background or even that you and me are friends. I figure you can fill her in on whatever parts of that you want to tell. Give you both something to talk about when you're stuck in rush hour traffic."

"Does she know I speak English?" Lo Manto asked, standing and turning away from the captain, staring through the thin glass window at the squad room, crowded now with teams of detectives working the phones and interviewing potential witnesses and prime suspects.

"She didn't ask," Fernandez said, getting up from behind his desk and standing next to his friend. "But my guess is she figures you don't. You want to play with that or not, I'll leave that up to you."

Lo Manto kept his head down, long hair flopping across his eyes, and then glanced over at Fernandez. "Do you think my niece is still alive, Frank?"

Fernandez ran a hand across his close-cropped

salt-and-pepper hair, styled to match the mustache of the same color. He kept his hair that way, rather than dye it or let it run long, in order to hide the fact that he was, at thirty-five, much too young to hold the rank he carried. Despite his youth, Fernandez knew the reality of the city and its unsparing harshness, especially when directed toward the most innocent of victims. And he also knew he could never lie to Lo Manto, whom he considered both a close friend and a great detective. "I wouldn't have let you come here if I felt otherwise," he said. "I wouldn't have wanted you to be here when we found her body."

"Does your information back up what Bartoni's street eyes told him?" Lo Manto asked. "Or does he come up short somewhere?"

"That old badge has some good sources," Fernandez said. "I wish to hell I knew who they were. Could use them to help plug up some of my other empty cases."

"It might not be a lift and it doesn't look like it's a sell," Lo Manto said. "We would have heard from someone by now if it had gone that way."

"She's definitely not a sell," Fernandez said. "I had my crew on that from the second I heard. Nothing's moved on the street fitting her description or age group in the last week. We also ran checks on all the skin sellers, put them through the ringer, from VICAP to fingerprints, and there's nothing and no one who matches up with Paula. So we're pretty good there. I'm with your boss all the way on this. I peg it as a lift."

"With me, not money, as the ransom," Lo Manto said. "If I was looking to pull a kidnap, I'd try to get back something worth a whole lot more than a cop from Naples."

"You cost the Camorra a lot of money all these years," Fernandez said. "Frankly, I'm surprised they've waited this long to make their move. The way you been hitting their operations, both here and in the old country, you're like an all-night ATM sucking off their savings. It's bad for business, and when this crew gets their business touched, they like to touch back."

"This new partner of mine," Lo Manto said.

"Jennifer Fabini," Fernandez said. "Works plain-clothes narcotics. Or did until you came to town."

"How'd she take the news?" Lo Manto asked. "About her baby-sitting job?"

"Other than demoting her back down to uniform, I can't think of anything that would have ticked her off more," Fernandez said with a laugh. "There was a lot of pissing and moaning about having to diaper-change a wop cop looking to act tough in the big city. Then she stormed out of my office and headed down to the gym. Let the heavy bag pay the price of her anger."

"Doesn't sound like it's going to be love at first sight," Lo Manto said, opening the door leading out of the office.

"I'll be happy she doesn't shoot you at first sight," Fernandez said. "But give her time. If I'm right about her, she's going to end up as good a cop as you and me.

With an outside shot at being better."

"If she's that good, then she's got a good reason to be pissed," Lo Manto said, shaking his friend's hand. "I wouldn't want to waste my days and nights baby-sitting a wop cop, either."

Jennifer Fabini stood in the bathroom, cold water dripping off her face, and stared into the steam-smeared mirror, dark eyes lit with anger. Behind her, she could hear the low talk and loud laughter of three other policewomen dressing for work. Fabini had on black jeans, black running shoes, and a thin black bra. Her blond hair was brushed back and pulled into a ponytail. She wiped her face dry with a white cloth towel and gazed at her reflection, for the very first time feeling old and trapped in a job she loved.

Fabini was two weeks shy of her thirtieth birthday and had been on the job seven years, the last three as a third-grade plainclothes detective. She knew, from the day she took the police exam, that everything she did on the job would be measured in some way against her father's talent and skill. So she worked both the job and her body hard, doing her best to minimize the questions and ease the doubts that came with being Sal Fabini's only kid. Jennifer ran for an hour every day, often around the dirt track near Riverside Drive, a few blocks from her cramped one-bedroom, third-floor walk-up. She also kick-boxed regularly and was one belt shy of black in karate. She stood five-foot-five and weighed a solid 115 pounds, but knew she could take down men twice her weight and inches over her height. And when she ran into a situation where a physical confrontation was not possible, she took them with a bullet. Her range scores had her at the top of her grade, her aim curving higher at far range, the better and more difficult standard for accuracy.

She worked hard at being a good cop, living with the weight of her father's immense shadow, which filtered down to even the youngest of rookies. She put in extra hours, working a case until it was broken, going beyond the time clock and staying on a possible suspect all night if needed. She kept her mistakes to a minimum and made it a point to learn from each one, knowing that every error she made would be magnified simply because of her father's history. She took classes at John Jay, focusing on new modes of detection, zoning in on the advances made in both forensics and DNA technology. She read thrillers and law books, took yoga to keep her body flexible and her mind sharp, and read old files on solved cases to study how the detectives pieced together the information and cracked the crime. She didn't smoke, preferred red wine to white, and hated to dance. She surrendered to only one vice—watching late-night cable reruns of old police shows, which she did sitting in the four-poster bed that ate up most of the space in her tiny bedroom, her cat Milo by her side and a pint of fat-free chocolate sorbet on her lap.

Physically, Jennifer was a blend of her father's dark,

handsome features and her mother's sheer Scandinavian beauty. She was asked out often by the detectives she worked with and those she met while killing time in the dim halls of 111 Centre Street, waiting to give testimony. She always found it easy to say no, holding strong to her desire never to date a cop. The majority of those who asked were either married or rebounding off a failed one, which made them easy candidates to brush off. Most cops make horrible husbands and even worse boyfriends, with only a rare handful able to shake off the burdens of the job and relax in the company of a woman. And if that woman also happened to wear a badge and carry a gun, it made the task that much more difficult. One of the reasons, Jennifer quickly learned, that so many female cops dated other cops was the reluctance of those not on the job to do so. "As soon as we took on this work, our chances of getting laid were brought down to fractions," her closest friend in the department, Connie Dutton, an eight-year veteran recently promoted to sergeant, once told her. "You go out with a cop, you gotta hear about the wife he can't deal with anymore or the ex-wife who never understood him or his work. All the usual cliché shit. And meantime, the only reason he's selling any of this to you is to get you into bed where *maybe,* if he's not too drunk or too stoned, he can deliver the goods to at least make one part of the night worth it."

"But the ones who aren't on the job don't seem at all interested," Jennifer said. "That's been my experience, anyway."

"Why should they be?" Connie said. "Men are as insecure as infants to start with. Then, here we come along, chicks with guns, badges, and attitude, and it scares the hell out of them. They don't know what to say or how to deal with broads like us. Think about it. We can shoot them, arrest them, or just plain kick their ass if we set our minds on it. And you know how the job makes us judge everybody we meet, and not always in a good way. So we meet an investment banker or a lawyer, well, we're thinking he must be ripping somebody off. We hook up with a newspaper or magazine guy, we figure him for a wannabe looking for an angle to make some dough with some publisher. We meet a doctor and we figure him to have botched some operation along the way or working some insurance scam that's going to take us down with him."

"So how'd you land a guy like Joe?" Jennifer asked.

"I caught some luck, I'll admit to that," Connie said. "We both go to the same church and sing in the same choir. Turns out we knew each other when we were kids, grew up in the same neighborhood in Brooklyn. Only he remembered me and I couldn't finger him out of a lineup. Anyway, he's a good man, happy at his work with Con Ed and happy with me as the woman in his life. And he's cool with what I do except for the worry end of it. But that'd be true with anybody that cared."

"Maybe I should start going back to church," Jennifer said. "Even join the choir. Who knows who I'll meet."

"These days, your choice comes down to one of two,"

Connie said. "A good man looking to give praise to the Lord or a pedophile trying to steer clear of somebody like you."

Jennifer tossed a starched white T-shirt over her head and stuffed it into her jeans. She walked over to her open locker, nodded to a uniform officer ten minutes shy of starting her shift, and reached for her gun and hip holster.

"Got something good working?" the officer asked her.

Jennifer knew the cop by face but not by name, and up to now had never exchanged anything beyond an occasional hello and a wave. "Not really," Jennifer said. "The captain asked me to hand-hold a detective in from Italy for a few days. Make sure he doesn't get lost in the crowd or, even worse, mugged."

"He good-looking at least?"

"Don't know," Jennifer said. "I'm supposed to meet him in front of the house in about fifteen minutes. Doesn't much matter, though, whether he is or he isn't. I'm not looking to go there."

"You think he speaks English?" the young officer asked.

"At best, I'm in a Chico Marx situation," Jennifer said. "At worst, not a word other than *pizza* and *pasta*."

"Why is he here?" the officer asked.

"He's looking for his niece," Jennifer said. "Here to help us out if he can. And get to see some of the sights while he's doing it."

"You don't sound happy about the detail," the officer said.

"You're right, I don't," Jennifer said. "But maybe I should be. It's been a while since I took a ride on the Circle Line, went to the Statue of Liberty, took the elevator to the top of the Empire State Building. They always say the one city you never really get to see is the one you live in. Well, now, here's my chance."

"I'd trade places with you in a heart tick," the young officer said as she put on her police cap and turned to walk out of the locker room. "I have to spend the next eight hours, maybe even twelve if I catch some OT, making sure a couple of high-enders from the UN don't catch a bullet going from their limo to the Plaza for a meeting with another group of big swingers."

"Maybe I'll stop by," Jennifer said, waving good-bye to the young officer. "I've never been inside the Plaza. My Italian shadow might like it too."

"You could share a *Breakfast at Tiffany's* moment," the young officer said over her shoulder, the thick wooden door slowly closing behind her. "If nothing else, it'll make the time go by."

Jennifer stared at the door, jammed her hip holster into place, and put on a thin black leather jacket. "I *hated* that movie," she said.

10

Pete Rossi sat across from the teenage girl and placed a cold bottle of Snapple iced tea by her side. The girl glanced at the bottle and then looked back up at the man. She was exactly what he expected her to be—just a few years older than his own daughters, slightly defiant in her manner, the tremble in her hands the only hint she was concerned about her plight. "You're going to be here for a few days," Rossi said. "But I don't want you to worry. Anything you need or want, someone will make sure you get. You're also free to leave the room and go outside, play in the sun, or walk around the property. There'll be somebody with you, but that's just for your safety."

"What do you want?" the girl asked.

"I don't want anything from you, Paula," Pete Rossi said.

"Then why am I here?" the girl asked. She looked around the big room on the second floor of a large, well-maintained house. It was a girl's room, much like the one she had with her visiting family, but filled with much more expensive furniture. She was angry at herself for having ended up in such a situation, breaking every rule her uncle had tried to cram into her, his wasted lessons repeated over and over, warnings never to fall for any line given her by a stranger gone unheeded. It was an old trap and she fell into it as easily as if she were a child in diapers. She believed the sincere young man behind the wheel of the shiny new black car. She trusted him when he told her that her mother in Italy was ill and she needed to get in with him and be rushed back to her host family, who would then book her on the first plane to Italy. He told her he was a nephew, the one she was supposed to meet at next Sunday's dinner, sent for her because everyone else was so busy making arrangements for her to leave.

She got into the car, surrendered to his concern, put on her seat belt, and heard the snap of the doors as they went on auto-lock as soon as the gears shifted. The man never raised his voice, not even when Paula watched with quiet panic as the car veered off the New York streets and onto the north ramp of the West Side Highway, heading toward the safety of the suburbs. He looked over at her several times, always with a nod and a smile on his face as he kept to the speed limit and easily switched from one lane to another. They drove for well over two hours, past the constantly ongoing roadside construction that seemed as much a part of New York life as traffic and potholes, the tall office buildings and apartment complexes disappearing in the distance, replaced by thick trees and suburban sprawl.

The man, thin, handsome, and well dressed, answered all her questions in a low-key and professional manner. He didn't raise his voice or move his hands in a threatening way, doing his best not to frighten the girl any more than she was. "Why are you doing this?" she asked at one point, mindful to keep her hands on her lap and her eyes fixed on the driver.

"We're just going for a ride," he said, keeping his focus on the road. "No one wants to hurt you and no one will. I know it's hard, but you should just try and enjoy the trip. It won't be long, we're just about there."

"It's not going to do you any good to ask for money," Paula said. "We don't have that much to give. I don't come from a rich family."

"Don't concern yourself with any of that," the man said in a reassuring voice. "Just keep thinking that everything is going to work out, and believe me, it will."

"*Believe* you?" Paula said, not hiding the anger in her voice. "I made that mistake once, remember? I'm not going to make it ever again. And you can *believe* that."

"You're probably hungry," the man said, ignoring her mini outburst. "And you must be thirsty, too. There's a cooler on the floor behind your seat. It's filled with drinks and a few sandwiches. Help yourself to whatever you want."

"The only thing I want is to get out of this car," Paula said.

"That will happen soon enough," the man said.

"You'll go to jail, you know," Paula said, her teenage temper grabbing the lead over commonsense silence. "You'll get caught and be sent to jail. Are you willing to take that chance? For someone like me?"

The young man looked away from the empty road and stared over at the teenage girl by his side. He admired her ability to choke back the fear and confront him, her grit and anger finding equal footing with the beauty that was only a few short years shy of coming to fruition. "I would take that chance for anyone," he said to her after a few quiet moments. "Especially for someone as valuable to us as you."

"Why am I here?" Paula now asked Pete Rossi, watching as he popped the top of the Snapple bottle with the palm of his right hand and loosened the cap.

"I need you to help me," he said. His voice was calm and soothing, a young man clearly accustomed to the company of children. "And my family."

"Help you how?" Paula asked, taking a quick sip from the Snapple. "I'm not allowed off the property. I can't use the phone or send any e-mails. And if I even raise my voice, I'm sure somebody will jump out and put a gag over my mouth."

"You don't need to do any of that," Rossi said, the right side of his face creasing into a slight smile. "Just having you here will give me all the help I need."

Paula stood, gently pushed the rocking chair she had

been sitting in aside, and walked toward a small window that faced out onto an expansive, beautifully manicured yard. "This is about my uncle, isn't it?" she asked, her back to Rossi.

"What makes you think that?" Rossi said. He was impressed with the girl's poise and quick grasp of her situation. He was a child of the Camorra, and in that guarded world there was little patience for teen tantrums or mood swings. The early years of a young man, or on the rare occasion a young girl, were expected to move swiftly from child to adult with no stops in between. Each waking hour was devoted to the lessons of the day, all geared to the time when each decision made would affect the success or failure of the Camorra family.

"Why else would you need me?" Paula asked, turning to face him. "What other reason is there to kidnap me and take me out here into the middle of nowhere?"

"You're a very smart young lady," Rossi said, his fingers toying with the bottle top. "As I expected you to be. And smart young ladies often understand that it's sometimes better to stop asking questions and just wait for the answers to emerge."

"Which means yes," Paula said, stepping closer toward Rossi.

"Which means it's time for me to get on with the rest of my day," Rossi said. "And for you to do the same."

"He's better than you," Paula said, her anger in check, her flushed cheeks the only outward indication that she felt at all uncomfortable. "He'll figure out where

I am and he'll come and find me. And you won't want to be here when he does."

"He may already know," Rossi said, hands in his suit pockets, smiling down at his irreverent young hostage. "And, taking into consideration travel and time change, he may be in New York, ready to sort through the pieces to get him from where he is to where he thinks you are."

"He won't fall for your tricks or be fooled by any traps you might try to set up," Paula said. "My uncle's a great cop and he's been a great cop for a long time."

"I hope you're right," Rossi said, losing the smile and turning serious for the first time since he had walked into the room. "I hope your uncle is all the things you say he is. And when this is all over, I want you to still think of him the way you do now. That will be your only comfort when you visit his grave to place fresh flowers on his headstone. And you'll be the only one to know, the only one to *really* know who it was that put him in that hole."

Rossi stared at Paula for a few brief seconds and then turned and walked out of the room, gently closing the door as he left. Paula stood in the center of the room, hands at her side, body trembling, her eyes moist and her throat dry. She looked to her right, at a four-drawer bureau topped with an assortment of ceramic statues of various Disney characters. She picked up one of the Seven Dwarfs, Dopey she thought, and threw him against the center of the wooden door. As she sat back down on the rocking chair, the ceramic piece shattered, sprinkling the floor with sheared edges.

Frank Silvestri sat on the park bench near the West 102nd Street underpass, a bag of birdseed by his side, and tossed small handfuls to the ground, watching as a platoon of pigeons swooped down and began pecking at the food. He kept his eyes on the birds as they fought over loose seeds, and ignored the two shadows who came up next to him, blocking the warm sun from his already tanned face. "You're twenty minutes late," he said, his eyes staying on the birds. "That puts us off to a bad start. And bad can only turn to worse, at least from your end."

"I'm sorry for that," one of the two shadows said. He was well built and young, brown hair hanging close to the edges of his zippered black polyester windbreaker. He kept both hands inside the front pockets of brown Timberland pants and was wearing new construction boots, laces undone. "We caught some traffic."

"On the subway?" Silvestri asked, not looking for an answer, throwing out a fresh handful of seed to the birds.

"We're here now," the second shadow said. "That should be what matters." He was huskier than his partner, older by a handful of years, his muscular body nicked and pocked by a series of scars, from bullet wounds to knife cuts. He was dressed lighter, too, in a clean white T-shirt, crisp blue jeans, and white Michael Jordan ankle-hugging sneakers, tied tight. He held a baseball in his right hand, moving it around with his fingers, gripping and massaging the stitching, flexing his grip on and off.

117

"Which one of you holds the leash?" Silvestri asked.

"You can talk to me," the one with the baseball in his hand said. "I'm Armand. This is my cousin, Georgie."

"Save the names for the dating service," Silvestri said. "I don't need to know anything about you other than the fact you're going to take a job and not fuck it up. We clear on that?"

Armand squeezed the baseball harder, his pale blue eyes staring at the man in the designer suit. He hated doing business with these old-time wiseguys, most of them talking in short bursts, their whole life run by a set of rules from another century, ones that nobody on this side of the ocean had ever even heard before. They were always preaching patience, their words crammed with examples of loyal soldiers who devoted decades of hard, solid work to their bosses before they earned their way into the power positions. The majority of the young Camorristas bought into that way of thinking, more than content to ease their way up the criminal ladder, with no greater ambition than to one day be an old don. Armand Castioni was not one of them. He was not a gangster who expected even to see old age, let alone be in the upper ranks of the Camorra if he did. He wanted in on the action now and had plans in the works that would accelerate his ascent into the inner circle. At the moment, he was middle-tier muscle and an occasional shooter, drawing a high-five-figure salary to deal with any problems that crossed the old bosses' desks. If Armand's plan worked, all that would change in six months.

"Can you hear?" Silvestri asked. "Or am I just talking to the fuckin' wind here?"

"I heard," Armand said in a low voice, avoiding eye contact with the older man. "And I got it. Keep the info to a minimum."

"We're taking a chance with you two on something like this," Silvestri said. "Up to this point, from what I've been told, you've handled every job that's been tossed your way and walked away clean after it was done. Now that can be because you're both real good, which from the looks of the two of you is a stretch for me to believe. Or it could be luck. Or it could be you've been out whacking tennis balls with baseball bats, standing up to lightweights. This here is a major-league step forward we're handing you. My advice will be to get it right."

"All we need to know is where and how soon," Armand said, brimming with confidence. "You can sleep easy after that."

"I sleep easy whether you get it done or not," Silvestri said. "You deliver for us, my boss ends his day with a smile. You fail and then the both of you are the ones having the night sweats. Either way it tags out on a good note for me. You get the full picture?"

"You made it clear," Armand said.

"The target's a cop," Silvestri said, throwing the last of the feed down at the hungry pigeons. "Not one of ours. A visiting badge from the other side. Even so, the brass here's not going to be too happy. Cop's a cop, no matter what country he's from or color he is. Which means there's gonna be heat on the two of you if it all goes down the right way. So, I hope you like Spain, because that's where you're both going to be living for about three months after the job's done."

"Why Spain?" Armand asked. "Why can't we just go back to Italy?"

"You might be right," Silvestri said, standing, his massive frame towering over the two men. "Why the fuck should we send you to a place where nobody knows you and nobody will even *think* of looking for you? When we could just send you back to your little hometown, where everybody knows you, including the cops."

"How much time do we have?" Armand asked, brushing aside the comment, bringing it back to business. "To get it done?"

"You take longer than a week, I'm going to worry," Silvestri said. "If we start getting close to two weeks, I'm gonna come hunt you both down myself."

"Where's the package?" Armand asked.

"That's the first good question you asked all day," Silvestri said. He folded the empty birdseed bag and handed it to Armand. "I'm gonna leave and you're gonna sit down and wait ten minutes, have a smoke, shoot the shit, whatever. Then, you walk out of the park, heading east. When you get to Fifth, tear open that bag and read what's written on the inside. That'll bring you to the package. Everything you need you'll find in there. The rest is up to you."

"We won't let you down," Armand said, sitting on the

bench, watching Silvestri move with slow, deliberate strides out of the park. "Me and Georgie, we're like money in the bank."

"That's too bad," Silvestri said, glancing over his shoulder at Armand and his silent cousin. "I bet my boss five thousand that the cop would take you both out the first move you made to make him dead. I figured I was looking at a sure thing. Makes me sad to think I might be wrong."

Armand waited until Silvestri was out of the park and was well beyond hearing anything he had to say. "I'll take out the cop," he said to his cousin. "And then one day I'm gonna be the one that takes out Pete Rossi's pit bull. And I'm gonna make sure to shove five thousand dollars in the asswipe's mouth. Make him sit there and gag on it, just before I put a bullet in his head."

"And then we feed *him* to the pigeons," Georgie said, free to speak now that Silvestri was gone, gazing down with disgust at the feeding birds. "He likes these flying rats so fuckin' much."

Pete Rossi walked down the center aisle of the freezer room, 250-pound hindquarters of prime beef hanging on thick hooks lining both sides. He was holding a steaming container of hot coffee in his right hand, his left slapping at the sides of beef as he walked past. In the rear of the room, he could see the man bound to the reclining chair, two of his crew standing over him, glaring down at him, waiting for Rossi's orders.

121

"Give us a few minutes," he told them when he got closer. Both were young, their biceps thick as thighs, veins bulging like cords down the sides of their arms. Rossi figured they spent as many hours juicing up as they did lifting, which would soon damage both their brains and their bodies, rendering their services totally useless to him in a few years' time.

He watched as they nodded and walked toward the thick freezer door leading out of the room, the sawdust from the floor sticking to their Puma sneakers. Then Rossi turned his attention to the man tied to the chair. He was in his mid-thirties, with a handsome face and a close-trimmed beard topped by a thick head of brown hair. He was in decent physical shape and had a light tan and manicured nails. "I told you when you first came to me about your troubles that this is how it would end," Rossi said to him. "I said to you, 'Charlie, don't get yourself into this because there's no way out for you.' But you said I was wrong. That you would make it work. And now look at where we are."

"I thought the money would come in faster than it has," Charlie said. "And I'm up to date with the payments. I haven't missed one since I borrowed. It's just the interest that's killing me. *Nobody*, not even fuckin' Donald Trump, can keep up with seventeen percent a week."

"But that's part of the deal, Charlie," Rossi said, taking a slow sip of his coffee. "I don't make money just by *giving* you money. If that were the case, I'd be working the losing end. Then, I'd be the one in the chair with all the problems."

"Then you might as well kill me," Charlie said in a matter-of-fact tone. "I'm better off dead than trying to scramble for the rest of my life just to pay you off. And you can take my share of the business too, for what the hell that's worth. And then I'd be finished with it, and even with all that you'll still be short the money you put out. So nobody wins. Not me and not you."

Pete Rossi tossed the container of coffee to the ground, the hot liquid quickly absorbed by the mounds of sawdust. "There are a lot of ways to die, Charlie," Rossi said, each word spoken slowly and with great care. "A couple of bullets to the head would be the easiest, but then that's only if I want to let you off light. Which I have no intention of doing. You lied to me. You gave me your word and you lied. And that bill is going to cost you a lot more than two bullets."

Charlie looked up at Rossi and swallowed hard, the cold of the room chilling the sweat on his forehead and damp shirt. A fearful panic filled his eyes, his lower lip trembling, his teeth chattering. "This is between you and me," he said in a soft voice. "It doesn't need to go beyond that."

"You're the one that took it there, Charlie," Rossi said. "Not me."

"What are you going to do?" Charlie asked, his voice reduced to that of a little boy cowering in a corner of a dark room.

"What you've forced me to do," Rossi said in a voice cold enough to frost the walls of the chilled locker. "My job."

"Give it another week, Pete," Charlie said, tears starting to edge down the corner of his eyes. "I'm begging you as a friend. One more week and I'll get you all the money plus all the interest. Please, Pete! Oh, Jesus! Please!"

Rossi stood in front of Charlie and looked down at the withering man, hands in his pants pockets, his eyes cold as a winter morning. "There are men inside your apartment right now," he said to him. "They're taking anything of value, anything that can be turned into fast cash. Your wife is there with them. When they're through with the jewels and the clothes, they'll start on her and they won't stop until they've had enough."

"You bastard!" Charlie hissed, his eyes wide with anger and fright. "You have a family of your own! How can you do this to somebody else? How can you live with yourself?"

"There are other men in your downtown warehouse," Rossi said, ignoring the questions, holding his look on Charlie. "You got a full inventory in there, fresh shipment just came in late last night. They're going to torch it all and burn it to the ground. The insurance check you'll get from the fire will be signed over to a third party and be used to cover the rest of your loan to me."

Charlie coughed up bile, spitting some onto the sawdust by his feet, letting the rest run down the front of his drenched shirt. He was sobbing now, his eyes closed, tears coating his face, the cold air giving it an icy sheen.

"I'm going to leave now and send the two men who were with you earlier back in here," Rossi said. "They've been instructed not to kill you, even though you may ask them to. They'll come very close and leave you wishing they had finished the job. You'll spend the night locked in here and, maybe, if you have any luck left in your life, you'll freeze to death. At some point early in the morning, if you're still breathing, you'll be dragged out and dropped off at the nearest hospital. From that moment, it ends between us. You won't owe me and I won't owe you."

"I'll pay you double what I owe," Charlie said, trying to make the most of whatever seconds he had before his future would be sealed. "And you won't have to wait. I can get it all to you by tomorrow."

Rossi ran a hand along a side of beef, the fat thick as a man's waist, and looked back at Charlie, for the first time showing a hint of anger. "You couldn't pay me what you owed on a weekly," he said. "But now you have enough to hand over twice what you owe? You draw a Win Five since you been locked in here?"

"It's not my money," Charlie said, the sweat running down his face at garden hose speed. "It belongs to one of my partners. But I have access to it. I can pull out as much of it as I need in an emergency."

Pete Rossi nodded and strode closer to Charlie, careful not to step in the vomit that had blended into the sawdust. "Do you have to be there?" he asked. "Or can it all be done with a phone call?"

"Either one," Charlie said, his voice reduced to a whimper. "All I have to do is call our principal banker and give him the code number. That gets me into the account. From there, I just tell him where I want it wired and how much is needed."

"How much is in the account?" Rossi asked. "Total?"

"Enough to cover double what I owe," Charlie said, starting to return to a normal breathing pattern, sensing that he at least had Rossi's interest and maybe that much would be enough to alter his plans.

"That's not what I asked," Rossi said. "I want to know how much is in the account, as of right now. Down to the last nickel."

"Six hundred and fifty thousand," Charlie said. "As of last Friday, which is the last time I checked."

"Have you ever borrowed against it before?" Rossi asked.

"Once," Charlie said. "About two years ago. We were about a hundred grand behind in bills. I made good on it as soon as we sold most of our inventory."

"And why didn't you use it to pay what you owed us?" Rossi asked. "If all you say is true, the money is just a phone call away. Then none of this would have been necessary. I'm sure your partner would have understood."

"I thought about it," Charlie said. "And I almost made the call a week or so ago. But my loan from you was personal. It had nothing to do with our business. My partner looks up to me like an older brother, and I guess I didn't want him to think I was just another gambling deadbeat in hock."

"He's going to think you're worse than that," Rossi said. "He's going to think you're the lowest kind of thief there is, and if he has any sense at all he'll wash his hands of you first chance he gets."

"I'll pay him back," Charlie said. "I'll do whatever it takes but I'll get the money."

"You're going to have to pay back *all* that's in there," Rossi said. "And I don't know if you'll be up to that. And frankly, I don't give a shit whether you are or not."

"I don't need to give it all back," Charlie said, taking a defensive mode. "I'm only taking out a little more than half, that covers double what I owe and makes it square between you and me."

"No," Rossi said, shaking his head. "You're going to make that call and you're going to empty out that account and then make arrangements to have the money wired to a third party. From there, it'll find its way to me."

"I don't *owe* you that much," Charlie said, raising his voice, steam coming out of his mouth. "And that would clean out the entire partnership, force us to shut the business. You just can't do that."

"I'm not doing it," Rossi said. "You are. You'll call your banker and transfer the funds to a number you'll be given. And you'll do that as soon as we ask you to."

"And what happens after that?" Charlie asked, afraid that he already knew the answer to his question.

"Then we go back to the original plan," Rossi said, walking toward the rear of the freezer room. "Nothing's changed. Other than the fact that my side of the table is now six hundred and fifty grand richer. It's been a pleasure doing business with you, Charlie. Enjoy what's left of your life."

"You're a fuck!" Charlie shouted out at him. "A heartless, no-good fuck! That's all you are. That's all you'll ever be."

Rossi turned and looked down the aisle at Charlie, struggling against the thick rope and reams of tape holding him in his chair. "It's all I ever wanted to be," he said to him.

Rossi opened the freezer door and walked out into the humid New York air. He stepped up to a black sedan, where the two men were waiting by the rear of the car, one holding the back door open.

"He needs to make a call," Rossi said to the one at the door. "Once that's cleared, he belongs to you."

"How do you want him?" the man asked.

"Take the head, hands, and feet," Rossi said in a manner as relaxed as if he were ordering a takeout lunch. "Get rid of those and then ship what's left of him to his family. I don't want it to be said that we don't care about the people who do business with us."

11

Lo Manto slid into the passenger seat of Fabini's four-door unmarked charcoal gray Chrysler sedan and snapped on his seat belt. He looked over at Jennifer, gave her a quick smile and a nod, and handed her a folded sheet of paper. She grabbed it, flipped it open, and gave a quick scan of what was written in pen across the top half. "What's in the Bronx?" she asked, handing the paper back.

"*Come?*" Lo Manto asked in Italian.

"Do you speak *any* English at all?" she asked, turning over the engine and shifting the car into gear, easing into the congested midtown traffic flow. "Or should I just talk to myself these next few days?"

"*Sì, sì*, English," Lo Manto said, nodding, a wide grin spread across his face. "I speak, yes, very well. In *Italia* I study for four years and I go to many, many movies. Like born in America."

"That's good for me to know," Jennifer said as she gunned the engine and ran a red light as she passed Fifth Avenue.

"Do you *parle Italiano*?" Lo Manto asked. "Fabini, yes? You are Italian, no?"

"I'm New York Italian," Jennifer said, not bothering to hide the frustration she felt over her new assignment. "That means I eat the food, but I don't speak the lingo."

"Is true of so many Italians in America," Lo Manto said, folding his hands behind his head and checking out Fabini. "They say they are Italian, but they don't learn to speak. It's such a *peccato* to not speak such beautiful words. Especially if the one speaking them is also beautiful."

Fabini shot Lo Manto a quick look and chuckled. "You can't be for serious," she said. "Not unless cops have a whole different way of talking back in your country."

"I am *molto* serious," he said. "It is what I believe in my heart to be true. In *Italia* we look for beauty in all things. Even in the police."

"Sounds great," Fabini said. "I guess we look at things a little bit different over here. We look for the bad first and sort of turn our backs on the good. That's true of most in this city. And it's even truer if you happen to be a cop."

"You like what you do?" Lo Manto asked.

"Most days I love it," Fabini said, wincing as her front end nose-dived into a crater-size pothole on the Bruckner Boulevard entrance ramp. "Even if I have to spend hours doing paperwork or cool my heels sitting outside a courtroom waiting to give testimony. It's all part of the same package."

"But today, you don't love," Lo Manto said. "Taking me to the Bronx. Making sure I don't get lost."

"It's not personal and I'm not looking for you to take it that way," Fabini said. "I would have hated this assignment no matter who it was I ended up sitting next to. I thought I was past working details like this, that I'd done enough as a cop to not be the precinct driver. But since you're there and I'm here and we *are* going to the Bronx, it looks like I was as wrong as could be."

"Maybe it's for a good reason your captain put you with me, no?" Lo Manto asked. "He thinks that if I help you and if you help me, together we are a good team. He's a smart man and smart men always have plans."

"Listen, I'm sure back in Naples, you're a pretty decent cop," Jennifer said, resigned to her situation. "I don't think the captain would treat you with the respect he does if you weren't. But you're not here to bust anybody and you're not looking to make a big score, so our entire partnership is based on me not getting lost behind the wheel and on not having you disappear outside the car. Clean as that."

"If you are so unhappy, I can ask for another cop," Lo Manto said. "The captain is a friend. He will make the change if I ask."

"That'd go over real well," Jennifer said in a sarcastic tone. "Then I get switched from driving you to working the sun shift in traffic. Your friend doesn't care for cops who ask out of assignments and he makes sure he gets his point across when they do."

"Then we make it work," Lo Manto said. "We learn from our time together. I teach what I know and watch and look how you do your job. That is maybe what the captain wants for us. If true, then, next time, with the next cop off a plane, you no have to drive."

"What's in the Bronx?" Jennifer asked, circling onto White Plains Road, driving under the shadows of the elevated subway tracks.

"A man I know," Lo Manto said, sitting up, his body language shifting from relaxed to a higher gear. "I think he has the answers to my questions. It would be nice to come out of his place with more than a *pancia* filled with coffee."

"You used to live around here, no?" Jennifer asked.

"Yes," Lo Manto said. "When I was a boy, this was my *quartiere*. How you say in English?"

"Neighborhood," Jennifer said, catching Lo Manto's look. "I took three years of Italian in high school. Some of the lessons stayed with me."

"Can stop next to that small store?" Lo Manto asked. "The one with the *giornali* in the front."

"Which one we going into?" she asked, easing the unmarked to a stop in front of a fire hydrant, its locked lid dripping water out of the sides. "The candy store or the bar next to it?"

"*I* go into the bar," Lo Manto said, opening the passenger car door, one foot fast on the pavement. "But you are free to go into any other store you like."

"I'm not supposed to leave you alone," Jennifer said.

"I don't like them, but those are my orders. And I'm going to follow them."

"What if I say please to you?" Lo Manto asked, tilting his head at Jennifer and giving her a casual smile. "The man I'm going to see doesn't like the police very much."

"I'll stay clear of you," Jennifer said. "I won't step on any of your action, let you two go over old times, play cards, drink coffee, watch a few hours of Italian television. Stay there as long as you want. You'll get no pressure from me. But just know that when you walk into that bar, I'll be the one that's behind you."

Lo Manto stepped out of the car and waited as Jennifer killed the engine, jammed an NYPD parking voucher on the dashboard, and walked away from the wheel. "Italian women, American women," he said as much to himself as he did to her. "There is no difference."

"There is with this one," she said, leading the way toward the dark glass and door of the corner bar.

"What?"

"I carry a weapon," she said.

Lo Manto walked into the room, wood floors shiny and waxed, sideboard lights on dim, the bar long and polished. There were three men in well-tailored suits sitting on swivel stools, hunched over shot glasses, their cigarettes left smoldering in thick ashtrays. Behind the wood, a bartender in a crisp clean white shirt and knotted red tie was filling the front freezer with warm, long-necked beer bottles. There were six small tables at one end of the bar area, each covered with a white linen tablecloth, silverware, and lit candles. From the middle of the room, Lo Manto could see the lights of the main dining room to his left, the sounds of a Sinatra song filtering down. He caught the bartender's eye and nodded. "Eduardo," Lo Manto said to him.

"In the back," the bartender said in a soft voice. *"Ti aspetta."*

"Do you like espresso?" Lo Manto asked Jennifer. She was standing next to him, her jacket open, her gun and shield covered by the front flaps, her eyes taking in the space and the occupants.

"You have any idea whose bar this is?" she asked.

"Yes," Lo Manto said to her, his voice now rougher, an angrier tone to it. "Everyone does."

"You gonna be good in here?" she asked, speaking in low tones. "You screw up with this crowd, you're a ten-minute ride away from the back of a cement mixer."

"You sit at the bar," Lo Manto said. "Enjoy your espresso, maybe even have a *dolce* to go with it, and listen to the music. It will relax you."

"I can't let you walk into trouble," Jennifer said. "What part of that can't you seem to work out?"

"Eduardo is expecting me," Lo Manto said, his eyes roving from Jennifer to the three suits at the bar. "He would find it an insult if I brought a stranger with me. *Ti prego,* please wait for me here."

Jennifer looked at Lo Manto and then toward the

back of the bar. She took a deep breath and slowly nodded her head. "I'll go your way," she said. "But if I even smell a whiff of trouble, I'm coming in. You *capice* what I'm bringing across?"

"Un espresso per la signorina, per cortesia," Lo Manto said to the bartender, walking away from Jennifer and heading toward the back room. *"Al bar."*

"I'd rather have American coffee," Jennifer said, pulling back a stool and sitting down, her back to Lo Manto.

"When in Rome, Signorina, do as the Romans," the bartender said. "And when in my bar, drink it the way it's served."

"I was always told you were the kind who liked to work alone," Eduardo Gaspaldi said. "Now here you come dancing into my place with a partner. And a woman, to top it off. One of us must be getting old and he's not sitting at my end of the table."

"Who she is doesn't play into what we need to talk about," Lo Manto said. "As far as you're concerned, she's a customer, killing some time, drinking a cup of your fresh coffee. Your business is with me."

"And what business would that be?" Eduardo asked, pushing aside an espresso cup and reaching for a half-empty pack of Lord's cigarettes.

"My niece went missing about a week ago," Lo Manto said. "You probably heard about it before I did. I came back to help find her and figured my best bet would be to come see you."

"This is a big neighborhood, Lo Manto," Eduardo said, striking a match to his cigarette. "Kids come and go all the time, for all sorts of reasons. It's not up to me to keep track. I run a restaurant. Not a school."

"You're a pimp," Lo Manto said. He pulled out the chair across from Eduardo and sat down, his elbows on the edge of the table, body leaning forward. "That's what you were when I left here and that's what you stayed. Back then at least you were using pros. Then, just like every other pool scraper, you got greedy. Started going after them young, banked on there being more profit in it."

"You're hot shit in Naples," Eduardo said, blowing a line of smoke toward the ceiling fan above his head. "But you're nothing here. You can't even make a citizen's arrest because you're not a fuckin' citizen."

Lo Manto moved like a coiled bobcat. He was off his chair and by Eduardo's side in a blur, a switchblade in his right hand, sharp edge jammed inside the stunned pimp's ear, his other arm wrapped around his throat. Eduardo's cigarette was still clenched between his teeth. "I'm invisible in this country," Lo Manto said. "Which means I can do whatever the hell I want. Especially to a scum floater like you. No cop, on the pad or off, is even going to miss lunch if they hear you're lying facedown in a back alley dumpster."

"I don't know anything," Eduardo said, his voice reduced to a stilted squeak. "If I did, I'd pass it on."

"The blade on my knife is thin," Lo Manto said. "And

I'm not that far from your eardrum. So make sure the next words you say mean something to me."

"Not even you would be that fuckin' crazy," Eduardo said, spitting the lit cigarette to the floor.

Lo Manto pulled the blade out of Eduardo's ear and then with a quick flick sliced a small piece off his lobe. He reached a hand up and covered the pimp's mouth, holding him in place, checking to make sure no one from the other room heard the commotion. "I just wanted to make sure it was sharp enough," he whispered into the man's ear, blood flowing down the side of Eduardo's neck and onto Lo Manto's jacket. "Talk to me, while you can still hear. And if you yell for your men, I'll move from your ear to your throat before they're off their stools."

"Word is she got into somebody's car," Eduardo said. "Not here, but somewhere in the city."

"Whose car?"

"Not one of the regular crew guys," Eduardo said. "More than not, an out-of-town hire brought in for the day."

"And he took her where?" Lo Manto asked, tightening his grip around Eduardo's throat, the ear and neck now coated in blood.

"Out of the city," Eduardo said. "Westchester, some-place like that. Not where the cops would think to look for her."

"She alive?" Lo Manto asked.

"Whatta you think, we print our own fuckin' news-paper?" Eduardo asked. "They don't tell me everything that goes on and I make it a habit not to ask a lot of questions."

"You won't need to ask *any* questions if you can't hear," Lo Manto said, scraping the knife against the side of Eduardo's ear.

"Killing her ain't part of the plan," Eduardo said. "That much I do know."

"What is part of the plan?" Lo Manto asked.

"Killing you," Eduardo said.

Jennifer slammed the car into drive and hit the gas, pulling out of the spot, swerving to avoid an oncoming gypsy cab. "I trusted you," she said to Lo Manto, her face red as a clay court, her hands squeezing the steering wheel. "I bought into your third-tier guinea sweet-talk bullshit routine and look what happens!"

"Nothing happened," Lo Manto said, wiping at the blood on his jacket with a cloth napkin he took from the bar. "My friend had an accident. He cut himself while we were talking."

"Cut himself with what?" Jennifer screamed. "What's he do, stir his coffee with a meat cleaver?"

"He's going to be good," Lo Manto said, looking to calm her down and get her to bring him to his next stop. "He said so himself. You heard, no?"

"You got something going on," Jennifer said. "And it's all well and good you want to get to it on your own. But, as long as you need me to drive Miss Daisy around town, it'd be better for both of us if you fill me in."

"Have you had lunch yet?" Lo Manto asked, tossing the blood-soaked napkin onto the backseat.

"No, but I *had* coffee," she said, turning right on a red light. "Four tiny cups of that Italian heart-grabber while I was sitting at the bar like a good little girl, waiting while you were doing a Sweeney Todd on the owner."

"We're very close to Eastchester," Lo Manto said. "That means we are very close to a wonderful meal. An *antipasto misto*, a bowl of pasta, and a glass of *vino* will put you in a much better mood. It might even make you smile."

"Taking you to the airport and shoving you on a plane back to Italy would make me smile," Jennifer said. "And let's not forget, we're on city time in this car, which means it's taxpayer money we're wasting while we're driving around looking for the latest Zagat five-star. They may not give two shits about stuff like that back in Naples, but it's pretty much a huge deal in New York."

"I will pay," Lo Manto said. "Both for the meal and for the gas. With my own money. It is what's fair."

"It's going to be your nightmare if I find out you're playing me," Jennifer said. "You'll regret it till the day you're on your deathbed."

"You are not married, correct?" Lo Manto said. "And no boyfriend as well. True?"

"What's that have to do with the price of tomatoes?" Jennifer asked, calming down, more agitated than angry. "I could have a *GQ* husband, six model kids, and

Rin Tin Tin waiting for me on the front porch, I'd still be in the pissed-off mood I'm in."

"You spend all your free time alone," Lo Manto said. "It is why you are always so fast to get angry. You have, *come si dice,* a short fuse. Like a volcano, you wait to explode."

"I suppose you got a nice, hefty Italian bride waiting for you back home," Jennifer said. "The kind that cooks all your meals, irons all your clothes, and serves all your needs. And maybe, seeing as how you're both a cop *and* an Italian, you also have yourself something even better on the side. That's the Kodak moment that flashes before my eyes."

"No," Lo Manto said, shaking his head. "I have no wife or girlfriend. I too spend all my free time alone. And like you, I get angry very fast. I am the one with the short fuse."

"It fits easier on a man," Jennifer said. "You don't get ragged on as much by your friends, your family, the others on the job. Everybody you know trying to pair you up with someone they wouldn't be caught in a grave with. All this massive effort just so, at the end of the day, you can end up as miserable as everyone else around you."

"Now I know you have never been to Italy," Lo Manto said. "To be a single man, as I am, in his late thirties, is *un grande problema.* There is always talk behind your back that maybe you are not right. *Mi capisci?*"

"The words *gay* and *cop* hardly ever make a Scrabble

match," Jennifer said. "No matter what side of the ocean you walk your beat."

"And then there are all the female cousins in faraway places who have never married," Lo Manto said. "And there are reasons found for us to meet."

"You would marry a cousin?"

"I would not, no," Lo Manto said with a shrug of indifference. "But many in Naples have. And in New York, too. I have an Aunt Claudia and an Uncle Franco, they are first cousins and have been married for close to forty years. And they are more in love now than when they were children. It is *una bella cosa* to see them together, holding hands, teasing one to the other. Some customs are much slower to break than others and some last so long for a reason."

"That would never work for me," Jennifer said. "I can't stand being in the same room with my relatives, never mind being married to one."

"Some are made for marriage and others are not," Lo Manto said. "And I think you are a better police officer, here and in Italy, if you have no family."

"Seeing how there's no sign of my *Bachelor* anywhere on the horizon, I'll have to agree with you," Jennifer said. "Not unless we throw Milo in the mix. He's been crazy about me for a lot of years."

"But you said you had no *fidanzato*?" Lo Manto said.

"If that means boyfriend," Jennifer said, "you're right. Milo's my cat and my friend and the one who listens to me bitch about my problems late at night when

141

nobody else cares. He cleans up after himself, never leaves a mess outside his box, and even likes to drink beer. He's as close to the perfect man as I'll ever get."

"Does he know about me?"

"There isn't anything that goes on in my life that he *doesn't* know," Jennifer said. "We keep no secrets between us, me and Milo. We're partners clean down the middle. Total trust."

"Even the *gatto* wants me back in Italy," Lo Manto said. "Well, soon he gets his wish and you both will be happy again."

"How soon?" Jennifer asked, hitting the brakes hard at a red light, ignoring the angry glances of the crossing pedestrians.

"I can't talk when my stomach is empty," Lo Manto said, dismissing her question with a wave of his hand. "I can't even think. We must eat now. That's a request even a great *gatto* like Milo would honor."

Jennifer stared at Lo Manto, shook her head, and hit the gas, running through the light, barely missing an oncoming Ford Taurus, the driver's right fist furiously slamming down on his horn. "Maybe I'll get lucky," she muttered. "Maybe I'll get food poisoning and be out a few days."

"Have the raw clams," Lo Manto said. "That usually works in Naples."

12

Felipe Lopez stood and watched as the man in the red sauce–splattered shirt slid a plain slice onto a paper plate and rested it on the counter. "You want a drink with that?" he asked.

"What I want and what I can buy ain't the same," Felipe said, reaching for the red pepper. "I got enough to cover the slice, so I'll just stick with that."

"Where you been sleeping these days?" the man asked, watching Felipe fold the slice and take a big bite.

"This a pizzeria or a police station, Joey?" Felipe asked. "You should be asking me how I like the pie, not where I get my mail sent."

"You're still on the street," Joey said. "That's why you give off with the smart answers instead of laying out the truth."

"I deal with it," Felipe said. "That's as much as I can do right now."

"The brothers at that school of yours came up with six months' worth of rent money a few weeks back," Joey

143

said. "At least that's what I heard. Handed it off to your father and told him to go find a place for the both of you. What happened there?"

"Six months of rent money can buy you four weeks of booze," Felipe said. "That's what happened. And that picture ain't never gonna change. Not while he's alive, anyway."

Felipe Lopez was fifteen and homeless. His father, Enrique, was an abusive alcoholic, out of work and in debt, living and sleeping in a string of downtown flophouses. He had managed to get it together enough to figure a way to scam Social Security out of a small disability check the first of each month, which he used to help fund his bottle habit. Felipe avoided him as much as possible as he moved from shelter to shelter in search of warm food, a cool drink and a clean cot. On some nights, usually during the school year, he would take advantage of a friend's offer and sleep on a fold-away in the boy's tight one-bedroom apartment. And some other nights he would crouch in the rear of a steamy tenement hallway, waiting out the hours until the sun came up. Either way, on the street or off, Felipe managed to stay in school. He scrounged together enough pocket cash to keep the mandatory uniform he had to wear clean and hold up to the demanding academic schedule devised by the Catholic order of brothers who ran the place.

Felipe was twelve the last time he saw his mother. She was just out of her teens when she met Enrique, and soon she was pregnant with his son. The marriage was always shaky at best, both husband and wife chasing demons of their own, trying to hold down low-paying jobs, with little time left over to care for an infant son. "She was laying flat out," Felipe once told a friend about that last day with his mother, "her eyes rolling like marbles in the back of her head, white foam bubbling up on her lips. She was holding the crack pipe in her right hand, held it tight like it was a winning lottery ticket. It looked like she was floating away. I said good-bye to her right then and there, in the middle of a crack den, in a room filled with junkies and pipe rats."

"She dead?" his friend asked.

"To me she is," Felipe said, shrugging his shoulders, his voice still navigating the border between adolescent and adult. "Probably to everybody else that knew her back in the day. Except maybe for her dealer. That lowlife will be the last set of eyes my mom will ever see before the drop-off into the OD."

The counterman filled a small plastic cup with crushed ice and Coke and rested it next to Felipe. "Use this to wash down the slice," he said to the boy. "My pizza's the best. With a drink, it's even better."

"I ain't one of Jerry's kids," Felipe said, ignoring the cold soda. "You looking to give something away, dial him up."

"I don't move nothin' for free," Joey said. "I don't care who it's for. You're gonna pay me for that soda, you just won't be paying me for it today."

"All right then," Felipe said, reaching a hand out for the drink. "Next time I walk in here, you and me be square."

"You keeping up with the schoolwork?" Joey asked. "Those brothers don't give a shit you live in a mansion or on the steps of a sewer, they expect all their boys to be pulling down straights."

"I get my A's no sweat," Felipe said. "And I don't mind the work, either. Gives me an excuse to hang in the library late as I want."

"You catch any buzz with that lady from social?" he asked. "I seen her around here the other night. She any help to you or just talking it to cash a weekly?"

"I don't let her anywhere near me," Felipe said, munching on the thin crust end of the pizza. "She's starting to catch wise I don't sleep anyplace steady. She nails it, I head straight for a foster home and I want no piece of that end."

"Where she think you're living?" Joey asked. "The Plaza?"

"There's a house up around Baychester," Felipe said. "Remember Jerry Botten? Old man lost a leg down the piers?"

"Extra mushrooms, heavy on the cheese," Joey said, wiping down the Formica top with a damp cloth. "I never forget a regular. He died about six, maybe eight weeks ago. Am I right?"

"That's him," Felipe said. "Now his two kids are butting heads over the house. Who gets it, who don't.

Until all that gets cleaned up, the place stays the way it was the day Jerry kicked. So that's the address I give the lady from social. She's been up there four, five times I heard looking for me. Walked away like a Jehovah's Witness, her hands and pockets empty."

"She go up to the school?" Joey asked. "Scope you out there?"

"It ain't like she's on me 24/7, Joey," Felipe said. "Came up there twice, figuring to nab me in the halls between classes. The brothers put some Jason Kidd moves on her and made sure she left same way she came in."

"Which leaves you where?" Joey asked.

"Here," Felipe said. "With you. Eatin' your pizza and drinkin' your soda."

"And you get the money for that how?" Joey asked, leaning forward, one arm bent across the countertop.

"I take off pizza places," Felipe said, flashing a wide smile. "That way I can score on cash and cheese."

"I'm talking to you serious," Joey said, genuine concern behind his words. "You're on the street, which is no place for anybody to be, let alone a kid still in high school. Shit happens out there and none of it is even close to being good. You can joke about it you want, maybe that helps you deal with it, but the real deal is short of laughs."

"I'm too old to cry, Joey," Felipe said. The boy stepped away from the counter. The smile was gone now. He was a wiry young man, thin and fast, a natural athlete with a handsome face and charcoal eyes set off by a head of hair as thick and dark as tar. "And I'm too young not to be scared. But this is my hand and this is what I gotta play. You can only do your best and hope for it, too."

Felipe excelled at playground basketball and was a solid enough player to work his way into the five-on-five rotation games that offered cash payouts to the winners. His six-dollar cut was usually enough to carry him for three days, sometimes four. He also competed with the homeless, the winos, and the rummies for the empty cans and bottles that filled the corner garbage bins or were left on the sides of curbs and in unlit hallways. But a full-day tour of that work never amounted to more than pocket change.

The boy never begged and he never accepted handouts, neither from the brothers at school nor from his extended street family. Not even from the do-gooders down at the Salvation Army. "I'll make my way out of this," he once told Brother Joseph, the school's American history teacher. He was the prime force behind convincing school administrators to ignore the boy's rising tuition bills and focus on his grades, making him eligible for one of the four yearly scholarships that were offered. "Maybe not in a way you'd like or want to see, but I'll do it. I'm not gonna be on the streets the rest of my life and I don't count on being found dead there either."

"So you steal," Brother Joseph said. They were in the school gym that day, a large, warehouse-size space, with a regulation basketball court, running track, and indoor bleachers. "You take what belongs to someone else and make it your own."

"It's what I need to do now, Brother," he said. "I'm as happy about it as you are, but it's keeping me alive. And I never take from those that have less than me."

"No one has less than you, Felipe," Brother Joseph said. "Even I have more in my pocket than you do."

"That was a choice you made," Felipe said. "I never wanted to be poor."

"One crime always leads to another," Brother Joseph said. "It's easy to move from stealing food to eat to robbing a bank or a restaurant at gunpoint. I've seen it happen too many times to too many kids the same age as you. I'm forty-two years old and sick of going to funerals, watching them bury people twice as young as me."

"Let's not make a U-turn here and put me on a wanted poster," Felipe said. "I steal candy bars, snack foods, a bottle of 7-Up maybe, take a bag out of the Chinese delivery guy's basket. Nobody's gonna die off of anything like that."

"Speaking of which," Brother Joseph said, his voice echoing off the thick walls of the empty court, "Denise in the cafeteria tells me we're missing one of the roasted turkeys that were delivered the other night. You wouldn't know anything about that?"

"No," Felipe said, shaking his head. "But you want, I'll look into it for you."

"I'd appreciate it," Brother Joseph said.

*

Felipe walked out of the pizzeria and into the thick and humid East Bronx air. This was the hottest city summer he could remember, and he was giving some thought to spending the night up on Ely Avenue, where he could always count on the fire hydrants being open full blast. A couple of hours under the spray of the ice cold water there would be more than enough to cool him down. Then, he could jump the brick wall at the dead end of Ely, sneak into one of the subway cars that were parked there, and spend the night on the number two line, moving between Manhattan and the Bronx. With luck, he might even catch an air-conditioned car. Either way, it had to beat the large cardboard box he had been using as cover the last two nights, his back and neck still sore from the cement floor that took the place of a mattress.

He was crossing against the light on East 235th Street, walking under the shade of the elevated subway, when he saw Charlie Sunshine coming out of Ben Murphy's Bar and Grill, his right arm pressed against his side, the sleeve of his loose-fitting blue bowling shirt tinged with blood. Felipe ducked behind a rusty iron pillar, the subway rumbling loud overhead, and watched as Sunshine lurched from the side of a parked car to that of a waiting one. Sunshine opened the rear door of a black Oldsmobile Cutlass and dove in. Within seconds, the driver had the car out in the traffic lane, moving fast toward the entrance to the Major Deegan Expressway.

Felipe checked the oncoming cars, then ran across to

Murphy's B&G. He opened the front door, his eyes forced to adjust to the near-darkness. Thin lines of smoke filtered through the air, the smell of cooking grease hanging heavy. The booths that lined the right-hand side of the B&G were empty, table settings in place, ready for the start of business. He walked slowly toward the bar, careful not to step on the broken glass that littered the center of the floor, the whiskey seeping out of the bottle forming a puddle near one of the stools. The television above the bar was tuned to the Yankee game on YES, Jim Kaat breaking down a Jorge Posada at bat. "Ben?" Felipe called out. "Are you in here?"

Felipe stopped when he heard a low moan coming from behind the bar. He made his way around the wood and looked down at the row of cracked slats that covered the dark blue linoleum. Ben was sitting in the center of the floor, just under the open cash register, his back resting against the cold steel door of a small fridge. He turned to look at Felipe, his chubby face bruised and bleeding, his bald head shining under the lights from the beer dispenser, part of his skull cracked and raw. The front of his white shirt was sopped with blood and a puddle of it was forming at the base of his spine. His legs were splayed out, the right one trembling slightly.

Felipe rushed to his side, got down on one knee and reached for his hand, holding it to his chest. "I'll call for an ambulance," he told him. "Get you to a hospital in about five minutes. They'll fix you up good once you're there."

Ben yanked at the boy. "You stay put," he said. "I want no ambulance. No hospital and no cops, either. There's no time or need for any of that."

"I can't just let you stay here like this," Felipe said. "We don't do something quick you're going to bleed to death. And I can't even think of what else to do. I gotta call for help, Ben. It's your only shot."

"Listen to me," Ben said to the boy. "Forget all that other shit and just shut the hell up and listen."

Felipe nodded. "I'm with you, Ben," he said, squeezing the man's hand tighter to his chest.

"That prick Sunshine came here for the money," Ben said. "And he left as empty as when he first walked in. Asshole."

"Why didn't you let him have it?" Felipe asked. "How much could there have been in the till? It ain't worth dying for less than a hundred dollars."

"How about one hundred thousand dollars?" Ben asked. "Is that something you would die for?"

"I don't know anybody with that kind of money," Felipe said.

"You're looking at somebody with that kind of money," Ben said, the blood now running down the front of his face, blurring the vision in one of his eyes.

"Shit," Felipe said. "You're moving a lot more beer and burgers than I thought."

"Five years ago, me and three other guys were in on a heist," Ben said, talking in slow spurts. "We got away clean, divided the money into four shares, and hid the

Paradise City

dough, acting like none of us even had it. We were going to wait the seven years, then pull it out and treat it like our own."

"Was Charlie Sunshine one of the four?" Felipe asked.

Ben snorted out what sounded like a laugh. "Charlie Sunshine couldn't find his ass with both hands," he said. "About six months after the job, one of the crew got nabbed on a break-and-enter in Brooklyn. It should have been a short stretch, but the cops had a bug up their ass about that first hit and tried to squeeze him to give up what he knew. He kept quiet and won a six-to-ten as his reward. Ended up at Comstock. Same tier as Charlie, who knew him from the neighborhood."

"And he told Charlie about the robbery?" Felipe asked. He reached his hands into the slop sink, rinsed out a cold cloth, and rested it on one side of Ben's head. "That how he found out about the money?"

"Nobody on my crew talks," Ben said. "That's why we pulled as many jobs as we did. We do the hits and then turn deaf and dumb. But Sunshine had hooked up with some of those White Power assholes in the joint, and they caught my buddy in a bad way. Beat him and cut him until he told Charlie what he wanted to hear. After that, they dumped him back in his cell and let the bulls find him there at morning call, dead."

"Sunshine's been out what—three, maybe four weeks?" Felipe asked. "Why'd he wait so long to come to you?"

"He played it cute at first," Ben said. "Started coming in, buying beers, sometimes a meal, acting for all the world like we was asshole buddies, me and him. I figured he was sniffing around and I had heard it was him that had done the punk city to my buddy."

"So why didn't you move on him?" Felipe asked.

"Maybe I'm not as tough or as smart as I like to think," Ben said. "And I sure as shit am older and slower than I want to believe. Or maybe I thought I could play him, laying it out that a slab of meat like Sunshine didn't have the onions to come and do what he did. I guess a hundred grand can buy you a crotch packed with balls."

"How'd you two leave it?"

"He said if he couldn't have the money, then he'd make sure I wouldn't live to spend it," Ben said. "Left me like you found me."

"I spotted him outside," Felipe said. "Watched him jump into somebody's car and head for the Deegan. He was holding his side, leaving drops wherever he walked."

"I broke a Dewar's bottle across the bar and sliced the side of his stomach with it," Ben said. "Ten, even five years ago, I would have been washing the floor with his blood. No sense crying over it now, though, he made the move and I let him. I just wish I had peeled a couple of hundreds off my stash and got one of those crazy Spanish kids up in Yonkers to blender Sunshine soon as he walked out of the joint."

"You want me to try and get you into the back room?" Felipe asked. "Get you to your bed?"

"No," Ben said. "I'm good where I am. But here's what you can do. Run around the bar, slap the closed sign on the front, and lock the door. Then, come back to me."

Felipe nodded, jumped to his feet, scooted around the bar, and ran toward the door. He was back by Ben's side in less than two minutes. "I pulled the shades over the front glass, too," he said. "This way nobody can look in."

"Good work," Ben said. "Now look behind you and reach a hand out for the center keg under the beer pit. Just roll it out and let it fall to the floor."

"Those things are heavy," Felipe said. "I don't know if I can move it all by myself."

"Don't worry about it," Ben said. "This one you can move."

Felipe walked toward the beer dispenser and crouched down, putting one hand on top of a large silver keg and wedging the other against its side. He tilted it toward him and watched as it fell with a tinny bang onto the wooden slabs. He turned back to Ben. "It's empty," the boy said.

"Not quite," Ben said. "Pull the top toward you. Unless it's jammed, it should just slide off."

Felipe nudged and twisted the top of the keg until the lid slipped off, rolling to the side, next to his black sneaker. He bent over to look inside the keg and saw three large yellow mailing envelopes, thick rubber bands double-wrapped around each one. "Grab what you see and bring them to me," Ben said.

Felipe shoved his head and arms deep into the pit of the barrel and pulled out the three envelopes, stood and walked them over to Ben. The bleeding man held the envelopes to his chest, staining them with his blood, a wide smile on his face. "This is what Charlie came to take away," he said. "And what he'll never have. Least not while I still have a say in the business."

"What are you going to do with it?" Felipe asked.

"Give it to you," Ben said, looking away from the money and up at the boy. "This way I'll know it's safe."

"Me?" Felipe said, stunned. "I don't have a place to keep my clothes. You're going to ask me to stash a hundred thousand dollars? There has gotta be somebody else you can trust. Somebody that's not me."

"Here's the deal," Ben said, ignoring the boy's plea. "You stash the cash until I'm well enough to move and until I figure a way to get Sunshine in a place where somebody who gives a shit brings him flowers every Sunday. Where it is I don't need to know, so long as it's safe and so long as you're the only one can find it."

"I can't even think of where that would be, Ben," Felipe said, a slight tinge of panic in his voice. "This is a huge haul. I don't want to be the one that messes it up for you. Not after all you went through to hide it."

"Don't worry," Ben said. "You won't. You'll figure a place for it. A good one. And now remember, you can't touch any of the money. Not a single dollar."

"I won't ever do that to you," Felipe said. "You're my friend and I don't steal from friends."

"It's not why I'm saying it," Ben said. "You're straight up solid, or I wouldn't have taken it this far with you. Sunshine's gonna be back, looking for that dough. So are the cops and any one of the other hoods chasing Charlie. This is a small neighborhood with a big mouth, especially where it comes to money. Word gets out that a homeless kid came into some dough, they'll all come looking for you. So you can't touch the money or even talk about it. Not to anyone. You readin' me on this?"

"You're covered, Ben," Felipe said. "Sleep easy on it."

"Then, when the time is right, I figure a little less than two years from now, give or take, you come find me and bring the money with you," Ben said. "Not all of it. Just half of what's there."

"What about the other half?" Felipe asked. "What am I supposed to do with that?"

"Give yourself a start, that's what," Ben said, looking up at the boy, wiping a stream of blood from his line of vision. "Get off the street and go fresh, find a place as far from here as you can. Don't be stupid with it. That's a lot of dough I'm resting on your lap, but you have no idea how fast cash like that can fly from your hand into someone else's pockets. Make it last and make it mean something."

Felipe took a few seconds to digest the plan. He didn't entirely believe it, though he had no reason to think he was being steered in the wrong direction. Ben had always treated him well, offering him a full meal for a few hours of backroom work cleaning up dirty dishes and washing down soiled rest rooms. But something about it all just didn't feel right: a hard-liner like Ben Murphy using a homeless kid to help skim away heist money from Charlie Sunshine and his messed-up crew. Felipe appreciated being trusted, but it all happened too fast and too easy. And if a move for the money was made, he would be in no position to fend it off, especially if Sunshine came at him with more than just the back of his hand.

"Why you picking me?" he asked. "Not like we're family or blood. Yeah, we're friends, but I know you have to be hooked up with a truckload of other people that are closer to you than I am. And I could split tomorrow, not say a word, leave you waiting out your two years only to find out that I'm in the wind. That's some chance you're taking with a lot of money."

"I picked you because you're in the here and now," Ben said. "None of the other people I know came walking through that door to watch me bleed. You did. That puts you at the head of a short line. And I need to make a move with the dough this second. Be nice if I had the time to come up with a Super Bowl game plan, but I don't. So it's you I'm forced to turn to and you that I'm counting on to hide the money. You don't want in, just say so and I'll go out another way. But decide fast and decide now."

"I won't skip on you—don't worry," Felipe said, reaching over and turning on the Bud sign above the bar, bringing a neon glow to the darkened room. "That was me running my mouth and putting it out there for you to see. But you needed to know it *could* happen but that it won't."

"I'm not worried," Ben said. "If I even had a twitch you were off the clock, I would have sat here and bled out, leaving the money to die alone with me. But if I hear you right—and even with all this blood loss, I think I did—you're in this now. Which makes you and me partners."

"I'm with you, Ben," Felipe said, reaching over and shaking the bar owner's hand. Even with the beating he took, bleeding as much as he had been, the grip was still firm and the boy knew there was a time when those hands were used for actions far more dangerous than a handshake. "I'll keep the money safe in a place no one but me will ever find."

"All right then," Ben said, releasing his grip. "Now you can call that ambulance you were so eager to call when you first walked in. Then take this money and disappear with it before anybody gets here."

"When I find a good place for it," Felipe said, "I'll let you know."

"I told you not to tell anybody about it," Ben said. "That includes me."

"You don't want to know where it is?" Felipe asked. "What if I pick the wrong place?"

"That would be a terrible mistake," Ben said, his voice a little harder now, the words thicker, not as slurred. "More for you than for me. Besides, I don't need to know where it is. All I need to know is where *you* are. Think of yourself as a map, kid. *My* map."

Felipe stared at Ben and nodded. He got to his feet and reached for the phone under the bar. "You care which hospital they take you to?" he asked, his back to the bleeding man.

"Any one with doctors will do," Ben Murphy said. He was holding the three packets of money, gazing down at them, a weak smile on his face.

13

Jennifer led the way out of Ciccino's, the Eastchester restaurant where she had just spent the past three hours having lunch with Lo Manto. "It's supposed to be a meal," she said over her shoulder, heading toward her unmarked car parked in the alley behind the building, "not a freakin' career move."

"I believe it is why so many of you Americans die so young," Lo Manto said, sliding on a pair of black wraparound sunglasses, keeping pace with Jennifer's fast-forward walk. He paused briefly and dropped to one knee, pulling up his socks and catching a glance at the passenger-side mirror of a parked car. The charcoal gray late-model sedan was still parked in the lot across the way, engine running, two men inside, one behind the wheel, the other in the rear, his face and shoulder braced against the raised window. Lo Manto had first noticed the car from inside the restaurant as he complimented the owner on the excellent variety and quality of the four-course meal. He looked briefly from the car, graciously accepted a complimentary after-lunch drink, and caught a quick glimpse of Jennifer rolling her eyes, out of boredom and dismay. He figured them to be professionals, shooters not robbers, after either him or Jennifer but not the restaurant. It was much too early in the day to count on any kind of a haul from the registers, and a broad-daylight robbery, even on a quiet stretch of road, was bound to catch someone's attention. Lo Manto also ruled out the possibility that the two men might be scouts, assigned to follow them, reporting their steps back to a cash customer. If that were the case, there would have been no reason for them to keep the car running, especially given how many hours the two cops had spent inside the restaurant. To Lo Manto's way of thinking, the entire situation was positioned to be a hit, and he was the most likely target. And if the two hit men had worked their end the right way, they would have narrowed down the area and zeroed in on the hot zone for their hit. That could only be the narrow walkway in the alley before he and Jennifer got to the car, and Lo Manto had less than a minute to make his move.

"Do you eat this big a lunch every day?" Jennifer asked, her back still to him. "You ask me, I don't think there's any way you could, not without showing up at the squad room looking like John Goodman."

"Who is John Goodman?" Lo Manto asked. "A policeman you know?"

He turned and saw the car's rear lights come on.

They were moving in reverse out of the parking lot, looking to make a U-turn onto White Plains Road. A hard hit to the gas would get them across the narrow two-lane road and into the restaurant's driveway in the time it takes a light to change from yellow to red. That would leave either cop just enough time to get to the unmarked, which was lodged in a corner of the tight alley, parked between a dumpster and a new Lexus.

"He's an actor," Jennifer said. "A terrific actor, but not somebody you'd describe as on the skinny side."

She turned when she heard the squealing tires of an oncoming car, a four-door sedan moving at high speed past the empty intersection and into the restaurant's narrow driveway. She looked at Lo Manto, who reached for her hand and pulled her along with him as they both ran toward the unmarked. "Get between the car and the wall," he told her, the first time he spoke without any hint of an Italian accent. "And if you have a drop gun on you, it'd be a good idea to let me have it."

"You speak English?" she said, brushing past the trunk of the car, looking to wedge herself against the smooth concrete wall. "I mean real English. Not that choppy shit you've been handing me all day."

"Actually, I speak four languages," Lo Manto said, his back against the wall, his knees pressed against the side of the unmarked. "We can talk about that later. But what I could really use now is a drop gun."

Jennifer hesitated. The car came at them at full speed, driver bearing down hard on the unmarked, the passenger in the backseat trying to get a bead on them with a nine-millimeter revolver. She pulled her service gun from her hip holster and crouched down, across from Lo Manto, aiming the barrel at the oncoming. "It's against regulations," she said without looking at him. "I could get into a big jackpot if I let you anywhere near it."

"And we can both die if you don't," Lo Manto said. "It's your call, Detective. But whatever you decide, do it now."

Armand Castioni and his cousin, George, had been following Jennifer's car since their initial stop at the bar in the East Bronx. "This guy's got some sack on him to just walk into that place," Armand had said. "Acting like he couldn't give a shit who owns it and whose turf he's stepping on."

"Maybe he don't know," George said. "Maybe he's just thirsty."

"And maybe one day you'll start to figure things out on your own," Armand said. "No, this guy's gotta have some muscle, enough to make the bosses nervous and put me and you to work."

"The broad with him is kinda cute, don't you think?" George asked. "I always figured women cops for dykes, but she looks way too good to go that way."

"Don't kid yourself, cousin," Armand said. "Half the good-looking women in this world, if not more than that, like to go swimming down by the shallow end of the lake. Been my experience, anyway."

"It's a shame if that's true," George said.

They followed the unmarked up into Eastchester and parked in a strip mall across the street from a small restaurant with blue stucco walls. Armand put the car in park and left the engine running, air conditioner on full blast. "This cop knows how to live," he said with a touch of frustration in his voice. "First a bar and now a restaurant. The badges in Naples must have it real sweet if he's any example. And I bet it's all on the arm. He ain't putting out of his pocket for nobody. Letting the broad pick up the tabs."

"He probably has a movie picked out," George said. "For after lunch."

Armand looked over at his cousin and shook his head. "He's not gonna have time for a movie," he said. "Or for anything else, for that matter. We do him when he comes out of the place. This is a perfect setup: one way into the driveway and one way out. We can make the hit and be on the road in less than two minutes, full out of the picture. Hop into the backseat and start to get ready. Soon as they move, we move."

George leaned over, looking out at the tight street, the half-moon strip mall not exactly bustling with activity. "It's the middle of the day," he said. "All anybody with eyes needs to do is look and they'll spot us easy. Why not wait till their next stop? Maybe it'll be dark out by then."

"What is anybody gonna see that's got you worried?" Armand asked, his voice steeped in controlled anger and confidence. "Look around you. It's like a desert around here. Me and you been in this car longer than you were in school and the only people I saw was an old man with a walker and his pissed-off nurse. Besides, by the time *anybody* sees *anything,* it'll all be over. Now load up your guns and make sure you hit what you aim at."

"Don't worry about me, cousin," George said. "Shootin' a gun is the only thing I've ever been good at and I'm only getting better. You just keep the car moving steady and I'll take the cop."

"You gotta take both cops, Georgie," Armand said. "Just one is only half the job."

"The lady ain't a target," George said, looking up from the revolver in his hand. "Or if she was, I didn't hear about it."

"She's *not* a target," Armand said. "She's a witness. And the worst kind at that. One with a badge and handcuffs. Two minutes ago you were worried about being seen in broad daylight. And now here you are ready to have your mug seen by somebody can put you away for a full load and you don't seem all that eager to pin her down."

"I thought we were only supposed to hit the one target," George said, sounding defensive, his eyes rotating from his cousin to the front door of the restaurant. "You know how crazy that head case Silvestri gets we don't do exactly as he says to do. I just wanna do what's right. For both of us."

"Putting both those cops on the ground dead," Armand said. "That's what's right. For you and for me."

*

Lo Manto rested the barrel of the .38 Special against the hood of the unmarked and aimed it at the driver of the car bearing down on them. Jennifer had handed over her drop gun, a second weapon many cops carry, with great reluctance. "If you have to shoot anybody," she told him, "make sure it's a clean hit. *I'm* not supposed to have that gun, which means you shouldn't be anywhere near it."

"I'll take the driver," he told her. His mind was already running at warp speed. He was taking in the situation, envisioning any one of four scenarios that could play out over the next several minutes. "You worry about the shooter. Aim for the glass just off to the driver's left. It won't be enough to kill him, but it'll get that gun out of his hands. But that's only *if* you hit him."

"Worry about your guy," she said, her back braced against the wall, her feet wedged against the wheel of her car. "He's coming straight for us. He hits this car and they'll be able to bury us both in an empty can of tuna."

"They'll ram into us whether we hit them or not," Lo Manto said. "On my signal, you get off your shots as fast as you can and make them count and then dive clear of the car. With a little luck, we'll get out of this still able to walk."

"Why *your* signal?" Jennifer asked. "Why not mine?"

Lo Manto gave her a quick glance and then looked at the car, now less than twenty feet away. "Because I'm your guest," he said. "And you shouldn't be rude to a guest."

Two bullets chipped the wall above their heads, dust and small chunks of cement dripping down on their shoulders, as the passenger in the backseat took aim and fired in their direction.

"Take your time with this," Jennifer said. "I don't want to rush you into anything you're not ready for."

"Now!" Lo Manto said.

Jennifer and Lo Manto each unleashed three rapid rounds and then they dove out from behind the body of the unmarked. Jennifer landed facedown on a pile of heavy black garbage bags, her knees scraping against gravel. Lo Manto, on the other side, landed with full force against the back end of the parked Lexus, his right shoulder taking most of the hit, which jarred the gun loose from his hand and sent it flying toward the center of the alley. They both turned their heads when they heard the heavy crash of car against car, metal crumbling, air bags popping, white smoke filling the air around them.

Jennifer was first to get to her feet, approaching the attack car with careful steps, her gun cocked and held down against her hip. She peered past the smoke. In the back of the car, a man was spread out across the leather seats, his face covered with lines of blood, his body motionless. She gave a quick look at the driver, slumped over the wheel, his head encased in the smashed windshield, his arms spread, engulfed in smoke and blood. She saw Lo Manto on the other side of the car, prying open the back door and reaching in to check on the shooter. She stepped closer to the car, her gun raised, ready to move in the event the man in the back turned on Lo Manto. Around them, a small circle of people had started to form, all eager to see the result of the commotion.

"We need to get an ambulance here fast," Lo Manto told her. "This one's still alive, but he won't be for long unless he gets some help."

Jennifer had a cell phone in her hand as she walked away from the car and toward the small crowd. "This is a crime scene," she told them. "You need to step back and keep clear of the area."

"Who are they?" one of the waiters asked. "The two men in the car?"

"They're not anybody you'll ever have a chance to know," Jennifer said, turning her back and making the call for a support team and an emergency unit.

Lo Manto walked away from the smoking car, picked up his gun, and made his way toward Jennifer, who was now leaning against the rear wall of the restaurant. "They should all be here in about three, four minutes," she said to him. "I got EMS coming for the guy in the back and a black van with a zipper coat for the driver."

"Do you want your gun back?" Lo Manto asked, holding out the .38.

"You hold on to it for now," she said. "Who the hell knows? A few more of your friends might show up and try to surprise us."

Lo Manto nodded and shoved the gun into the back of his waistband. "You did very well," he said, looking over his shoulder at the damaged cars and bodies. "You hit soft flesh with two of your shots and got very close with the third."

"I'm a cop, or did you forget?" Jennifer said, shaking her head. "That's why I'm the one with the two guns and the shield."

She stared at Lo Manto, feeling the yank of the short leash on her temper getting tighter, concerned over the attempt made on both their lives. She had been too angry to ask Captain Fernandez any relevant questions about Lo Manto when she first got the baby-watch assignment, too quick to write it off as another visiting cop who needed someone with a driver's license to take him around town. She had sulked out of the captain's office, steeling herself for what she thought would be, at best, a mundane ride-along week. Their morning together had played right into the dull scenario she had so clearly dreaded and envisioned. But it was all a different game now, with shots fired and one guy splayed out across the front end of his car and a shooter lying in a pool of blood in the back, his body stilled by two of her bullets. All of it because some cop from Naples with a New York accent thicker than hers had hopped on a plane and come back home.

"You hurt?" Lo Manto asked, looking past her as an ambulance and local squad car arrived, each with siren running silent and doors swinging wide as soon as they entered the tight parking area.

"I'm good," Jennifer said, glancing at the two EMS workers rushing toward the smoking car. "But you and me need to find ourselves a quiet place where we can sit down and talk all this out. I thought I signed on to be your tour guide. But after this, it looks to me like a bodyguard is more what you need."

"What makes you think I know anything more about those two than you do?" Lo Manto asked. "I don't know your street history. They could have just as easily been gunning for you."

"Sell that brand of bullshit on some other corner," Jennifer said, moving away from the wall and standing directly across from Lo Manto, staring up at him with hard eyes. "It was you that first spotted them, which to me means you knew enough to look out for a tail shaving our backs. It was almost like you were ready for it, expecting the move to come, just not all that sure from which direction. None of that adds up to a cop on a visit here to score a few days of R-and-R with friends from the old neighborhood. It's more like a cop that's running toward a case. Maybe it's the one dealing with that missing niece of yours, I don't know. But if you and me are going to keep seeing each other, let alone talk to each other, I *need* to know."

Lo Manto stared back at her for several moments, staying silent, strands of his long hair falling over his face. He had made it his business to steer clear of partners for most of his career, preferring to walk in and out of his cases on his own time, letting the suspect and the crime dictate the pace. When he did work with other detectives, in Italy or on joint task forces in New York and London, he would still find the time to veer off course and venture out on his own. He would walk the dark streets of cities both strange and familiar into the early morning hours, working out the moves and the motives of his prey in his mind. He had always believed that the best cops were always the loners, the ones who were tied down neither to the demands of a family nor to the weakness and whims of a full-time partner. But as he looked back at Jennifer Fabini, at her eyes that while blazing with anger also amplified her beauty, he came to the realization that he either needed to trust her or go back to Fernandez and have her taken off his watch. That wouldn't sit too well with the captain, who would be forced to balance their friendship with the responsibilities of his job. Lo Manto would be left with little in the way of wiggle room and no say in who Jennifer's replacement would be, assuming it would even get to that point. Fernandez would be well within his jurisdictional powers to restrict Lo Manto's movements, and might even go so far as to confine him to the cheapest room at the nearest hotel while the search for his niece played out. He couldn't afford the lost time, waiting out the back-and-forth calls that would take place between Fernandez in New York and Bartoni in Naples, stewing in the precinct while the two men decided in which direction he would be allowed to move. If he was going to have a partner in New York, it would have to be the wired-up young woman glaring at him, her arms folded across her chest.

"You with me?" she asked, her words ringing with frustration. "Or you already thinking about what to order for dinner?"

Lo Manto turned away from her and surveyed the scene behind them, where a crowd of police personnel had gathered. Two uniforms and a team of detectives were staring at the body in the front seat of the car, while the EMS crew was slowly easing the wounded man out the rear door. A forensics team was taking photos, dusting for prints, and scanning for bullet fragments. "Unless you do it different here than we do it in Naples, we're both going to have to spend an hour or so talking to these people and answering all their questions," he said to her. "Then, I would imagine, back to the house, to answer even more questions."

"That's the picture I'm getting," Jennifer said, scanning the scene. "On top of that, the shooting happened beyond city limits. *I* have no police power here, and I sure as hell know that *you* don't. Which means we have to answer to cops who might not be as friendly as the guys in the Bronx."

"Throw the blame all at me," he told her. "While you're doing that, try to find out as much as you can about the two in the car. See if they're locals or out-of-town hires that were brought in for the one job. The more we know about them, the better we can figure out what our next move is going to be."

Lorenzo Carcaterra

"How do we handle the little matter that the gun in your hand, the one whose bullets took out the driver, just happens to be mine?" she asked, still dubious as to Lo Manto's true intentions.

"It fell out of its holster when you hit the wall," Lo Manto said. "I picked it up and, given the heat of the moment, there really wasn't anything you could do to stop me without risking both our lives."

"You're a little too good at this," Jennifer said. "Lies come shooting out of your mouth faster than you worked that trigger back there. But then, you've probably been through this dance a few times before."

"I've never met a good cop who wasn't a good liar," Lo Manto said. "They're usually the ones that break the rules and they're the ones with all the valid reasons as to why they had to do it."

"I'm walking the edge of the surf here for you," she said, stepping even closer to him, her voice now almost a whisper. "The worst that can happen to you is someone hands you a plane ticket to Rome and drives you out to the airport. But if I get tagged, I'll be picking up hot lumps of shit down at the K-9 pound until my retirement party. Before I do any of that, I need to know what it is I'm stepping into here."

Lo Manto reached out a hand and rested it on Jennifer's elbow. "If you want me to trust you," he said to her in a reassuring manner, "I need you to trust me."

Jennifer looked over Lo Manto's shoulder and saw the two detectives walking toward them, one a woman

174

in a sky blue short-sleeved blouse, the other an older man in a worn plaid jacket with a gleaming head tinged with sweat beads. "I'll back you up on this," she said to him. "But if it doesn't play out fair and you leave me to take the hit, the next time you see me with a gun in my hand it'll be aimed at you."

"Not exactly the most romantic proposal I've ever been offered," Lo Manto said, giving her a slight smile. "But one I'd be a fool to turn down. I'll take a step back and leave you to handle Will and Grace and the Internal team back at the house. *If* you're good enough to get us past them, then I'll tell you everything you want to know."

"What about the captain?" she asked. "He's your friend, but he's my boss and he's a good bet to be more than pissed over this news."

"If he's as good a friend as I think he is, neither one of us should have a problem," Lo Manto said.

"And if he's not?"

"Then it won't be just you shoveling shit with the K-9 units," Lo Manto said, turning to face the two detectives. "I'll be right there next to you."

14

Pete Rossi took several long sips from a tall glass filled with espresso and chipped ice, his face a benign mask of indifference. He was sitting across from Silvestri, listening as the older man filled him in on the botched shooting in Eastchester, one of his hired guns dead, the other on a hospital respirator, clutching on to what was left of his life. Rossi had been taught many lessons during his years spent under the strict schooling of the men assigned to instruct him in the ways of the Camorra. No rule was more crucial to his ability to function as a modern day boss than the demand that no betrayal of emotion ever be shown outside his inner circle. Rossi absorbed the lessons that were passed to him by dons as powerful as his father had been and as vindictive as the legendary Carlo Robuto, a ruthless man who controlled the streets of Naples for well over two decades. Rossi had twisted and shaped those lessons to the contours of his own personality, so that now they were as natural to him as breathing.

He was keenly aware of his weak areas, of the temper

that could often flare violently out of control, attacking with a fierce anger all that stood in its groundswell. Rather than bury the temper, he learned to control it, to unleash it when it best suited his needs, allowing it to strengthen, not weaken, his position. He seldom would speak first in any setting, whether a formal business meeting or an informal family gathering. He had learned to treat his day-to-day life as if he were in the middle of a long poker game and all the other players were only interested in the cards he held in his hand.

"Bottom line is this," Silvestri said, downing the last of what had been a tumbler filled with scotch and ice. "We took a chance and sent two amateurs out in the ring, hoping they would get lucky and score a knockout. We were wrong and they ended up dead or close enough to it for it not to matter."

"They connect back to us in any way?" Rossi asked. He rested the iced espresso on a glass holder, careful not to spill any drops onto the polished veneer of his oak wood desk.

"Not even in the same area code," Silvestri said. "They came to us through a third party. I met with them once and the payout was handled with me clear out of the picture. They supplied their own weapons and they came up with their own plan. None of our people were anywhere near them and wouldn't know them if they died on their front lawn."

"The one in the hospital," Rossi said. "What odds is he looking at?"

"You ask me, the kid was half a potato *before* he got shot," Silvestri said. "Now he's looking at total vegetable and that's only if he pulls through."

"I don't think he's going to make it," Rossi said, his voice firm and direct. "Do you?"

"No," Silvestri said, understanding that his don was not venturing an opinion but stating a fact. "It don't look good, no matter which way you turn the dial."

"Which leaves us still with an unresolved problem," Rossi said. "One that's going to be harder for us to solve the next time."

"We need to wait two, maybe three days before we try again," Silvestri said "Give the situation time to simmer down. Maybe we catch some luck and the people here will be as fed up with him as we are and send him packing back across the ocean."

"Their decision won't matter to him," Rossi said, settling deeper into his leather chair, his head pushing back against the rest. "Nor, for that matter, should it. He won't leave without the young lady we're holding. That means he won't leave until he figures out where she is and who it is that has her."

"How long you think that will take him?" Silvestri asked.

"Not very," Rossi said. "He's held back a bit working minus the freedom he had in his own city, but New York is as much home to him as Naples. He has to be a bit more creative in getting things done, but that's never been a problem for him. He can adapt to any situation.

If things had gone down a different path, he could have easily been raised the same way I was, taught by the same people who schooled me."

"Do we use the niece as bait?" Silvestri said. "Hold her out to lure him in?"

"He's already been lured in," Rossi said impatiently. "He's here. He's where we want him to be. That seems to have been the easy part. Getting him dead is proving to be a bit more of a challenge. Make this your priority. Clear everything else, pass it to whoever needs to deal with it. This man, this cop, is your only mission. And I expect it to be a successful one."

Silvestri stared at his don and nodded. He had been a member of the Camorra long enough to understand the importance of such an order, spoken in a rare and direct manner. Pete Rossi's family had suffered many personal losses, in manpower and in business, due to Lo Manto's aggressive actions both on the streets of Naples and here in New York. The dozens of other factions of the vast enterprise that ruled the crime roost in both cities had sustained equal amounts of damage, but they seemed content to write it off as the price of doing business. They were not as willing to waste the time, energy, and dollar commitment required in the vain pursuit of a lone cop. With Rossi, the level of anger and frustration seemed to go beyond the mere loss of men and money. Rossi had crossed a crucial and discernible line, delving into the personal, the one arena that all the great dons of the past had done their best to avoid. And now, by direct order, Silvestri had been pulled into the line of fire as well. "I won't fail you," he said with as much conviction as he could muster. "There's only one way that cop from Naples gets back on a plane to Italy. That's in a coffin."

Pete Rossi stared across at Silvestri, his face as solid and unflinching as it was when their conversation first started. He reached for his glass of iced espresso and took a long swallow, wrapping his fingers around the cold base. "You're not the first to say that," he said. "He's been fighting the organization for fifteen years and no one has yet put him in a grave. A few have come close, but more have gone down than walked away."

"I'll take care of the hospital situation first," Silvestri said, once again feeling the harsh weight of his don's unspoken words. "Then our friend from Naples will have my full attention."

"I hope you still have it in you to win," Pete Rossi said to him. "For my sake and even more for yours." He then stood up, pushed his chair back, and walked slowly out of the office.

The hospital room was all ruffled shadows and quiet darkness. An IV drip was hanging off an iron pole and a TV hung in the corner next to the shuttered blinds. The young man in the bed was asleep, his eyes fluttering, his face grimacing with every jolt of pain that shot through the open wounds in his body. His head was bandaged, caked blood coating the center, under which were buried the dozen stitches required to seal shut the thick vertical cut caused when he banged violently against the doorjamb. Six hours earlier, he had been wheeled into surgery, where a team of doctors worked quickly and with calm precision to remove the two bullets lodged in his chest cavity. Within two hours and after a great deal of blood had been lost, they had managed to remove all but the smallest of the fragments fired from the barrel of Jennifer Fabini's gun. As the doctors left the operating room to wash off the bone matter and toss out their stained gowns, they were relieved to have accomplished as much as they had in such a short span of time and realistic enough to know that their work had done nothing but delay the inevitable. "If he lives to feel the sun on his face in the morning," one surgeon said to a nurse walking by his side, "we'll have more than done our jobs."

"I haven't seen that much blood loss in years," she said, a bit shaken despite more than a decade of operating room experience. "He was close to a bleed-out by the time we got him to the table."

"What put him there?" the doctor asked, tossing off his mask and gloves and dropping them into a blue canister.

"Shoot-out with the police," the nurse said. "At least that was the rumble among the EMS crew that brought him in."

"It always ends up that way," the surgeon said. "Especially these last few years."

Lorenzo Carcaterra

"How do you mean?" the nurse asked.

"I do my best surgical work on criminals," the surgeon said. "Seems a shame and a waste, any way you look at it."

The door to the room slowly opened and a young man in a white lab coat walked in. He had a blue cap over his head and a mask dangling in front of his blue shirt. His brown deck shoes made no noise as he stepped on the cold floor, making his way toward the side of the bed. The young man stood against the edge of the bed, staring down at the damaged body of a mob wannabe who would never make it to his twentieth birthday. He reached behind him and grabbed a pillow from the empty green chair to his left. Gripping it with both hands, he shoved it down atop the silent, battered face of George Castioni. He held it in place for several minutes, bearing down with all his weight, waiting patiently for what little life there was left in the shooter's body to dissipate. Once he was convinced the man in bed was no threat to the living, he tossed the pillow back onto the chair, yanked the IV out of the dead patient's arm, and took three steps back. He then reached a hand into his waistband, pushed the white lab coat off to the side, and pulled out a nine-millimeter with an adjustable silencer screwed onto the barrel. He aimed the gun at the body in the bed and squeezed off two rounds, one to the chest and one through the closed right eye. The two quick pops forced the body to lurch forward and then

182

drop back down on the bed, fresh blood oozing out of both open wounds. "Sorry about that, Georgie," the young man said before putting the gun back against his hip and heading out of the room.

Gaspaldi sat in the back booth of the empty Chinese restaurant. He sipped a small cup of tea, filled with three teaspoons of sugar, waiting for the burly man to squeeze his way into the booth. "You always this late?" Gaspaldi asked, more curious than irritated.

"My clock shows I'm ten minutes past the meet time," the burly man said. "For me that's pretty good. Truth be told, it's goddam fuckin' excellent. Besides, I didn't hear you screaming about this being an emergency."

Gaspaldi suppressed a laugh, showing only a quick smile. He allowed very few people he did business with to talk to him the way the burly man usually did, but he had grown a soft spot for his antics over the years, and he often let the disrespect go without comment. Besides, only a handful of soldiers in the crew were as ruthless and efficient in their work as the burly man. Gaspaldi had wasted a great deal of energy attempting to groom other members of the Rossi crew in the hopes that they would one day be in a position either to replace or bolster the burly man, but he had yet to find any fit to fulfill such a cold-blooded destiny. The burly man had never known failure in any assignment, always bringing the matter before him to its painful conclusion. Given the hunger Pete Rossi seemed to have for Lo Manto's blood, it seemed foolish to turn to anyone else. The future of the cop from Naples would soon be in the hands of the burly man.

"You hungry?" Gaspaldi asked. "Want to order something before we get down to it?"

"I'm starving," the burly man said. "I'm so hungry I could eat the ass off a dead Polack. But you'd have to shoot me before you'll get me to put my mouth anywhere near this chink shit they call food."

"Have some soup," Gaspaldi said. "Nobody can mess up soup."

"These people put cat in everything they eat," the burly man said. "Soup included. I'll grab something at Mario's later. There I know what goes into the pot."

"Let's get to it, then," Gaspaldi said. "How much do you know?"

"You got a cop you want disposed," the burly man said. "You tried once and came away with empty hands, looking like a team of gang-bangers out on their first hit."

"You can get a full background check from the usual place," Gaspaldi said. "Take a few days to study it and then play it any way you want, so long as the problem gets fixed."

"The same go for anybody might be with him?" the burly man asked. "He's a foreign. NYPD keeps close tabs on visiting cops, stays on them like a wino on a bologna sandwich. Need to know if I can take out his watchers, too, if it comes down to that."

"I don't care if the commissioner himself walks him to

take a piss," Gaspaldi said. "He goes down. Anybody gets in the way, take them, too. We'll deal with any problems that may cause after the fact."

"What can you tell me about the cop?" the burly man asked. "I mean, something not in the file I'll get later."

"He's good," Gaspaldi said. "Better than any badge we ever went against. I don't mean shooter good, even though he's solid in that department. I'm talking smart good. Plans out his moves, goes in anticipating all the angles, makes it his business to know his business. Don't expect to catch him off-guard. That ain't gonna happen. Not with this guy."

"Why's he here in the first place?" the burly man asked. "Why isn't he back in Italy arresting some guy for pinching some broad's ass?"

"A family member went missing," Gaspaldi said. "He's here to help find her. He hasn't got it narrowed down yet as to who did the lift and why, but he's too smart a guy not to work it all out pretty soon."

"Was the lift done to get him here?" the burly man asked. "Or we talking two separate situations?"

"That doesn't fall under your umbrella," Gaspaldi said. "If it did I would have said so by now. I've given you all you need to know."

"Except to tell me how much," the burly man said, irritated and anxious to get out of the empty restaurant and step back into the warm, humid air.

"Same as you always get," Gaspaldi said. "Plus expenses."

"Not good enough," the burly man said. "This ain't an old wiseguy on the run, hiding out in some black neighborhood on Long Island, thinking we would never look there, let alone go in after him. This is a cop and that comes with a whole set of its own headaches, not the least of which is the death penalty if I get nabbed."

"He's an *Italian* cop," Gaspaldi said. "That carries no weight here—at least not the kind you need to worry about."

"A badge is a badge, no matter what country's stamped on his passport," the burly man said. "And that makes it a risk. Now for me to make that risk worth my time and maybe my life, I'll need double the usual stack and enough on the expenses to cover a three-week vacation on a warm spot of sand."

Gaspaldi drank the last of his tea and waved over a waiter standing with his arms folded in a corner of the room. "That's a heavy dose of bling bling," he said to the burly man, watching as the waiter moved toward their table. "A lot more than we've put out before. Especially since it's to take out only the one guy."

"You came to me, as I remember it," the burly man said. "You want to reach out for a cheaper gun, that's your call. I gave you my price and there's no movement on it."

Gaspaldi handed a folded-over twenty to the waiter, waving away the check the young man had written out for the tea. "What's left is yours," he told him, and waited as the kid cleared away the empty cup and pot and nodded his thanks. Then he turned his attention back to the burly man. "I'll meet the asking price," he said. "Just make sure it's done right. There's no miss on this. Bigger eyes than mine are gonna be tracking the job. It don't go the way we want and you're still walking, there'll be money put out to change that. You hear the words okay?"

"You know how I work," the burly man said. "I don't take a nickel until the package is delivered. If the cop is good enough or lucky enough to wash me away, your guys are out of pocket nothing. So, save the Joe Pesci hard-ass lectures for the rookies. This ain't my first fuckin' barbecue. And I don't plan on it being my last."

"It's on you, then," Gaspaldi said, easing out of the booth, his stomach rubbing against the flat edge of the Formica table. "Me and you are done here."

"Glad to hear it," the burly man said. "Now I can finally get out of this shit hole and get myself a decent meal."

"I still think you would have liked the soup here," Gaspaldi said as he walked toward the white exit sign next to the darkened coatroom. "Shame you didn't try it."

Felipe Lopez stepped out of the basement apartment and dropped a small plastic bag into the garbage can closest to the curled black iron gate. He walked up the two short steps, undid the bolt lock, and swung the gate out, stepping onto the sidewalk in front of the four-story

187

building. It was early in the morning of what was shaping up to be another day of intense summer heat, and the street was empty except for a jogger finishing his run in what passed for the cooler hours. Felipe felt for the ten-dollar bill in the rear pocket of his torn jeans, making sure the folded money that Mrs. Claire Samuels had handed him a few minutes earlier was still there. He had been running errands for Mrs. Samuels for about two years now, starting just around the time her husband, Eliot, fell face-to-the-floor dead in the small foyer of their two-bedroom, rent-controlled apartment. She didn't need much: milk, juice, eggs, half a pound of ham, and bread were what she usually sent him out for and what she seemed to live on.

He stopped in to check on her twice a week, usually Wednesdays and Sundays, taking out her trash and bringing in the mail, tossed in a pile in front of her locked door. More often than not, she insisted he stay with her for breakfast, both eating their sandwiches and drinking small glasses of orange juice as they sat in front of a TV screen, watching the latest news on MSNBC. They seldom spoke, preferring the peace of each other's company, but when they did, it was more often Mrs. Samuels who took up the majority of the conversation. She talked about a city she once knew and one he was much too young to have seen, a time when their neighborhood was alive with the sounds of newly arrived immigrants, each eager to put his or her stamp on their new home. She talked about her husband, Eliot, and about how hard he had worked running the local laundry, putting in twelve-hour days in front of the heavy-load washing machines and large tumble dryers, the short brown apron tied around his waist always filled with quarters. She would shake her head slowly, her words coming out in spurts, the pain from her withering lungs apparent as she remembered the money her husband wasted betting on the horses and sitting in on the weekly card game held in the back of Giacomo's Deli. "We would have had a nice big house," she'd say to Felipe. "Like the ones on Ely Avenue. Maybe a car and money in the bank for a vacation. We would have had all of that. Instead, all Eli had was his laundry and his debts. And when he died they came to see me, the men he owed all his money to, and they took his business. Made me sign the papers over to them in the kitchen."

"Why didn't you just say no?" Felipe had asked her. "The debts were your husband's, not yours."

"Then I would have been dead, too," she said. "And the business would still belong to them."

Most of the time, when she wasn't remembering the lost days of the neighborhood or the defeated dreams of her husband, Mrs. Samuels would tell Felipe stories about cities in Europe he had only read about in books and foods he had never even heard of, let alone tasted. She recalled her days growing up an orphan and being shuttled off from one family to another, until she was placed in a home that was run by nuns in Salerno, in southern Italy. It was where she lived until she was one week shy of her eighteenth birthday and saw her Eliot for the first time at a local café, in a meeting arranged by his parents and the mother superior. Mrs. Samuels spoke of her early years living in a strange city in a foreign country, finding work as a seamstress in a downtown sweatshop. She gave birth to three sons and survived brutal summers without the aid of fans or air conditioners and winters warmed only by the heat from a lit gas oven.

Felipe liked listening to her stories as both of them sipped tea, the television playing in the background while outside the sounds of the neighborhood rose to greet the day. She never asked about his life and his struggles living without a home and family, and he offered up little in the way of information. She knew all she needed to know about him from her landlord, Luis, a wiry, wobbly little man who had initially convinced her to trust the boy enough to let him into her home, to help with her errands and serve as a buffer against the ravages of loneliness. She had never asked him to spend a night on the couch next to the crowded bookcase, its wooden boards sagging from the weight of first editions long left unread, regardless of how beastly the weather outside or how poorly prepared for it the boy seemed. Felipe never asked to stay, nor did he mind not getting the invitation. He accepted the relationship for what it was, grateful for the time they spent together and the money she paid him. They made no demands on each other, content to let it remain as it had been from their first day together.

Felipe never stole from Mrs. Samuels. He had ample opportunity to lift silverware, riffle through the jewelry box she kept hidden under the night table near her bed, or even grab the small television on those rare occasions when she fell asleep while listening to the morning news. But he never did, and if asked, Felipe would have no easy answer as to why not. He liked the woman, but he also liked the guy who managed the neighborhood Key Food, and over the years he had lifted enough groceries out of that supermarket to put them on the verge of bankruptcy. Maybe it was because it was too easy to steal from someone who had so little to take. Or maybe he only stole what he could eat or wear. Or it just might be he didn't want to disappoint an old woman who, without ever saying a word, seemed to expect so much from him. And he wasn't ready to let her down.

Felipe trusted Mrs. Samuels and knew of no better place to hide the packets of money given him by Ben Murphy than in one of the dark corners of her apartment. He also felt confident that if she ever did find the three thick packets she wouldn't simply pocket them— she'd ask the questions she needed answers to, the money still resting safe in her hands. No one he knew would ever think he would have access to that kind of cash. And no one putting the hard squeeze on Murphy would even consider a look in his direction in their mad search for a hundred grand. In the event they ever did, or if Murphy caved and gave in to the pressure, they would look everywhere but in the basement apartment of a withered widow. Her husband was long dead, her friends had been gone for decades, and her three sons' lives were all tragically cut short before they even got a taste of middle age. Leaving the three thick packets of cash behind the tattered volumes of Sherlock Holmes stories was as safe as placing them in a bank vault. Now, as he jammed his hands into the front pockets of his blue jeans, all Felipe Lopez had to do to see half that cash land back in his lap was to stay alive on the streets of the city for two more years.

Paula walked along the edge of the thick privet hedges, feeling her way toward the rear gate, avoiding the glare of the row of outdoor floodlights buried in the ground that illuminated the back end of the Rossi property. She had managed to climb out the small window of her room, the one that looked out onto the garden, just as dusk had settled on the property. She crawled down the side of a small tar-shingled roof and then, using the gutters as a balance beam, worked her way along a corner of the stone house, moving with great care from the edge of one rock to another. She was standing on garden soil more than two hours after she had escaped from her room. She steered clear of the video cameras mounted on either side of the six-foot iron gate that could be opened only by key or electronic eye, her back braced against the sharp edges of the brick wall that lined the end of the property. She wrapped her arms around the bricks and began a slow shimmy up the side, cutting and scraping her arms and knees as she worked her way to the top. All around her was silence and darkness and shadow, the two-way street beyond the gate deserted. She had no idea where she was or in which direction she should head once she got to the top of the wall and jumped into the grass and leaf clearing below. She only knew that once she got there, she would be free.

She struggled to the top of the wall, her legs cut and bleeding, the flesh on her right arm torn, the palms on both her hands open and raw. She looked back at the main house. A few lights were still on, and tall trees helped to hide most of it from view. She then turned away and jumped the six feet onto what she hoped would be nothing harder than grass and thick piles of shrubs. She landed with a muted thud, the left side of her face brushing against a rose bush, a long row of scattered thorns quick to break skin and draw blood. She lay there for several long minutes, catching her breath, her eyes closed, enveloped in the silence of the darkened countryside. She was tired, sore, and frightened, alone now, ready to walk down a dark and winding path, hoping to find help by the time the morning sun lit the sky. She got to her feet, brushed the leaves and the grass from her body, tried her best to ignore the pain from the cuts and scrapes, and began her journey into the darkness.

*

Pete Rossi had watched her every move from his study, sitting in a thick black leather chair, the wall above him filled with video monitors that covered the property from every possible angle. He smiled when he saw the girl scale the wall and jump down on the other side to safety. "Nobody can get in or out of here," he said to the thin man standing behind him. "That was one of the things you said to me when you put all this equipment in. And that I'd sleep safer than if I was the president of the United States. You remember saying any of that, Chris?"

"I remember," Chris Romano said. "And what I said then still holds. Don't let what you're looking at fool you, boss. Let's not forget, we're *letting* her get away. If we wanted to nab the kid, we could have done it at any point, from the minute she left the room to the time she scaled the back wall."

Rossi glanced away from the monitors, looked over at Romano and smiled. "She did pretty good out there," he said to him. "I wasn't too sure she'd even make it off the roof. She's got nerve, scared as she probably is, to make a move like that. Most kids, if they were going to skip at all, would have done it in daylight, give themselves a chance to see where they're going. This one flies off in the middle of the night instead, when she figures nobody's going to be looking her way."

"I got three on the outside, following her on foot," Romano said. "Then two cars in place a half mile down whichever end of the road she decides to take. Wherever she's gonna end up, they'll be right there with her."

"They should only surface if there's trouble," Rossi said, turning to look back at the monitors that now revealed nothing but hedges and trees. "I don't want anything to happen to that girl. She's not the target. She's only the bait."

"There's a tracking monitor in her wristwatch," Romano said. "In case the field team loses her, even for a blip, they'll be able to pick her up within seconds."

"What if she takes off the watch?" Rossi asked. "Or loses it? What then?"

"I had a backup put in on her small waist pack," Romano said. "And a third one was inserted in the glow light on her right sneaker. She might lose one of those things, maybe even two, but not three."

"I hope that's true," Rossi said. "We have no window built into this to be wrong. On anything."

"You think she'll find him?" Romano asked. He was in his mid-twenties and cover-boy handsome, with chiseled features, olive skin, rich dark hair, and eyes the color of a crow. He had lived in the Camorra since he was a six-year-old boy, given up by an impoverished family in Naples that brought him to their local don and swore their allegiance to the honored ways. He was flown to the United States and placed with a family who lived in wealthy Westchester County, in New York. There he was placed in the best private schools and allowed to display his strengths and talents, which in his case happened to be in the field of electronics. After college, Romano was brought in to work for Pete Rossi and placed in charge of the security system for all the family enterprises, both legal and not. Romano was a wizard at placing surveillance detectors in places no one before him had even thought possible. He scored his first major coup when he secured a mini-camera in the front snap of the bra of a young secretary who was in debt to the family, and had her capture all the sealed details of a planned merger between two major financial institutions. The tape that was then shown to the principals involved allowed the Rossis to squeeze millions from both ends of the table in return for silence and a future chunk of profits.

"Either she finds him or he finds her," Rossi told Romano. "Any way it works is fine by me."

"We'll have eyes up on him by tomorrow," Romano said. "I needed a little time to get close to the car, his room, that lady cop he rides with. Once we get it all in place, we'll know where he's going even before he does."

"Maybe," Rossi said, not sounding as confident as the young man to his right. "You're not the first to think you're two steps ahead of this cop. Dozens of others came into it feeling the same way. They're dead now or so deep inside a prison cell they pray they'll wake up dead. That's why it's us who are in it now. We need to bring this all to an end. So let's be confident *after* it's over, not before."

Romano nodded, knowing enough not to push the matter any further. "I didn't farm the drops out on this one," he said. "I'm laying them in myself. Make sure they're done the right way. We should start getting video on him by tomorrow, day after at the latest."

"Keep Silvestri informed with every step," Rossi told him. "He's working his own end and I don't want there to be any traffic on this. Let's keep it clean and simple, with every free hand knowing what the busy hand is doing."

"I'll keep him in the main loop," Romano said, slightly irritated. "Like I always try to do. But you know how Silvestri feels about what I do. He's as Old World as grappa, thinks all this electronic work belongs on a shelf at Radio Shack. And nothing I say, do, or show him is ever gonna budge his way of thought."

"Work out your problems with him, not with me," Rossi said in a dismissive tone. "Just stay focused, the both of you. I'm going to clear the table of this cop and I don't care who needs to die for that to happen. On his side or on mine. So make living your incentive to get the job done."

"What if he's in my way?" Romano asked. He sensed an opening, a chance not only to impress his boss by taking down the cop, but also to rid himself of an internal obstacle to his rise up the Camorra hierarchy. "Silvestri, I'm saying."

"I'll tell you the same thing I told him," Rossi said.

"Clear the path and get the job done. Is that clear enough?"

"Like a waterfall," Romano said.

15

Lo Manto walked down a busy street of the neighborhood where he had once lived, glancing at the crammed storefronts and changed landscape. It was late in the afternoon of what had been a long day filled with dozens of difficult questions that brought forth few satisfactory answers. Captain Fernandez and Jennifer had taken the brunt of the blitz, first from the team of detectives who drove down from Westchester primed to grill two cops who had dared to shoot and kill on their turf, and then from the truth seekers in NYPD's Internal Affairs Division. Lo Manto had been involved in enough force-of-arms situations to know it was often best to stay silent, answer only in short sentences, and play the room as ignorant as a bell ringer. He and Jennifer kept to their stories, both admitting only to the bare bones of the facts, avoiding as best they could any reasons or motives for the actions that took place outside the small restaurant. After the interrogators had packed up their audio equipment and left, content that they had gathered enough information for one day, Lo Manto and Jennifer had to sit and face the very real wrath of Fernandez.

"You handed out enough of your bullshit to maybe walk away from the IA squad without any heat coming down on your ass," he said, pouring his fourth cup of black coffee of the afternoon. "But now, right here, the two of you better start talking the truth. I hear just one word that's not right and I'll carry your ass back to Kennedy Airport myself."

"Did you get a background make on the shooters yet?" Lo Manto asked. "I hate having to leave it to a guess as to who hired them out."

"The driver was local product," Fernandez said. "Three rungs below a wannabe player. He took a hard gamble. Taking you out might have impressed enough of the dark shirts to help put him in the game."

"Who put out the deal?" Jennifer asked.

"Could have come from any one of the main Camorra crews," Fernandez said, sipping his coffee. "If I had to bet, I'd put my cash on the Rossi outfit, since Gian's last job in Naples cost them a score. And they've got a history of giving low-enders an occasional play; costs them nothing but talk."

"And still no word on my niece?" Lo Manto asked.

"She's invisible right now," Fernandez said. "A couple of runaways were found dead near the Jersey Turnpike the other night, but descriptions didn't match up. I got as many of my people on it as I can spare. She's out there, we're gonna find her—much sooner than later."

"So what happens now?" Jennifer asked, sitting across from the captain, her hands folded in her lap, looking more like an innocent college girl than a street-hardened cop. "To the two of us, I mean."

"That all depends," Fernandez said to her. "On the both of you being square with me on this shooting. On Gian here telling me what he's really up to and what his plans are. And on whether or not you still want a piece of all this. It might be best for your career and maybe even your life if you walked away from it now. You won't get any arguments out of me if you do."

"There were shots fired today," Jennifer said, looking from Lo Manto to the captain. "I want to be in this to find out why it was I had to put a man in an ICU. And better still, why he was aiming to put me in the morgue."

Captain Fernandez sat in his chair, braced his feet against the side of his desk, and folded his hands against the back of his neck. "Then it looks like it's your move, Gian," he said to Lo Manto. "It's time for you to take us down the right road."

"I'm not keeping anything from you," Lo Manto said, turning his back to Jennifer and the captain, gazing out at the bustling squad room outside the glass office. "I wouldn't be here looking for answers if I was. I'm as much in the dark about this as the two of you. I might have a better gauge on who the shadows behind the door calling in the decisions could be, but even then it's more a guess than a sure bet."

"You're telling me you have no idea why those two losers tried to stick you against the wall after lunch?" Fernandez asked. "And remember, Gian, this is me you're talking your shit to."

"I know they're Camorra," Lo Manto said with a slight shrug. "So did you as soon as you heard, and Jennifer would have figured it out quick enough. That doesn't make any of us special, it just means we know the turf we walk on. Besides, who the hell else would be gunning after a cop from Naples?"

"They had to know you were here, then," Fernandez said. "And they had to know you were coming. It takes time to set up the meeting, work out the plan, and put the hit in motion. That doesn't just happen overnight. So, even before you got on the plane to get out of Italy, they were working their phone lines."

"Which also means they knew *why* I was coming," Lo Manto said. "That takes my niece out of the runaway category."

"And puts her where exactly?" Jennifer asked.

"In their hands," Lo Manto said. "Just as Bartoni had suspected."

"That a name I should remember?" Jennifer asked him.

"Only if we get to know each other better," Lo Manto said.

"I've got a call out to both Jacobs and Rivera," Fernandez said. "One of my best young homicide teams. You're going to need some help on this, they're as good as it gets."

Lo Manto caught Jennifer's look of disappointment, her lips pursed, her jaw set tight, her eyes lit with anger. "I didn't come here so I could stand in your office and tell you what to do," he said to the captain. "You're the one with the stripes on the jacket, not me, and I respect that. But I came to you as a friend. And as that friend I'm asking you to leave this the way it is, with me and Jennifer. She knows the streets and I know the enemy. That about covers as much as we need. Two more cops, as good as they might be, could bring more trouble than we're already looking at. And none of us wants to see that happen."

"You're okay with that?" Fernandez asked, pointing a finger across his desk at Jennifer.

"Yes, sir," she said. "I am."

"You wanted out of this not too long ago," he said. "Told me you'd rather work the horse detail, as I remember it. Now the two of you are tighter than Lucy and Ricky. I'm always amazed at how far a nice lunch and a shoot-out takes you."

"I want to help find the girl," Jennifer said, not backing down, staring at her boss with a hard set of eyes. "And the ones who grabbed her. There's nothing more to it than that."

Fernandez leaned back in his chair and looked away from the two detectives. He stayed silent, lost in his thoughts for several long moments, leaving both Lo Manto and Jennifer with little to do but wait. "I'll back you both," he said, finally. "But only as far as I can. If this gets out of hand, if bodies start to fall and I start getting heavy heat from the borough command, then I'm going to do what needs to be done. And that's the best deal I put on the table. As a captain and as a friend."

"Then it's the one we'll take," Lo Manto said.

Lo Manto sat gazing out at DelGardo's crammed store, his back against the glass window, a cup of espresso in his right hand. "I don't think this place has been painted since I was a kid," he said. "Yellow walls then. Yellow walls now."

"It'll get painted when it needs to get painted, no sooner than that," Carmine DelGardo said. "When Michelangelo finished the Sistine Chapel, he didn't rush out, pick up a few gallons of Benjamin Moore, and slap on a second coat of paint, am I right? No, he left it alone. Same with me and this place."

"I didn't realize I was standing on holy ground," Lo Manto said, sipping his coffee. "I would have dressed better."

DelGardo dropped a Supremes LP on a dusty old stereo turntable and carefully placed the needle on the first track. "You been in town couple of days," he said, as the sweet voice of Diana Ross filled the small store. "And already somebody tried to take you out. Or did I hear that wrong?"

"What else did you hear?" Lo Manto asked, resting

his empty cup on a countertop, next to a stack of sugar-free gum.

"That you might as well have been on *America's Most Wanted* for a full hour," DelGardo said. "That's how many guns and shooters are gonna be coming your way. Be safer for me in downtown Baghdad than to be seen with you."

"And what about my niece?" he asked. "What's the word on her?"

"They're playing a strange hand of poker with that one," DelGardo said. "The Camorra took her and they're letting everybody on the street know it. They're calling you out to come get her. They're using her, like that fake rabbit at the dog track. Anything it takes to nail your ass, that's their end-of-the-day goal."

"And what do you think I should do about that?" Lo Manto asked, helping himself to a pack of gum.

DelGardo walked down the center aisle of his small candy store. He was a tall man, thick head of white hair combed back, his full white beard trimmed and neat. He wore a cream-colored loose-fitting short-sleeved shirt and gray slacks, the creases sharp enough to draw blood. He had clear blue eyes and pale white skin and a large tattoo of a serpent's head running down the side of his right arm. He was a confident man who had survived decades working outside the law, trusting only those he knew would take the bullet when the word wouldn't do.

"It don't matter what I think," DelGardo said. "You already made up your mind on that end, otherwise you wouldn't even be standing here. I know they got gum in Italy and I know you didn't miss seeing my skinny ass. Which makes it down to where and when and who's on your side and who isn't."

"They been to see you?" Lo Manto asked.

"I do most of my business with the Camorra," DelGardo said. "And we're both doing fine by it. They like me, they don't like me, none of that matters. All that counts is the cash that moves from one hand to the other."

"When I start making moves, they might start looking your way," Lo Manto said. "Find out what you know. I'll try to steer it clear from you, but the older crew runners will know our history."

"That's my worry," DelGardo said. "I do business with them; I'm not part of them. We butted heads before and I'm still here. They can come and ask all they want. And maybe they like what they hear and maybe they get pissed. Either way, it won't spoil my sleep."

"I'll need some equipment," Lo Manto said. "And enough supplies to get it done the right way. Whatever happens, to me or to the plan, I'll make sure you get paid."

"I got no money worries," DelGardo said. "And it won't be the first time I carried your freight. But I want to give you some advice in return for my free ride on the gear."

"I can always use a good lecture," Lo Manto said.

"I'll keep it sweet," DelGardo said. "You're in New

York now, ready to start a game where you don't know all the rules. You ain't back in old Napoli, where you know all the players, those with badges and those without, those that can be trusted and those that should be tossed. You've been away a lot of years and those task force jobs you come back to work on here and there don't count for shit. You should know that even better than me. Right now, at least from where I sit, you're walking into this blind as Stevie Wonder."

"You have a real shitty bedside manner," Lo Manto said to him. "You need to work on it a bit. Maybe open with a joke before you tell your patient he's about to die."

"This ain't the time to go at it subtle," DelGardo said. "You've caused these people a lot of grief and they're looking for a taste of the get-even. Been my experience, they usually hit what they aim at, especially if they want it bad enough. You're good, I'll grant you that. If you weren't, I'd have been at your funeral years ago. But you always go into these situations alone and one of these times just that is gonna be enough to rise up and bite you on the ass."

"I'm working this with a partner," Lo Manto told him, preferring to leave it at that and not have to go into any further detail.

"It better be that friggin' bullet-eating robot from *The Terminator*," DelGardo said. "Any less ain't gonna be of much help."

Lo Manto pulled a folded sheet of paper from his shirt

pocket and handed it to DelGardo. "That should pretty much cover all I need," he said. "If you think I missed a spot here and there, add it to the list."

DelGardo flipped open the paper and glanced over the neatly written list. "The first three I can have by tonight," he said. "The middle three by tomorrow, late in the afternoon. The last two I gotta check on and get back to you. With some luck, they'll be in your hands day after tomorrow. *If* you're still alive."

Lo Manto opened the rickety wooden door leading out of the store. "It might be worth getting killed, then," he said, glancing over his shoulder at DelGardo. "Just to stick you with a tab."

Lo Manto was walking past the El on East 238th Street, heading for a first-floor apartment on Boyd Avenue, when a heavy rain began to fall. He lifted the collar of his thin leather jacket and walked along the doorways of the storefronts that lined the street. A heavy jolt of thunder and a flash of lightning brought the rain down in an even heavier rush and Lo Manto ducked into the first open doorway he found, nestled in between a shuttered pizzeria and a small lingerie shop. He stood with his back against the row of mailboxes and ran a hand across his thick hair. The glass-paned door to the main lobby was ajar, the buzzer long ago rendered useless. Lo Manto opened it and slowly stepped inside, the hall filtered in darkness, an overhead twenty-five-watt bulb close to the rear exit the only visible light. He walked to the base of the first-floor steps and eased himself down on the cracked cement, faded flower patterns dotting its edges. He leaned back and took a deep breath, taking in the murmurs and smells of the building. The sounds from inside the small, stuffy apartments were a mixture of muffled conversations and flashes of television game shows and soap operas. Anyone home at this hour of the day was either retired, unemployed, or getting ready for the late-night shift at one of the nearby sweatshops. Lo Manto's hair was wet, and now droplets of water bounced against the collar of his jacket. He closed his eyes and leaned his head against the cement wall. He was cold, hungry, and tired as his mind rushed through a methodical breakdown of his current situation. The next move now belonged to him and he couldn't be passive about it, which required him quickly and quietly to gather as much street info as he could and then hit one of the major Camorra spots, either an after-hours gambling operation or a club that brought in half their weekly through drug sales. This would serve both as retaliation for the botched attempt on his life outside the restaurant and as a shout to the outfit that he wasn't quite ready to pack his bags and run back home. At the same time, he needed to smoke out which of the Camorra crews had lifted his niece and pinpoint where she'd been dropped. He was still gambling that she was merely the hook to reel him in and would thus remain unharmed, but slivers of doubt were starting to cloud that end of his thinking, specifically the lack of any contact between him and the lifters. On this one, Lo Manto knew he couldn't afford even to make anything close to a wrong move.

He opened his eyes but stayed still when he heard the rustle coming from behind the stairwell. He stretched out his legs and kept his body relaxed but primed to move as he listened to the sounds of rustling clothes and a quiet, muffled cough. He looked to his left and saw the shadow on the wall, hunching over, folding items, and placing them in what appeared to be a small bag. Then the shadow stood upright and moved away from the dark shade and toward the vestibule. Lo Manto watched a boy, about fifteen, walk past the stairwell, a plastic bag slung over one shoulder, his head down, ready to head out and brave the late afternoon storm.

"If you give it another twenty minutes, you'll save yourself a soak-through," Lo Manto said, his words directed at the boy's back. "You're walking into the heart of it if you head out now."

The boy, Felipe Lopez, turned and looked over at the man sitting on the steps. He wasn't a familiar face and he didn't figure to be a tenant, though he did have a neighborhood look to both his outfit and his manner, sitting there casually, indifferent, acting like somehow this was where he belonged. "The rain's gonna be falling down on my skin, not yours," Felipe said with a shrug. "So long as you're in here white and dry, I don't see it as your problem."

"Is Eduardo's still where it used to be?" Lo Manto

asked the boy, ignoring his display of street attitude. "Next to the dry cleaners, on 241st?"

"No reason for it to move," Felipe said. "Place is always packed. Even people who leave the neighborhood drive back every Saturday to grab a meal."

"Well, if Ida's still doing the cooking, then there's a good reason to burn through a tank of gas," Lo Manto said. He stood up, watching the boy tense as he did, anticipating his next move. "The food in there is better than in some restaurants in Italy."

"That I wouldn't know," Felipe said. "I never ate there."

"Why not?" Lo Manto asked, standing now, arching his back, cracking the stiffness out of the muscles. "Not big on Italian food?"

"Not big on money," Felipe said. "And I think they're one of those places that expects you to pay after you eat."

"You hungry now?" Lo Manto asked.

"I'm always hungry," Felipe said.

"I'm in the mood for baked clams and maybe some stuffed shells," Lo Manto said, walking toward the boy and the front door. "And I hate to eat alone. I can order more if there's two of us."

"I don't usually eat with strangers," Felipe said. "It's never a good idea."

"I never do," Lo Manto said, holding open the front door and waiting for the boy to walk past. "They're not to be trusted. Now, it's a good seven blocks in a heavy

211

rain, which means we're running it. First one that's there gets the table and orders the wine. And if that ends up to be you, make sure the wine's red and make twice as sure it's a Brunello."

"What if I get there and you never show?" Felipe asked, stepping into the small vestibule, staring at Lo Manto, the rain outside coming down hard enough to cause pain. "I'm the one gets stuck with a bottle of wine that probably costs more than I'm worth."

"If that happens, then you'll know," Lo Manto said, moving slowly toward the assault from above, gearing up for his dash through the streets of the East Bronx.

"Know what?" Felipe asked.

"That I was one of those strangers that shouldn't have been trusted," Lo Manto said. He smiled at the boy, turned, and ran out into the heavy rain in search of a restaurant and a meal.

They were halfway through their entrée, Lo Manto savoring a mixed grill of squid, shrimp, scallops, eel, clams, and mussels and a large tomato and red onion salad while Felipe devoured a steak pizzaiola, garlic mashed potatoes, and a side of marinated eggplant. They had muscled their way through the rain, jumping huge puddles, dodging passing cars that plowed water thick as waves onto the sidewalks, weaving in and out between street and curb until they reached the restaurant. They left their jackets, drenched and dripping, with a young coat-check girl with long, tapered nails, dark curly hair, and a gentle smile. They were escorted to a table in the back by an elderly man with a hunched-over walk wearing a tuxedo that had survived the better part of a decade. The restaurant was quiet, with only half the dozen tables filled, mostly with elderly customers looking for a warm plate and a dry room. Italian instrumental music flowed from the corner speakers on low volume.

Lo Manto ordered for both of them, speaking in Neapolitan dialect to the headwaiter, a tall, graceful man with white hair and a relaxed and gentle manner. The man nodded as he noted the order, offering his opinion on the choice of wine, smiling when the young boy asked for a Coke with no ice to start. They sat in silence as they waited for their first course to be placed in front of them, a cold antipasto platter filled with fresh-cut salami, prosciutto, sopressata, and a variety of cheeses. Lo Manto filled his bread plate with olive oil and heavy dashes of red pepper and acted as if he didn't notice when the boy did the same. The boy was on his second glass of Coke, his antipasto plate wiped clean, when he spoke. "You're not from here," he said to Lo Manto. "But you act like you are. What's the deal with that?"

"I used to live around here," Lo Manto said. "Many years ago. I left when I was about your age, when my mom moved me and my sister to Italy. But I've been back here and there."

"To see family?" the boy asked.

"No," Lo Manto said as he finished off the last of his

antipasto and poured himself a fresh glass of wine. "Any family I have is in Naples. Here, I have a few friends and enough enemies to fill this restaurant."

"That why you picked me to eat with?" Felipe asked.

"It's nice to sit across from a friendly face," Lo Manto said with a slight smile. "It helps you enjoy the meal more."

"The food's supposed to be even better in Italy," Felipe said. "Least that's what I read in the books at school and hear from the Guidos in the neighborhood. Plus, you have friends and family there, so you always have somebody to eat with, right?"

"Yes," Lo Manto said, his eyes briefly looking past the boy toward a young couple in the rear of the restaurant, their backs to a framed portrait of the Bay of Naples, locked in a long, passionate kiss.

"Then why you even bother coming to New York?" Felipe asked. "You tryin' to get an old apartment back, something like that?"

"My work brings me back," Lo Manto said.

"What kind of work does that?" Felipe asked. "Makes you go back and forth all the time? And don't pay that much on top."

Lo Manto laughed, wet hair flopping against his ears and neck. He lifted his wineglass and took a slow drink. "What makes you think I don't make a lot of money?" he asked. "For all you know I'm richer than Donald Trump."

"You're in a leather jacket, polo shirt, and Gap

214

jeans," Felipe said. "Show me a picture where you got Trump decked out in an outfit like that."

"He might dress better," Lo Manto said, leaning back in his chair as a waiter put a steaming bowl of pasta mixed with beef and pork braciola between his knife and fork. "But he can't tell a guy not to leave town for the weekend. When I'm working, I can do that."

Felipe rested his fork against the edge of his bowl of penne sitting in a thick marinara sauce. He pushed his chair back a few inches and placed the palms of his hands on top of the table. He stared across at Lo Manto, his dark eyes now no longer open and friendly, colored instead by a fresh coat of fear. "You a cop?" he asked, his mouth suddenly dry, his boyish voice minus its earlier spark.

Lo Manto nodded, jamming a forkful of pasta into his mouth, his expression betraying no emotion. "Not here, though," he said. "But back in my city, Naples. I work homicide and narcotics cases, mostly. So unless you're involved in either of those two areas, you can relax and go back to enjoying your meal. I try to make it a practice not to arrest anyone I share a dinner with."

"What about after dinner?" Felipe asked.

"I thought we'd go for a walk and talk," Lo Manto said. "Give us both a chance to burn off some of the meal and maybe get to know each other a little bit better."

"You don't need to waste your time getting to know me," Felipe said, picking up his fork again and jabbing

215

at his pasta, tension in his body starting to ease. "I try to steer clear of cops, no matter what country they come from."

"Don't blame you there," Lo Manto said, breaking off a thick chunk of warm bread. "You have to be careful who you trust in life, especially when it comes to cops. We'll see how it goes, you and me. If by the end of our walk, you want to head your own way, it'll be with no hard feelings. I expect the same from you, if it turns out I'm the one looking to say good-bye."

"You got something in mind?" Felipe asked. He was, at the very least, curious. He had never spent this much time alone with a cop, let alone sat down and shared a meal with one. He liked Lo Manto, ignoring the signals from his street antennae warning him to take heed, able to relax and find comfort in his company. Other than the fact that he wore a badge, eating with him was no different from having dinner with any other straight-up local from the neighborhood. Only Lo Manto ordered from the higher end of the menu.

"I've been away for a long time," Lo Manto said. "Some things have stayed the same, but there's a different feel to the area from when I was your age. If I had the time, maybe I could navigate my way through it. But I'm up against the clock and could use a good pair of eyes out there. Somebody I can depend on when I reach out with a question I need answered in a hurry."

"I won't stool for you," Felipe said, "if that's where

this is going. I don't go that way, for one. And pointing fingers around here is the death penalty."

"I wouldn't ask you to do that," Lo Manto said. "And a stool is not what I need. I can get that on my own."

"What do you need then?" Felipe asked.

"A partner," Lo Manto said.

16

Jennifer sipped from a cold Starbucks Frappuccino, her driver's side window down, engine on her unmarked parked in idle. Lo Manto sat across from her, reading the sports section of an Italian newspaper, a hot cup of coffee resting on the dashboard. It was early morning on what promised to be another hot and humid New York day, the storefronts along East Gun Hill Road still shuttered, a few shop owners hosing down the sidewalks, watching the dirt and debris flow over the curb and toward the half-moon sewer mouths.

"What did you and Fernandez talk about after I left his office?" Jennifer asked, setting her sweaty plastic cup in a slot under the radio. "And don't dodge the answer. Good or bad, I'd like to hear the truth. I think off of yesterday, I earned that much."

Lo Manto put aside his newspaper and grabbed his coffee. He took several slow sips, placed the cup back on the dash, and turned to face Jennifer. "He needed to decide if you were going to be a part of this or not," he said. "If you were good enough to deal with the action that's gonna happen and the heat that follows. He laid out your strengths and your weak spots."

"How'd I score?"

"You're here," Lo Manto said. "And you're in it. That's all that should matter. At least for the time being."

"Going into a situation, any situation, with a reluctant partner is not a place any cop wants to be put in," Jennifer said. "Especially this cop. I need to know if you want me in on this or you're going to look to ditch me first chance you get."

"I don't want anyone but me," Lo Manto said. "It has nothing to do with how good I think you are. It has everything to do with me not wanting to see another cop get hurt. This is my battle. I fight it every day in Naples and I usually fight it alone."

"Did Fernandez offer up those two homicide bozos again?" she asked. "Jacobs and Rivera? To take my place?"

"They weren't the answer, either," Lo Manto said. "He could have told me Frank Serpico was coming out of retirement and looking to partner up, it wouldn't have mattered. I like to work it by myself. Nothing personal against you or anybody else."

"But he said no," she said, raising her voice above the din of a passing bus.

"He said it was either with a partner or a ticket back to Naples," Lo Manto said. "And I wasn't ready to go back home."

"So, we're stuck in the middle with each other," she said. "No matter how much either of us dislikes the idea."

"I like you, and based on what I saw yesterday, I think you're street solid," Lo Manto said to her, gazing at her unlined face, taking in her sharp features, her bright eyes, her lips pursed and primed for either a smile or a pout. "And I don't want to see you go down for something you should have no business being in. This isn't about babysitting a wop cop anymore. Truth is, it never was. It's about taking on a crime family."

Jennifer took a deep breath and gazed out her open window. "When do we start?" she asked, turning back to face Lo Manto.

He pointed to a small florist sandwiched between a tanning salon and a bar. "As soon as the flower man opens for business," he said.

Jennifer stood in the middle of the shop, bending over to smell the buds on a potted gardenia. The man behind the counter looked up from a mound of paper and smiled at her over the crease of his glass frames. "Help you with anything?" he asked.

"Got an old aunt just home from the hospital," Jennifer said. "She likes plants. Lookin' for something to cheer her up."

"Can she get around?" the man asked. "Or she have to stay in bed?"

"Does it matter?" Jennifer asked, unable to completely

bury the cop attitude. "It's just a plant."

"A plant that needs to be watered," the man said, his condescending tone ripe with derision. "If your aunt can't get around to keep the dirt and leaves fresh, then you might as well buy her flowers. There, water or no water, they'll be dead in three days."

Jennifer walked away from the gardenia plant and headed toward the counter. The man took off his glasses and set aside his paperwork. He was tall with a solid build and a thick head of brown hair. He had a curved scar at the base of his lower lip and two rows of teeth as white as a freshly painted kitchen wall. "I'll take a dozen roses, then," she said. "Yellow ones. Be nice to have something in the apartment that's gonna die before my aunt."

"Now you're using the main brain," the man said, a smile creasing across thick skin and a thin mustache.

"Maybe not," Jennifer said. "Since a plant wouldn't have put as big a dent on my credit card bill."

"It's for family," the man said. "Can't put a price on that."

"You would," she said, "if you ever met my aunt."

The man stepped out from behind the counter and walked toward the refrigerated glass cabinet that kept the flowers fresh. "I'll pick the best ones I have," he said, walking with a slight limp. "Pretty enough to bring a smile to even the meanest face."

Jennifer leaned her elbows on the counter, the square of her back resting against the edge, and looked around the shop. "You work here alone?" she asked, watching as the man slid open a glass door and pulled out long-stemmed yellow roses, their petals not yet ready to blossom.

The man stopped choosing the roses and turned to look at Jennifer. There was a harder tone to his voice, a harsher glare to his eyes. "Does it matter?" he asked.

"Just trying to make a little small talk," she said, sensing his shift. "No need to get hormonal on me."

"We can talk about the weather," the man said, his manner once again soft. "That's always good for a few minutes."

"Can I get these flowers delivered?" she asked. "My aunt lives about six, seven blocks from here."

"She just got home from the hospital," the man said, walking back toward the counter, stems of the dozen roses resting firmly in his right hand. "Might be nice to show her a pretty face along with these flowers."

"I'm starting a new job today," she said. "And I don't want to be late first time through the door. My aunt was a career woman. She'd understand."

The man nodded, resting the flowers on the counter-top. He pulled out a long sheaf of clear plastic and rested it flat on the Formica surface. "The cards are over next to the frames," he said, reaching for a pair of cutting shears. "Find one you like, write something nice, and I'll staple it to the flowers."

Jennifer walked to a display case crammed with frames of various sizes, scanned a shelf of greeting cards situated just below, and picked one with the smiling face of an angel on its cover. She lifted it out of its slot, flipped it open, and grabbed a pen that was on the middle shelf. Signing her name, she slipped the card into a small envelope and walked back to the counter to hand it to the man. He took it with his right hand and with his left stapled it to the clear plastic paper now wrapped around the roses. "These should be there sometime between four and five," he said. "So long as she lives in the neighborhood, like you said."

"She's down the street from the old Wakefield Theater," Jennifer said. "Brown brick building with all the flowers in front. Right off White Plains Road. Third floor. Under the name Rosetti."

"There's an additional five-dollar delivery charge," the man said. "I don't do it myself. I use a Puerto Rican kid from next door whenever I need a run made, which these days isn't too often."

"Not a problem," Jennifer said. "Just add it the bill."

"That totals it out to forty-nine dollars with the delivery," the man said. "Unless there's something else you want."

"There is one more thing I'd like," Jennifer said. "But it won't cost either one of us any money."

The man adjusted his glasses and looked at her, his eyes still and stripped of any care or emotion. "And what would that be?" he asked.

"I want you to get on the floor, face first, legs spread, hands folded behind your back," she said, opening her

223

black jacket just enough for him to see the gun jammed in her waistband. "Please."

The man stood with his back straight, hands resting flat on the counter surface. His dark eyes glared at Jennifer, the friendly smile replaced by a tight-lipped scowl. "There are some places you walk in, rob, and get away with, the owner happy just to make it out alive," he said, in a matter-of-fact tone. "This just isn't one of them."

"Tough talk for a florist," Jennifer said. "Now, get down on that floor like I told you to do."

"And if I don't?" the man asked. "How nasty you going to bring it?"

Jennifer stared at the man for several seconds and took one long deep breath. "Tell me your name," she said.

"Is it important?" the man asked.

"Very," Jennifer said.

"George," the man said. "George Palmero."

"And I figure you to be what, sixty, little past that, maybe," Jennifer said, shifting closer to the edge of the counter. "Am I right?"

"Close enough," George said with a slight shrug.

"Now I asked you to take to the floor in a nice way, George," Jennifer said. "Like I would any man that's around my father's age."

"And if I don't?" George asked again, his defiance not backing down in the face of the threat. "Then what?"

"Then I'll shoot you until you fall," Jennifer said in

the calmest of tones but with a slight hint of an edge to her soft voice. "Just like I would any man around my father's age. Including my father."

George slid his hands slowly off the counter and placed them at his back. He then dropped to his knees and stared down at the splintered wooden floor. Jennifer made her way behind the counter and stood over him, a pair of cuffs in her right hand. "You won't live long enough to spend what's in the register," George said to her, not turning his head, his body still as stone.

"I don't want your money," Jennifer said, slapping the cuffs across his wrists with two quick moves. "Or your flowers."

"Then what?" George asked.

Jennifer looked down and made eye contact with the older man, a wide smile crossing her face. "I'm going to take the whole damn store," she said.

Lo Manto scaled the red stone wall and dropped to the other side, facing the back of the flower shop, its door dead-bolted shut. He glanced around, surveying the hard ground littered with plastic garbage bags and piles of bound newspapers. The walkway was narrow and dark, while above him the windows were drawn shut and painted black. He stepped around a dozen empty cardboard boxes and glanced down the steps of a basement lit only by a small overhead light bulb. He pulled the .38 from his waistband, rested it at his side, and began a slow walk into the semidarkness below.

He braced himself against a chipped wood wall, watching four young men gently place sealed packets of heroin inside long white boxes filled with tissue paper and fresh-cut flowers. They would then close the boxes, wrap them with different-colored ribbons, and place them inside supermarket shopping carts lined up behind them. There was a fifth man in the room, shorter and much older than the others, his body bent over a wooden butcher's slab, a ladle in his right hand and a surgical mask wrapped tight around his mouth and nose, pouring white powder into small, clear sandwich bags. A radio was playing somewhere in the darkened room, the sultry voice of Laura Pausini filtering through the murky air.

Lo Manto rested his head against the edge of the wall and closed his eyes for a brief moment. He had been witness to scenes like this so many times across so many years in both New York and Naples, and they never failed to leave him with feelings of sadness and anger. This dank and humid place, along with hundreds of other such spots spanning across two countries, was the feed from which the Camorra drew its power. This was the first stop on their march to riches. The legitimate end of their operations, from banks to brokerage houses to real estate agencies, all profitable enterprises that allowed their empire to grow and prosper, would not be attainable were it not for this first step. The heroin trade was at the heart of the Camorra strength and rested beneath the waves of their prosperity. In order to reduce their power, it was crucial that the steady stream of heroin income, which brought roughly $750 million a month into the criminal coffers of two cities, be decreased.

Lo Manto moved away from the wall and stepped into the center of the room, his gun pointed at the men working at the large wooden table. They lifted their heads when they saw him, dropped the heroin packets, raised their hands, and took several steps back. With a nod and a glance from Lo Manto, the old man put down his ladle and stepped in with the other four. They were illegals, more fearful of deportation than jail time, working off the loans their families back home had taken from the Camorra in return for their sons' entrance into a better life in a more prosperous country. He looked into the faces of the four young men and saw withered bodies and tired eyes gazing back. They fit the label of Camorra victim just as easily as the addicts in whose veins the white poison they were preparing for transport would flow. They would never know America as the vaunted land of opportunity. The only memories they would compile were of rooms such as this one, the long hours of many long days spent working the mule trade, under the orders of the unseen powers that ruled their lives.

He spoke to them in Italian, knowing their English would, at best, be weak. He signaled them to leave by the back way and told them not to worry, they had nothing to fear from his hand. He stood to the side and waited as they stripped off their dusty white aprons and slipped off plastic gloves, tossing both to the ground and nodding a silent thanks his way as they exited. Lo Manto held up his hand and stopped the old man as he was pushing aside a shopping cart and moving toward the rear steps. He walked over to him, grabbed his right arm, and turned it over, gazing down at the thick skin just above his wrist. Lo Manto ran a finger across the small tattoo of a black crow gripping the edge of a knife with its beak. "Camorrista?" Lo Manto asked the old man.

The old man nodded his head. "*Sì,*" he said, his slate blue eyes hard and defiant, his upper body rock hard despite his advancing years.

"Which family?" Lo Manto asked in English. He figured the man to have been in the States long enough to understand the language. "And whose drugs?"

The old man smiled, flashing a row of white teeth, newly capped and cleaned. "I say a word to you and I die," he said. "It's better to stay quiet and wait until they kill you. Then I come back here to work."

"My name is Lo Manto," he said, letting go of the old man's arm. "I'm a cop from Naples. I can't arrest you. I can't even tell you what to do."

"Then why are you here?" the old man asked. "Did you come all the way to America just to die? Even if you do nothing else, if you stop right now and get those boys back in here and let us finish our work, they will still make a lesson of you. Just for the interruption."

228

"Then there's really no reason for me to stop now," Lo Manto said. "Is there?"

"I won't tell them anything," the old man said. "And I'll make sure the boys do the same. But only if you go now."

"I want you to tell them," Lo Manto said. "I want you to tell them everything you saw and everything that's going to happen. And don't forget my name. This way Pete Rossi will know who to hunt down."

"Who told you I know anybody named Pete Rossi?" the old man asked, inching his way toward the steps.

"You just did," Lo Manto said.

Lo Manto walked past the pile of empty boxes and strewn wrappers and pushed open a large wooden door. He stepped into the flower shop and nodded at Jennifer, still standing over George, her gun holstered and her arms folded across her chest. "You stop for breakfast?" she asked, slightly irritated. "A kid with a box cutter and a pack of matches would have been home in bed by now."

"I ran into an old friend," Lo Manto said, easing in next to her behind the counter, gazing down at George. "And I gave you some time to make a new one."

"I don't think I'm his type," Jennifer said. "He doesn't seem to like girls who bring their own handcuffs."

George lifted his head and stared up at the two detectives. "Joke all you want," he said, his lips curled in a snarl. "Enjoy yourselves now, while you still got the chance. You'll both be dead before it's dark out."

"See what I'm saying?" Jennifer asked. "Not exactly somebody you can bring home to meet the folks. Unless your folks are parole officers and even then it's a bit of a stretch."

Lo Manto reached down and lifted George to his feet. He looked past the old man's shoulder and saw thin lines of smoke creeping their way from under the back door. "I'm going to have my partner take the cuffs off," Lo Manto told him.

"Those are the first sensible words to leave your mouth since you got here," George said. "It won't save your life, but it does show me you're not one hundred percent stupid."

"Let me ask you a question, genius," Lo Manto said. "How long you think they'll keep you alive after they hear about what happened?"

"Nothing happened," George said, his words lacking the confident edge they had held only seconds earlier.

"First you let a girl take you down," Lo Manto said. "That has to be worth two pins to the knees for sure. Then you let a wet wop like me come through the back door and torch the place. I mean we're looking at what? I'm figuring about thirty thousand just in lost flowers."

George looked away from Lo Manto and Jennifer and turned a panicked eye toward the back door, plumes of smoke filtering through now, the thin lines swallowed up by the flames licking at the side panels. He looked back at Lo Manto, his forehead drenched in sweat, his lower lip trembling. "You're right," he said, his voice cracking. "They got no choice but to kill me. But with me they'll do it clean and fast. You and the girl, they're gonna make suffer."

"Can you blame them?" Lo Manto asked. "Half a million in heroin going up in smoke. That's enough to make even the calmest Camorrista's blood bubble."

"Why'd you do all this?" George asked, following Lo Manto out of the flower shop, Jennifer trailing them, smoke licking at their backs. "You wanna die, it would have been easier and less painful for you to just toss yourself off a building."

Lo Manto turned to face the front of the store. Flames were rushing down the length of the shop, the heat melting the flowers and cracking glass and vases, George next to him, Jennifer leaning against the side of a parked car. A small crowd had gathered around the three and in the distance the squeal of fire engines could be heard. He looked over at George, the tough talker from earlier now reduced to a frightened old man, well aware of his own sealed fate. "There's no fun in dying alone," Lo Manto said.

He stared at the old man, smoke engulfing them both, then nodded, turned, and walked toward the unmarked car parked farther up the street.

Pete Rossi eased the bow of his forty-two-foot yacht into the thick foam of the oncoming wave, bracing for the bounce that always followed. He was shirtless at the wheel, on the top deck of the two-tiered vessel, fighting the squalls and the whitecaps in the middle of Long Island Sound. It had been a hot and humid day, but the winds had picked up with the setting sun, bringing with them cooler temperatures and choppier waters. Rossi shifted the directional gears into neutral, watched as the bow of the twin-engine boat dipped into the hard Atlantic, and released his grip on the wheel. He turned his chair in a half-circle and leaned back, his dark eyes on Silvestri, his body tense and coiled.

"You ever wonder how he even knows which of our places to hit?" Rossi asked, not expecting much of an answer in return. "And when? Here, Naples, it doesn't seem to much matter. It's like he's got a map in his pocket. Or better yet, a voice on the other end of a cell phone."

"He may have one or two of our guys locked down as informants," Silvestri agreed. "But no matter who they are, there's no way they'd know all our spots. We go out of our way to keep a tight lid on those. A street skel might know one, with a wild amount of luck, two, but no more than that. And no major locations. I can count on one hand the number on our side that could even come close to a guess on all the places we use."

"What did the fire cost?" Rossi asked. "Both money and time."

"There was a little bit over half a million in pure down in the basement," Silvestri said, wiping a line of sweat from his forehead with two fingers of his right hand. "Totals out to at least five times that on the street.

The suppliers on the other end are going to have to wait no more than two days before we get a fresh batch in their hands. Should be business as usual by Thursday."

"Except the operation will still be three million short," Rossi said, his voice calm, the high level of his anger apparent only in his tense demeanor. "All because one, that's right, one cop knows where to hit and when. He's got somebody close to me feeding him and that's a name I need."

"He's hit us in Naples and in New York," Silvestri said, pulling a cigarette from a half empty pack in his shirt pocket. "And we got nobody out there with knowledge of both ends. The way it's set up, it's just not possible. To my eyes anyway."

"Then your eyes are very wrong," Rossi said, standing now, walking with relaxed ease around the edges of the boat, waves lapping at its side. "Or they're not seeing all that they should. There's one of ours with lips close to this cop. That person must be found."

"I'll get on it soon as we dock," Silvestri said, resigned now to putting in motion a task with results that would be all but impossible to achieve.

The organizational structure of the Camorra was shaped like a giant squid, every tentacle operating independently but each one firmly attached to the large head at the center. This allowed the varied enterprises to run their multibillion-dollar operations without fear of any high-level infiltration. While its Sicilian counterpart in the organized crime hierarchy, the Mafia, had often been brought to the brink of ruin solely on the basis of informants able to share a vast knowledge of their overall methods of doing business, the Camorra historically sustained few such defections. Every member, regardless of rank or status, was fed only the information that enabled him to move the venture he was involved in to its next logical step. This allowed true power to remain in the hands of the reigning don, and the very best of these leaders made it a point to trust no one. Silence was the Camorra's most valuable weapon. No one had ever managed to infiltrate the top tier of the organization, and Silvestri had serious doubts that Lo Manto, despite his sporadic successes down the years, would be the first.

"Where are we with the girl?" Rossi asked. He had turned off the engines and dropped anchor, allowing the boat to float over uneasy water three miles from the Long Island shoreline.

"She found her way to the Metro-North station," Silvestri said. "It was either too late or she got lucky, but nobody came around asking her for a ticket. Our guys boarded it in time and rode with her into the city."

"She try to contact her uncle?" Rossi asked, reaching into an open cooler and pulling out a sweaty bottle of Deer Park water.

"Not yet," Silvestri said. "She spent her night on a ticket-holder's bench in Grand Central. Got up at the start of rush hour and started walking around the terminal."

"Our guys still with her?" Rossi took three large

gulps, then rested the bottle in an open slot on the side of his chair.

"They're pissing and moaning about it," Silvestri said. "But they're with her. She hasn't been out of their sight since she left the house."

"And that's the way it better stay," Rossi said, pulling the unlit cigarette from Silvestri's mouth and tossing it over his shoulder and into the water. "And make sure that when we move against her uncle, she's nowhere in sight. I'm looking for the cop to go down, not the kid."

"They're on her like Elmer's," Silvestri said. "She leads, they follow. Or they go down. I couldn't have made it any clearer."

"Once you relay all that, have them report to somebody else," Rossi told him. "I want you on this cop full-time. Go back in and get into his background. I'm talking beyond what we already have. Grab it from day one."

"The profile we got is pretty detailed," Silvestri said. "It tracks him from his first year in high school. I know more about this badge than I do about my own wife."

"We're missing something," Rossi insisted. "There has to be a card in this deck we haven't found. We're not just another case to this cop. We're very personal to him, have been from day one. Now, it could all just be about his father. With some people that's enough, and he might be one of those. But I don't think so. I think there's something at play here. The sooner we latch on to what that is, the sooner we pin him to the mat."

"You want me to use the info we already have?" Silvestri asked, "or start it all from scratch?"

"Work off the basics," Rossi told him, "and then think beyond them. This guy's a good cop, smart on the street, never makes a move unless he's standing on sure feet. But there's lots of guys out there like that. Maybe not in his league, but close. There has to be something he has or knows that gives him that extra tick, makes him anticipate what we do even before we go out there and do it."

"That ain't gonna be all that easy to find," Silvestri said. "Given that it's out there to start with."

"If it was easy, we would have had it already," Rossi said, his raspy voice filled with an impatient edge. "The fact we don't means that it's buried deep enough to lay hidden from everybody's line of sight."

"I'll put a call out to Naples," Silvestri said. "See what we can dig up there. There'll be somebody, another cop, a friend, maybe even a relative, who can give up more than what we're already holding."

"Put it out there on all levels," Rossi said. "From street to suite, anybody ever crossed his sight, I want to hear what they have to say."

"How close can we get to his family?" Silvestri asked, the implication of his words clear and apparent.

"We already got his niece," Rossi said. "You want to touch the sister, that can best be done through her husband. He's not straight blood, so he might be willing to give up some information in return for knowing his kid's safe."

"What about his mother?" Silvestri said. "What I get from the other side is that they're close. She doesn't talk much about her time here and he don't ask. I think that's what they both want us to think and see. I bet she knows a lot more than she lets on. It would make sense to try and get close to her."

"Do it clean," Rossi said. "Don't go to her direct. You can get just as much from the ones in her circle as you probably could out of her mouth. And make sure she doesn't sniff it out. I don't want her tipping off her son."

"We got another shipment in place to move by midweek," Silvestri said. "We can put a hold on it a few days, let the waters calm a bit, give us a chance to deal full-out with this cop."

"*We* decide on how we run our business," Rossi said, his handsome face flushed red from anger and the glare of the sun. "Not some badge chasing our tail. And besides, if he's on to our every move, he'll figure something's not right if we make any changes to our plans. Leave our world as is and plan on rocking his heavy."

"He seems awful calm about his niece," Silvestri said, glancing away from Rossi, his eyes focused on the spray of the waves as they bounced against the side of the boat. "That bothers me. Instead of flipping his informers about our next deals, he should be hounding them about the kid, but he's not. Why do you suppose that is?"

"Maybe he's got eyes on her that we can't see," Rossi said. "But even with him, that's a bit too much to expect.

It might be he just doesn't care. But he's not cut that way, either."

"Which leaves us where?" Silvestri asked.

"Looking for answers you better find," Rossi said. "Otherwise, it won't just be him I'd be planting in the ground."

Paula walked slowly through the crowded hall. She stared up at the majestic ceiling of Grand Central Terminal, taking several moments to marvel at the shapes and designs of the stars and planets, each one seemingly floating on a weight all its own. She was hungry and tired, despite a restful night in the security of the waiting area. More than anything, she was impatient, eager for her plight to come to an end. She brushed strands of hair away from her eyes, ever mindful that she hadn't washed or showered since she'd escaped from her locked room. She stood off to one side of a large circular information booth, a rush of people closing in, eager to have their questions regarding times and tracks answered by the indifferent attendants sitting behind a safety glass shield, who grudgingly dispensed their knowledge, barely audible without the power of the mike pressed close to their lips. She looked beyond the dashing throng of pedestrians, each desperate to catch a train. She walked toward the dining course at the bottom shell of the terminal, her eyes darting from right to left, seeking out a place to eat.

The two men in leather jackets and tight jeans

watched as she walked past, their arms resting casually on a ticket counter, above them the times and tracks for a long list of arrivals and departures changing as quickly as a stock market ticker. The taller of the two, thick dark hair gelled back, the collar of his black shirt buttoned, a folded morning edition of the *New York Post* in his right hand, lowered his eyes and shook his head. "You ask me, Otto," he said to the heftier man next to him, "this kid is in a rush to nowhere. She isn't even close to a clue as to where she's going. If this is all she got planned, she woulda been a whole lot better off just staying in the damn room."

"Maybe you're right, maybe you're not," Otto said. "Either way, we stay on her. We lose this kid, our wives get to go to two funerals next week."

The tall man slid the newspaper onto the counter and started to walk after the girl, Otto by his side. "You'd think, though, by now anyway, somebody would have made a move to help this kid," he said in a low voice. "If for nothing else, to show her they at least cared."

"It hasn't been that long—a couple of days, tops," Otto said. "These things take time to play themselves out. But then none of that should even be of any concern to you. What you have to be worried about is to see the move coming and be ready to jump when it does."

"Think it'll be from the cop?" the tall man asked, easing past a mother and her young daughter, their arms filled with packages, both rushing for a departing Westchester train. "Or a face we don't know?"

"Doesn't matter who moves, Freddie," Otto said, keeping his gaze focused on Paula as she walked past a bookstore display. "What matters is that we nail his ass before his hands touch the girl."

"Looks from here like she's headed for a meal," Freddie said, brushing off the bump he felt from a passing businessman in a tailor-made suit.

"About damn time," Otto said. "I could use a slice, too." Then, watching as his target veered to the right, "But I think she's making a pit stop first."

Paula let the cold water run over her hands. She stared at her face in the stained mirror. Her long hair was greasy and in need of a combing, her eyes puffy from days of fitful bouts of little sleep. She cupped her hands, lowered her head, and splashed the icy water on her face and forehead. She repeated the gesture several times, not noticing the man standing in the last stall, his eyes focused on the closed door. He watched as an elderly woman in a tan jacket dried her hands, tossed two paper towels into an overstuffed bin, picked up her small valise, and left the bathroom. The man then eased his way out of the stall and walked toward the girl, who was still bent over the sink, splashing cold water on her face. He put a hand on the center of the girl's back, freezing her in place. Her body was as still as stone, running water the only noise in the bathroom.

"How do you like New York so far?" the man asked the girl, smiling at her in the mirror.

Paula looked up. Her face exploded into a smile and she turned and rushed to hug the man. *"Zio,"* she whispered, holding him tight enough to feel both his muscles and the muzzle of his gun. "I knew you'd show up. I didn't know where or how, but I just knew you'd find me."

The man gently kissed the top of the girl's head and lifted her face up toward his, gazing into her clear, innocent eyes. "I'd have to die not to find you," Lo Manto said, smiling at his niece.

"I can't wait until I take a shower," Paula said. "And after that, I'm going to eat the biggest meal you've ever seen."

Lo Manto looked away from his niece and glanced at the closed door. "That's going to have to wait a bit," he said. "There are still a few things I need to finish, and I can't get it all done without your help."

"Uncle Gianni, please," Paula said with full teenage frustration. "You've done your job. You rescued me. You're here and I'm safe. There's nothing left for you to do. Except get me to a shower and then take me to lunch."

Lo Manto heard the door handle turn. He grabbed Paula and pulled her into the first open stall. He closed the door, snapped the lock, and jumped onto the toilet seat, crouching so as not to be seen by the middle-aged woman who had just entered. He signaled his niece to stay silent. They both relaxed as they listened to the clacking of the woman's pumps as she entered the stall nearest the far wall and closed its door. Paula took a deep breath and turned to face her uncle. He was crouched on the toilet, his eyes trained on the floor, where the tips of a pair of men's loafers were visible. She saw her uncle effortlessly move his right hand under his jacket and pull out his gun.

The man must have stepped to the sink, because they could hear water running. Lo Manto pointed to Paula and gestured for her to open the stall a few inches and step out. Before she could move, the middle-aged woman came out of the last stall. "What are you doing in here?" she asked the man, her tone angry but her manner calm. "This is the ladies' room."

"I know," Freddie said. He was polite but to the point. "The men's room is flooded. Guy outside said I could wash up in here. Said this was empty."

"He was wrong," the woman said, stepping to the base of the sink.

"I see that now," the man said. "I'll get out of your way."

Lo Manto nudged Paula forward and unlatched the door. He moved off the toilet seat and drifted with the shadow of the door, his feet against the base of the bowl, his back arched between stall and wall. Paula walked out slowly, staring at the man and talking to the woman. "What's he doing in here?" she asked.

Freddie held up one hand against both ladies. "Relax, you two," he said. "I made a mistake. And now I'll fix it all by leaving."

Freddie stared at Paula, looked at the empty stall behind her, and gave a quick glance at the woman by the sink. He bowed his head, a curt smile on his face, then turned and walked out of the restroom. The woman turned to Paula as soon as he left, talking to her as she dried off her hands with a sheaf of brown paper towels. "Don't dawdle in here," she said. "He might be back. In fact, more than likely, he will be. That's what guys like him do. If one of us was in here alone, it might not have ended the way it did."

"Don't worry," Paula told her. "I'll be out in less than a minute."

Lo Manto stepped out of the stall just as the restroom door closed behind the woman. Paula turned and glared at him. "Can we get out of here now?" she asked.

"Listen to me, *cara*," Lo Manto said, both hands gently grasping his niece's shoulders. "That man who was just in here is one of the two following you, keeping you safe until you lead them to me."

"And what happens then?"

"They'll make their move and try to kill me," Lo Manto said. "Which is exactly what I want them to do."

"Why?" Paula asked. "We're here together now. We can just leave. The two of us. I lost them in the bathroom, we can easily lose them in a crowd. You don't have to fight them anymore. Let it come to an end. Before one of them does kill you."

"These things don't just end with someone walking away," Lo Manto said. "Too much blood has been spilled for that to happen now. I'm too close. They know it. And I know it."

Paula stared into her uncle's eyes. She had heard all the stories about him, beginning when she was just old enough to walk. She later added a dose of reality to those sagas by reading through the scrapbook of his police exploits that her mother kept. Even at her tender age, she knew her uncle as a determined man, absorbed by his quest to clear the streets of Naples of the blight caused by the Camorra. Her mother thought Lo Manto the saddest man she'd ever known. In Paula's eyes, he was the bravest, a lone hero waging a battle against a force superior in strength and coated in brutality and deception. She knew he would give his life for her without an instant of hesitation and would kill anyone who even threatened to do her harm.

But she knew more about him than his crusade against the Camorra. He was the uncle who showed up the day after Christmas, with a car crammed with gifts and a warm, easy-to-forgive smile. He was the one who sent her a birthday present a month after the day and who had dressed as a hospital orderly to be the first to see her open her eyes after she got out of emergency surgery. He took her to old movies, exposing her to the neorealism of Vittorio De Sica, Roberto Rossellini, and a young Federico Fellini. He took her to outdoor productions of Italian classics and was also first on line with her in the summer, both eager to see the latest silliness from the comic westerns of Bud Spencer and

Terence Hill. He took her ice skating, bought her CDs of the hottest groups, both American and Italian, and walked with her through the corridors of every museum in Naples, sharing his knowledge of the works on display and the lives of the men whose magical brushes created them.

He was an important part of her young life and she would do anything not to lose him. And now, here, in a urine-streaked bathroom in the bowels of Grand Central Terminal, he stood in front of her and asked for help.

"Tell me what it is you need me to do," Paula said.

17

Jennifer sat alone at a small table in the back of a poorly lit room, the blue glow of a computer screen lighting her face, a large cup of Starbucks to her right, legal pad and pen at her elbow. She was in the records room in the basement of One Police Plaza, attempting to piece together the life of Giancarlo Lo Manto. One of the lessons of the job that Jennifer swore by was always to know who it is you're giving your back to. In the span of less than seventy-two hours, Lo Manto had gone from an Italian cop she was ordered to keep an eye on to a full-blown partner with whom she was about to walk side by side into a Camorra shooting gallery. She had already been targeted and shot at, forced to pump bullet holes into an adversary bearing down on her, and she still wasn't sure why. All she knew about Lo Manto was what she had seen for herself and heard from a few other cops, who knew him only by reputation. To a savvy street vet like Captain Fernandez, Lo Manto came off as a young Sherlock Holmes, using guile and instinct to capture his prey, matching his brain to the enemy's brawn and walking away with both his life and a solid arrest.

The younger cops painted a different portrait. They saw Lo Manto as an Italian Dirty Harry, quick-tempered and with a hard-won taste for action. He was a cop with no qualms about pulling a gun and shelling out the barrel into a criminal's chest. He was an action junkie, his addiction fueled by the crime-ravaged streets of Naples, where he was free of the barriers of search and seizure and Miranda warnings. He worked his cases hard, wild bull-charging against the various Camorra factions as if he were on a mission that only he could accomplish. He squeezed his informants, spread the word among his street sources, and displayed an uncanny ability to hit Camorra hot spots hours after a fresh six-figure connection had been completed. Jennifer had heard Lo Manto referred to by some of the cops who had worked with him on the various task forces as a "loose cannon with a brain," but wasn't put off by that assessment. In fact, she found she didn't mind riding alongside a cop as determined and daring as he was, willing to risk it all for the chance at a takedown. What bothered her, however, and what she was hoping to get at least the glint of an answer to from the computer files on Lo Manto, was the darker side of his personality.

Her cop antennae were raised high enough for her to realize there was more to his quest than merely another notch on his arrest record. There was a secret that drove

Lo Manto, forced him to go head-to-head against the best of the Camorra, challenged him to bring them down, and not only defeat them but leave the gang under a rubble of ruin. Jennifer reached for her coffee and took several long sips, rubbing the ache from her neck muscles with her free hand. She clicked onto the Intelligence Division site and typed in his name and her code and then waited the few minutes it took for the information to be processed. She leaned in closer to the computer, tossing the empty coffee container into a nearby bin, and began to read about the man who had, in a short span of time, become the first partner she ever had who would willingly give his life for her in the heat of battle.

"Been looking all over the building for you," Captain Fernandez said to her, in a voice not even close to being a whisper. The sound of his words startled her, forcing her to drop her pencil and bump her leg against the base of the computer desk.

"Looks like you found me, Cap," she said, trying to put on a smile and eager to get one back in return.

Fernandez grabbed a brief glance at both her notes and the computer screen, watching her move with a degree of unease as he did. "I catch you in the middle of something?" he asked.

Jennifer gently eased her chair away from the computer and stood up, inches away from her captain, her manner calm and at ease. She had grown to trust and respect Fernandez in her years working under his command and felt there was no reason to keep the truth away from him. "I'm trying to learn as much as I can about my new partner," she said.

Fernandez smiled. "And you figured a computer would tell you what it is you need to know?"

"I figured it was a good place to start," Jennifer said. "Other than what I've seen and heard for myself and some rumblings here and there, I don't really know all that much about the man."

"Why do you think you need to know any more than that?" Fernandez asked. "He'll be there for you if the time comes and you'll be there for him. That's as much as I ever wanted to know about any of my partners."

"It's not enough, Cap," Jennifer said. "He's planning on going up against some pretty heavy guns, top-tier action. And it's not just because they had the cubes to lift his niece. With him, it goes miles beyond that. I'd like to know why."

"He know you're doing this?"

"I didn't tell him," Jennifer said. "But if he's as good a cop as everyone says, then I'm sure he figured it to be a move I'd make."

"What are you looking to find?" Fernandez asked.

"His history would be one," Jennifer said, sitting back down, wishing she had a fresh cup of coffee. "Give me a sense of him if I knew his background, family details. Also, see the kind of cop he was over in Italy, read about some of the busts he took down, some of the criminals he chased. I guess I just feel like I need more answers than what I already have. I can't really put it into words."

Fernandez folded his arms across his bulky chest and took a deep breath, leaning the weight of his body against the edge of a wall. "He's always been a hard puzzle to crack," he told her. "There's a special kind of fuel to Lo Manto that makes him run harder and tougher than most any other cop you'll come across. I've worked with him on half a dozen task forces and I've never seen a badge that had a better understanding of who it was he was up against than Lo Manto. He doesn't let you in on much; guess that comes out of all those years working alone and not being able to trust anybody. But when he gives birth to a plan, my advice would be to make sure you do all you can to follow it."

"You ever work with him over in Naples?" Jennifer asked. "See him in action on his own turf?"

Fernandez nodded. "About three, maybe four years ago. We were on a three-month operation, NYPD working the cash angle and Lo Manto dealing with the heroin in Naples. He went at it full-tilt night and day, making snap decisions that kept him a jump ahead, moving the players, cops and crooks, like they were all pieces on one big chessboard. He had more street informants than any twelve cops, reaching out to people from all walks, knocking on the most surprising of doors. At the end, the Camorra was out four million in cash and just as much in smack. The bust made page one in both countries, but Lo Manto made sure to keep his name clear of any newspaper story."

"So, he's not a glory hog," Jennifer said. "I didn't get

a feel of that from him. He seems to be more about the case he's on than what road solving that case will actually take him down."

"How important is all this to you?" Fernandez asked. "Getting to know about Lo Manto? Figuring out his inner clock?"

"He's not the only cop who likes to know all the answers before he goes through the door," she said. "Besides, it might help us work together better."

"Have you thought about asking him?"

"How far would that take me?" she asked, smiling at the question.

"I imagine he'd duck and dodge it pretty well," Fernandez said. "But at the very least, it would be entertaining to watch."

"You think I'm wasting my time?" Jennifer asked. "You've been through these clips and files. Am I going to learn anything I don't already know?"

"That depends not on where you look, but how you look," Fernandez said. "But no, you're not going to get all your answers down here. Just a lot more questions."

"Then where, Cap?" Jennifer asked. "Where do I look?"

"You want to know Lo Manto, then you forget Naples, forget the busts, forget he's even a cop," Fernandez said. "You go back to the East Bronx, to his neighborhood. To the closed doors that may not ever open for you. All your answers will be there, on those streets, with those people. They're not going to be all that easy to find. I tried a couple of times and I came away empty. But that's where they are. That's where the truth can be found."

Jennifer nodded and turned back to the computer screen. Fernandez unfolded his arms, moved from the wall, and began to walk away, heading down the narrow passage between computer and file drawers. He was halfway down the hall when she lifted her head and called out to him. "Hey, Cap?" she said in a voice loud enough to draw stares from the faces at the surrounding cubicles.

Fernandez stopped and turned back to look at Jennifer. "Was wondering when you were going to ask how I knew to look for you down here," he said with a smile.

"Well?" she said, hands stretched out, her shoulders arched against the soft recline of the roll-back chair.

"Lo Manto told me," he said. He gave her a wink and a wave and continued on his way out the front door.

The burly man rested his arms on the edge of the roof, his body spread out across the tar, gazing down at the crowded street below. The afternoon sun bore down heavily on his black jeans and T-shirt, the light leather jacket tossed off to one side, the back of his thick neck streaked with thin lines of sweat. He kept a set of binoculars wedged near his right elbow, next to a long, silver thermos filled with hot espresso. He had an unfiltered cigarette dangling off his lower lip and a set of wraparound shades protecting his eyes from the heated glare. He had a rifle scope in his hands, focusing the eyepiece on the stairs of a tenement building across the street. Once he felt he had his target within the required distance, he made a mental note of the temperature and degree of tilt, taking into account wind velocity, range of motion, and other potential hazards, regardless of how minute. He had briefly toyed with the notion of attempting an early morning or evening shot, reducing the power of the sun and of passing cars and pedestrians, but had cast aside both possibilities after reflecting that he would be replacing the unknown factor of glare with the equally troublesome issue of shadows. Besides, the burly man took jobs these days as much to test his skill level as he did to fill his bank account. And there was no greater challenge to a professional shooter than a moving target drenched in sunlight. It would make the head-only hit and the $75,000 cash prize that came with the result all the sweeter.

The burly man had been born to money; both his parents were renowned doctors and medical scholars. He was raised in the warm grasp of luxury and wealth but found comfort in neither. He was eight when a wayward uncle gave him a hunting rifle and nine when he made his first kill, a buck grazing along the rush of a north Maryland stream. It was at that very moment, the second the hot bullet seared its way through flesh and bone, that young Gregory Randell had found his true calling. That was three decades ago and now the burly man, known within his chosen profession as "Flash" because of the speed with which he dispensed of a target, was coming close to the end of the line, ready to put away his rifles and scopes and settle down for a more peaceful and benign way of life. He had killed many more than he could ever count since that first drop in the Maryland woods, never bothering to distinguish between human prey and animal trophy. This was going to be his final conquest. He had grown weary of the business, tired of the endless late-night phone calls and meetings with quiet men whose names he never bothered to learn. He had remained fearless throughout, not concerned with either prison or betrayal, knowing that the men he dealt with wanted nothing more than to rid themselves of an annoyance and were willing to put up large blocks of money rather than stand up to their foe and pull a trigger and end it on their own clock and dime. In all his years as a paid assassin, Flash Randell had never lost his taste for the kill or his love for all the little steps that needed to be taken in order for a job to be completed in the desired manner. What he had grown weary of and had decided to do without weeks ago was the business end of a hit man's life. It left him cold and tired, listening to the drone of millionaires as they fretted over his payment schedule and whined over the accrued expenses that were so crucial to the job he performed. And if he failed, a fate that he had yet to experience, it would turn him from hunter into prey, another prospect of his trade he didn't relish.

He turned away from the street and lifted his face up toward the sun, his eyes closed, the front of his shirt wet with cool sweat. This was his last target, his last hunt. And he would make it his best.

The killing of Giancarlo Lo Manto would be one hit no one would ever forget.

Lo Manto stood on the third step of the tenement stoop and looked down at Felipe Lopez. The boy's eyes shone like dark beacons when he spoke, the weight he gave to each word more that of a seasoned adult than of a young teen living hand-to-mouth on hard streets. "You got more people looking for you than we got looking for that Osama dude," Felipe told him. "Only difference is the price on your head is a lot lower and you got no rock tunnels to hide you from sight."

"Who's looking the hardest?" Lo Manto asked. He reached into the front pocket of the boy's blue T-shirt and grabbed a fresh pack of cinnamon chewing gum.

"Depends on which way you mean hard," Felipe said. "Who's dangling the most cash or who's got the most people out on the street?"

"Give me both," Lo Manto said. He looked away from the boy, his eyes casually running the length of the street, a sea of strange faces, empty of emotion, burdened with their own concerns, blankly walking past them. "Hard numbers if you got them."

"Word is anybody brings you in, dead better than alive, gets to cash out," Felipe said. "Walk away with enough money in their pockets to live crime-free for a year, maybe two. That's on talk from your crowd."

"That offer open to anybody?"

"If you got two legs and a halfway decent pair of eyes, you make final cut," Felipe said. "They don't seem to care who brings you down, so long as down you go."

"You see any new faces around the neighborhood?" Lo Manto asked. "Not the usual set of basement knock-offs, but Samsonite leather, real dealers."

"No one face to point to," Felipe said. "But a lot of whispers about a shooter brought in just to put a few pins through your back. Guy's supposed to be good, is what I hear. If he misses you, or just wounds you, it'd be the first exam he ever failed."

Lo Manto sat on the third step of the stoop and stretched out his legs, resting his arms and shoulders against the hard, cement base. He looked over at Felipe and gave the boy a smile and a slight shrug. "We must be running on the right track," he said. "To get them to give us all this unwanted attention."

"Or maybe you're the kind of guy that just pisses people off," Felipe said. "And from what I hear your problems ain't just with the Italians and their shooters. Once words make their way uptown and down, every wannabe from goomba to Crip who can get his fingers on a Glock is going to be aiming it at you."

Lo Manto stared at the boy for several seconds, the sun warming both their faces, their eyes shaded by the brims of baseball caps. "I brought you into this to be my eyes and ears," he told him. "And that's what I expect you to do and keep doing. But the second the heat gets turned up, you're out. I'm paying you to listen, not to take a bullet."

"Truth be told, you're not paying me all that much to make either play," Felipe said. "I can make a fast and solid twenty a day just picking cans and bottles up and down the West Side."

"That for real?" Lo Manto asked, giving the boy the slightest of smiles. "Then why'd you say yes to the offer? Run out of trash bags to bring in your haul?"

"Not even close to being true," Felipe said. "I was looking to try something different and this sounded easy enough to do."

"Seems fair," Lo Manto said. "Just keep floating under everyone's radar. Don't ask too many questions and don't go near anyone your gut tells you can link you to me."

"These guys are careful about what they say to begin with," Felipe said. "But you grew up here. You know how information gets passed around. The places and faces may have changed some since you left, but not the way the bad go about their business."

"This shooter everyone's got their ear out for?" Lo Manto asked. "You pick up a name?"

"Just his street name," Felipe said. "The hard faces on the crew call him Flash. That sound like anybody you ever crossed with before?"

"I'll get someone to run the name through the

system," Lo Manto said. "If we come up with a face and his real ID, then maybe he's nowhere near as good as he might like to think."

"He don't have to be great," Felipe said. "Sometimes just lucky is enough. I just hope he don't miss by much and end up hitting some innocent guy doing nothing but standing by."

"You mean an innocent like you?" Lo Manto asked, a smile inching across his face.

"Like something like that never happens," Felipe said. "Last three library books I read, all had somebody in them got shot when they had nothing to do with anything. Meantime, the hero? He walks away clean, like not even a strong wind come his way."

"Maybe you're just reading the wrong kind of books," Lo Manto said.

"Maybe so," Felipe said. "But the same holds true for newspapers, TV, and movies. In all those places, same thing happens. Guy like you walks away clean. Guy like me gets one through the head."

"I'll do my best to change that," Lo Manto said, taking a quick scan of the nearby rooftops.

"If you do, you'll be the first," Felipe said. "Besides, I'm not too worked up about it. Just aware, that's all."

Lo Manto stared at the boy, marveling at his ability to ignore his surroundings and his plight and assume command of his situation. In so many ways, he reminded Lo Manto of the destitute street kids in Naples, kids who lived a hand-to-mouth existence, supplementing what they got from begging on corners with what they could steal from local grocers and merchants. These were children forced by fate and circumstance to deal with daily life as adults, bearing the responsibilities of broken homes and splintered families as they brokered for food and shelter, clothes and medicine. They shared a bond with Felipe, each moment of their tattered days etched across their rapidly aging faces. And he could see it all in their eyes, dark, penetrating, filled to the brim with equal doses of sadness and determination, anger and humility.

On the streets of Naples, Lo Manto was respected if not revered by the thieves. They knew he would never arrest them and felt they could always seek him out, knowing he would come through with whatever the emergency need of the moment happened to be. In return, they trusted him with information, giving the Italian detective hundreds of eyes and ears on the streets of his city. He never treated them as beggars or crooks and always paid for the street info he was given with a meal or a cold drink or a doctor's referral. He made them feel as if they were all partners in a joint venture, keeping intact their dignity and never making it appear that he felt sorry for them in any way.

In New York, Lo Manto was counting on Felipe to fill the void of his Naples informers. It was a lot to place on one small set of shoulders, but he felt the boy came to the table armed with a certain edge, an ability to read the temperature of the streets and understand the subtle

difference between rumors and facts. There was a sense
of purpose to Felipe, but not lost in all the tough talk and
bravado was the fear he had learned to live with and
embrace as if it were a winter coat designed to shield
him against blasts of arctic cold. It was a fear Lo Manto
had detected in others from the very first day he carried
a badge. It was a fear whose primal origins he clearly
understood. A fear he had come to respect.

A fear that Lo Manto felt every day of his life.

"Thanks," he said, walking away from Felipe and
heading toward the elevated subway station. "It's nice to
know I'll be missed."

"A guy with money is always missed," Felipe shouted
after him. "Even if he is a cop."

Jennifer closed the police folder and shoved it under her
car seat, watching as Lo Manto quietly approached the
idling unmarked. She pressed a button, rolled down the
passenger side window, and waited until he reached for
the door handle. "A cup of coffee would have been a
nice touch," she said to him.

Lo Manto jumped into the seat next to her, slammed
the door shut, and smiled. "I never drink coffee before a
meal," he said. "Or a shoot-out."

"Which are we planning?" she asked.

"A rooftop two blocks up, there was a guy with a rifle
scope spread out just beneath the edge," he said. "I was
right across the way. He could have taken his shot then.
I gave him plenty of time and open space to do it, but he

didn't make the move."

"You like doing that, do you?" she asked. "Standing out in the street, making yourself a clear and open target, just waiting to see if a guy with a gun has the cubes to take you out?"

"It helps to pass the time," he said, shrugging.

"Making a move on the guy might have knocked another hour or so off your day," she said. "Unless you're just eager to find out how good a shot the guy is."

"I wasn't alone," Lo Manto said. "And neither of us seemed ready to make the jump to the next step."

"And now?" she asked. "Where's that put us? Given that he's had enough escape time to shave, shower, and find his way home."

"He didn't run," Lo Manto said, his voice filled with its usual calm. "There'd be no need for him to do that. The man's a pro and the only reason he was seen was because he wanted to be seen. He wanted to let me know he was there and that we'd be going up against one another."

"You two have done this before?" she asked.

"We came close a couple of times," Lo Manto said. "Once in Naples and once here while I was on a joint task force. I had heard they had offers out to him, but he passed on them each time."

"You ever figure out why?" Jennifer asked.

"Money's the only reason," Lo Manto said. "It's why guys like him do the work they do. He enjoys the planning, the prep work, following the target and then taking it out. But you bottom-line it and the only reason he tugs at that trigger is for the money."

"Which means they either upped their offer or he lowered his asking price," Jennifer said. "Either way, that paints a very attractive bull's-eye on your back."

"Don't worry," Lo Manto said. "It's just me he's getting paid to take out. He doesn't get extra for the collateral damage."

"I'm not worried," Jennifer said, slow-to-surface anger and frustration etched in her words. "If I was, I'd be talking to you from a much safer location."

"He's warned me," Lo Manto said. "The next time there'll be no glint in the sun. He'll just take his shot."

"My guess is you have some sort of a plan," Jennifer said.

He turned to look at her, the sharp cut of the sun coating her face and hair, highlighting her natural beauty, making him wish, ever so briefly, that she wasn't a cop and that they weren't parked in an unmarked planning a move against a shooter paid to end his life. It would be so much simpler if they had the rest of the day to talk, to get to know each other in a slower, steadier way. Both Lo Manto and Jennifer had suffered through the hard lessons of on-the-job relationships. They often grew not out of love or passion but from an under-standing of the job that needed to be done. There was an artificial quality to love affairs between cops, feeding into the isolation and loneliness of the profession, the long hours spent together and the adrenaline rush that came from the actual work. Few of the romances blossomed beyond much more than dalliances, which lasted as little as a weekend or as long as six months. And when they did end, it was often on a harsh note: the partnership ruined, the friendship severed. Lo Manto always felt it was best to resist the temptation, that to stray too close, even to such an alluring flame, would only lead to a bad burn.

"So," Jennifer said, coaxing him out of his silence. "What are you going to do about the shooter?"

"Duck," Lo Manto said. "This way, if I'm at all lucky, I'll throw off his timing."

"I'm serious about this," she said. "And you better damn well be, too."

"Okay, then," Lo Manto said. "If I can't duck the shooter, then that leaves me with only one choice."

"Which is?"

"To kill him first," Lo Manto said.

He stared into Jennifer's eyes for several long seconds and then turned to look at the pedestrian traffic clogging the streets of the East Bronx on an otherwise peaceful summer day.

Joey "Tugs" McGraw sat on an empty crate in the darkness listening to the loud voice, the words banging with an echo against the thick wooden slats of the long-abandoned pier. He had a large Florida orange in one hand and a shearing knife in the other, quickly cutting the fruit into four thick chunks. He chewed on the fruit and listened as the voice and the footsteps that followed in its wake both grew louder. "Your end, you looking at an easy million, maybe even a million-two," the voice said. "And for what? Just for showing up, making a pickup one day and a drop the next. This were any easier, I'd take my kid out of school and hand the job over to him."

"Why don't you do just that?" McGraw asked, staring up now at the face behind the voice. "Nothing I can see stopping you."

The man was tall, standing an easy six-foot-four in loafers, and big, packing a hefty 250 pounds across a massive frame. Some of it was fat, the bulge around his middle bigger than it used to be eight years ago, when they closed their first deal. But most of it was muscle, his hands wide as a picture frame and thick as coiled rope, the knuckles around them chipped and raw. McGraw had seen the shattered flesh and splintered bones that had been at the other end of those hands and he didn't want to even begin to count the number of bodies they had helped to kill.

"Because the kid's only in the fourth grade, wiseass," Reno the Squid, the man behind the voice, said. "And he can't drive. Otherwise, why talk to you when I can talk to him? At the very least, he does as he's told."

Reno the Squid had a voice that ricocheted off the ears, each word a garbled and hoarse blend of sound. Not much was known about the Squid's early years, other than that he had made his way to New York from

Naples in his late teens, working his way up the intricate Camorra ladder, proving indispensable in whatever activity he was given. He had an affinity for the drug trade and, before he was much past his twenties, set himself up as the Camorra's most trusted dealer. In the decades since his arrival, he had built a powerful network working the harbors of both cities, putting him in charge of a drug ring that netted a yearly profit estimated by mob insiders to be in excess of $150 million. He structured his drug deals in tiers, making it all but impossible for law enforcement to detect who was at the receiving end of the cash and who was supplying the drugs. Reno the Squid was never seen with so much as a cigarette in his hand, living a sedate suburban life in a four-bedroom colonial twenty minutes outside the city limits. He had a one-bedroom apartment in the center of Naples, which he had inherited from his mother. He listed his income at $75,000 a year plus a profit-incentive $25,000 bonus, working for a lower Manhattan contracting firm. He had no criminal record and steered clear of known Camorra hangouts. He changed his cell number every six weeks and had an unlisted home phone, which neither he nor his wife nor their two sons ever used to make outgoing calls. He was the very model of the perfect Camorrista, benign and law-abiding on the surface, brutal and treacherous below it.

He stepped closer to McGraw, leaning down and staring with dead eyes at the much shorter, less stocky man. "Deal is all set to happen on Tuesday," he said. "It should be clean and it should go off the way it was planned out. Anything happens that changes that, I expect you to deal with it. Understood?"

"These people I'm meeting, they been cleared?" McGraw asked. "I like to keep my surprises limited to birthday parties."

"Two men, one woman," Reno said, nodding, his eyes giving a quick scan of the vast emptiness around him. "The men are German, have a bit of an accent, but you won't hear much of it, since they treat talk like it was work."

"Why the woman?" McGraw asked.

"She's the bank," Reno said. "The Germans can move the drugs, but they can't lay out the cash to buy in large supplies. She can."

"You've done business with her before?" McGraw asked.

"Couple of deals over the last five years," Reno said. "They all went off clean. Just like this one will."

"She good-looking?" McGraw asked, a snakelike smile inching its way across his pockmarked face.

"You'll meet her on Tuesday," Reno said, not bothering to return the smile. "But I'd be careful. Men have a way of dying around her. Since I've known her, she's had five different partners, always men, always European."

"What happened to them?"

"Ask her yourself," Reno said. "It'd be a nice way to break the ice. But close the deal first. Give her the drugs on Tuesday. Get the cash on Wednesday. You want to fall in love, get married, move to Maui? Do it on Thursday."

"I'll close the deal," McGraw said, tossing the orange skins onto a corner of the pier. "As I always do."

"One more thing," Reno said. "There's a cop from Naples in the city. He's hit the bosses more than a couple of times down the years. Some way, some how, he gets wind of when and where the deal goes down, takes both the drugs and the money. They don't want to see it happen with this one."

"Why should it?" McGraw asked with a shrug. "You don't tell people your business, I don't tell anybody mine. Not a lot of ears get to hear what we work on. I'm not worried unless you're telling me I got something to worry about."

"You only have something to worry about if this cop hits this deal," Reno the Squid said. "That happens, though, it won't be the bosses you need concern yourself with. It'll be me."

McGraw pushed aside the wooden crate he was sitting on, stood and glared up at Reno. "This cop or any cop comes close to this, he'll be taken care of. Just like always. So save your breath on the threats. They don't work on me."

Reno the Squid nodded and quietly turned away from Joey McGraw, disappearing into the mist, dust, and darkness of the empty pier, the heavy bounce of his step the only sound to be heard.

*

Jennifer, driving with one hand, gently eased the unmarked into the slow moving traffic of the Henry Hudson Parkway. Lo Manto sat next to her, his hands cupped around a large container of Starbucks Caffè Verona. "I hope you got a good reason for us to be sitting in this?" she asked him, working the brakes as the car inched its way forward.

"I hope so too," he said.

"Want to share it?" she asked.

"You're impatient," Lo Manto said. "Want to know things right away, sometimes even before you should. It's natural for a woman to be that way. But it might not be the best thing in the world for a detective."

"What are you saying?" she asked, her temper ready to spark. "I'm not a good cop? Just because I dared to ask you a question?"

"You go up like a match, too," Lo Manto said. "That could be one more thing to hold you back."

"Hold me back from what?" she said, her right hand slapping the steering wheel in sheer frustration.

"You got great cop instincts," Lo Manto said, sipping his coffee as he talked. "Doesn't take you long to read a situation or size up an opponent. And you've learned how to bury the fear. You go out there without even a thought of the risk."

"Enough with the praise," Jennifer said. "Get to the *but*."

"You lose control," he said. His voice was calm, direct

but soothing, as if he were a doctor offering a medical opinion about a rare ailment to a junior physician. "Whether it's due to temper or impatience, it doesn't matter. You have to learn to work it in your favor, make it a strength, not a weakness."

"And if I do that, then what?" she asked, glancing his way. "Just out of curiosity."

Lo Manto placed his cup in the holder next to the heater and leaned against the headrest, closing his eyes for a brief moment. "Then nobody can touch you," he said. "You'd be better than a good cop. You'd be someone that they can't figure out. And that would make you both dangerous and feared."

They drove in silence for a while, the sedan slowly winding its way past the quiet streets of Riverdale. The day was hot and muggy, the humidity coming off the warm tar of the road in waves. They had all the windows up and the air conditioner running at medium cool, neither one quite ready to brave the harsh heat of another brutal New York summer. "Is that what you are?" she asked, veering the car into the speed lane. "Or at least think you are?"

"It's what I try to be," he said. "I need to control the situation, be ready to take it where I need it to go. You can't always do that, but you can at least try. You give up a lot, though, in return for that."

"Like what?"

"A reasonable chance at a personal life," he said. For the first time since they met, she sensed a degree of sadness in Lo Manto, a melancholy longing for a less complicated existence. His time away from New York hadn't done much to chisel down the rough edges and street attitude that came from living in a city without much give to it. And his years working the alleys and hallways of Naples, bringing down the dealers and the doers who preyed on impoverished soil, only added to the hard core. But there was a soft spot beneath all of Lo Manto's steel-like determination, a gust of warmth that was unable to shake totally free of its southern Italian roots. "Once you learn how to control the action on the street, it isn't long before it becomes a habit and you look to do the same with the people in your life. Which, I suppose, explains why most cops are either single, divorced, or talking to a bartender instead of their wife."

"Or worst of all," Jennifer said, "married to other cops."

Lo Manto nodded and smiled. "We're just about there," he told her. "Grab a right up ahead."

Jennifer switched lanes, looked up at the signs and then back at Lo Manto. "What's at the Cloisters?"

"Great works of medieval art," he said. "A cool place to walk and talk. A nice restaurant to have lunch in. And two drug dealers who want their deal to go down without any problems."

The two men stared with indifference at the centuries-old cross at rest behind a thick glass display case. They relished the coolness of the dark rooms, a pleasant break from the crushing heat outside. The taller of the two wore a short-sleeved black shirt, an Armani jacket, and tan slacks. He gazed away from the cross and stared at the small group that had gathered, studying their faces and watching their reactions to the works around them. The museum was crowded for this early in the day, the clock just shy of eleven, a good two hours before the lunch break began. It was a typical blend of museum visitors, bored junior high school students on a class trip, senior citizens out on a rare excursion, and academics gazing at the works as if they possessed a secret knowledge available to few others. The tall man wasn't interested in any of them.

He tapped his program against the shoulder of the man next to him and nodded for them both to move on. "He's not anywhere in this group," he said. "Let's check some of the other exhibits."

"There's a lot of history in this place, Terry," the other man said. He was shorter, with hair hanging down just to the tips of his shoulders, a scarred but still youthful face and a pleasant manner. "I didn't know this was even here until we got the job."

"Come back on your own time, you want to see more," Terry said, shaking his head with impatience. "For now, we're here on somebody else's nickel."

They stepped away from the group and wandered through the cool, dark halls. Terry, with his razor-cut hair and trim body, looked more like a high school art history teacher on an outing than a Camorra dealer in search of his score. He usually preferred to work alone, allowing himself ample time to make the cash-for-powder transaction. But this was a short-notice job, spliced together at the last minute to make up for excess street demand, and he was forced to bring in the blocker who walked by his side. Bruno Magro was destined to be nothing more than a minor leaguer with limited skills, a paid gunman who made himself useful on such jobs for the simple reason that he was good with a gun and quick to use it. He was unafraid to spray bullets into a crowd, bringing down anyone who interfered with the making of the deal.

Men like Bruno were used as sacrifices. They were told very little if anything about the actual operation, content to be allowed in on a Camorra job, always hopeful that it would lead to more work, bigger jobs and eventual entry into the secret society. It would never happen. The men and women of the Camorra were chosen at the earliest age, many as young as six, and trained in their ways until they reached adulthood. They were put through the best schools, educated toward their strengths, and then put out into the real world to ply both their legal and illegal trades. Terry was the son of a Neapolitan streetwalker who handed him over to a local Camorra family when he was two days shy of his seventh birthday. In return for the gift of her son, his mother was allowed to keep her wages for the week. Terry was encouraged to develop his strengths, the prime among them being an intuitive facility with math and geometry. He graduated from high school in Naples, then undergraduate studies in England and a graduate program in New York. By the time he was handed the last of his diplomas, Terry Fossino was a high-level Camorra drug operative, making six-figure buys and moving the cash through an intricate system that went through six different banks in five countries before settling in as clean money in a Camorrista account in Rome. Terry was one of the many poster boys for the Camorra system, a criminal enterprise functioning at its highest levels.

Terry steered Bruno into a darkened side area, several feet away from the line of passing visitors, both men leaning their backs against a cool wall. "You sure this is the spot they said?" Bruno asked, a nervous twitch creasing the tones of his voice. "I mean, everything looks the same to me in here. How can you be sure?"

"If they're not here in five minutes, then we'll know either I was wrong or they didn't show," Terry said, his manner as calm as a surgeon.

"What happens if that happens?" Bruno asked, gazing up at Terry through the dark shield surrounding him.

"I'll have to blame someone for the mix-up," Terry said, his tone even more casual than before. "Might as well be you."

Bruno let out a short, nervous giggle. "Very funny," he said. "I just love working with a comedian."

Terry Fossino stared down at the emptiness around

Lorenzo Carcaterra

him, his eyes following Bruno's squeaky voice, and knew that no matter how this exchange played out, the young man before him was the wrong man. If captured by the police, he would fold in the back of the squad car and tell all he knew before the ride to the station house ended. If apprehended by a rival gang, he would give up the drop spot and the names of the dealers and doers minutes into any pressure applied. Within the short span of a few seconds, standing in the cool darkness of a medieval museum, Terry Fossino had made a decision about another man's life. This would be Bruno Magro's last job.

Terry stiffened when he felt the barrel end of a gun jab hard against the side of his rib cage. He took a deep breath; he had been in enough tense situations to know better than to either move or speak. He relaxed his body and waited for the figure holding the gun to make himself known. "Reach for your partner's gun," a male voice said, the words spoken in low and calm tones, "with your left hand and let it slip to the ground. And keep this in mind. My gun is already on your flesh. If you move in any way that makes me uncomfortable, I'll pull on the trigger three times before you can put me down."

Terry reached a hand out into the darkness and slid his fingers across Bruno's waist, grabbing hold of his partner's nine-millimeter. "What the hell are you doing?" Bruno asked, trying to move away.

"Let me have the gun," Terry told him. "And just shut the hell up."

Terry held the gun by the barrel and let it fall to the floor, its bounce echoing slightly in the chamber hall. He turned his head toward the voice by his side. "Want mine too?" he asked.

"I would," the voice said. "If you had one. But you haven't strapped on a gun in over twenty years. And I don't think you'd pick a museum as a good place to start."

"So what do you want, then?"

"Your clothes," the voice said. The shadow shifted slightly out of the cool darkness and into the slants of light, his face and portions of his upper body revealed. "Along with the fifty thousand in cash in the side pockets of the Armani."

Terry glared at the man's face, searching it for any signs of fear or trepidation. He found none. "You won't be able to spend it," he said in a low voice. "I'll make sure you're dead before you can even crack a twenty."

"I don't plan on spending it," Lo Manto said, stepping further into the light. "I'm going to give it to a charity. And not to worry, I'll make the donation in your name."

"The money's not mine, either," Terry said. "And the man whose pockets it came out of hates charity."

"Just another of Pete Rossi's many weaknesses," Lo Manto said, smiling. "Now lose the clothes. Both you and your friend."

"We could say no," Terry said.

Lo Manto moved the gun against Terry's elbow. "It's

no to the clothes or no to your arm. And put this in your thoughts. If I pull the trigger, I won't want the soiled jacket."

Terry, his angular face red and trembling with anger, nodded and eased one of his shoulders out of the jacket. Lo Manto stepped back and waited as it was handed to him. "Now take off the rest of them, both of you, and kick them over toward the corner," he said.

"You got the money," Terry said. "That should do you."

"I haven't been here long," Lo Manto said. "And you guys have had me on the run since I got off the plane. So, because of that, I haven't had any time to shop. Between the two of you, I should find something nice to wear."

"I'm not taking my clothes off," Bruno snarled. "I'd rather you kill me than leave me here naked."

Lo Manto stepped closer to the shorter man, stared at him for several quiet seconds, and then slammed the butt end of his gun against Bruno's lips, the strength and speed of the blow chipping three of his front teeth. He then whirled the gun away from Bruno and jammed it under Terry's chin, forcing his head to thud against the stone wall. "I'm late for lunch," he told them. "And I'd hate to leave without the clothes."

Terry unbuttoned the front of his trousers and let them drop to his knees. Bruno, thin lines of blood running down his jaw and onto his neck, tossed off his shirt and put it on top of Terry's jacket. Lo Manto stood back two feet and watched. Once the two men were naked, he handed Bruno a museum shopping bag. "Put the clothes and the shoes in there," he ordered. "Don't bother folding them. Except for the jacket. I'm going to wear that now. This way I get to go to lunch in style. My line of work, I can't afford to buy Armani."

"I'll see that you get buried in it," Terry said, his brown eyes glaring at Lo Manto.

"My mother would like that," Lo Manto said. "She always complains about the way I dress."

Lo Manto held the gun against his waist, took the shopping bag crammed with clothes and shoes, and walked toward the lit area of the museum. "Be careful on your way out," he warned the two naked drug dealers. "The floors can get a little slippery. I would hate to see you get hurt."

Frank Silvestri stared at the young man standing across from him nervously sipping a container of coffee, his navy blue J. Crew shirt drenched through with sweat and smeared with stains. "You lost the shipment how?" Silvestri asked, his thick fingers gripping a thin ballpoint pen. "Tell it to me slow. I don't want to miss any of the important parts."

They were alone in the rear stall of an empty stable, two men in tan jackets guarding the front entrance. It was nearing dusk and shadows filtered across the stacks of hay and piles of blankets and saddles spread throughout the large space. Silvestri's men had picked up the courier as he ran in a panic along Fort Washington Avenue, his feet bare, the small leather satchel in his hand emptied of the drugs he had been given earlier in the day, filled now, instead, with bottles of hand cream. The young man was doing all he could, using the last ounces of what remained of his strength, not to cry.

"This lady came up to me inside the museum," the young man said, his words rushing out in a nervous burst of energy. "Told me she was lost. Asked if I could help her find her way out of the museum. Show her how to get back on the highway heading downtown."

"And this you did, despite being told by all involved not to talk or look at anybody, not even the pickup team?" Silvestri said. "Did I get all that right?"

"We were right near the exit," the young man said. "I didn't think it would take no more than three, maybe four minutes."

"When did she pull the gun?" Silvestri asked.

"How do you know she had a gun?" the young man asked, curiosity nudging aside his fear.

"Because if she didn't have a gun and you handed over fifty grand worth of smack to a pretty face all because she told you to, it's going to go down for you a lot uglier than you can even imagine," Silvestri said.

"When we got close to her car," the young man said, sweat pouring off his body as if released from a stream. "She jabbed me in the spine with the barrel, took my pack and tossed it in the back of her car."

"You get a make and model?" Silvestri asked. "A partial plate number? Any fuckin' thing I can use to find this bitch?"

The young man shook his head. "Sorry," he said. "I just wasn't thinkin' the right way. She caught me off-guard, wasn't expectin' anything like that to happen."

"No shit you got caught off-guard," Silvestri said. "I would have been better off sending that retard from *Rain Man* to make the drop. At least he woulda come back to me with some numbers."

"I don't know what to say," the young man said, anticipating his sealed fate. "I screwed up real bad. Believe me, it won't ever happen again."

"That's right, Raymond," Silvestri said. "It won't ever happen again. Least not with you holding the stash."

Silvestri reached out an arm and put it around Raymond's thin shoulders and walked him closer to the rear of the darkening stable. The young boy dragged his feet as they moved, sneakers kicking up small mounds of dust and strips of straw. "Give me another chance, Frank," Raymond pleaded. "I'll do right by you. I swear to it."

"There's no hurry," Silvestri said, reaching a hand into his jacket pocket and pulling out a knife with a curved six-inch blade. "We need to close this deal first before we talk about doing another."

"What's there left to do?" Raymond asked.

"The make-good," Silvestri said. He jabbed the blade

deep into Raymond's chest cavity and held the young man up with one arm, staring into his eyes, watching and waiting as the life slowly seeped out of his body.

18

Charlie Sunshine waited inside a dark corner of the stairwell, a set of brass knuckles wrapped around his right hand. He kept a small-caliber handgun wedged down the back of his right boot and a jagged-edged knife closed and dangling from a thick chain around his neck. His hair was slicked back, gelled and packed with enough grease to lube the underside of an SUV. His breath came in rapid spurts, his frail chest reacting to the painful throbbing of a recent asthma attack. The right side of his body was heavily bandaged and tapcd, the fifteen stitches running across his rib cage, the result of the slash job done to him by Ben Murphy's broken bottle, slow to heal.

Sunshine knew Murphy had moved his heist money, he just wasn't sure where the new hiding spot was or who had picked it. But he did know that the first person to follow him into the bar the day of their confrontation was the homeless kid, Felipe. Sunshine knew the kid worked the bar on occasion and it wouldn't be out of place for him to be there on a quiet morning before the regulars started to stream in. So, had he stayed a few hours and walked out of the place dirtier than when he had come in, with maybe a few extra dollars in his pocket for the work he did, Charlie would have dismissed any notion of the homeless kid being involved. But the word from his eyes on the street put the boy in the place less than an hour and then saw him split minutes before the EMS truck arrived to tend to Murphy's wounds. That was more than enough to put the kid under Sunshine's scope, following his moves, watching to see if his behavior had shifted since the day in the bar, looking for any signs to indicate the boy had even come near a major score.

The kid had also been spotted around the neighborhood in the company of a cop, further fueling Sunshine's suspicions that the boy had fallen on top of a score. The cop was a new face to Sunshine, tabbed as an export by the whispers on the street, no doubt tipped to the boy's play and cut in for a slice of the cash action. The cop's main function was to be Felipe's shield, his brace against any attempts to zone in on the money, a perfect cover to keep the dust of a predator from his feet. But no cop, especially a badge from a foreign zip code, could protect Felipe Lopez twenty-four hours a day.

Sunshine wedged his body tighter against the cold edges of the wall when he heard the entrance door open. He turned his head enough to glance down the shaded corridor and see the boy sitting in a corner of the vestibule, his head down, slowly tearing away the cello-phane wrapper on a bologna and American cheese sandwich. Sunshine waited two minutes, making sure no one else was following Felipe into the building, and then, with quiet steps, came out from the shadows. He walked as if in the center of a cloud, his flat, torn black boat shoes barely registering a mark as they moved across the stained marble hallway floor. "I hate to eat alone," Sunshine said to Felipe. "Bet you feel the same way, no?"

Felipe looked up, careful to hide his fear and surprise, disguise the anger he felt for allowing himself to be nabbed off-guard. He prided himself on his ability to stay a step ahead, to survive on the harsh streets with natural instincts and the skill to read the signals on any potentially dangerous situations. He knew in an environment such as the one he lived in, the one factor he needed to always depend on was keeping his safety antennae on high alert. "I don't mind," Felipe said, his voice calm and in control. "It gives me some time to think things out."

"Looks like you got yourself a good sandwich there," Sunshine said, spreading a smile exposing small rows of brown, crooked teeth. "That must have put you back a wagonful of empty cans."

"It's only money," Felipe said with a slight shrug and a quick bite of his sandwich. "Besides, you gotta eat, right?"

"And you gotta live, too," Charlie Sunshine said. He

leaned his body closer to Felipe, his thin shadow eclipsing the boy's, shrouding him from the sultry glare of the encroaching sunlight. "So, you go ahead and finish that sandwich you got for yourself. It looks way too good to let waste. While you do that, you keep your ears perked and listen up to what it is I gotta say to you. That seem easy enough to follow?"

Felipe nodded. "You talk," he said. "And I eat."

"That bartender Murphy passed something on to you that I'm pretty sure belongs to me," Sunshine said, his foul breath raining down on Felipe, who was slowly munching away at what was left of the sandwich. "You hand it over and I let you live the rest of your days free of me. And who knows? There might even be a reward in it for you. Which is a lot more than that old drunk would have done."

"What kind of a reward are we talking about?" Felipe asked, downing the final piece of the bread, his eyes casting about, looking for any escape options.

"Five hundred dollars," Sunshine said, face and eyes disappearing into the cool shadows of the vestibule. "Maybe even a thousand if there's more there than I think."

"And what do you think is there?"

"Don't fuck with me, you little shit," Sunshine said, his anger kicking into high gear. "The bartender was sitting on his cut of a long-ago heist. A cut he was supposed to hand over to me. Instead, for reasons I have yet to figure out, he gave it to you. Now none of that is gonna matter, not so long as you put it back where it belongs. In my hands."

Felipe shook his head and stared up at Sunshine, trying to make out his features in the sharp light. "If I had what you think I have," the boy said in tones as calm as he could manage to keep them, "then why would I bother sticking around here, waiting for a guy like you to come along and stake his claim? I'd be drilling an umbrella into the hot sand down in PR. Not sitting in a ratty hallway, eating a stale sandwich and breathing your snake breath."

Sunshine reached down and slapped Felipe hard across the right side of the boy's face, turning the skin red, the edge of the brass knuckles raising welts on the dark flesh. "I start with the hand," he said through gritted teeth that looked loose enough to topple with a soft flick. "Then I'll move to the knife if I have to. So save yourself some pain and tell me what I need to hear."

"What you need to hear is that I don't know anything about any heist money," Felipe said. His right eye had begun to tear and the slap caused his ear to ring. "Any money Ben Murphy gave me was cash he owed me for working the place. And if that's what you're after, I can't help you there either. I already spent it."

"I was hoping you were smart," Sunshine said. "I guess I was wrong about that."

He reached under his shirt collar and pulled out the knife, snapping it open with his right index finger. He leaned down closer to the boy, anger and madness joining and uniting as one. "You'll need your tongue to talk and your ears to hear," he snarled. "The rest now belongs to me."

Sunshine lifted Felipe by his hair, standing him up to his feet. He jabbed the sharp end of the knife against the boy's right palm, the touch of the tip drawing blood. "Think of this as your last chance, little Rican," he said to him. "After that, I won't stop until you beg me to."

Felipe glared into Sunshine's eyes and smiled. "Do what you came to do," he said. "But remember, without me, there is no money. And on your own, you wouldn't find it if it was hidden in one of your pockets."

"Maybe so," Sunshine said. "But I'll make sure you won't get a chance to spend it either."

"Then it's a waste of a good haul all around," Felipe said. "Nothing for me and even less for you."

Sunshine stuck the blade into Felipe's hand, causing the boy's legs to give and his vision to blur. The sharp pain was the only relief that kept him from keeling over. "If I ain't getting the money," he said into the boy's ear, "then I might as well enjoy myself some other way. And I'm looking to have myself a good time."

The hard blow caught Sunshine right between the base of his head and the bridge of his shoulder. It was sharp and direct and sent a shooting pain down the center of his body, forcing him to release the knife and hold on to the wall for support. The second punch landed in his left kidney and had him gasping for breath. He whirled around slowly and caught the third blow flush to the center of his face, smashing the bones in his nose and sending his blood spraying through the small vestibule. Lo Manto stood over Sunshine and pulled a white handkerchief from his rear pocket, then he leaned over toward Felipe and yanked the knife out of his hand and tossed it against the wall behind them. "Wrap this around the wound," he told him. "Tight as you can. Then keep your arm elevated. It'll help stop the bleeding."

Sunshine, head still resting on the cold tiles, coiled two arms around Lo Manto's left leg and opened his mouth, ready to clamp down on some skin and bone. Lo Manto lifted his right boot and stomped on the side of Sunshine's face, the thick end of his heel snapping the hood's head back, sending three chipped teeth and a mouthful of blood tumbling to the ground. Lo Manto stared at Sunshine for several seconds, waiting to pounce again in the event he moved, then turned his attentions back to Felipe. The boy was standing by his side, his lithe body still shivering, his warm eyes watery and looking as if they were about to melt. The white handkerchief wrapped around his hand was now a hard shade of red, his fingers trembling, thin rivers of blood running down toward his elbow. Felipe lowered his head and leaned it against the center of Lo Manto's chest, resting it there, allowing the fear to wind its way through his body. Lo Manto raised his left arm, embraced the boy, and brought him closer to his side. Felipe was crying now, his shoulders shaking with every sob, the brave front he had put up against Sunshine's menace fast melting away. He shed the cover of the tough and gruff street survivor, tossed that heavy shield to the ground and allowed himself briefly to be a frightened little boy. Lo Manto let his tears flow, granted him the silence and the respect such moments demanded, content to gently rub the back of the boy's head.

Lo Manto was angry that Felipe had been hurt. Especially by a low-tier street scavenger like Sunshine, now sprawled and bleeding several feet to his left. But he was also pleased to see him release his fears and find comfort in his trust of Lo Manto, a man he had known for less than three days. He often wished he had known someone when he was that age who could help him unleash the burdens he felt, let loose the anger that raged inside. He had, much like Felipe, learned to maintain a constant guard against weakness, never showing that side of himself to anyone, especially a foe. Lo Manto had spent so many years burying deep any sense of fear and vulnerability that he doubted now if he could bring it to the surface even if he wanted. If his enemies only knew the truth about the cop they felt had no heart.

"I'm sorry," Felipe said, lifting his head, looking up at Lo Manto, his face washed with a veneer of tears. "I don't usually do something like that."

"You don't usually get stabbed every day," Lo Manto said. "You should see me when I get shot. I sound like an old woman at a funeral."

Felipe smiled and wiped at his face with dirty fingers, glancing down at Sunshine. "I should have figured he would have moved against me sooner than later. Guy like him can't stay away from money for too long."

"What makes him think you have any money that someone would want?"

"Because I do," Felipe said. As he spoke the words, he realized he was entrusting someone with a secret he had promised to keep only to himself. And while he liked Lo Manto and clearly trusted him, it was still something he felt uncomfortable doing. "It was a gift to me from a local guy who owns a bar. Only I can't touch it for at least a couple of years. Nobody can."

"Where is it?" he asked.

"In a place where nobody would think to look," Felipe said with a quick nod toward the bleeding man on the ground. "Especially a bottom feeder like Charlie Sunshine."

"He would have made you tell him," Lo Manto said. "Making people give up information is the only thing guys like him are good at."

"Do you want to know where it is?" Felipe asked. The pain in his hand was shooting up into his arm now, the blood flow slowing to a trickle.

"What makes you think I'd care?" Lo Manto asked. "It's your money and it's hidden in your place."

"But you're a cop," Felipe said with a fast shrug.

"Not that kind of cop," Lo Manto said. "I don't want

a cut of it and I don't want to know where it came from. Those are things you never need to tell me. Doesn't matter if we stay friends for just a week or for the rest of our lives."

"The guy that gave it to me, I used to work for now and then," Felipe said. "He told me to use it to get an honest jump on life. Get away from the way I have to live now."

"That's great advice," Lo Manto said, resting one hand on the boy's shoulder. "I hope you take him up on it."

"I plan to," Felipe said. "If I live long enough."

Lo Manto smiled and led Felipe out of the vestibule, both of them stepping over the still body of Charlie Sunshine. "On that end, maybe I can help you," he told the boy. "For starters, find a doctor and get that hand of yours stitched up."

"And don't worry," Felipe said as they walked into the hot sun and heavy air. "I promise I won't embarrass you and cry in front of the doctor. And I won't faint on you either."

"I wish I could promise you the same," Lo Manto said. "But to tell you the truth, needles always make my head go a little light. So anything could happen in there."

"I'll cover for you," Felipe said, smiling up at him. "You can count on that."

"I know I can," Lo Manto said.

*

Paula sat on the edge of the fire escape, her thin legs hanging over the side, buffered by two rusty railings. She had half a vanilla ice cream cone in her right hand. Overhead, the late afternoon sun was being over-shadowed by an advancing army of thick clouds, each weighed down with heavy pockets of rain. She licked at the ice cream running down the side of her hand, the cool taste refreshing to her dry throat. She had been on the move since earlier that morning, following her visit with her Uncle Giancarlo in the downstairs bathroom at Grand Central Terminal. She had made her way uptown, into the Bronx, mixing long walks down hot steamy streets with quick rides on air-conditioned buses, always shadowed by the two tiring Camorristas stepping on her trail.

She found the tenement building on Ely Avenue, a five-storey walk-up with a shiny brown door, sandwiched between a bakery and a florist, just where her uncle said it would be. She squeezed into the narrow alley, made her way into the backyard crammed tight with fresh flowers, fruits, and vegetables, and jumped up to catch the lower tier of the fire escape steps. She went up to the top floor, pulled the Ray's ice cream bag out of her small waistpack, and sat down for the first time that day. She was tired and weary, still confused as to why her uncle didn't just grab her and bring her to a safe spot, even though she could now see the dangers he faced with much clearer eyes. She also knew that her escape from the Rossi compound was not the result of her brilliant planning and execution but only one more devious device to ensnare her uncle in a trap that ultimately would lead to his death.

She glanced down at the lush garden below and spotted the two men who had been on her trail since the night she walked from the compound. They were partially hidden by long rows of tomato and basil plants, crouched down, their knees brushing up against thick mounds of brown dirt. They seemed tired and possibly frustrated, knowing even less about her plans than she did, wondering where the hell it was this young runaway was leading them. Paula was startled, nearly dropping the last piece of the ice cream cone, by the whispers of the old woman at her back. She turned her head slowly and saw the dark, hard-lined face smiling at her behind an open window, her full features hidden by the curtains rustling in the soft breeze. "Face forward and listen to what I have to tell you," the old woman said, her voice low and raspy, coated with a heavy Italian accent. "I am a friend of your uncle."

"Is he okay?" Paula asked.

"He has the heart of a saint," the old woman said with a chuckle, "but the soul of the devil. He will one day die, but not in any way his enemies would expect."

"Where is he, then?"

"Doing what he needs to do," the old woman said. "And now it is time for you to be brought to a safe place and end your chase with these thugs."

"How?" Paula asked. "They're right in the garden

below me. They can see every move I make."

"That is a pretty dress," the old lady said, switching gears, making an attempt at softness. "My granddaughter has one just like it. Same color, same design. She's also about the same age as you."

"Maybe we can meet someday," Paula said, trying hard not to show her frustration. "I don't think now would be a good time, though."

"You're wrong," the old woman said firmly. "Now would be the best time."

"Only if you want to risk her life, too," Paula said. "Those two down there see me with anybody, they'll have no choice but to shoot. I don't think that's what you'd like to see happen."

"Get up slowly," the old woman said, her voice in full control of both the situation and her emotions. "Pick up your pack and walk toward the steps leading down, but stay close to my window."

Paula closed her eyes for a moment and took a deep breath. She then lifted her legs through the thin bars, glancing down at the two men below, who were pretending not to notice her and were busy plucking ripe red tomatoes off thick vines. She grabbed her pack, fingers still sticky from the ice cream cone, and eased toward the steps down the fire escape. She had her left hand out, pressed firm against the worn brown bricks, only inches from where the old woman stood behind the open window. She turned her head slightly and looked through glass panes, past the breeze-blown curtains, and made eye contact with the old woman, smiling up at her with a nod of her head. She was close enough to smell a chicken roasting in the oven and a fresh pot of sauce percolating on top of a small gas range. The old woman leaned closer to the sill, chunky hands rich with veins gripping the splintered wood, her head peering out the open window. "Get in," she said to Paula. "As fast as you can."

The old woman took three steps back, away from the window, and braced herself against one side of a wall. She watched as Paula dove in headfirst, catching herself on a small wooden coffee table nearest the couch. The old woman grabbed the waistpack from Paula and then turned to a young girl standing in the shadows, handed it to her, and then helped lift her out onto the fire escape. The girl, same age and height and in the same outfit as Paula, and with her hair combed in the same haphazard manner, began a slow walk down the fire escape steps. Within seconds, the switch had been made and the girl was soon out of sight. Paula stood stunned in the middle of a darkened living room, the drapes once again blocking out the sunlight, keeping the room surprisingly cool. "What the hell just happened here?" she managed to ask, her mouth as dry as an empty swimming pool. "Those guys will figure out soon enough that they're chasing a different girl. Then, they'll come here looking for you and expecting to find me."

"By then I hope it will be too late," the old woman said. "Since there will be nobody at home for them to find."

"How will we get out?" she asked. "One of them will make sure the backyard stays covered. The other will probably head toward the front of the building. And it won't take them very long to call for help."

"That is why we must not waste any time," the old woman said. "We need to get to the basement before they realize my Regina is not you. Once we get there, we can use the underground steps and come out three buildings down the street, right next to the gas station on the corner. There will be a car waiting for you there, with a driver who has known your uncle for many years. On the road, you will hand him your wristwatch and sneakers. He'll know what to do with them."

"And he'll take me where?"

"Where your uncle asked us to take you," the old woman said.

She reached for Paula's hand and led her out of the narrow apartment, grabbing a shoulder bag as they ran. The woman was stout of figure and short in stature and moved at a faster clip than her age would indicate. Her thick gray hair was combed straight back and held in place by a small battalion of bobby pins and she wore a medallion of the Blessed Mother around her neck. She had a thin angular scar running down the right side of her face and her breath reeked of stale tobacco. Her name was Assunta and she was the widow of Alberto Conte, murdered in front of his three children nearly twenty-five years ago because of his refusal to pay any further tribute to the Camorra bosses who ran the New

York waterfront. Since then, since the morning she watched four hefty men lower her husband's casket into the cold ground of Woodlawn Cemetery, Assunta had waged a private war against the members of the criminal organization that so callously had ended his life. She helped rescue those they sought, found refuge for the innocents they looked to kill, and dispensed funds to those in need of paying off massive debts. Declaring her own war against the members of the Camorra had made her an underground legend, a woman who worked in the shadows and brought harm and chaos to those who had given her such a great deal of pain. The Camorra had become Assunta Conte's lifework and she thrived on it.

Much like her godson, Giancarlo Lo Manto.

The old woman and the young girl raced down the tenement steps, eager to reach the basement before one of the Camorristas made it to the front door. Assunta led the way, her thick right hand using the rickety wood railing as a guide, often taking the cement steps two at a clip. "What if we don't make it?" Paula asked, her lungs burning from the run, fear starting to creep into her words and thoughts. "What if he catches us in the lobby?"

"You will let go of my hand and head to the basement," Assunta told her in a voice as strong as honed steel. "I will deal with the Camorrista."

They crossed the second landing and ran toward the first. Paula could feel weariness and age start to creep up

on the old woman, the rasping in her lungs loud enough
to echo off the cold walls. A handful of the bobby pins
had fallen away, freeing strands of her hair now left
hanging loose and wet with sweat against the sides of her
beefy neck. Paula's back was drenched through and the
laces on her right sneaker had come undone. She was
having trouble catching her breath as they ran into the
large lobby, the walls covered with tattered, old framed
photos of the Italian countryside, a sealed-up fireplace
in the center, its black brick opening filled with a fresh
bouquet of flowers. She pulled her hand free from
Assunta and came to a stop. The old woman never lost
a step, continuing down the side corridor leading to the
large red basement door. She released the latches and
swung the door open, for an instant peering down the
darkened steps below. She then turned to Paula, waiting
as the girl came running toward her, her hair flowing
wildly against the coolness of the shuttered air.

It was then that the old woman saw the gunman walk
into the shadowed darkness of the lobby. His steps were
heavy, their echoes bouncing against the thick walls.
Assunta could see the gun in his right hand, hanging
down low, primed and ready to be fired. She put her
hands on Paula's slight shoulders, her fingers squeezing
the soft skin. She leaned over and kissed the girl on the
forehead and gave her a warm smile. "Be careful as you
go down those steps," she said. "When you get to the
bottom make a quick turn to the left. Keep going until
you get to the boiler. Next to it, you'll see an opening in

the wall. Run through that as fast and as far as it will take you. That leads to a short stairwell up to the street. Once you're there, you'll see a black car with the engine running. Get in and let the driver do the rest."

"What about you?" Paula asked, glancing past the old woman's girth at the approaching shadow. "Aren't you coming with me?"

"I will see you again, little one," Assunta said. "This I promise you."

Paula looked into the old woman's hard eyes and nodded. She then turned and ran down the narrow steps, disappearing quickly into the darkness below.

"That was a big mistake," the man's voice said. He was standing behind Assunta now, the gun poised at waist level. "She's not going to make it. And neither are you."

Assunta hung her head and turned slowly toward the man with the gun, her right hand wedged inside the front pocket of her checkered housedress. "You would kill an old woman and a child?" she asked.

The man with the gun let out a low chuckle. "Only if they're in my way," he said. "And right now you are in my way. The girl, too. But with her I have to wait. There will be a time for her to die."

"But not at your hand," Assunta said.

She turned to face the man with the gun, her large bare feet flat on the hard surface, her back braced, her gaze steady. She moved the fingers of her right hand, buried inside her dress, and pressed them around the grip and trigger of the old handgun that had once belonged to her husband. She fired off three rounds, each one catching the man in the center of his chest, the second shot bursting through a great artery. The man's gun fell to the floor an instant before he did. He went down with a heavy thud, the front of his head landing against the edge of the stairwell, the skin ripped open and gushing blood. The old woman stared down at her target, watching him bleed out for several seconds, and then turned away. She locked the door to the basement and then gently sidestepped the flow of blood filling the area around the man's body and walked back up to her apartment, the gun in her dress still smoking and hot.

Pete Rossi stood in the center of the restaurant's large kitchen, surrounded by an array of pots and pans hanging from a series of shiny hooks nailed into the four brick walls. He ran the cold water tap on the stainless steel sink, slowly rubbing his hands together under the rush of the icy flow. He reached over, grabbed a cloth napkin off a side cabinet, and watched the water soak it through. He turned off the tap, squeezed dry the napkin, then spread it across his face. He kept it there, allowing its fresh smell and cool touch help wipe away the strain of the last several days. He leaned his head back, took a deep breath, and pulled the cloth from his face, tossing it back into the empty sink.

It was only then that he turned his attention to the shivering man standing across the room, staring at him

299

with eyes filled to the brim with fear. Rossi walked over to the stove and reached for a small espresso pot, thin lines of steam flowing out of the spout. He pulled a cup from the cabinet above his head and poured out the thick black liquid, filling it to the lip. He took several slow sips, the hot coffee warming his chest, the biting taste of the espresso coating his throat. The man across from him was now visibly shaking, his right hand braced against the side of a wooden hutch to help steady his legs. Rossi walked closer to the man, stopping next to a Viking stove, and clicked the oven on to four hundred degrees. "What is it that makes you so afraid?" Rossi asked the man in a low voice. "Is it me? Or is it the fact that you failed me? Failed the very people who depended on you to succeed?"

"I had the back covered," the frightened man, Otto, said, the words barely audible. "The kid didn't get out that way. I was told to stay put and that's what I did."

"And while you were busy staying put, one of my men died and the girl I asked you not to lose went into the wind," Rossi said. "So, it really doesn't matter then, does it, that you had the back covered?"

"What was I supposed to do, Mr. Rossi?" Otto asked. "What if she had come out that way and I wasn't there to stop her? Then, I'd still be in the same jackpot I'm in now. Only worse."

"How long have you worked for me?" Rossi asked, resting the empty coffee cup on a clean white counter.

"It'll be six months come November," Otto said.

"And up till now, every job I been on has gone off without a hitch."

"I never concern myself with the ones that have gone as planned," Rossi said. His words were measured, direct, a mob boss dictating to an underling not deserving to be in the same room. "It's the ones that fail that get my attention."

"It was not my fault, Don Rossi," Otto said, sweating out each word, swallowing hard to keep his voice free of the panic running through his body like a river. "I did all I could to keep that cop's niece under our eyes. The job did not fail because of me."

"But you're the one that's here," Rossi said to him. "Your partner's dead. The girl is somewhere safe. And you are here with me, in the warmth of a large kitchen, watching me drink my coffee."

"I will find her for you, Mr. Rossi," Otto said. "I swear to you, I'll track her and bring her back to you alive, like you wanted."

"I don't want her back," Rossi said with a shake of his head. "And I don't want you to find her. All I asked was for you not to lose sight of her. The girl was never my target. She was my lure. And now, because of you and your dead friend, she's gone. And so is the plan that she was to play such a key part in. Which means since I no longer need the plan, I no longer need you."

"It's the cop you want, Mr. Rossi," Otto said, straining out every word, well aware that a decision about his life had been made long before he even entered the room. "I could take him out for you. All I need is the chance and your say-so."

Pete Rossi turned and opened the door to the large oven behind him, a burst of intense heat warming his face. "You are out of chances," he said to the young man standing behind him. Rossi pressed down gently on a black button in the middle of a phone hanging on a side wall, next to a framed photo of his father, looking young and stylish in a brown three-piece suit and brown fedora. Within seconds, three men in dark clothes stepped into the kitchen, circling Otto. "Strip him before you throw him in," Rossi told them as he headed out of the room.

Panic filled Otto's young body, each muscle trembling now beyond any control. One of the three goons reached over and held him by the elbows, preventing him from falling to the floor. "You can't do this, Mr. Rossi," Otto managed to say. "You just can't do this to me."

Rossi turned to Otto, shrugged his shoulders, and smiled. "Don't worry, Otto," he said. "I wouldn't waste a new oven on you. I was just testing to see if it worked. But you will die today."

Pete Rossi locked eyes on Otto and stared at him for several long seconds. He always argued against keeping men like this in the organization, even if they were used for only the simplest tasks. They often failed in their duty, and on the few occasions when they did manage to succeed, they bragged about it to the first set of good ears they could find. It was too much of a risk for the Camorra to take. The outfit should always strive to bring in the best recruits, the smartest and sharpest available talent, and have them work their way up from the most menial chores. If it was good enough for a Fortune 500 corporation, it should be good enough for the most elite criminal organization in the world.

"Don't waste any bullets on him," Rossi ordered the tallest of the three goons. "Bury him alive."

Joey Tugs McGraw rested the suitcase filled with pure heroin on top of the shiny brown table. He gazed up at the man standing across from him and nodded. "I see your hands are empty," he said. "And there's no bag anywhere near you. I hope that doesn't mean you forgot to bring the money."

"The money's in the car," the man said in a voice that was steady, calm, and assured. "All of it. Down to the last Andrew Jackson."

"How about, then, you go and get it," McGraw said. "Since that was a big part of the deal. And I'll wait here while you do."

"Open the suitcase," the man said. "And step away from it. I need to make sure the product is in there and that it's as good as I was told. For me, that was an even bigger part of the deal."

"Well, now that we made it very clear we don't trust each other," McGraw said, "how do you want to play this out?"

The man took a deep breath and rested his hands inside his jacket pocket. He pulled one out slowly and pointed an open pack of gum at McGraw. "I usually chew three at a time," he said. "The extra one in there is for you, if you want it."

McGraw shook his head. "Knock yourself out," he said. "Chew three, four, put the pack in your mouth if you want. I really don't give a shit. I came here to close a deal and leave with some cash. If I want to blow bubbles, I'll hang out with a kid."

The man undid the gum wrappings and placed one slice after another in his mouth. "How about you take the suitcase and we both go outside?" the man asked McGraw. "I pop the trunk and you look at the cash, while I check out the dope."

"In broad daylight?" McGraw said. "That your idea of clever or did some moron read it to you this morning?"

"You have a very negative attitude to be doing this kind of work," the man said. "That either means you're new to this end of the business or this is your first shot at a big haul. Either way, I get no comfort from it."

"I don't give a shit what you get from it," McGraw said, spitting out the words, a small bubble forming at the edge of his lips.

"Nor should you," the man said. "But here's something you should give a shit about. You need to leave here with the money and I need to leave with the dope. And we're going to have to do that soon. Otherwise I turn and go back to where I came from, which puts you back in your car as well. Except I don't have to explain to the Squid why you still have his dope and don't have his money."

"I'll throw that to you," McGraw said. "No sense in me catching blame for any of this shit."

"You can try that," the man said. "That might buy you an extra ten minutes or at least a long enough time for the Squid to figure out which knife he wants to use to slice you into little pieces for his fish tank. He'll come looking for me again. But only to tell me that you're dead and he's sending somebody who knows how to close."

"How do I know if I go outside you don't have three or four guys waiting for me?" Tugs McGraw said. "Waiting for your nod to take me out?"

"Like you said, it's broad daylight," the man said, resting his hands hard and flat on the table. "And I never needed a nod to take anybody out. I do my own blood work."

Tugs McGraw's eyes moved from the man to the suitcase, beads of sweat coating his upper lip. "We move to the car, you go out first," he said. "Then head right for the cash. Any move that don't look right to me is gonna be followed by a bullet. We clear?"

"As a glass coffee table," the man said.

The man turned and led the way out of the small office, down two flights of concrete steps, and out through a glass door to the tree-lined street. Tugs McGraw was several steps behind, the suitcase in his left hand, his right in the front pocket of a thin jeans jacket, fingers wrapped around a .38 Special. The man walked toward a near-empty parking area, heading for a black late-model sedan with New Jersey plates. He stopped, turned, and waited as McGraw drew closer and pointed to the car at his back. "I need to pop the trunk," he said. "Everything you'll need to see is in there."

"Do whatever it is you need to get it done," McGraw said. "Just do it slow and know I'm eyeballing every move you make."

"I'm counting on it," the man said.

He stood in front of the trunk, slid the key into the lock, and popped it open. He moved aside and waited as McGraw stepped in next to him. Tugs glanced down into the trunk and jumped several steps back when he saw the muscular young man in the leather coat bound and gagged, his head resting on a gray valise filled with the cash McGraw was expecting to bring back to the Squid. McGraw pulled the .38 from his pocket and dropped the suitcase to the ground. "I warned you not to screw with me," he snarled. "Now all you went and done is give me a solid reason to make you dead."

"Don't you even want to know who I am?" Lo Manto asked, standing with his hands spread apart. "Otherwise, how will the Squid know who it was you killed?"

The sharp edge of the barrel end of a nine-millimeter wedged against McGraw's neck froze him in place, preventing him from giving Lo Manto an answer. "Ease your finger off the trigger," Jennifer said to him. "And don't push your luck. I don't care if my partner lives or dies. So you can only imagine how that makes me feel about you."

"I think she does care," Lo Manto said, stepping closer to McGraw, watching as he let his gun slip from his fingers, catching it as it came off his hand. "She just says that to annoy me and scare the piss out of guys like you."

"You gonna take the money *and* the drugs?" McGraw asked, his voice cracking from fear and the tension. "You have any idea what the Squid will do to you for something like that?"

"I can only imagine it'll be ugly," Lo Manto said, tossing the gun into the open trunk. "Maybe not as ugly as what he's going to do to you for letting it happen, but still not a situation I'd want to have to face."

"You're not going to arrest me?" McGraw asked, surprised at the very thought.

"I can't," Lo Manto said. "I have no authority in this city. And my partner behind you, just dying to put a round into the back of your head? She's not looking to make a bust. She just wants to go home and get away from all of us."

"We were making a drug deal," McGraw said, losing any pretense of tough. "You can't let me walk away from something like that. I don't care what end of the world you're a cop in. That's an arrest you just gotta go and make."

"I've never met anyone so eager to go to jail," Lo

Manto said. He leaned against the trunk of the car with his arms folded, watching Jennifer holster her piece and step back from McGraw. "But I didn't see any laws broken here. If anything, I'm just borrowing your suitcase. Airline lost one of mine on the trip over here. And I'll get it back to you, first chance. So you can leave anytime you want. I know the Squid's waiting for you and I don't want you to be late on account of me and my partner."

"What's the deal?" Tugs McGraw asked. "What is it you want? It ain't like the cops to just hustle and take a bag of cash and a haul of dope and leave the doers free. So unless the two of you are going to cut that up between yourselves, there's something else we need to talk about."

Lo Manto tilted his head against the overhead sun and glanced over at Jennifer. "Now didn't I tell you he wasn't as big an idiot as you thought? Job like this, you don't just hand off to the first two morons with guns and a car. You give it thought and pick out the movers from the top tier."

"Deal didn't go down, did it?" Jennifer asked. "Still makes them shaky to me. Guy in the trunk was ready to give up the money even *before* we pulled guns on him. And this other one followed you out of the office building like a puppy without a leash."

"She does have a point," Lo Manto said, turning his full attention back to McGraw. "And seems to have made up her mind. You're going to have to give me something to help convince her you can deliver. Otherwise, you're free to go. The Squid is probably dying to hear all about your adventure."

"It's him you want, am I right?" McGraw said. "You don't care about me or that other loser in the trunk. And why the hell should you care? Neither one of us brings you anything. Everything we know you already know. But the Squid's a whole other story. You rope him in along with the money and that dope and you'd have yourself a hefty catch."

"All that's true," Lo Manto said. "But listening to a mouthful of tough talk from you isn't going to bring me the Squid. And until I hear something that does, you're a clear man, free to go about the business of your day."

"I can get you to the Squid," Tugs McGraw said. He was standing close enough to the open trunk to see the curled-up man in the dark leather coat, silver tape double-wrapped around his hands, feet, and mouth, sweat pouring out through every open pore. "You just let me know when and I can make it happen."

Lo Manto stared at McGraw and shook his head. "I just got off a plane," he said, the harsh tone of his voice catching Jennifer off-guard. "Not a boat. I'll set up the deal with you. Even give you the money to show the Squid this transaction went down without a hitch. Then we'll step back and wait for you to set up a meet. A one-on-one between him and me. But if you shuck me at any point, play me for the wop with a badge, I'll find you and kill you cold. And if I end up dead, I'll make sure someone breathing does the job for me. You want to think about it or you ready to make a call?"

McGraw had trouble catching his breath, trying to come off as calm and composed, but feeling his weakness below the surface. He didn't know who this cop was or where he was from, but he believed he was as serious as suicide and would waste him as easy as a paper target at a shooting range. He owed no allegiance to the Squid and for that matter might even benefit from having him out of the way. Use it as a way to take a step up to the next level, start playing with the major league team, setting up the deals instead of always working the risky end of the business. He might even maneuver it so he could end up playing both sides against the middle, with this cop providing the ultimate in the way of a protective shield. McGraw looked across at the cop, trying hard to ignore the danger that floated across the man's dark eyes, and nodded. "I'm your man," he said. "Tell me what it is you want me to do."

Carmine DelGardo stood in the center of the pool hall, the three forty-watt bulbs above him offering the only light in the long, dusty room. He leaned against the side of an old table and shot a six ball into a corner pocket with practiced ease. Frank Silvestri took a sip from a tumbler of bourbon, pulled a stool from the empty bar, and sat down. "You think of ever maybe putting a fresh coat of paint on this place?" he asked DelGardo. "You know, spruce it up a little. Make it seem like you give a shit if anybody comes here to play or not."

"You want a game, you'd play it in a snowstorm," DelGardo said. "Pool players don't give a rat's dick about paint. They only care about the cash laying on the felt."

"How's that candy store of yours doing?" Silvestri asked, lighting a thin cigar and blowing a line of smoke up toward the dark ceiling. "Even there, I don't think you had a customer since the first Bush was in the White House."

"I invest for love, not for profit," DelGardo said, leaning over to line up his next shot. "Besides, you don't play pool and you don't eat candy. And I own both buildings, so I know you're not here to collect rent. So, there's a reason for this meeting. I just ain't heard you mention it yet."

"The call is out for four top shooters, the best around," Silvestri said, his voice low, direct, and strong. "The don wants them in place before the week is out. Half a million in cash to each. He expects them to all work together, function as a team. And they all get the money, regardless of who brings down the target."

"That news don't make my heart beat faster," DelGardo said. "I ain't shot a gun since I was a kid. And I *missed* what I was aiming to hit."

"The target's a friend of yours," Silvestri said. "That cop from Naples. The boss wants him flat and out of the picture. And he wants it done by this time next week."

DelGardo hit his shot, then stood up as he chalked his

pool cue, his manner cool and indifferent, as if he were being given an update on the week's weather. "How hard can that be?" he asked. "One badge up against four top-tier shooters. Two million in cash waiting on the table. Once word gets around, there are gonna be more hit men in this city than there are Arab cabdrivers."

"The cop's been a hard target up to now," Silvestri said. "But even with help, I don't see how he walks from this one. They're going to be lined up on every corner taking their shots."

"So you should be happy, no?" DelGardo said with a shrug. "What I hear, he's been a nasty thorn in your rib since he first pinned on the tin. Maybe you should have moved down this road a few years back. Saved yourselves a ton of money and a belly full of grief."

"Which way you going to go on this?" Silvestri asked.

"There ain't many ways for me to go," DelGardo said. "The call's already been made. Shooters are starting to pack and check their clip loads. Not many places for me to bring this news."

"You can go back to your candy store and keep doing whatever it is you do in there," Silvestri said. "Or you can reach out to a friend and spread the word. Give him a heads-up. A feel for what's about to come his way."

"That leaves my door open for two questions," DelGardo said, taking a slow walk around the pool table. "What's in it for me to do that and what's in it for you to ask?"

"The cop's been an issue for too many years,"

Silvestri said. "On the matter of him going down, its never been a question of *if* but *when*. You're his friend, known him since his puppy days. You'll be doing him a favor, is all. Give him a chance to fire back before he goes down. There isn't anything you can say or do that is going to change the end result. He's going to die whether you talk to him or not."

"Okay," DelGardo said. "That covers why I might want to help the hothead. It still don't explain your end of it."

"Let's just say I'd be paying off a debt," Silvestri said. "No more to it than that."

"Not like somebody in your line of work to be owing somebody in his, if you catch my float," DelGardo said. "At least with me and him there's a history, what with his papa and all."

Frank Silvestri stood, his large shadow dominating the light in the musty room. "You're not the only one with a history, candy store man," he said. He tossed his lit cigar to the ground, finished the last of his drink, and walked out of the pool room, the sound of his heavy steps bouncing off the chipped walls.

19

Jennifer checked the name written on her notepad, closed it, and jammed it back into the rear pocket of her jeans. She walked up the well-maintained tenement steps and pushed open the polished wooden door leading into the foyer. She gently pressed down on the buzzer to the fifth-floor apartment and waited for a voice to come crackling over the silver intercom box. Instead, the buzzer by the door handle went off, and she was let into the building that a day earlier had been a crime scene. She walked up the first-floor steps, glancing off to her right at the large blood circles still staining the ornate cement, a long strip of yellow police tape blocking any access to the area. She had been at so many of these scenes in her years as a cop, the modern-day symbols of a life taken, that it would be easy to be indifferent to what passed before her eyes. She had learned early on the lessons of keeping it all a safe distance away, of treating any crime she was called into as a puzzle that needed to be solved, and never to cross the deadly line into the personal. It was a lesson that had been hammered home on an almost daily basis by every cop she had ever met, from her father to the instructors at the Academy to her first partner and up to and including Captain Fernandez. Still, despite the mental adjustment to the hard ways of doing a difficult job, Jennifer Fabini had never quite managed to shake off the cold finality of a murder.

Assunta Conte opened the door to her apartment a moment before Jennifer's second knock. She glared through a set of clear, sharp eyes at the younger woman and took two steps back. "You want to come in, I won't stop you," she said. "But I told the other cops everything I knew and did. They seemed happy with the answers when they left."

"I'm not here about the shooting," Jennifer said as she stepped into the apartment. "It's not my case. Even though from what I hear, it came down pretty clean. And I don't think anybody's going to make an issue of the gun charge."

"You want some coffee?" Assunta asked. "I just made a fresh pot. I always make more than I should drink. It's a bad habit. But when you get as old as me, all that's left are bad habits."

Jennifer nodded. "If it comes with milk and two sugars I won't pass it up," she said.

"Comes with pastry and biscotti, too," Assunta said, padding off into her large eat-in kitchen. "The coffee helps jump-start your heart, but it doesn't do much for your stomach. That's why you need that side dish."

Lorenzo Carcaterra

Jennifer followed her into the kitchen, pulled a wooden chair away from the thick, hand-carved table, and sat down. She watched the old woman reach into a cabinet and pull down two large cups, moving with a speed and dexterity that belied her years. She gave no emotional indication that less than twenty-four hours earlier she had stood with feet planted solid and pumped three bullets into a predicate felon and dropped him dead, allowing a young girl to escape to safety.

The kitchen was Italian-American Bronx. The walls were papered with a rich pastel flower arrangement, a row of commemorative plates featuring the images of President John F. Kennedy and Pope John XXIII lining one side of the room. An Italian calendar, with each month highlighted by a drawing of Jesus or a saint, the holy days of the Catholic year highlighted in red ink, hung from one of a series of white cabinets. The slop sink was filled with soapy water and soaking clothes, the old woman's chore for the afternoon. The back burners of the small stove were covered by two large pots, one slow-boiling a red sauce swimming with fresh fish, the other keeping the pasta water at a simmer. The odors of food mingled easily with the harsher smells of cleaning liquids, and it all quick-flashed Jennifer back to childhood and her Grandma Francesca's kitchen in Queens. She would do her homework, while the chubby old woman she knew for too short a time sang Neapolitan love songs and whipped up enough food to feed a family of twelve, always insisting on making four times more than was required. Those were the special moments of a childhood shortened too harshly by her mother's death, and Jennifer held on to them as if they were her only remaining possessions.

Assunta sat across from her and slid a large cup of coffee her way. She then reached behind her and placed a platter of Italian cookies and pastries between them. "I warn you," she said, "I make my coffee very strong. It's how my husband used to take it. It's not for everyone— this I know."

Jennifer put the cup to her lips and took a long, slow sip. The coffee was as thick as roof tar and had a sour licorice taste to it. It burned her throat and chest going down and the aftertaste was one that lingered. "It's got a kick, that's for sure," she said to the old woman. "You can't get anything like this at Starbucks."

"And it's better for you," Assunta said as she wrapped her heavy hands around the large cup in front of her and drank down half the coffee in two quick swallows. "Helps keep the head clear. Makes it easier for you to ask me your questions."

"You're a brave woman," Jennifer said. "You saved that girl's life yesterday. And you took a man down to do it. That's not something that's easy to do. I haven't seen as much of life as you have, but I've seen enough to know that."

"Maybe we both have just done what needed to be done," Assunta said, finishing her coffee. "It is how we have chosen to live our days. You with a gun and a badge and me with the memories of my husband."

"I came here because I need your help," Jennifer said, her eyes square on the woman's layered face. "I don't know why you'd give it to me. But I figured you cared enough for Lo Manto to risk your life for him. And he cared enough for you to trust his niece would be kept safe. That's pretty much all I have to go on."

"It's always easier to trust the old," Assunta said. "We have very little time left to betray the ones we have come to love. Age forces us to keep our circle small."

"You've known Lo Manto since he was a boy," Jennifer said. "You knew his parents. You know what he was like here and why he left. And you know him as a cop. And you're the only one that has all the answers."

"That depends on the questions," Assunta said. "And the reasons they are being asked."

"The only reason worth asking," Jennifer said. "I want to try to keep him alive. And while I'm at it, maybe duck and dodge a few bullets myself."

"Gianni's very good at doing that on his own," the old woman said. "He has been for a very long time."

"It's different now," Jennifer said. "This isn't just him against a small band of hoods he can track through informants and phone taps. There are a lot of people out there looking to bring him down. I don't know for sure how many, but I've been a street cop long enough to know something's building and the two of us together aren't going to be any match to handle it."

"But you are still with him," Assunta said. "You can leave him alone or pretend to be sick. Even ask your boss to put you with someone else. I have nephews on the police force. I understand how they work. You stay, though, because you choose to stay. So, then I must ask the first question. Why?"

Jennifer pushed the coffee aside and rested her elbows on the table. "Part of it is because it's my job and I don't like to walk away from one until it's done," she said.

"That's the cop part," Assunta said. "The woman part is what interests me. What does that answer tell me?"

"I don't want to see him get hurt," Jennifer said. "I could help him more if I knew what it is he's going after. I've only been working with him a few days, but that's long enough to find out that these busts, shoot-outs, setups he's in the middle of go way beyond just normal police work. It's personal with him, and I think it's something that started here, when he was a kid."

"His father was murdered," Assunta said. "By the Camorra. The Rossi family end of the business. But those facts, I'm sure, are all in his police folder. And you seem like a smart enough someone to have already read those."

"There's more to it," Jennifer said, reaching over and placing a hand on top of the woman's folded grip. "He's buried it and maybe so have you. I don't know yet. But I'd like to find out before I leave here."

"You care for him," Assunta said. "I can hear it in your voice. See it in your eyes."

Jennifer smiled and sat back in her chair. "I've only

known the guy a few days," she said. "It's a little too soon to turn this into *Casablanca*."

"How long should it take?" Assunta shrugged. "I knew my husband less than an hour before I came to believe he would be the one man I would always love. There is no clock on a woman's heart. It just drifts away on its own time."

"Maybe under different circumstances," Jennifer said, feeling her cheeks heating into a full blush. "But not the way it is right now. We've never even talked about it."

"Which means he doesn't know," Assunta said, her smile flashing a row of brown teeth and tobacco-stained gums. "That's always the best way."

Assunta stood, grabbed the empty cups from the table, and moved them over to the sink. "Let me finish my sauce and wash the dishes," she said. "Once that's done, I will go into the back bedroom and rest on my bed. You leave and go for a nice walk, take as long as you need. Bring the key from the small saucer in the hall with you. If you come back, wake me and then I will give you the answers you seek. Answers that my own godson doesn't even know. But I tell you this now. Think on it hard. For the easiest answer is not to come back at all."

Eduardo Gaspaldi stared out at the waves lapping against the side of the large boat docked alongside the abandoned pier. He lit an unfiltered cigarette and took a deep drag through clenched teeth, letting the late afternoon sun warm his face. He pulled the lid off a small container of hot tea and wrapped his hands around it, warming his thick, beefy palms. The four shooters were waiting for him down in the hull of the ship, all newly arrived, their gear in tow, eager to accept the lucrative job awaiting them. He had devised what he felt would be a strong plan, one designed finally to entrap a man who had haunted him for the past fifteen years. Gaspaldi and Lo Manto had first crossed paths in Naples back in the late eighties, when he was running a small brothel less than ten miles from the center of the city. It was a protected site, the weekly payoffs to both the police and the Camorra insuring his safety and allowing him to do business free of any worry. In the first three years of operation, Gaspaldi's end from the eight girls he kept under his roof totaled out to a neat and clean $4,800 a week.

Then, in what Gaspaldi felt was a legitimate dispute over an unhappy and frequent customer, he slashed the face of a young prostitute with the jagged edge of a broken bottle of Campari. The girl, Rosalia Ventura, was a seventeen-year-old runaway from a small town in northern Italy. She was dragged out of the brothel and brought to a nearby hospital, where her face was stitched and she was kept overnight by the elderly nun who ran the emergency room. At some point during that night, while the young girl slept soundly and sedated, the nun placed a call to a young cop working undercover vice. The cop went to the hospital, talked to the nun, checked on the girl, and came to the brothel looking for Gaspaldi. "You're two days early," he said to the cop, assuming he was there for the pickup. "Come back on Monday. I'll have the cash for you then."

"You won't be here on Monday," the cop, Giancarlo Lo Manto, had said to him. "No one will. This place will be empty."

"And where are we all going?" Gaspaldi answered with a loud laugh. "Church?"

"The girls will be sent to a shelter," Lo Manto said. "And you will be in a hospital bed, with tubes running into your arms."

Gaspaldi lunged for Lo Manto, who sideswiped the bigger man and pushed him down to the floor. Lo Manto reached for a bottle of red wine, broke the front half across the top of a wooden table, and jabbed it into Gaspaldi's chest, puncturing his right lung and leaving him with a ragged scar and a heavy wheeze for the rest of his life. Lo Manto straddled the bleeding Gaspaldi, lifted his head so his eyes gazed up at him, and put the sharp end of the bottle against the pimp's exposed throat. "When you leave the hospital, you leave this city," he told him. "I see you now, here, on the floor of this shit hole. If I see you in Naples again, I'll kill you."

Two weeks later, Gaspaldi had moved to New York and begun his climb up the Rossi family ladder. He was not the type they usually sought, but he knew how to manage a brothel and, over the course of time, would learn both the drug trade and the restaurant business.

He became someone the Camorra valued, a six-figure earner who could be counted on to bring in a steady stream of income and take a prison fall if one came their way. Pete Rossi also knew he could throw Gaspaldi's body to the federal wolves if they needed to make a tabloid bust.

Gaspaldi had managed to avoid Lo Manto on the occasions the detective made his way back to New York as part of a series of high-profile joint task forces. Until this latest visit, when Lo Manto had walked into his bar unannounced less than a week ago and sliced off a piece of his ear. He had no choice then but to ignore the cop's action and allow the Rossi plan to take shape. But now, with four shooters sitting on a stash of two million in cash just waiting for the go-ahead, Gaspaldi could finally put into motion the moves that would eliminate a man he had grown to loathe. He finished off the last of the tea and tossed the empty container into the water below. He took a deep breath of the harbor air, allowing the spray of wet salt to coat his face and fill his lungs. Then the pimp from Naples turned and walked toward the stairwell leading to the bottom tier of the ship, ready to approve a plan to kill an Italian cop on the streets of New York.

Lo Manto stood with his back against the rooftop door. His hands were braced against the side of the brick walls. It was late at night, a light, misty rain coating the hot tar ground, the city not yet cooled down from an oppressively humid day. The lights from the top-floor apartments surrounding him cast the area in a shadowy glow. He shifted his feet slightly and checked the rounds in his .38 Special. Lo Manto did not, as a rule, go into a situation anticipating a shoot-out. In fact, he made it a practice to avoid it as much as possible. He had steered clear of the shoot-first mentality that becomes the reflex of so many cops after a number of years on the job. He preferred to bring his prey in standing. But on this night, he wondered if that philosophy would stand a chance.

This night Lo Manto was going up against Reno the Squid.

Lo Manto walked the edge of the roof and peered over. He moved toward the rusting steps leading down to the fifth-floor fire escape, gripped the bars, and stepped over the edge. He stopped to gaze out at the wide streets and low buildings of the East Bronx neighborhood where he had spent the bulk of his childhood. These were the streets that shaped him, giving his life its purpose and direction. They were the streets where he had played ball, walked to school, run under the cool flow of open fire hydrants, learned the words to favorite songs by the Rolling Stones, Bob Seger, and Frank Sinatra, and kissed a girl for the first time. He had served as an altar boy at the local Catholic church, dutifully working both the scattered crowds of the Saturday five o'clock mass and the packed house on Sunday morning at nine. He began his first job, after school and on weekends, at Dellwood's Dry Cleaner. He spent four hours a day alongside the owner, Murray Saltzman, a stoop-shouldered, hardworking widower who filled Lo Manto with sorrowful stories of lost lives and ruined bodies left in the wreckage of a war and a hatred he would never come to understand. Saltzman was the first non-Italian Lo Manto had ever met, a deeply religious man who ate cottage cheese every day for lunch and laughed at his own rendition of stupid jokes. A man who had built a business with a small loan from his wife's father and had worked it six days a week, twelve hours a day for close to forty years. Lo Manto grew to respect him as a man and love him as a friend. Mr. Saltzman opened Lo Manto's young eyes to the short stories of Irwin Shaw, the comedy of Mel Brooks, and the genius of Sid Caesar. He also took him to his first Broadway play, a Sunday matinee of Arthur Miller's *Death of a Salesman*. "It seemed so real," Lo Manto said to him as they walked toward the subway for the ride back up to the Bronx. "And so sad."

"It's about life," Saltzman said to him. "How can it then not be real or sad?"

Murray Saltzman also exposed Lo Manto to his first taste of Camorra treachery. For years, the old man had reluctantly paid a weekly tariff of fifty dollars to the Rossi family. In return, the dry cleaner was allowed to stay in operation and not be bothered by any of the local thugs. Lo Manto would watch as each week a tall, slender young man would come into the shop, stand with an arm draped over the cash register, and smile as the old man counted out the five ten-dollar bills. Mr. Saltzman would usually stay quiet the rest of that workday, going about his business, his mind in another place.

"Why does he take your money?" Lo Manto once asked him. He had been in the shop close to six months and had exchanged hard glances with the young collector in the tan jacket on more than one occasion.

"Because that is how he earns his," Mr. Saltzman said, "off the hard sweat of other people. I thought it would be different in this country. Not like it was for me back home. But it is all the same, no matter which end of the ocean you live on. There will always be those that take. In Europe it was your life. Here it is your money."

"What if you didn't pay?" Lo Manto asked. "What would happen then?"

"I never asked," Mr. Saltzman said. "But I know it wouldn't be good. Not for me and not for my store."

"Still," Lo Manto said, "it's not right what he does. The money doesn't belong to him. It belongs to you."

Mr. Saltzman put an arm around the boy's sturdy shoulders. "You will learn soon enough, my young friend," he told Lo Manto, "that most of what happens in this world is not right."

A month later, the Rossi crew doubled Mr. Saltzman's tariff, kicking it up to one hundred dollars a week. The old man was having trouble meeting the payments and keeping up with the other expenses of the shop.

"You need to let me go, I would understand, Mr. Saltzman," Lo Manto said to him late one night as they were shutting the front door and turning on the alarm. "I don't want to leave you in a bad spot."

"I let you go, Gianni, then who would be left to listen to my stories?" Mr. Saltzman answered. "You don't just work for me. You're my friend. And I like to keep the few friends I have around."

Ten days later, Murray Saltzman, a short, distinguished white-haired gentleman who had survived two concentration camps and had seen his two younger sisters buried alive, was found dead in the back of the dry cleaner's, his body wedged inside the steam presser, his throat slashed to the bone. He had missed only one payment in all the years he ran his business, but that was one payment too many for the young collector with the crooked smile.

Lo Manto didn't see the young Camorrista again until three months to the day Murray Saltzman was buried. He came into Carmine DelGardo's candy store to pick up a carton of Marlboros and a six-pack of Budweiser. He took the cigarette carton and the cold beer from DelGardo and turned to walk out of the store. "This is the U.S. of A., smartass," DelGardo said. "You pay as you go."

The collector turned and stared at DelGardo, his eyes giving him a hard glare. "You don't want any trouble with me," he said in a low voice.

"And I won't get none," DelGardo said. "So long as

you leave cash for what's in your hand or put the smokes and drink back where you found them. Either way, won't ruin my day."

The collector stood near the door, smiled at DelGardo, and dropped the six-pack and the cigarette carton to the floor. "I'll be back some other time," he said. "When you're not in such a bad mood. Maybe then you and me can drink some beer and have a few smokes. How's that sound to you?"

"Like a morning in hell," DelGardo said, turning his back to the collector.

The collector opened the door and slid out, turning his attention to his next target in the neighborhood. Lo Manto looked up at DelGardo and placed two quarters on the counter, flashing him a pack of Juicy Fruit gum. "That guy have a name?" he asked.

"He's got a lot of things, that dickwad," DelGardo said. "A name's only one of them."

"What is it?"

"Reno Senzani," DelGardo said. "But that's only to his mother and some miserable Hungarian skank he keeps on the side. Everybody else calls him Reno the Squid."

"Why they call him that?" Lo Manto asked.

"They say he's into so much shit that he's gotta have at least eight arms to carry all that cash around," DelGardo said. "You know, like an octopus. Besides, the skinny fool likes the name. Thinks people will remember him better."

"He's right," Lo Manto said.

*

Lo Manto started his descent down the fire escape and stopped at the first landing. He peered into the window, gazing down at a large, well-maintained living room filled with imported furniture and ornate paintings. The Squid had his back to him, a bottle of wine in one hand, a thick glass in the other. Lo Manto stepped back and looked at his watch. He had arranged with Joey Tugs McGraw to meet the Squid down at the Chelsea Piers at two in the morning. McGraw was supposed to tell the Squid that Lo Manto was a dealer from Italy looking to dump a high-six-figure load of pure heroin on the New York streets. He was in a rush to make the deal happen and would be willing to take less than the full freight from anyone who pulled the merchandise from his hands. Lo Manto figured that McGraw passed only some of that information on to the Squid. He counted on some form of betrayal coming into play and decided it would be in his best interests to jump the gun and meet the Squid an hour earlier at a cozier spot. He checked his watch. It was twelve minutes past one in the morning.

Lo Manto thought now would be the best time to pay a visit to the man who murdered Mr. Murray Saltzman.

The loud hum of the 8,000-btu air conditioner drowned out any noise Lo Manto made on the thin fire escape steps. He watched and waited until the Squid, his jacket off, two semiautomatics at rest on a small coffee table next to it, sat down on his leather couch and spread his legs. He sipped from the glass of red wine in his right hand and channel-surfed with the remote in his left. Lo Manto looked down at the window and saw the latch was closed. He shifted the .38 to his waist and took a deep breath, his jaw working the three pieces of Bazooka bubble gum.

He was in the living room and on his feet in less than fifteen seconds. The sound forced the Squid to his feet, his glass shattering on the floor, red wine spilled on his trousers and the leg of his couch. Lo Manto stared at the Squid and smiled. "I love reunions," he said. "They help bring back so many memories."

"I should have killed you when you were a punk-ass little kid," the Squid said. "Instead of waiting till now to get it done."

"But you were busy in those days, remember?" Lo Manto said. "Besides, you liked your targets older, as I recall. That way they didn't have the strength to fight back."

The Squid looked at the broken window and the shattered glass resting in a circle around Lo Manto's feet. "I don't remember the rules in Naples," he said. "But in New York breaking into someone's apartment is a crime. An even bigger one if you're a cop."

"I don't figure you to be the type of guy who would put a complaint out," Lo Manto said. "Especially since what happened was an accident. I slipped on the wet fire escape and couldn't grab the railing in time."

The Squid turned away from Lo Manto and gave a

quick glance to the coffee table, his two guns resting side by side. Lo Manto caught the look. "Ten seconds, if you still have the instincts and the speed," the detective said to the Squid. "Get to the guns, grab them in your hands, aim them my way, and start pumping out bullets."

"There's time for you to die, cop," the Squid said, a thin smirk spread across his face. "I waited this long. It could hold a while longer."

"Am I keeping you from something?" Lo Manto asked. "A deal you need to close? A pickup you need to make? An innocent old man you need to torture and kill?"

"Not me," the Squid said. "I got all night to be entertained. There wasn't shit on the TV. Then you came along to spice it up a bit."

Lo Manto stepped away from the window, his boots crumbling the glass beneath them, and walked deeper into the living room. He saw the suitcase, the one that Tugs McGraw had brought to their meet, resting on its side next to the television set, the channel tuned to an MSNBC documentary. "Okay by you if I take a look around?" Lo Manto asked. "I'm thinking of maybe getting a place of my own in the area. This way, it works out right, we could be neighbors again."

"I don't think you'd like it around here much anymore," the Squid said. "The place isn't the same as when you lived here. Not as many Italians and a lot more blacks and Ricans. Not as safe as the old days. That's why I carry the guns."

"I wonder how they feel about having a lowlife piece of shit in their neighborhood doing drug deals?" Lo Manto asked.

"You have to ask the spics and the niggers, you want an answer to that," the Squid said. "I don't deal shit. If that's what you heard, then you heard wrong."

Lo Manto picked up the suitcase, tossed it on the coffee table, and popped it open. Inside were four individual kilo bags of heroin. "Then all this dope can't belong to you," Lo Manto said, looking away from the packets and at the Squid. "You know, a narc comes walking in here, even by accident like I did, he's going to think this is stuff you're planning to move. He might not be so quick to toss the blame to the blacks and the Puerto Ricans. He might look to impound your ass, instead."

"I don't know how that got there," the Squid said, barely compressing a smile. "And even if I did, so what? What are you going to do? Arrest me? This ain't Naples, wop cop. You got no weight on these streets."

"So then we'd both be in trouble," Lo Manto said. "I don't know about you, but I can't afford to get into another jackpot. My boss back in Naples, Inspector Bartoni, he has no patience for cops who bring him problems. But if there are no drugs, then you and me, we're both in the clear."

"You're starting to bore me, cop," the Squid said. "And I hate it when I get bored."

The Squid looked past Lo Manto, down the narrow

hallway corridor to his right, at the slow-moving shadow of Joey Tugs McGraw gently easing his way into the living room. McGraw held a gun in both hands, walking in bare feet and stepping gingerly on the Asian carpet that lined the hall, anxious not to make the wooden panels under the hand-sewn tapestry creak. Lo Manto caught the look and ignored it. Instead, he threw the Squid's two guns into the open briefcase, lifted it and carried it into the kitchen. He turned the tap on the cold water faucet and let it run at full speed into the empty sink. "I am very impressed," he told the Squid. "I would never take you for a man who owned a Braun tap. That's top-of-the-line. The more I hear, the more I believe that crime does pay."

"Maybe you should think about switching sides," the Squid said. "Or do what every other cop I know does. Work both ends of the room."

Lo Manto reached over and pulled a large kitchen knife out of a wooden sheath and sliced open the first bag of heroin. He turned it over and flipped it into the sink, watching as the white powder melted under the force of the running water as it slid down into the silver drain mouth. He looked up and saw a mixture of horror and anger cross the Squid's face. "Relax, dealer," Lo Manto said. "It's not like your bosses are going to blame you for all this prime-time dope being flushed. Like you said, they can throw the weight against all those black and Puerto Rican people."

"I am going to take my time killing you," the Squid

said. "Do you worse than that old Jew you used to like so much. Make you scream like I made him scream."

Lo Manto cut open the second bag of heroin, tossed it in the sink and moved the knife to his left hand. He pulled the .38 from his waist, moved toward the Squid, and stopped two feet away from him. "You know how they say a cop can never use force against an unarmed man?" Lo Manto asked. "You heard that, right?"

The Squid nodded, his eyes shifting slowly from the cop to McGraw, now standing at the edge of the living room. "Yeah," he said. "What about it?"

Lo Manto lifted his .38 and fired a single shot into the Squid's right leg. "That's only true in New York," he said. "We don't really have that law in Naples."

He watched as the dealer reached down and grabbed at his knee, the force of the bullet sending a seismic shock wave through the Squid's body, blood gushing through the small hole in his jeans just below the kneecap. Red blotches ran down and formed thick puddles on the orange-shaded Oriental rug. The Squid was too stunned to scream, his eyes wide, his lower lip cut and bleeding from the bite he put on it.

Lo Manto looked away from the Squid and followed the shadow that was moving to his left. He turned around, braced his knees, and fired four shots into the foyer, three of them hitting Joey Tugs McGraw, one finding the center of his heart. McGraw's two guns fell to the ground and he followed, facedown and dead.

The Squid jumped on Lo Manto, squeezing down on

the detective's neck with the full strength of both hands, his good knee shoved against the younger man's back. The force caused Lo Manto to drop his gun to the floor, the thick hands around his throat cutting off his breathing passages. "Get ready to taste it, cop," the Squid said. "Get ready to die."

Lo Manto reared up and jammed the butt end of one elbow into the Squid's open wound. That forced the dealer to ease up on the hold around the detective's neck. Lo Manto rose to one knee, turned, and drove the knife he held in his left hand deep into the center of the Squid's stomach. He held it there for several long seconds and then lifted the knife up, shredding bone, tissue, and skin as he made his way to the Squid's chest. Lo Manto got to his feet, the Squid's hands now wrapped tightly around his wrists, his head trembling, eyes red and bulging. White foam mixed with blood oozed down the sides of his mouth and the veins at his neck were engorged. Lo Manto pulled away from the Squid, shoved the hands down, and took a step back. He then lifted his right leg and kicked the knife deeper into the Squid's chest, sending the dealer crashing back onto the leather couch. He flopped down to one side, his head hanging off the edge of the couch, eyes still open, dead.

Lo Manto looked down at the Squid and shook his head. "I'm sorry it took me so long, Mr. Saltzman."

He stepped over the body of Joey Tugs McGraw and went back to the sink to finish flushing down the final two bags of heroin.

*

Jennifer sat on the bench across from the polar bears at the Bronx Zoo, holding a small paper bag filled with roasted chestnuts. The early morning sun warmed her face, the soft breeze blew strands of hair across her eyes. She smiled when she saw a small parade of children, led by an eager group of parents, point and stare with wonder at the massive bears flopping around in the cold water or stretched out over the shiny stones that served as their home. The Bronx Zoo had always been a sanctuary for Jennifer, a place to retreat when the problems of the day seemed strong enough to over-whelm her. She would come there as a child, in her starched Catholic-school uniform, spending a few morning hours gawking at the animals, giggling with her friends, and losing herself in the dark recesses of the reptile room. She would sometimes go there with her mother, the two of them quietly walking the expansive grounds, taking comfort in each other's company. Most of the time Jennifer went by herself, considering it her own special place to make decisions or face the truth about the realities of her existence. She went there the day after she was accepted as a member of the Police Academy and on the morning she was made a third-grade detective. She spent four long afternoons in the zoo, frozen to a bench across from the elephants, in the days after her first police shoot-out.

And she went there the day after her mother's funeral.

Jennifer cracked open two of the chestnuts, tossed the skins into a garbage bin to her right, and watched as Assunta slowly walked toward the bench. The old woman sat on the far end, draping a large blue handbag between them. "I didn't think you would come," Jennifer said. "But I'm glad you did."

"The buses were running late," Assunta said, staring out at a cluster of smiling children. "And I don't move as fast as I once did."

Jennifer looked over at her and smiled. "I heard you were moving pretty fast the other day," she said. "Outran one shooter and put down another."

"There was no man with a gun chasing me to the zoo," Assunta said, nodding to one of the children, a girl with a short ponytail who had sent a wave her way. "If there was, I would have been here before you."

"I thought this would be a good place for us to have our talk," Jennifer said. "It's safe and it's quiet. And we can always find a place to eat if we get hungry."

"I only eat in my house and what I cook with my own hands," the old woman said with a slight shrug. "I don't like dirty kitchens and surprises."

"Tell me about Lo Manto," Jennifer said. "Not the things I already know or can find out on my own. I need to know the things that are buried and never talked about. The things only a handful of people know and remember."

Assunta turned and stared at the young detective. She liked the hard edge that came with the soft face and the warm eyes that hid a determined nature. She sensed that she cared for Lo Manto and in many ways was similar to him, especially in the manner she approached her profession and the guard she placed around her demeanor. The old lady had been through enough to know that she was sitting next to a woman with her own set of secrets and her own thirst for revenge. "To know those things, to truly understand them, to come away without any questions, there is something bigger than Lo Manto you need to know about," Assunta told Jennifer.

"What is that?" Jennifer asked, tossing the bag of chestnuts into the garbage.

"You must know about the Camorra," Assunta said.

The reign of the Camorra began in the sixteenth century with the Spanish conquest of Italy. There, the Spanish Garduna evolved over time and slowly emerged as an early incarnation of the Neapolitan Camorra. What began with a series of weekly meetings of a dozen local men looking to gain a foothold in their occupied and poverty-stricken land grew with swift speed and deadly silence across the centuries to become the most powerful branch of organized crime in the world. From their earliest days, the Camorra was ruled by a body of bosses who referred to themselves as the Grand Ruling Council. While the Sicilian-based Mafia stretched its tentacles across small towns, the Camorra concentrated on big cities, specifically New York and Naples. The first known member to arrive in America was an extortionist named Alessandro Vollero in 1916. He was chased and hounded by the first true police hero of the twentieth century, Italian-American cop Joseph Petrosino. The determined young detective, who worked to rid his neighborhood of the predators swooping down on the innocent, was ultimately murdered in his fruitless attempt to return to Naples and crush the Camorra on their own soil.

Lo Manto had studied all of Petrosino's tactics and strategies and adapted them to his own form of police work, adding heavy doses of lethal force to his methods. On the day Lo Manto was made a detective in Naples, Inspector Bartoni gave him a framed photo of Petrosino to be used as a steady reminder about the war he would wage and the sacrifice it would demand. Lo Manto placed it in his living room in Naples.

In time, the Camorra ruled every Italian neighborhood in the two cities, dictating who worked and who didn't, who ate and who went without food, who lived and who needed to die. The bosses who ran the gangs had no qualms about shedding the blood of their own people, and their legends spanned the Atlantic, growing in strength and power with every kill. Pelligrino Morano, a Coney Island thug, was the first of the famed Camorrista dons to build his power base in New York. He was soon followed by the likes of John "Lefty" Esposito, Luigi Bizarro, and "Torpedo" Tony Notaro. They made fortunes by controlling the income of others, running the piers, the meat, fish, and produce markets, garbage pickups, and construction contracts that were handed to them by the corrupt politicians of their day. In return for steady work and a weekly paycheck, they demanded a 30 percent cut of a worker's wages. In turn, they then handed over 5 percent to the elected officials in the five boroughs and doled out a 3 percent commission to the police precincts scattered throughout the area.

"They became rich men on the backs of poor," Assunta told Jennifer. The two were taking a slow walk now, ambling their way toward the large swimming area filled with seals and attended by screaming children and tired adults. "It is always the fastest way to a dollar. In this or in any other country."

"Fastest way to a prison sentence or a bullet to the head, too," Jennifer said. "Most hoods never live long enough to spend much of the money they steal."

"That is true of most gangs," Assunta said, "but not of the Camorra."

By the end of World War II, after the collapse of Il Duce's dream and the destruction of Italy at the hands of the American, British, and German forces, the country was at its most vulnerable. Naples was by far the most destitute and ravaged city in all of Europe and the Camorra seized the opportunity. The local dons, intent on adding to and solidifying their power base, came up with an ingenious and chillingly methodical way to guarantee the future success of their criminal empire. On the surface it would have the appearance of an act of charity and was soon embraced by many in the area who turned to the Camorra as the only way for their children to escape the hard walls of an impoverished life. "It was the devil's plan," Assunta said. "If a working man had a debt to the Camorra, he was offered three choices. He could pay it off. He could die. Or he could hand them his youngest son, to be raised as one of their own, schooled by them, taught to live in their ways."

"So they stole kids from their families?" Jennifer asked, turning to face the old woman, the sun warming both their backs.

"Sometimes the families were so poor, so desperate to keep their sons alive that they would give them to the Camorra," Assunta said. "The children were fed well, sent to the best schools, and put on a path that would make them a lot of money. The mothers and fathers never saw them again."

"How many boys are we talking about?" Jennifer asked, the stunning revelations even managing to pierce her tested police armor. "And over how many years?"

"Hundreds at the very least," Assunta said. "Across many decades. They were schooled to their strengths. If a boy had a head for numbers he would be sent to business school. If he was better at science, he would go to medical school. With this system, it did not take long for the Camorra to have one of their own in any business you could name."

"The same go for over here, too?" Jennifer asked.

"That did not start until much later," Assunta said.

341

"But by the time Lo Manto was a boy, it was the rule here as well."

Nicola Rossi was the first Camorra don to institute the ways of Naples in the city. He felt that it was even more important to develop young minds with a sharp business sense to slither their way into the top levels of the major brokerage houses and financial institutions. His long-term approach was one that envisioned New York as the city that would supply the organization with the brain power it needed to consolidate its base, while Naples supplied the muscle. The two cities combined would then be indestructible and guarantee each other's success.

"Lo Manto's father was a good man but a weak one," Assunta said. The two were sitting at a small table in an outdoor café, each drinking an iced cappuccino. "He had a mad hunger for gambling but no ability for it. He was always in debt to Don Nicola's moneylenders. Most times he and his wife got the money together and paid off the loans. Then, there was one time when he could not."

"And that's why they killed him?" Jennifer asked.

Assunta looked across the table at the young detective, smiled, and shook her head. "No," she said. "That is why Lo Manto *thinks* they killed him. He was told his father stood up to the Camorra, tired of paying a large part of his salary to criminals, fed up with having to hand over loans at such insane interest rates. That was what he was told and that was what he believes. To this very day."

"He's a good cop," Jennifer said. "A great cop if you listen to some. He could find the truth if he wanted."

"We find the answers only to the questions we want answered," Assunta said. "And even then, we don't always believe what we hear."

"So what did happen?"

Assunta took a long sip of her cold drink and stared hard at the young lady she was about to entrust with a secret so very few people knew and so many died without revealing. A secret that once brought out into the open could only lead to more bloodshed and death. She took in a deep breath, sat back in her iron-railed chair, and raised her round face to the hot sun.

"They were going to kill him. The order had already been put out," Assunta said. "There was no money to be had and Don Nicola knew he would be unwilling to give up his only son. That left the Camorra with death as their only option."

"Did Lo Manto know any of this was going on?"

"A parent can hide a great deal from a child, no matter how bright the boy," Assunta said. "And the neighborhood, either because of fear or out of respect, knew how to stay silent as well."

"And his dad was murdered by the Camorra, right?" Jennifer asked. "That part is still true."

"That part will always be true," Assunta said. "Only the reasons behind the murder have been hidden."

They stood and began to walk again, this time making their way to the zoo exit, the old woman resting her left arm on Jennifer's right, both as calm and relaxed as a mother and daughter enjoying a rare day together. "Lo Manto's mother went to see Don Nicola," Assunta said, her voice low now, as if sitting around a campfire and telling a horror tale long handed down. "She was much braver than her husband and went looking for a way out of the mess he had made of their lives. She told the don to spare her husband's life and forgive the debt. In return, she would give him a son. But not the one she had with her husband, not Gianni. She would give Don Nicola a son of their own, one who would have Rossi blood rushing through his veins."

Jennifer stopped walking, staring across at the old woman, the harsh reality of what she had just been told landing on her with the force of a large wave. "Did he agree?" she asked, her voice equally as hushed.

"What don would not?" Assunta said. "To have a child with a beautiful woman, to take from her what no one else would dare touch. It is the purest taste of power."

"And did they have a kid together?" Jennifer asked, afraid she already knew the answer.

Assunta nodded. "They had a son," she said. "Born two months before Gianni's sixth birthday, at a local clinic. I was the midwife."

"Pete Rossi," Jennifer said.

"The don that Giancarlo Lo Manto so much hates, the one he has waged war against for these past fifteen years, and the one who carries the weight of the blame for his father's death is his younger brother," Assunta said. "He fights against his own blood every day of his life."

"And his father was killed not because of any debts," Jennifer said. "He was shot dead because he found out about the affair and went to see the don about it."

"He did not suspect the truth until the night of the baby's birth," Assunta said. "He was walking down a corridor, a small bunch of fresh-picked flowers in his hand, when he saw Don Nicola and his men come out of his wife's room. He stepped into a dark corner and listened as he heard them all congratulate the gangster on the birth of such a fine and strong son."

"Did he go see his wife?" Jennifer asked. "Try to figure out that it was him that put her in such a spot?"

"He was like most men, too proud and too filled with anger to admit their own errors," Assunta said, shaking her head. "He left the clinic and went out into the night, a lost man."

"Lo Manto was old enough to know his mother was having a baby," Jennifer said. "He had to ask what happened."

"What he asked and what he was told were two different tales," Assunta said. "The truth never played any part in the story of his early life."

"But they stayed in the neighborhood until Lo Manto was about fourteen," Jennifer said, standing in front of her car, opening the passenger door for the old woman. "And his mom gave up her baby at birth. Why wait so long to move away?"

"She secretly cared for little Peter until he was just about six years old," Assunta said. "She was allowed to visit him three times a week and sometimes enjoy a Sunday meal together. Then, soon after that, the boy was taken away, sent off to begin the journey that would lead him to his current place. She gave herself time to mourn her lost child and her dead husband. Then she planned the move back to Naples."

"And his father waited all those years, knowing his wife was caring for another man's child before he went and made a move against the don?" Jennifer asked.

"Lo Manto's father loved his wife very much, and for a while, it was easier for him to leave his hatred buried inside a bottle of wine," Assunta said. "But as it always does, hate travels at its own pace, and seeing the grief he had caused the woman he loved proved too heavy a burden for him to continue to carry. Death at the hand of the don became the easier choice."

"That sad woman," Jennifer said. "All these years with all that pain and not able to share it with anyone."

"And worse," Assunta said, "living and knowing that each day her only two sons fight a war with each other that can only lead to the death of one or both."

"I figure if Lo Manto doesn't know anything, then Pete Rossi knows even less," Jennifer said.

"He is one of theirs, has been since he first took a breath," Assunta said. "He is a Rossi. A Camorrista don. To expect a heart to beat beneath that chest would be asking for a miracle from Christ."

Jennifer opened her car door and got in. She jammed the key into the ignition and turned the engine over. She let it idle for several seconds, staring out at the crowded streets, the noise of the passing traffic blending into the background. She then turned and faced the old woman. "I know this wasn't an easy thing for you to do," she said. "And I don't know why you decided to tell me, but I'm glad you did."

"The problem with being told the answers to the questions we ask is that they often only lead to more questions," Assunta said. "You have been given a heavy burden. It is one you can choose to carry with silence or act upon. That is something only you can decide."

"I'll figure something out," Jennifer said. "I only hope whatever it is, it's the right way to go."

"If there is a right way, you will find it," Assunta said, shielding her eyes from the sun. "I wouldn't have told you any of this if I didn't believe that."

"People will die, especially if I make a mistake with this," Jennifer said. "I have to make sure before I make the next move."

"People always die," Assunta said. "For reasons both good and bad. It's only a question of when."

Jennifer nodded and then shifted the unmarked into gear and swung it out into the Bronx traffic.

347

20

Pete Rossi stood on the New Rochelle Metro-North platform reading the morning edition of the *New York Post*. He was focused on the sports section, glossing over a half-dozen articles detailing the previous night's Yankees–Red Sox game. He ignored the Amtrak train that came rumbling in at four-fifteen, on its way down from Boston, making the local stops into Penn Station. He walked over to a freshly painted blue bench and sat down, stretching his legs, careful not to wrinkle the crease on his hand-stitched Rocco Ciccarelli suit, and avoided the pedestrian traffic hustling to get on and off the train. He flipped from the sports pages to the business section, checking on a number of his recent stock transactions and catching up on the latest in scandal and gossip. He took his eyes off a blind item about a corporate executive involved in mutual fund manipulation and glanced across the platform at the burly man.

Rossi nodded, stood, and walked toward the steps

that led to an overhead tunnel that would take him down to the other end of the station. He took his time, gave no hint of a rush, aware that the burly man was there on his clock and would wait all day and all night if Rossi deemed it necessary. He initially had reservations about agreeing to the meeting, always on the prowl for any hint of betrayal from within his inner circle, conscious that in the life he led he could expect full and undivided loyalty from no man. It was also not a practice of his to meet with anyone directly connected to a contracted job. He always made an effort to cover those tracks with as many layers as possible. He had been a careful crime boss, aware of the numerous obstacles that could ensnare him and bring with them a multi-decade federal prison sentence. Rossi seldom spoke on the telephone and when he did the conversations covered only the most innocuous topics. He had his cell phone number changed every two weeks, always keeping two in use, one for incoming only and the other for outgoing. He made sure he showed up for work on a daily basis at the investment firm he ran and reported his income legitimately and paid his fair share of taxes on a $500,000 yearly salary. The stream of $7 million that came to him personally as the don of the Rossi crime family was funneled through a complex system of offshore bank accounts, European brokerage houses, and midwestern bond exchanges. He had a dozen different management firms hired to handle his money, each one moving large amounts of cash and stocks every day, washing it through another dozen multinational front companies and fifteen individuals unknowingly allowing their names to be used.

Rossi was a very wealthy man who gave himself very little time to enjoy the powers of his position. He sent his children to the best private schools, spared no expense when it came to his wife's lifestyle, adorned his Manhattan brownstone and country mansion with the finest in furnishings and electronic equipment. He worked every day, including weekends, his Camorra training allowing him little time to waste on leisurely vacations and idle hours spent in the company of close friends. The best of the Camorra dons lived their daily lives as if they were cloistered monks, keeping at arm's length the weakening pleasures of heavy drink, drug use, and affairs with women with high profiles. Whatever passions a don did crave, he handled with a heavy dose of discretion. It was the secret to a long reign and an even longer life.

Rossi stepped onto the north end platform and stood next to the burly man. "Let's walk," he said. "There's a coffee shop three blocks up. We can talk on the way there."

"I appreciate you agreeing to see me like this," the burly man said. "I know you don't usually do the meets."

"You said you had important information to give me," Rossi said, his manner detached, his words cold and distant. "I like to hear news like that firsthand."

"Truth be told, there's two ends I need to touch base

with you on," the burly man said. They stopped at a red light, both standing silent, letting the late afternoon traffic slither past. The burly man shifted his feet from side to side, trying to calm his nerves, still not sure he had made the right call by putting himself in a one-on-one position with the don. He had worked exclusively for Pete Rossi the past six years, handling assigned hits on both ends of the ocean. But this was only the second time he had stood close enough to the young boss to touch him and the first time they had ever exchanged any words. The burly man, Gregory Flash Randell, had been a paid hitter long enough to know the hard rules of his world. He had crossed a line by making direct contact with a sitting don, eliminating the middlemen he had always been instructed to call. His life now depended on how crucial the information he would impart to Pete Rossi would be perceived to be. If it was deemed important enough for the boss to take notice and then action, his mission would be a success and he could count on scaling the heights of the mob kingdom, having earned the eternal gratitude of a man who trusted no one. If, on the other hand, he was passing on street rumor as fact, handing over names that had already been checked and cleared by Rossi and his crew, he could count on being chopped and dropped, another summertime floater lost in the depths of the Hudson River.

"I know there are going to be four heavy hitters going down after that Italian cop," Randell said as they walked across the street, both careful not to step in the wide potholes that dotted the crossing. "They'll try and drop him somewhere out in the open. It's a smart move and they'll no doubt go in with a good plan."

"What's your point?" Rossi asked, disguising his surprise that the paid shooter knew as much as he did. Hit men traveled in a business that was ruled by tight lips and the need to keep their work hidden from even the friendliest eyes. It was unlikely that Randell had heard about the four hires from anyone connected to the hitters, since there would be no need for them to advertise their acceptance of the assignment. That left Rossi nowhere else to turn except in the direction of his own camp. It was there that the names were first floated and the plans for the execution drawn up. And it would be there that any signs of betrayal would be found.

"I'd like to be kept in on that job," Randell said. "I don't want any part of the group that you got working. I'm sure they got their orders and will do their best to see them through. But I still want to go at the cop. And I won't charge you anything close to what the street says is going into their pockets."

They were standing across from the train station, their backs against a chain-link fence, the heat of the day heavy enough to lift. "Why are you telling me this?" Rossi asked. "And why now?"

"I won't move without permission," Randell said. "I never go in without the supplier wanting me on the scene. The word gets to the four hitters, they take it the way they take it. Them I don't really care about. You I do. You shake your head on this, I walk away from it, act like we never met. You keep me in the game, then I promise you, when that cop goes down it'll be my bullets that do it."

"You follow boxing at all?" Rossi asked Randell.

"A regular fan, nothing big," Randell said. "I catch all the fights they show on HBO, but other than that I don't go crazy over it."

"That's more than enough to cover my example," Rossi said, locking eyes with a tall brunette in a tight black skirt moving gingerly in high heels across the ruined pavement. "Any man can go down at any time. No matter who it is. And most of the time, he never sees the blow that sends him to the canvas. He just drops. And if I'm betting for a knockout to happen sometime that night, then I don't really care, either. The only worry I bring to it is that the guy I bet against is out of the game."

"A knockout's in the cards," Randell said. "You can rest easy on that end of the bet."

"What's a bet like that run a man?" Rossi asked, turning away from the woman but not before throwing her a casual smile. "Given the odds and the opponent."

"A quarter of what the current spread is now," Randell said.

"Seems like a fair bet to make," Rossi said. "I would lay my own money on something with that kind of payback."

Rossi moved away from the fence and started to walk down the narrow street, Randell by his side. "You said there were two things you had on your mind," Rossi said to him. "I figure boxing was one of them. Now, it wouldn't make much sense for me to leave here without hearing about the other."

"I've been in my end of the business a lot of years," Randell said. "Was born into it I guess you could say, a hand-down profession."

"I want to hear about somebody's biography, there's a TV channel for that," Rossi said, not bothering to disguise his irritation. "You have something I need to hear then let me hear it."

"You got a mouth inside your operation," Randell said. "And it talks into that Italian cop's ears whenever it gets the urge. It's one of the ways he's always a step ahead of you, both here and on the other end of your business."

Pete Rossi stopped in the middle of the street and glared at Randell. "Listen to me well, shooter," he said. "If you have a name, tell me. If you have the proof, show me. This isn't *Jeopardy!*. I don't want to ask a lot of questions. I just want the answers."

Randell looked around, cars and trucks rumbling down the choppy street, a straggle of pedestrians inching their way past them, many rushing to catch the next train into the city. "You sure this is a good place to have that kind of talk?" he asked.

"It's the *only* place we're going to have that kind of

talk," Rossi said.

"It's one of your capos," Randell said. His mouth was dry and parched, tiny balls of sweat running down his neck. He stood in the glare of the late afternoon sun as it began its slow descent toward dusk and knew he had just put his life on the line on a nowhere street in New Rochelle.

"Before you tell me a name, tell me how you know," Rossi said.

"This capo was born in Naples and is related by marriage to the badge," Randell said. "He's been feeding him the inside from his first day at cop school. That's how he gets the jump on the deals that are in play."

"How long have you had this information?" Rossi asked.

"For sure, less than a week," Randell said. "Truth, though, I suspected it for about a year or so. Not the related end. Just that he was the main feed."

"Based on what?" Rossi asked. "He take out billboard ads?"

"I had a job overseas a little less than ten months ago," Randell said. "One from out of your group got caught dipping a few fingers into the profit pot and the word came down the line to erase."

"Get to it," Rossi said. He was walking as he listened, head low, hands jammed inside his pants pockets, breaking down the shooter's information and disguising the anger he felt at the possibility that a key adviser had been working with Lo Manto for years. An insider, someone who had earned the trust and respect of the don, had broken the sacred seal of the Camorra, and Rossi had been the one who allowed it to happen. He knew that if word of what the hitter was spreading indeed proved to be true, then the crack in Rossi's steel façade risked being exposed. It was a situation that required Rossi to act with swift and deadly precision. That meant taking out not only the informant but the shooter who made him aware of the situation.

"I was a day away from the finish line," Randell said. "All going as per the schedule of the deal: I go out for a late dinner, come back to the hotel, get ready, and head to the site. Instead, less than an hour into my meal, I was out of the restaurant, crouched down on the back of a motorboat, Italian cops hot on my tail. And the target went in the wind, under full custody protection."

"Dominic Murino," Rossi said. "I read about that one. He was on the hide at a small seaside town in Cassino. The papers I saw said that experiment failed because of a weak plan. And excess exposure on the bidder's end."

"You know my work and how I do it," Randell said, jabbing back at the dig to his pride. "I wouldn't be at this game for as many years and playing it at such a high level if I didn't know how to cover every track. So my end was steam-cleaned. The reason I got trapped and my score walked clear was because somebody talked. And that was a somebody played on your team."

"Name the player," Rossi said, stopping to light a cigar with a thin butane lighter. "And back up the talk."

"Frank Silvestri," Randell said. "Him and the cop's mother are cousins, linked up back to the old country. He's loyal, by and large, dedicated to what he does and what you ask him to get done. The only time he ever crosses it is when it comes to that cop you're hunting. He puts the feed bag to him on a regular basis. Not every job, mind you, but enough to keep him on your case and you on the move."

"Why'd you wait this long to tell me?" Rossi asked. "A week is a lifetime in some circles, especially ours."

"I needed to be a thousand percent sure," Randell said. "I can't risk coming to you with this kind of talk and not have the paper to back it up."

"But you came today," Rossi said. "So that means you rid yourself of any risk."

"There's no risk when you got the proof," Randell said. "And that I got the other day. Soon as I knew for sure, I worked to set up the meet with you."

"Do you have it on you?" Rossi asked. He turned a corner and walked across North Avenue, making his way back toward the train station and the adjacent lot, where he had parked his new black Mercedes 600SL. "Ready to hand over?"

"I got enough with me to make you a believer," Randell said. "And it's fresh. Less than five days old."

Pete Rossi stopped, tossed the cigar to the pavement, checked the time on his watch, and stared over at

Randell. "The meeting is over," he said. "The next train to New York should be arriving in about six minutes. You can take it or walk to wherever it is you need to go or find a cab. Whichever way, it's not a decision I need to know about."

"What about the packet?" Randell said, sounding as confused as he looked. "I hand that to you now or sometime later?"

"You don't need to show it to me," Rossi said. "All I cared about was that you had it and no one but you had seen it."

"Only two people know what we talked about," Randell said. "And that's us. I don't bring anybody to the table that doesn't need to be there."

"Then our business is done," Rossi said.

"Don't you want me to at least tell what your guy told the cop?" Randell asked.

"You already did," Rossi said. "You just were too busy talking to notice." He turned away from Flash Randell and walked down a sloping hill toward his parked car, quietly working out the details to three murder plots in his mind.

Lo Manto stepped onto the IRT number 2 train seconds before the doors closed at the East 233rd Street station. He walked through three cars, using poles for balance. The cars were filled with a wide array of New Yorkers. Students gazed out with tired eyes at the nondescript buildings along the elevated route. Exhausted construction workers were heading home from bone-weary ten-hour shifts. A collage of old men and women sat arched forward, their eyes squinting at folded-over newspapers and thick magazines. An urban blend of young women, Walkman pads resting over their ears, eyes closed, listened to music in sync with the rhythmic motions of the subway.

He found a seat in front of a subway map, the various lines slithering their way from one borough to the next, all linked by a random series of letters and numbers. He turned to his right, glancing over at Carmine DelGardo, his head buried deep inside a *New York Post* story detailing a multiple murder at a dance club in downtown Brooklyn. "This must be important," Lo Manto said, staring straight ahead at the abandoned buildings that still dotted the streets of the South Bronx even after decades of political promises. "I don't think I've ever seen you away from the store or the pool hall. What happened? They burn down?"

"Stick to the badge work, wop," DelGardo said, still immersed in the story. "Your jokes just flat-out suck."

"I could sing you a song, if that's the way you want to go," Lo Manto said with a wide smile. "You spend as much time in Naples as I do, you pick up a lot about music."

"Not enough to warm my ears," DelGardo said. "But let's save all that shit for later. We got business."

"We're on the local," Lo Manto said, resting the back

of his head against the hard edge of the subway map. "Plenty of time to cover all your bases."

"You got yourself two big problems," DelGardo said. "And both of them are gonna come down faster than a bullet."

"Start with one," Lo Manto said.

"The Rossi crew is onto your inside hand," DelGardo said. "Some hired gun calls himself Flash dropped the words right into the don's ears. Put the guy out on a thin branch. I'm not saying it's going to be today or even tomorrow. But if it were me sitting where you are, I'd expect him to disappear real soon."

Lo Manto looked past DelGardo, staring at a middle-aged woman in a faux fur, her eyes fixed on the hard-cover book spread open on her lap. She was thin, with long brown hair covering half her face, her beauty clear and unlined, her features proudly daring the arrival of old age to tend to their chore. "What's the second problem?" he asked.

"Four guns and two million dollars in cash," DelGardo said. "Each one with their scopes aimed down at your head. My guess is they're going to come at you on the street, work together and hit you from any direction you could turn. And they ain't gonna leave or get to take their cash until they zipper a black bag over your dead ass."

The subway screeched into the Tremont Avenue station, side doors slipping open, a crew of Hispanic kids in high-top sneakers and baggy jeans jumping aboard, laughing over a story whose punch line was left on the platform. "You have any names?" Lo Manto asked. "On either the shooters or their handlers?"

"Nothing solid yet," DelGardo said. "But you have to think they're coming off the top of the charts, given the dough that's being shelled out and the target they've been asked to take down. My money tells me there's no local talent in this bunch. These are Armani imports."

"You work on that end," Lo Manto said. "Tab the hitters coming in from overseas. It's a better bet that Rossi would lay both his trust and his money on shooters from out of the country. I'll move to get my inside man to a safe place outside."

"Might already be too late for that," DelGardo said. "Nothing those wild Italian cowboys hate more than a guy breaks rank, and they like to deal with shit like that in a heart-attack hurry. He could be dead now for all I know, but he'll be dead soon, that's straight and sure."

The train was now submerged in darkness, entering the main tunnel at East 149th Street, zooming like a runaway toward the first big city stop at 125th. Lo Manto stood up, holding on to a high bar, looking down at DelGardo, folded newspaper still on his lap. "I get off the next stop," he told him. "I'll reach out to you when I'm back up East again. You get some solid street information before then, get it to me through the relay."

"Next stop is Harlem," DelGardo said. "You don't have enough people that are ready to put bullets in your ass? You want to go piss off some black gangsters now, too?"

"You can come with me if you want," Lo Manto said. "Make sure nothing bad happens."

"The only way I get off the train in Harlem is if you carry me off," DelGardo said. "I only walk the streets of one neighborhood. That's the one I was born in and the one I'm going to be more than happy to be found dead in."

"There's nothing to worry about," Lo Manto said, stepping off the train. "They're all southern Italians up here. Just like you and me."

Carmine DelGardo smiled and waved a fast good-bye. "That the case," he said, as the doors were closing and Lo Manto was heading down a long flight of steps, "then you can walk without fear."

Jennifer was leaning on the front of her car, arms folded across her chest, a bored look stretched over her face. Lo Manto came up to her left and handed her a container of black coffee. "I didn't know how you liked it," he said. "So I kept it simple."

Jennifer took the cup from his hand and lifted the lid. "This is good as is," she said. "I like it regular, milk with two sugars, but I've been trying to cut back on calories."

Lo Manto took a sip from his coffee and smiled. "Americans are always trying to lose weight," he said. "They move from one diet to the next, willing to try anything in order to stay slim."

"What are you saying?" Jennifer asked. "That Italians don't diet? That they don't care about how they look?"

"They very much care about their appearance," Lo Manto said. "It's just not as big an obsession with them. Their day is built around the big meal, not spent avoiding it. Food is as important to them as friendship, love, and religion. It is one of the keys to who we are. You want to understand an Italian, find out what he likes to eat."

"That hold true for you as well?" Jennifer asked.

"Why?" Lo Manto asked, staring at Jennifer above the lid of his coffee container. "Do you want to get to know me better?"

Jennifer held his look for several seconds and then turned away, catching a glance at the traffic moving across Lenox Avenue. "There a good reason we're standing here drinking coffee in the middle of Harlem?" she asked, attempting to shift the conversation back to police business. "What's next after this? A ride on the Circle Line?"

Lo Manto started to walk against the oncoming traffic, still drinking his coffee, his eyes giving a quick check to the street action along the avenue. It was late-afternoon crowded, old women straining to pull their groceries back home, plastic bags stuffed inside squeaky carts. Middle-aged men mingled in front of candy stores, a steady diet of cigarettes and chatter filling their time. Most of the shops were crowded and the wide street hummed with fresh activity. It was a working-class neighborhood with a lowering crime rate, bracing for the onslaught of a new gentrified generation, moving in with speed and pockets crammed with money, eager young faces looking to turn old tenements into fresh-faced brownstones overnight. "I don't know if we have time for that today," he said to Jennifer as he tossed his empty container into a full trash bin. "Maybe tomorrow if the day breaks our way."

"What's a visit to New York without a ride up the Hudson?" Jennifer asked, words dripping with sarcasm. "But before I rush out and get us a couple of tickets, can you give me a hint why we're here?"

"I want to spend some time with an old friend," Lo Manto said, stopping in front of a dark gray building with a façade that hadn't been cleaned in decades. "Thought you'd like to meet him, too."

"Is this someone else you knew back from when you were a kid?" Jennifer asked as she pushed her way through a glass-and-old-wood revolving door into a long, dark lobby that smelled like stale beer.

Lo Manto wheeled through the door and led Jennifer toward the rear and a worn and creaky elevator. "I hope you're not afraid of dogs," he said to her, ignoring her question. "Moe's a friendly enough guy, at least once he gets to know you. But Little Moe is a whole other story. The kind of dog that wants to be liked *and* respected, and if he feels that he's not getting either one, he does something about it."

"How's he get along with you?" Jennifer asked,

stepping into a shaky elevator car, watching as Lo Manto pressed the button for the sixth floor.

He put a hand in his pocket and pulled out a small packet of dog treats. "He loves me," Lo Manto said. "But that's because I come with bribes."

The elevator door clanged shut and the two detectives rode the rest of the way in silence.

Blind Moe Ravini was once the numbers king of the East Bronx, and he held on to that title for more than forty years. He would be driven into the neighborhood twice a day, the first time very early in the morning to collect and the second after the last horse race was run at dusk for the payoff. As he got older and aging bones made it more difficult for him to get around, Moe let his team of runners do the bulk of his legwork. After a long day taking bets and collecting slips, paying off both the police and the winning hand, Blind Moe Ravini was driven back to his Harlem office building where he put in a few more hours making calls to the bosses and reporting the day's policy take. Little was known about his personal life, other than he had a wife and a son living somewhere on a farm he owned in Georgia. Even less was known about his early years or how he came to run the numbers operations in three of the five boroughs in New York. He materialized one day as if dropped from a thick cloud, a tall, muscular, blind-at-birth man, the only son of a black cleaning woman and a white Camorra bookkeeper. Blind Moe made his rounds with the aid of a silver walking stick and a thick-jowled English bulldog who was more lookout than guide. He seldom spoke and no one from any of the neighborhoods where he plied his trade ever saw him eat. Wherever he went, his large sedan and driver, Black Jack Curry, were always within the distance of a shout, the man behind the wheel as silent as his employer. Blind Moe seemed devoted only to the art of the numbers game, taking the bet, dropping the action and waiting for the payout to be handed over.

Lo Manto first met Blind Moe when the boy was just shy of his fifth birthday. That was the first time his mother entrusted him with her daily one-dollar bet on her lucky number, 213. He remembered handing the blind man the folded-over slip of paper, whispering the number as his mother had told him to do and gently placing the dollar in the palm of his right hand. That first morning, Lo Manto leaned over to pet the top of the bulldog's head, only to get a growl in return. "You're lucky," Blind Moe said to the boy. "You caught Little Moe in a good mood. You try that tomorrow and you might leave behind a finger along with that dollar bill."

Lo Manto followed the same pattern every morning for the next seven years, the bet never larger than a dollar, the number always the same, the conversation never lasting longer than a minute, the bulldog only growing nastier with time. Still, Lo Manto grew comfortable with the arrangement and looked forward to placing the bet each morning, making the corner of East

238th Street and White Plains Road his first stop on his way to school. He liked Blind Moe and learned to ignore the growling and barking of the various dogs by his side.

One spring morning, Lo Manto, then just approaching his twelfth birthday, placed his bet and had just about turned the corner, heading toward his first class of the day, when Blind Moe spoke to him for only the second time. "You like coffee?" he asked the boy.

Lo Manto turned and faced Blind Moe. "Yes," he said.

"Keep the dollar then," Blind Moe said. "And tomorrow come back with two cups. One for me, one for you. I like mine with lots of milk and four sugars. You can take yours any way you please. And that's only if you got the time and are willing."

"I'll pick them up on my way," Lo Manto said. "You want me to get something for the dog, too?"

"He don't need nothing to get him started in the morning," Blind Moe said. "Other than a bowl of water and some biscuits and he's got himself plenty of both. You and me are the ones that could use the kick."

The next morning, Lo Manto left the apartment fifteen minutes earlier than usual, stopped at Dick's Deli, bought two containers of coffee, and walked them the two blocks over to Blind Moe's corner spot. The containers burned his hands as he walked. He stood in front of Blind Moe, the unleashed bulldog lapping up cold water from a large blue bowl to his right, and waited for the numbers boss to acknowledge his presence. "Am I supposed to guess which one has the sugar in it?" Blind Moe finally asked. "Or is staying quiet just your cute little way of telling me there ain't no difference between the two cups?"

"This one's yours," Lo Manto said, holding up the container in his right hand. "I grabbed a few extra sugars in case you wanted more than what's already in there."

Blind Moe took the hot cup, put it to his lips, and finished off half the coffee with one long swallow. "In my book, a good cup of fresh, sweet coffee runs a tight second to being with a beautiful woman," he said, staring down at Lo Manto, his eyes hidden by a thin pair of wraparound sunglasses. "My guess is you're still a baby when it comes to that end of the pool, so you're just going to have to take it on my say-so."

Lo Manto sipped his coffee slowly and smiled. There was an empty wooden crate up on its side, nestled between Blind Moe and the dark brown bulldog. "Okay with you if I sit down?" he asked.

"Fine by me if it's fine by Little Moe," Blind Moe said. "Just don't want to hear any lip if you start to run late for school. I'm already where I'm supposed to be. But you got an empty classroom waiting on your end, with one of them nuns standing up against the board."

"They're not as tough as they want us to think they are," Lo Manto said, sitting down, the dog eyeing him with suspicion. "They talk it, but you can see in their eyes they don't mean any of it."

"Things have changed then since I had them in school," Blind Moe said. "Back then, they were some scary chicks buried under those starched white uniforms. I know men that did a long stretch of hard time that didn't come off as tough as any one of those nuns."

"I didn't know you went to Catholic school," Lo Manto said, not bothering to hide the surprise in his voice.

"What, you think I was born on this corner?" Blind Moe asked. "I put my years in, like you doing now. Except they jammed me into a special school, a lot different than where you go. A place for kids who can't learn what they can't see."

"What did they teach you?" Lo Manto asked.

"The ladies preached the truth," Blind Moe said. "They drummed it home. They said not to expect anything from anybody because I was blind except for pity and that shit don't pay any rent. They told me to use what I had and not piss and moan about what I didn't. They couldn't teach me how to see, so they taught me how to hear. And that lesson has given me a lot of frequent flyer miles."

Blind Moe Ravini could hear it all. He used the handicap he was born with to help strengthen his other key senses. While others talked, Ravini listened and, through the years, that one fact helped build his power base. Strangers, friends, and foes all felt they could talk in front of Blind Moe, confide in him, seek advice from the man who seldom spoke. He was the ears of the East

Bronx, keyed in on every deal and scam even before it went down. He didn't need his eyes to tell him who the primary players were, along which lines criminal affiliations were divided, and who among the street dealers and climbers were living under the Rossi scope. He gathered all the information and stored it, building a mental database of detail, logging all the comings and goings, blessed with the ability to do business and operate without interference by simply standing still and taking bets on an isolated corner of the East Bronx.

Lo Manto knocked on a heavy wooden door, turned the knob, and walked in, Jennifer close behind. The corridor was blanketed in darkness and he could hear the hard scuffle and scrape from the paws of a large dog running toward them. Jennifer instinctively reached for her gun. Lo Manto tore open the bag of dog biscuits and slid two into his right hand. He waited until the bulldog was close enough for him to hear the growl coming from deep within his chest. *"Sono io,"* Lo Manto said to the approaching dog, knowing that Ravini had trained them all to respond only to Italian commands. *"Fa il bravo e sietate."*

The bulldog slid to a halt and sat on his rear haunches. Lo Manto felt for a small coffee table and clicked on an ornate lamp. He looked and saw a large bulldog, wet tongue hanging off to the side of his thick jowls, sitting and patiently waiting for his treat. He moved toward the dog and put out his right hand. The dog lapped the two biscuits from his palm and crouched down to enjoy his special surprise. "You learned enough to make it past a dumb dog," Blind Moe said. "But what makes you think you got the smarts to get past me?"

Lo Manto walked over to Blind Moe, standing in the doorway between the foyer and his office. He was much older now than when they had first met, his short Afro tinged with patches of gray, his beard streaked with white. He still had the wraparound shades but maneuvered around the office without the need of a cane. "I figure you'd just be happy to hear my voice," Lo Manto said, reaching out a hand and resting it gently on Blind Moe's shoulder. "That would be enough to get me in."

"Cut the kiss-ass," Blind Moe said, "and tell me about the woman."

Lo Manto glanced over at Jennifer and motioned her closer. "She's a cop," he said to Blind Moe. "NYPD asked her to keep tabs on me. See that I don't get into any kind of trouble."

"I already figured that on my own," Blind Moe said. "Didn't think you'd come all the way down to my neck just to show a girl a blind man's office. That ruled out a date from the get-go. And the only women around you are either ducking bullets or aiming them. Based on the lack of any perfume, I bet she fell on the side of the badge."

"I would have cracked open the Chanel if only I knew," Jennifer said. "A girl needs some heads-up time. But I'm stuck on short-notice detail."

Blind Moe smiled. "She's got some smoke to her," he said to Lo Manto. "I like that. It'll do you some good to get a whiff of that. Might help to keep you nailed in your place."

"You got some time for me?" Lo Manto asked.

"You came in with a beautiful woman and a pocket full of dog treats," Blind Moe said. "That's more than good to get you both a cup of coffee and fifteen minutes of my time. That enough to hold you?"

"Depends on what you have to go with the coffee," Lo Manto said, following Blind Moe into his office, watching as the old man clicked on an overhead light as he moved through a large space cluttered with cabinets, old photos resting against the sides of gray walls, bookshelves filled with jazz and blues LPs, all lined up in alphabetical order. Two floor-to-ceiling windows dominated the center of the room, offering a full view of the wide expanse of Lenox Avenue.

"I could have shot the two of you for breaking and entering," Blind Moe said, walking to a small corner of the office where a kitchenette was set up, "and would have walked away clean as a just-washed baby. Now I'm supposed to come out with a platter of appetizers."

"I wasn't asking for me," Lo Manto said, sitting in a thick mahogany chair across from Blind Moe's desk. "But we do have a guest. Thought it would be nice to offer her a little something to munch on."

"She wants something she can ask," Blind Moe said. "I ain't ever known a cop to be shy. Or a woman for that

372

matter. And she covers both them bases."

"I'm good with just the coffee," Jennifer said. "I don't need anything else."

"Good," Blind Moe said, his back to both of them, pouring out three large cups of coffee. "Then there'll only be two of us wishing we had something to eat."

He put milk and sugar in each cup, not bothering to ask how either cop preferred to drink it. He turned around and walked the two cups toward them, vibrantly aware of how soft Jennifer's skin felt as it brushed against the side of his hand. He walked back to the kitchenette, picked up the third cup, walked to his large desk and sat down in the thick black leather rocking chair, cradled in the middle of the well. He pressed a button next to the old rotary phone and soon the sounds of John Coltrane filled the room. "Okay," he said, sitting back, "let's get to it. What is it you need?"

"I want to know what you heard about a call out to set up a high-end shooting for hire," Lo Manto said. "Supposed to go down sometime in the next few days. By the weekend, maybe early into the new week, but no later."

"Help me with the target," Blind Moe said. "What poor fool are the shooters looking to bury?"

"Me," Lo Manto said.

Felipe sat back in his wooden seat, front row of the loge overlooking first base, waiting for the start of the game between the Mets and the Braves. His right hand was in a tight white bandage taped across his palm, five stitches needed to seal the wound inflicted by Charlie Sunshine's blade. Felipe loved both baseball and the Mets and had been thrilled when Lo Manto came across with the two tickets, plus enough money to cover a visit to the Diamond Club, but still played it close and tried not to appear too eager. "This is a lot of money to be shelling out," he'd said to the detective. "And I didn't do anything to earn this."

"Don't worry," Lo Manto told him. "None of it is coming out of my pocket. The seats belong to the captain and he can't make the game and didn't want them to go to waste. I promised him I'd find them a home."

"No strings?" Felipe asked. He had known Lo Manto for only a few days, but had him pegged well enough to know there was always some plan brewing with every action he took, even one as simple as a night at a ballpark. "I can go and not have to worry about anything or scope anybody out?"

"I want you to sit back and enjoy the game," Lo Manto said, handing over the tickets and the Club pass. "Have as many hot dogs and peanuts as your stomach can handle. And pay for what you eat. You have enough money in your pockets. There's no call to lift anything from anybody."

"There's two tickets here," Felipe said. "You going to come with me?"

"I've got a meeting I can't miss," Lo Manto said. "But

a baseball game can run forever, especially with a team like the Mets. If I get a chance, I might stop by and grab a few innings."

"So I go in alone?" Felipe asked, sensing that something was in play. "Do nothing but root root root for the home team?"

"Just you and about thirty thousand die-hard fans," Lo Manto said. "And one guy who won't care who wins or loses. He'll just be there with his eye on you. At some point, figure around the fourth, maybe fifth inning, he'll come down and grab the empty seat next to you."

"I knew it sounded too good," Felipe said. "There's a catch to every free ride."

"He's going to stay for no more than an hour," Lo Manto said. "When he's decided he's had enough of the hits, runs, and errors, he'll get up, throw a smile your way, and head for the exits. He'll leave behind a Mets warmup jacket and a yellow envelope shoved inside one of the sleeves. The jacket's yours to keep. The envelope has to get to me."

"It sounds way too simple," Felipe said. "What if it doesn't go down the way you mapped it out?"

"You worry about watching the Mets," Lo Manto said. "Let me worry about watching your back."

The score was tied 1–1 going into the bottom half of the fourth inning. Felipe had his feet resting flat against the blue iron rail, Mets cap on his head tilted forward. He was on his second Cracker Jack box and had already

seen Mike Piazza take a hanging curveball deep. Kevin
Millwood was on the mound for the Braves, peering in
to the catcher for the sign, looking to jam up the Mets
leadoff hitter, Jose Reyes. Felipe leaned forward, hands
wrapped around his knees, and focused on the action
below. The first pitch was fouled off down into the left
field corner as the crowd began chanting for a hit. The
boy turned away from the game and looked up at the
tall, beefy man as he slowly made his way down the thick
cement steps and sat in the open seat. On the next pitch,
Reyes lashed a sharp single to center field and glided
down toward first base. "Looks like I got here just in
time," the man said as he snapped open a bag of peanuts
and placed a large container of beer by his feet. "Maybe
even get to see them score a few runs."

"That might be tough," Felipe said. "Both pitchers
are on the mark, tossing nothing but strikes for the most
part. Only hits have been on mistake pitches."

"You sound like you know the game pretty well," the
man said, offering Felipe some peanuts. "You play for
your school team?"

"I'm in a league with some of my friends," Felipe said.
"Nothing too organized. Just some pickup games when
we got enough of us to play a full nine."

"What position?"

"That depends on what time I get there," Felipe said.
"If I'm early, I get the pick of what I want and that's to
pitch. If I'm late, they usually toss me behind the plate
and keep me there till the end."

The man sat back, the ground around his feet soon crowded with empty peanut shells, and focused on the game for a few batters. Felipe glanced at his hands, thick-skinned and scarred, a large, oval-shaped ring wedged onto his right pinky. They were the hands of a hitter, someone that would be comfortable in a brawl, content to let his skill and his zest for punishment decide the night's outcome. His clothes were tailored and expensive, a sharp contrast to the man's imposing physical presence. The overhead lights highlighted the white in his thick mound of hair and, when he turned to look at Felipe, the boy could see the ragged ends of thin scars that dotted the skin around his dark eyes. "You're a new face to me," he said to Felipe. "How long have you and the cop been friends?"

"Long enough for me to be here with you," Felipe said, still not sure on what side of Lo Manto's fence the man next to him fell.

"Relax, little man," he said. "Me and you are on the same team with this one. If you got any worries, don't let them come from my end. Me and your cop pal go back decades, not days."

"I figure you for a friend," Felipe said. "I don't think he'd put me next to you if it was the other way. Still, it's always better to go in the water one step at a time."

"I don't blame you there," the man said. "It's worth the dough you pay to be careful. But for now, there's nothing for us to do but kick back and watch the game. In a bit, I'll get up and hit the head. When I come back,

I'll have a few things with me. I'll leave them on the chair and be on my way. With any luck, that's about as exciting as our night together is gonna get."

Felipe nodded and smiled. "You throw a Mets win into that mix and I'll sleep happy tonight."

Tony Collins and Rock Pullman, two Camorra gunmen, waited in the walkway leading to section 421A, watching Frank Silvestri talking to the Hispanic kid next to him as if he didn't have any cares. They were assigned to ride tail on Silvestri, check on his moves and motives, and take him only if and when an opening allowed them to make a clean break. The word down from their boss was that it would score them higher points with the don they had never met if they could come back with some positive information that would pin a traitor tag on Silvestri. They had been on him for two days, but so far had detected nothing that would give off any such indication.

"You sure you heard right?" Collins asked. He was in his mid-thirties, an Italian by birth who had been adopted and then abandoned by the elderly couple who found the troubled child too difficult a burden to carry. He was raised in the States by a Camorra crew boss who used the boy's taste for violence to the advantage of the family. "This guy's doing a flip on the crew?"

"That's the impression I was given," Pullman said with a slight stutter. He was younger, stronger, and much more dangerous than his partner, quick to flare and even quicker to draw a gun and empty the barrel. He had been in the business less than three years, after he had bailed Collins out of a setup in a downtown dance club. The move, made more out of instinct than any sense of honor, resulted in the shooting death of two low-level drug dealers and a high five-figure offer to follow Camorra instructions. So long as those instructions involved someone taking a bullet, Rock Pullman was a happy man.

"So, how do you explain him going to a ball game with a spic from the Bronx?" Collins asked, ignoring the screams of the crowd for a Mets rally.

"It's not my job to explain where this old sandhog goes," Pullman said with a shrug. "We just need to figure out his game plan. This thing with him and the kid might just be a night at a ballpark. If so, we waste a few hours, nothing more."

"That were so, he would have come with the kid," Collins said. "Not just show up four innings into the game. Ain't like he's coming from a job or anything. The guy was in a bar up until he got in his car and hit the highway."

"Maybe the kid's a safe way to either make a drop or a pickup," Pullman said. "Of what is what I can't figure."

"Whatever it is, it's something," Collins said. "None of it, the ballpark, him with the kid, don't feel right to me."

"You ask me, we waste this old fuck right here,

tonight," Pullman said. "We'll never get a better setup than what's in front of us now. Everybody, left and right, up and down the entire ballpark, will do nothing but panic. We make the hit and then just walk out, like nothing happened. We do that and we score points in a big way and maybe finally get noticed for the work we do."

"They wanted us to pop him, they would have made it clear," Collins said. "But if they said a word about it, they didn't spread it out my way."

"This guy's going to take some heavy slugs," Pullman said. "We wouldn't be on his tail if it wasn't so. It's just down to a question of who and when. Let's make it tonight."

"And what happens if that's the wrong move for us to make?" Collins asked. He stopped a beer vendor and overpaid for two large containers that seemed to be all foam and no brew. "Which parts of the city you want your bones buried in?"

"This guy was a made crew boss long before you and me were born," Pullman said, reaching for one of the containers. "Taking out a somebody like him is how reputations are made. And no matter what else happens, bringing him down and dealing with all the shit that might follow is a whole lot better way to go than being sent out as errand boys."

Collins drank his beer, looked out at the vast ballpark, the sounds of the hometown crowd ringing in his ears, and weighed his options. He knew the wiser move was to do as they were told, follow Silvestri, note his contacts and venues, and report back. The riskier call was to do what had not been asked, bring down a Camorra boss they already suspected of being on the endangered list. Collins realized such a move would be seen as either forceful and brilliant or reckless and foolish and it was now on his shoulders to decide which way to go. He downed the last of his beer and tossed the empty container to the hard ground at his feet.

"Let's waste this old fuck."

Silvestri wiped shell dust from his black button-down shirt and jacket and ran a hand across the front of his mouth. He looked over at Felipe, the boy totally engrossed in the give and get of a tie ball game. He envied the kid his youth and his freedom, his ability to get lost in something as mundane as baseball, millions of miles removed from the worries of the criminal life. He had heard enough about Felipe to know the boy had a firm handle on most of what came his way, had been steeled against the hard rules of daily life, and had learned to disguise his fears. He knew how to handle trouble and had learned to think on his feet and let the moment dictate his motions. Frank Silvestri looked at Felipe and saw the same fierce gaze that he saw in Lo Manto when the cop was that age. It was a look that signaled both determination and an unwillingness to cave in to any danger tossed in his path. It was a look that grew out of the harsh lessons of street life and the pain of personal loss. And now it was time to put all those lessons to good use.

"I was supposed to hand you an envelope wrapped in a Mets jacket," Silvestri told Felipe, both standing now during the seventh-inning stretch. "You're going to have to settle for just the envelope. I don't have the time to get you the jacket. I have to make my move before then."

Felipe looked at Silvestri and then at the faces that stood gathered around their section. They were either men in jackets and ties rushing to a game after a long day at a crazed office or fathers with their sons, both wearing gloves and hats, eager for a foul ball to come their way. The rest were senior citizens, grateful for a night away from the lonely sounds of an empty apartment. None of them looked like shooters out for a kill.

"You need me to come with you?" Felipe asked. "Maybe I could help."

Silvestri shook his head and followed it with a chuckle. "Lo Manto said you had the cubes," he told the boy. "I appreciate it, but the day comes I can't handle two would-bes, then they earned the right to put me down."

"They followed you into the game?" Felipe asked.

"I didn't see them at first," Silvestri said. "Caught a glimpse when that little guy from short hit a home run. They're down to my left, waiting in the walkway."

"What do you want me to do?" Felipe asked. He

watched as Silvestri pulled a long yellow envelope from deep inside his jacket pocket.

"Lo Manto needs to see this," he told the boy, and handed him the envelope. "Make sure that he does."

"What about you?" Felipe asked, watching as Silvestri buttoned his jacket and began a slow walk up the concrete steps. "What are you going to do?"

Frank Silvestri turned back to Felipe and gave the boy a wink and a smile. "What I was born to do," he said.

Silvestri sidestepped a young couple holding hands, the girl's head at rest on her boyfriend's chest, both holding a beer, alone in a crowd of thirty thousand. He was moving to his right, heading toward home plate, looking to get out of the stadium and into the parking lot, where the darkness and the rows of cars played more to his hand. He didn't need to turn around to know the two ghosts were on his tail, following him as close as they could, still deciding when to make their move. Even if they succeeded in putting him down and ending his venerable Camorra run, Silvestri knew they would not last long in the dark life.

Silvestri walked down a garbage-littered ramp, heading for the Gate A exit. He moved slowly, looking to anticipate what lay ahead, the options that made the most sense. Even though he had been at this dance so many times across so many years, the adrenaline rush still felt fresh, his body coiled but relaxed, ready to pounce in any direction, his mind cleared of all clutter, free only to thoughts of a kill. Silvestri had been a crime boss for more years than he could count, and normally such a time away from the down and nasty would work to weaken his actions. But at heart, he was a street soldier, his instincts better suited to a fight in an empty parking lot than to the walls of a sterile conference room.

Silvestri was walking down the center aisle of parking area A2 when the first bullet zipped past him and shattered the windshield of a black Ford Explorer. He pulled a .38 from his hip holster and rolled to the ground with the agility of a man half his age. He came up on one knee, his gun hand poised over the hood of a steel gray Honda Accord, staring out into the neon darkness, listening for the slightest sound that would tip off the location of the shooters. He controlled his breathing, the noise from the ballpark reduced to background, waiting for the one small mistake that would dictate the flight of his first bullet.

The sneaker skid came to his left, beside a battered light pole, between a blue van and a dented station wagon. He turned his hand, held his gaze steady, and fired off two rounds, then waited for the grunt that soon followed. Silvestri leaned against the side of the Honda and rested his head on the tin door, his eyes closed, as relaxed and at ease as if he were on a family picnic. This was the only way he could imagine to face death. He figured the second shooter to be crouched down somewhere, nervous, confused as to what his next move should be. It was the advantage of age over inexperience, and Frank Silvestri was going to play that hand straight through to the end.

He opened his eyes when he felt the hard end of the nine-millimeter press against his right temple.

"You should have waited until we were both dead before you go off and take a break," Rock Pullman said. He was leaning down, body reeking of cold sweat and stale beer, breathing heavy, right leg twitching beyond his control. "I guess that sort of shit happens when you get to be as gray in the beard as you."

"What do you and your bleeding friend over there expect to pick up by doing this?" Silvestri asked. "It's not that I really give a fuck, just curious is all."

"You know how it plays," Pullman said. "We take out a top player like you, we score a few points. You score points, they give you more time in the game. Before you know it, you're the one sitting on top snapping out the orders."

Silvestri laughed and rested a hand across his left knee. "You can kill me," he said, "and you can go out and then kill ten more just like me. Even twenty. Won't mean shit. The closest a low-end skel like you is ever going to come to a boss is if one decides to pay his respects at your wake. Other than that, the pope has a better shot at becoming a made boss than you."

"Maybe that's true," Pullman said. "I guess I'll find out soon enough. But at least I had the goods to take you out of service."

385

"Somebody had to," Frank Silvestri said.

He shifted his head and gazed up at an ocean blue sky crammed with stars. Behind him a loud roar came out of the park, echoing off the empty cars and into the darkness of the Queens night. "Sounds like they won," he said. "It's good to go out with a win."

Rock Pullman planted his feet and fired three bullets into Frank Silvestri's head, the first close-contact hit killing the career criminal in an instant. Pullman took a step back and watched as the old man's body jolted to the right, his face landing against a front tire. He stepped over Silvestri's body, jammed his hot gun back into the rear of his dirty brown jeans, and ran across the parking lot. He found Tony Collins leaning on the front bumper of a late-model sedan, blood running down the side of one leg. "You good enough to walk to the car?" Pullman asked, gazing down at the wound. "I can give you a hand, you need it."

"How far away you figure the car is?" Collins asked, his face lit with sweat.

"Not much more than a mile," Pullman said. "If we go out through the open gate down this side and jump the divider and head toward the Boulevard it might save us some time and you a little bit of pain."

"Let's get it done, then," Collins said. "The sooner we get out of here, the sooner I can get this leg looked after. Maybe even find a doctor willing to yank the bullet out."

"I know a guy runs a clinic in Jamaica," Pullman said. "I got his card somewhere on me. I'll throw him a call and see if he'll help bail us."

"He a real doctor?" Collins asked, starting to limp alongside Pullman, both heading for the open gate leading out toward Grand Central Parkway. "Or one of those Indian guys with a matchbook degree?"

"Does it really matter where the fuck he went to school?" Pullman asked, heavy anger in his voice. "All that counts is that he takes the freaking bullet out."

They moved past the row of darkened cars, overhead lights casting a circular glow on their path, the stadium behind them shining and rocking as if it fell from the sky. With each tender step, Collins left behind a dotted blood trail, the sharp pain from the bullet that penetrated his shin running up his leg and causing his body to shiver despite the heavy heat of the night. Pullman dragged him along, less out of friendship and more with an urgency spun from the knowledge that someone who left the game early was bound to have heard the shots and alerted stadium security.

They were about fifty feet from the chain-link fence, its twin gates open wide, when they spotted the un-marked car.

It was parked parallel to the road, the figure of a man standing alongside the front end of the vehicle. "Who the hell is that?" Collins asked, squinting his eyes to get a better look.

"Too early for the cops," Pullman said. "They don't show until the crowds start to build. And they're usually in black-and-whites. Could just be a guy waiting for one of his friends. We'll know as much as we need to know when we get closer."

"Keep your gun handy, just in case," Collins said. "We took our one big chance tonight by whacking a made guy. Now's not the time for us to go and get careless."

"Maybe we should take him anyway, no matter why he's here," Pullman said. "Whether bystander or trouble, we drop him, we take his car, and motor our ass right out the gate."

"We already got us a car," Collins said, his voice a low rasp, his face pasty white. "All we need to do is get to it."

"And at the rate you're moving, that could be by tomorrow's first pitch," Pullman said. "By the time we get to it, who the hell knows how many cops will be here. And none of them need to be Batman and Robin to follow that blood trail you're leaving behind."

"Us killing that old-timer might go over good with the bosses," Collins said. "We don't know for sure, but at least there's a chance. This other guy you want to drop turns out to be a civilian, they'll only see it as trouble, and that won't be good for either one of us."

"Then keep your trap shut and only cop to the one drop that works in our favor," Pullman said. "Either that or stand here and bleed to death. Your life, your call."

They were about twenty feet from the man and could start to make out his features. He was standing on the far side of his car, his hands on the roof, down flat, eyes glaring in their direction. He hadn't moved since they first made the spot. "We could use some help here," Pullman shouted out to the man. "You got a minute? My friend tripped down one of the escalators and hurt his leg. It's bleeding pretty bad. I think he's going to need a few stitches."

"There's a first-aid center in the ballpark," Lo Manto said. "Could have saved your friend a couple of pints of blood by making that your first stop."

"We didn't even think of that," Collins said, his voice cracking in the night. "I just thought I could make it to the car and maybe get to a hospital. It didn't feel as bad when it happened as it does now."

"I've never bandaged a scrape before," Lo Manto said. "At least nothing as bad as what it looks like you have. I did take a couple of bullets out of a few people, though. In some ways that's much easier to do."

"Not as easy as putting one in," Pullman said.

"That all depends on how good you are," Lo Manto said. "My guess is you got enough to take out an old man with too much time on his meter. But anything better than that and you're going to get wasted."

"You saying that's you?" Pullman asked.

"I'm saying you got a chance to find out," Lo Manto said.

Rock Pullman yanked the nine-millimeter from the back of his waistband and pointed it at Lo Manto. Collins held a .38 in his right hand, the pain in his leg causing the fingers to twitch. "You can just walk away,"

Pullman told Lo Manto. "All we want is the car. You can get to keep your life, you do it this way."

"I live for my car," Lo Manto said.

Pullman fired two rounds and Collins managed to get off a single shot. Lo Manto ducked behind his sedan and disappeared. There was silence for several long seconds, the two gunmen peering into the semidarkness, trying to get a gauge on their target. "Maybe the shots scared him off," Collins said. "Could have made off into that grass field there and be on the main drag by now."

"He didn't seem the type that scared easy," Pullman said. "It sounded like he wanted a fight."

Collins peered over at the car, saw exhaust fumes coming out of the muffler, engine still in idle. "That car's just crying to be taken," he said. "We can stand here and wait out this asshole. Or we can take his car and split."

"You move for the driver's side," Pullman said, looking behind him and at his sides. "I'll stay back and give you cover. Any noise you hear not coming from me, shoot at it and then worry about what it was later."

The large round rock came hurtling from the left side of the parking area and landed with a muffled thud against the back of Tony Collins. The force of the blow combined with the surprise sent the gunman to his knees, the .38 in his hands falling to the ground next to the car's right front tire. Pullman swerved instinctively toward the direction from which he thought the rock was thrown and fired off two rounds, both shots echoing in the space close to the highway. Behind them the crowd was beginning to trickle out of the stadium and head toward the gates. Squad cars were starting to roam down the aisles, ready to monitor the flow of outgoing traffic. "Forget about the car," Pullman said. "We just gotta get the fuck out of here. We're going to be surrounded in two or three minutes."

"I can't walk," Collins stammered, still on his knees and sounding dazed. "My leg is bleeding pretty bad. I won't be able to make it out any way other than by car."

Pullman looked down at his fallen friend. He saw the whirling lights heading toward him and heard a woman's scream, close to where he had left Silvestri's body. "Then forget about you, too," he told Collins, turning to sprint out of the stadium and down a darkened street leading toward an access road.

Lo Manto came from behind a parked black van, gun in his right hand. He ran up behind Collins, stopped, waited for the wounded man to look at him and then coldcocked him with the butt end of his pistol. Collins fell over backwards, his head hitting the pavement with a soft pop. Lo Manto picked up the chase, running full out for the side road, leaving the wounded shooter behind for the arriving cops to handle. He hurdled the grass embankment and ran full bore down the middle of the road, ignoring the oncoming traffic and the blaring horns. He couldn't see the man he was chasing but could hear the echoes of his footsteps on the pavement, figuring him to be no more than two hundred yards ahead, off to his left, heading toward Northern Boulevard.

Lo Manto picked up his pace, jumped over a fallen wooden police barricade, and crossed the divider leading to the main drag just outside the confines of the stadium. The streets now were teeming with men, women, and children, all happy and weary and eager to get home after a late-night extra-inning game. Lo Manto dodged and scurried past the slow-moving clusters, closing in on the tiring Pullman, who was out of shape and slowed by a two-pack-a-day cigarette habit. Lo Manto ran against a red light and a long line of oncoming traffic and stopped at a corner near the elevated subway station, his gun in his right hand. Pullman, his lungs burning and his face beet red from the long chase, stood across from him, his back to the glass panel of a Duane Reade drugstore. He had the nine-millimeter at his side. "Pick out anybody you want," he shouted at Lo Manto. "And that's who gets the next bullet. You don't let me leave here— somebody that shouldn't is going to die."

"You killed my friend tonight," Lo Manto said. "He shouldn't have died. At least not at your hand."

"And now a stranger's going to take it in the head," Pullman said. "Unless you step back and away."

"Why kill a stranger for all the wrong reasons," Lo Manto said, taking two small steps forward, "when you can kill me for all the right reasons?"

A handful of pedestrians had slowed their steps when they spotted both Pullman and Lo Manto with their guns drawn, and now shielded themselves behind a newsstand. "I'm going to leave that call up to you, cop,"

Pullman said. "If you back off, let me go my way, then nobody here has to die. Not even you."

Police sirens blared behind them and three squad cars came to a screeching halt on opposite ends of the corner. The uniformed officers swung their doors open and jumped out of their black-and-whites, weapons drawn, each in a shooting position, poised to fire at either Pullman or Lo Manto.

"You might fly that plan of yours by me," Lo Manto told Pullman. "But I don't think it's going to sit too well with the crew behind us. They look as serious as a car wreck."

"Look ready to drop you just as easily as they would me," Pullman said. "They don't seem too sure which one of us is the cop and which one isn't. I could let that play out to my benefit."

"It's not something I would bet my life on," Lo Manto said.

The double door to the drugstore swung open and an elderly couple stepped out, the man bracing his stooped shoulders against the steel bar, waiting patiently for his wife, who clutched a plastic shopping bag in her right hand. Pullman turned his gaze away from Lo Manto and toward the old man and woman. He lowered his gun and took three steps in their direction.

Lo Manto ignored the police weapons drawn against his back, shoved his gun into the side pocket of his thin leather jacket, and ran full out at Pullman. He caught the shooter at mid-waist, the force of the hit causing

393

them both to land hard on the glass, cracks running along the center like arteries down an arm. Pullman's gun fell out of his hand, skidding along the chipped concrete street. Lo Manto lowered Pullman's dark brown corduroy jacket across his shoulders, locking his arms into place. He then leaned back and landed two hard punches flush against the gunman's face, raising instant welts along his right eye and cheek.

Pullman struggled to free himself from the grip of his jacket and the force of Lo Manto's shoulders pressed against his upper body. But Lo Manto was now a mad bull unleashed, the fury of his anger over the death of Silvestri beyond anyone's control. He had grown to respect and love Frank Silvestri, a brutal man who had known and helped him since his earliest days, a stone killer who had shown the fatherless boy nothing but acts of kindness. Silvestri was his main source inside the Rossi crime family, but he acted not out of disloyalty to his crew, but out of friendship for a young cop. He never gave Lo Manto too much information, forcing the detective to plot his moves based on the small nuggets tossed his way. They seldom spoke, knowing that to do so might prove fatal to both. They also made it a point never to be seen in public together. They communicated through third-party link-ups or through coded messages strategically placed in newspapers or on clear-channel cell phones. It was a relationship that spanned more than thirty years, and both men knew it was inevitable that one day it would come to an end. But neither Lo Manto nor Silvestri, the cop and the crook, would have placed much stock in it coming down at the hands of a crawler like Rock Pullman.

Lo Manto slammed his right knee into the center of Pullman's stomach and stepped back as he heard the loud gasp. He reared back and sent a closed fist crashing onto the bridge of Pullman's nose, shattering muscle and tissue and sending a stream of blood in a circular pattern in the air. The uniformed officers had eased their way around the backs of their squad cars and were now within inches of the two men. Lo Manto was too laced with anger even to notice them. He stood there, in front of an all-night drugstore, and rained punishment on the man who had killed his friend.

Lo Manto was soaked through with sweat, leaning his damp head of hair against a pane of glass as he watched two uniformed officers hovering over Pullman's beaten body. Lo Manto's breath was coming out rushed, his chest muscles pounding, his heart racing, his knuckles swollen red and tinted with blood. One of the uniforms came over to him and stood by his side. The officer was in his late twenties, moving like a young Denzel Washington with a razor cut and arms thick enough to crush bone. "You on the job?" he asked. "Or just a part of the party mix?"

"I'm a cop," Lo Manto said through hard puffs of breath. "On special assignment. You can check with Captain Fernandez over at the Four-seven."

"I figure this guy you worked over is hooked up with

the other shooter, the one we found out cold in the stadium lot," the officer said. "And that links them to the guy with the three bullet holes in his head."

"Bag their biologicals," Lo Manto said, slowly easing his way into controlling the crime scene. "And run their guns for prints and a yellow, and the bullets through ballistics. This guy bleeding was the primary. The one by the car was his partner."

"We'll need you to come over to the house and fill out a DD-5," the officer said. "Make the bust official."

Lo Manto looked at the young man and stared at the name stenciled on his ID tag. "I don't want the bust, Officer Thompson," he said. "It's all yours. I'll give you a statement that will back up your heroic actions. It'll be on your captain's desk by morning."

"But the collar belongs to you, Detective," Officer Thompson said.

"Won't take you long to piece together what happened," Lo Manto said, pushing himself away from the drugstore window. "And what you can't get on your own you can pull out of the two losers in cuffs."

Lo Manto patted Officer Thompson on the shoulder and began a slow walk toward the elevated subway. "I can get one of the black-and-whites to give you a ride," the officer called out.

"I could use some time alone," Lo Manto said. "Clear my mind a little. It's been a long night with a few even longer ones ahead. You could do me one solid favor, though."

"Does it involve breaking the law?" Officer Thompson asked, wide smile spread across a handsome face.

"Not this time," Lo Manto said. "I hot-wired a car and used it to block off the parking lot entrance. Can you see it gets back to the guy who's still paying it off?"

"This someone you know or should I just go and check the registration in the glove compartment?" Officer Thompson asked, holding the smile.

"He's a friend," Lo Manto said, returning the grin and easing his way up the stairwell. "And I'm betting he likes me enough not to get completely pissed that I stole his car and had you return it."

"Share the name," Officer Thompson said.

"It's my captain," he said. "Frank Fernandez."

Lo Manto bounded up the steps, his energy returning as he disappeared into the dark void, looking to catch the number 7 express that was rumbling into the station.

21

Jennifer Fabini walked into the main foyer of the pristine brownstone and stood facing an oil portrait of a distinguished elderly man dressed in a stiff white shirt and hand-stitched dark blue jacket. The floors were sanded down to their original wood, shiny and bright in the early morning light. Large bay windows filled the space leading out to the street, the soundproof and shatter-resistant glass easily drowning out the traffic inching its way crosstown. There was a library off to her right, the thick wooden door to the room partially open, the bookshelves inside running floor-to-ceiling, each row packed with leather-bound classics printed in two languages. There were white marble steps to her left leading to the upper floors, the center of each thick step padded with an ornate Venetian rug. The entire place reeked of hidden power and cloistered riches, each nickel built on the strength of an illegal workforce.

The man came out of the small room next to the front door, walking with silent steps toward her. He was dressed in a light blue suit with a matching shirt and red tie, his loafers were spit-shined, and his manner was quiet and reserved. "Mr. Rossi asked that you wait for him in the library," the man said. She figured him to be no more than twenty and fresh out of school, his voice still giving a hint of its southern Italian origin. "And to see to it that you were comfortable."

He bowed slightly, turned, opened wide the door to the library, and gestured for Jennifer to precede him. The room, filled to the brim with close to a thousand books, had the smell of old pages and fresh polish. The leather furniture and antique lamps dotting every corner seemed dwarfed by the sheer majestic reach of the dark oak shelves that had been hand-carved in a small alley in the Spaccanapoli section of Naples. "May I get you something to drink?" the young man asked. "An iced tea or a hot coffee? Whatever it is that you prefer."

"An iced tea would be good," Jennifer said.

"Make that a pitcher, Mario, with extra ice," Pete Rossi said, standing with his hands in his pockets, leaning against the doorway and staring across the room at Jennifer.

Mario nodded at his boss and quietly walked out. Rossi waited until he was deep down the hall and on his way to the kitchen before entering the library and gently closing the door. "Find a chair that looks comfortable to you, Detective," he told her. "And I'll do the same."

"Have you read any of the books in this room?"

Jennifer asked, sitting in a deep red leather chair, its thick arms and width nearly swallowing her small body whole.

"About half," Rossi said. "And, if I live long enough, I will make my way through the other half. How about you? Have you read all the books in your library at home?"

"That wouldn't be hard," Jennifer said, trying to hide the fact that she felt ill at ease in the company of the Camorra don. "All I have are paperbacks. Thrillers and historical romances, mostly."

"In that case, feel free to choose any book that catches your eye," Rossi said. "Consider it a gift, from me to you."

A knock on the door got their attention and they waited in silence as Mario, holding a silver tray filled with two large glasses, a bowl of ice cubes, and a pitcher of cold tea mixed with slivers of lemon, walked in. He placed the tray on a small table and poured out two half glasses, filling the rest with spoonfuls of ice cubes. He handed a glass and a thick napkin to both Jennifer and Rossi, bowed, and headed back out of the room.

"I didn't come here to borrow a book," Jennifer said, resting the glass and the napkin on the floor by her feet.

"I figured as much," Rossi said. "What I haven't quite figured out as yet is why you are here and what you expect to leave with, other than me in handcuffs."

"That may happen some day," Jennifer said. "Just not today."

"Good to hear," Rossi said. "It's such a beautiful morning outside. I would hate to ruin it by having to spend the day in a holding cell."

"I need to talk to you about your family," Jennifer said. She was doing her best to hide the fact that she was as nervous as she had ever felt in someone else's presence. This was a long way removed from a buy-and-bust and bringing in two low-level dealers. And it wasn't as clear-cut as a shoot-out in a tenement stairwell, with one lucky bullet deciding the final outcome. This was a detective with a clean record sitting with the biggest mob boss in New York and asking for a favor that, if it was granted, could get both of them killed.

"What about my family?" Rossi said, sitting back in a leather rocking chair, studying his glass of iced tea cupped between both his hands.

"Look, it's not like me to beat around in circles," Jennifer said. "I have something to tell you. Maybe you know about it and maybe you don't. My guess is you know as much about this end as Lo Manto does and that's pretty much nothing at all."

Rossi stiffened at the mention of the detective's name, his eyes betraying both his concern and curiosity. "What kind of part's he play in this?" he asked. "Did Lo Manto ask you to set up this meeting?"

"He doesn't know I'm here," Jennifer said. "If he did, I think he'd take a shot at me quicker than even you would."

"I'm not in the practice of taking shots at anyone,"

401

Rossi said, slowly regaining the control he always kept on his emotions. "And if I were, it wouldn't be at women. Not even a policewoman partnered with a blood enemy."

"What do you know about your mother?" Jennifer asked, jumping into the heavy flames with both boots, deciding that there was no tactful way to broach the subject. She stared over at Rossi and noticed the resemblance to Lo Manto. They both had the same hard and handsome features, their hair thick, their eyes as dark as a rainy night. Some of it could be written off as southern Italian bloodlines. But there was something else that tipped it toward the tale told to her by the old woman, Assunta Conte. It was the way Rossi read the moment and the motive. Both he and Lo Manto had that innate ability to anticipate what direction a conversation would take and what was really being said beneath the multiple layers of lies and distortions. They used an opponent's body language to help telegraph to them the truth of the situation, using the movements as if each was a road map into a person's very soul.

"You're the first cop to ever ask about my mother," Rossi said, resting the now empty glass on his desk. "And I hope the last."

"It's a first for me too, believe me," she said. "But I wouldn't be doing it if it weren't important."

"This can't be police business," Rossi said. "So, let's start by ruling that out. Which puts you into personal waters, and before I let you take a dive into that deep pool I need to hear a solid reason as to why you need to know."

"Why don't I tell you what I managed to dig up?" Jennifer suggested. She reached for her large black shoulder bag and pulled out a thick manila envelope. "You tell me what's true and what's not. And then we either go forward from there or stop it dead cold. I'll leave that totally up to you."

"Make it quick," Rossi instructed. "And even better, make it good."

Jennifer opened the folder and flipped aside a few pages, holding the last one in her right hand. "According to your birth certificate filed with the city of New York, you were born in a small clinic, in lower Manhattan, long since closed," she began. "You are the only son of Nicola Rossi. The slot next to your mother's name was left blank. I don't know what you were told the reason for that was, but I do know whatever you were told it wasn't the truth."

"And you know this how?" Rossi said. "Neighborhood gossip, maybe? Or did one of those Italian gasbags fill your head with ideas you know nothing about? My mother's name is not on my birth certificate because she abandoned me and my father as soon as she could get out of the hospital. Since she didn't want me as a son, my father figured we go all the way with it and not put her down as a mother."

"She didn't abandon you," Jennifer said. "At least not when your father said she did."

403

Rossi leaned forward, elbows on the edge of his desk, hands folded across his face. "Keep going, cop," he said, his voice hard, direct, laced with venom. "Finish what it was you came here to tell me."

Jennifer closed the folder and jammed it back in her handbag. She stood and walked over to the desk, standing close enough to Rossi to pick up the scent of the expensive cologne he had splashed on his face earlier that morning. She sensed that while her presence had piqued his anger, her words had aroused his curiosity. She wasn't exactly sure how much he knew or suspected about his mother, how much had simply been suppressed, and how much was buried long before he had any chance to discover the truth. And she had no way to gauge how he would react to what he was about to hear.

"Your mother was a brave woman," Jennifer said. "And a tough one. She had to be to go through with what she did and still be standing long after it was over. She had a husband, a decent man with a bad gambling habit. The kind of man your father made money from, taking everything he could, until there was nothing left to take. Or almost nothing."

"Did my father tell him to gamble away money he didn't have?" Rossi asked. "Or did this loser go and do all that on his own?"

"He laid down all his own bets," Jennifer said. "And your father built up the interest payments. The man paid off most of the time, usually late, but still working within the well of reason."

"Then the guy's lost any right to complain," Rossi said. "The easiest play to make for a man like him is to turn and walk away. He does that and nobody can touch him or his family. But they can't walk away. The action means more to them than what they got at home, and they'll give up anything and everything to keep placing the bet, dreaming for that one big score that is supposed to change it all. It's a score that never looks in their direction. Not in this life, anyway."

"At least until the day your father calls in the final tab," Jennifer said. "The man is given three choices. Pay the loans. Give up your life. Or give up your youngest son. My guess is that most men would choose either to pay off the money or take the bullet. It seems the easiest of the three ways out."

"Which way did our hero go?" Rossi asked, words dripping with disdain. He had been raised in an environment that looked down on weakness, despising the actions of those who allowed themselves to be vulnerable.

"We'll never know," Jennifer said. "He never got a chance to make his choice. Your mother made it in his place. She threw a fresh card on the deck, one that not even your father had considered."

"Which was what?"

"She offered to give him a son of his own," Jennifer said. "One they would have together. A son that bled Rossi blood, not the blood of a much weaker man."

"My father agree to this?" Rossi asked. His eyes

405

betrayed no emotion, his body as still as an ancient statue.

"Why wouldn't he?" Jennifer asked. "Why take a risk on some kid you know little about when you can raise one who carries your name and your genes? A son who would grow up one day and run the family business. Be as good a don, if not a better one, than he could ever be. A son of his own."

"Nice story, Detective," Rossi said, relaxing the muscles around his neck and shoulders and sitting back in his chair. "And I appreciate you taking time away from chasing down criminals to come here and entertain me. But we both have business that needs our full attention and I think it's time we got back to it."

"That woman was your mother," Jennifer said. She was braced for the reaction, not sure in what shape or form it would take, anger or denial, indifference or histrionics. If Rossi had anything of Lo Manto in his veins, she figured now would be the best time for it to come to the surface.

"I'm going to humor you for a few more minutes," Rossi said. "Let's just say, for argument's sake, this little tale of yours is true, and my father had a fling with some woman whose husband was buried in a financial hole. Let me take it one more step forward. Let's say I concede to you that this sad, pathetic woman could well have been my mother. Giving you all of that, handing it over to you without any questions attached, it still comes out to a big so-what. It means nothing to me and it doesn't touch me in any way."

"You're wrong on that count, Rossi," Jennifer said. She had one hand flat on his desk now, leaning forward, her blonde hair hanging low and partially obscuring the right side of her face. "It does mean something to you and it does touch you. Touch you in a way a man like you would never even dream was possible."

"Tell me how?" Rossi said. "Lay it all out for me. Once that part is history, I'll expect you to turn around and get the hell out of my house."

"Your mother had two sons," Jennifer said, staring down at Rossi as hard as she had at any criminal she had ever been up against. "The one with your father and another with her husband."

"Finish it," Rossi ordered.

"The one she had with her husband is Lo Manto," Jennifer said, silently shaking as she spoke the words. "The cop you want so much to see dead is your brother."

Pete Rossi pushed his chair back and stood. He walked over toward the bay windows and stared out at the passing traffic. He placed his hands inside his pants pockets and took in slow, controlled breaths. The cop who stood behind him had swung open a door he had long kept slammed shut and bolted. Even as a child, Rossi had never totally bought into the story of his mother abandoning both husband and son in search of a life with more meaning than the one she was destined to lead. Then, as an adult born and reared in the Camorra fashion, he found it even less likely to carry a candle close to the truth. He had long suspected he was the bastard son resulting from one of his father's many flings. Don Nicola Rossi was a stickler in all the ways of the Camorra save for one. He was weak and vulnerable when it came to women and seduced and conquered as many as crossed his path. He was a man who happily substituted passion for love, sex for romance, a quick dalliance for a long-term relationship. Rossi learned early on to bury any curiosity he might have had about his mother, content instead to accept the constructed story that had been placed in his path.

Rossi glanced down at an old man walking past his building, a small dog leading him on his leash. The man looked to be in his late seventies, long past the days when he had to heed a clock and a boss, yet he still dressed as if he were off for a day at the office. His suit was old but sturdy, his shoes worn but shined, his tie rigid and tight. The old man had lived long enough to know that appearances could often disguise foibles, serving as a mask for our true selves.

"What did you expect would happen once you told me?" Rossi asked Jennifer, his back still to her, the morning sun warming his face. "A family picnic, maybe? Or a cozy dinner between me and the cop to kick around some old memories? How is this information going to change anything that exists between me and Lo Manto?"

"I didn't know what your reaction would be," Jennifer said. "Tell you the truth, I can't imagine it's going to change anything at all between you and him. Maybe it's not supposed to. I don't know that part, either. I just figured it was time you heard the real story and I was the only one around willing to tell it."

"Does he know?" Rossi asked. "Did you share your dark little saga with him as well?"

"If he does, he didn't hear it from me," Jennifer said. "And for what it's worth, I don't think he has a clue."

"Odd, don't you think?" Rossi asked, turning now to face her. "The great detective unable to piece together the clues to his own story."

"Neither could the great don," Jennifer said. "So I'd go easy on giving out pats on the back."

"Then we all made a mistake, Detective," Rossi said, walking toward her. He placed a hand on her elbow and started to escort her out of the library and into the foyer. "This one sad perhaps, but acceptable. It's the next one that will determine the true direction of all our lives."

They stopped at the front door, Rossi waiting as Mario opened it, letting in a warm blast of air and heavy doses of sunshine. On the street, just to their left, two girls played a fast game of jump rope, their giggling filling the morning with happy sounds.

"What are you going to do now?" Jennifer asked.

"What I was meant to do," Pete Rossi said, the power of the gangster stitched across each word.

The four shooters sat in the back room of the small restaurant, each quietly finishing a large meal. Gaspaldi was at the head of the long table, sipping his third glass of red wine, staring at the men, running through their bloody résumés in his mind, content that he had finally found the right mix of hitters to take out a cop he so hated. He waited as a young, thin, and nervous waiter came through the thick red curtains separating the private dining area from the main part of the restaurant and jotted down mumbled coffee and dessert orders on a crumpled notepad.

"Hold on to that order for about twenty minutes," Gaspaldi told the waiter. "Give us a chance to digest our meal and catch up on old times."

The waiter nodded and walked silently out of the room. Gaspaldi reached down and pulled a thick folded spreadsheet from a briefcase by his feet, and brought it up to the table. "Clear some of this shit out of the way," he ordered the four men around him. "I want to go over this one final time."

"You're acting like a virgin on his wedding night with this job," the shooter sitting at Gaspaldi's right, Elmo Stalli, said. "We've all done this work for a long time and we've been good enough at it to stuff our safe deposit boxes with cash. And there's four of us aiming down at one cop. Where's all the worry come from?"

"Old age," Gaspaldi said. "Bad knees. A horrible marriage. A mother in the hospital. In other words, who gives a fuck where my worries come from? Why don't we just worry that I get the right bang for all those bucks that have been doled out like penny candy? And if that means we go over the plan a half-dozen more times before I call it a night, then that's what we'll do. Anybody not good to go with that?"

The four men each nodded as they poured themselves wine refills. They sat in stony silence as Gaspaldi opened the spreadsheet and rested it on the cleared table, careful not to get any smudges on the designs and street locations drawn across it. "Let's take it from the start," he said to them. "Who moves first and where?"

"I'm there," Carlo Bertz said. He was the youngest of the assassins gathered, a muscled British expatriate who had been working as a paid gunman for fifteen years and had notched twenty-seven murders. He had extensive military training, was an expert marksman with both a pistol and a high-powered rifle, and could take out a target as far as three hundred feet in the distance. "On the roof of the six-story building on the corner. I hold my shot, keep the target in my scope, and wait for him to be fully exposed."

"I fire first," John Rummy said. He was of German and Italian ancestry, a professional killer for thirty of his fifty-four years and a wounded veteran of four civil wars and three government uprisings. He used the bulk of his money and time to fund right-wing takeovers of shaky regimes throughout the world. He liked to mark his kill at close contact, not afraid to look in the eyes of the men he had been paid cash money to murder. "But I hit to stop not to drop, the wound not severe enough to bring him down. He'll give chase and I lead him out into the middle of the narrow street."

"Sounds good to me so far," Gaspaldi said. He always found professionals of any stripe to be pleasant company, none more so than hit men. They went about their work in a calm and direct manner, the business not a good haven for those who were quick to panic. They very often brought to the table an odd and sometimes exotic array of hobbies and were as curious about life as they were indifferent to death. "Mifo, it's your turn."

"I work the lead car, parked in the middle of the street, engine idle," Mifo said. He was a rare killer, a man who brought his targets down not with bullets but with the blunt and brutal force of an automobile. He was born somewhere in Southeast Asia and fell into his chosen profession quite by accident. He had been a teenager in love with fast cars and clean, power-fueled engines who harbored a dream of one day racing on the famed Formula One tracks that dotted most of Europe. He longed to drink from a champion's cup and wrap his arms around the ravishing beauties who often came with such victories. Instead, he was speeding along a highway in Poland, revving the engine on a Fiat 124 as fast as a meager four cylinders could take it, when he zoomed past an embankment and crashed head-on into a dazed young woman flagging down help in the evening mist, flares lit on her left and right, her stalled car parked and smoking in an off-lane one hundred yards to her back. The girl died on impact. Mifo, due in part to the half-empty bottle of Russian vodka lying on his front seat and the levels of alcohol in his bloodstream, ended up with a five-year vehicular manslaughter conviction and a new career path. "The shooter on the street leads him up my way. At two hundred and fifty feet, give or take, I shift gears and aim square for the cop. I hit him and keep moving, make a left on the corner, right at the next, one more quick left, and onto the highway leading out of the city."

"That just leaves you," Gaspaldi said, pointing at Stalli. "If you got your part down, then we can get that waiter back in here with our coffee and pastries."

"I wait inside the hallway at 238 East 234th Street," Stalli said. He was a known face to Gaspaldi, a Camorra shooter who began picking off targets in the woods outside Naples as a child, starting with rabbits and pigeons and graduating to his first murder at seventeen. He got into an angry dispute with a local grocer over the price of three farm-fresh tomatoes and settled it with a hunting rifle rather than a conversation. The killing of a sixty-seven-year-old fruit vendor forced Stalli underground, and his escape was helped by several junior members of the Camorra, who were always on the lookout for a man quick to pull a gun and fire it. He ended up in a small town to the north, earning his keep by toiling as a busboy in a local restaurant. He spent his evenings in the quiet company of paid Camorra hitters, each imparting his wisdom and techniques to the willing young man. "If he's still moving and breathing after taking the street hit and the bump from the car, I make my move. I pump as many bullets his way as I can pack in my guns and pockets and then head for the subway ride downtown and out of the picture."

"And once the cop is down on the ground?" Gaspaldi said. "What happens to him at that point?"

"I pull on my high-power and put three garlic slugs in his upper torso, front or back, it makes no difference," Bertz said, lighting a French cigarette. "Anybody happens to be in the way, curious as to who went down or just looking to help, gets taken out just as fast. I then lock up my gear, jump down to the next roof, and get out as fast as I came in."

"Any other questions you want us to answer?" John Rummy asked, pushing aside his empty glass of wine.

"Just one more," Gaspaldi said, not bothering to hide his smile.

"What is it?" Elmo Stalli said.

"What kind of booze do you want to go along with that coffee?" he asked.

Lo Manto sat in the front pew of the empty church, facing the altar. The shadows of the lit votive candles bounced off the four walls around him, the faces of the silent saints staring down. He loved old churches and liked them even more when he had them all to himself. Here, he found a serenity that eluded him in all other areas of his life. He had served as an altar boy in this weathered old building, wearing the white cassock and dark surplice, working early afternoon masses, the ones that attracted the true believers. Most of the parishioners were elderly, often praying for the souls of loved ones long gone, themselves painfully approaching a funeral mass and the smoking of the incense.

For the briefest of moments, Lo Manto had toyed with a religious life. He was attracted to it not because of any specific calling or spiritual thoughts, but because he knew from the priests he had spent time with that they got both their first-rate education and extensive travels on the nickel of the Church. It was his best friend from school, Hank Somettri, who, at the age of fourteen, offered the sagest advice. "If it's free school and travel you're after, then join the army or the navy," Hank said. "At least that way, you can still get laid. But if it's something else you're after, then my thinking would be to get laid *before* the Roman collars get their hands on you."

"It was only a thought," Lo Manto said, a bit defensive. "It's not like I'm eager to spend my life in a monastery."

"Tell you the truth," Hank said. "Sometimes I think even living in a monastery would be better than staying in this place the rest of our lives. Be nice to get away from all the shit that goes on around here."

Lo Manto never answered his friend that day. He knew his family was in deep financial trouble, both to the government and, even worse, to Camorra loan sharks. Hank's father had been out of work for close to eighteen months, and his mother's housecleaning jobs brought in just enough to cover the food bills. Every hour of each day, the family found themselves deeper in debt, buried in a hole from which there could be no escape. The Camorra waited until Hank turned seventeen. By then, Lo Manto had been living in Naples for over two years, but kept in touch with his friend with regular letters and the occasional phone call. "They want me to go work for them, Gianni," Hank had said to him in the middle of their last phone conversation. The boy's voice was filled with dread, a somber feeling of helplessness etched in each word he spoke. "And I don't think that's something I can do."

"Then you need to get out of there," Lo Manto told him, the memory of his father's death still fresh in his mind. "Don't wait, Hank. Just tell your parents to pack and go."

"Go where?" Hank said. "Where can we go that they can't find us if they want to make the effort?"

Two weeks later, Hank Somettri was killed crossing White Plains Road near Our Lady of Mercy Medical Center, hit from behind by a dark blue van with no license plates. His grave was still fresh when the boy's father was found slumped on a bench in a small park in lower Manhattan, a bullet in the back of his head. Neither killer was ever apprehended. The Camorra let his mother live, allowing her to mourn the loss of her family for the rest of her days.

Lo Manto sat back in the pew, lowered his head and

closed his eyes. He had been waging his war against the Camorra for close to two decades and still there was no victory in sight. He had confiscated millions of dollars in drug money, disrupted the flow of their business operations, and arrested and killed more than fifty high-ranking members of the massive criminal organization in two countries. Despite his efforts, the Camorra was as powerful today as it was the night of his father's murder, still trolling the waters and stripping the shore of all its wealth, leaving in their wake battered bodies and ruined lives. He had watched the casualty count mount by the day. He had seen with dismay the destructive effects of the physical and emotional pounding given to the innocents who were mere prey to the Camorra quest for power and control. And he could do nothing to bring it all to an end. "There will always be so many more of them than there will be of us," Inspector Bartoni had told him early on in their time together. "That must be accepted as fact. Ours is a battle not fought for victory but for justice. It is the one lesson you must never allow yourself to forget."

But the words of Inspector Bartoni were lost on Lo Manto. He was not content with the occasional rush of justice. He was not satisfied with a drug bust or the takedown of a Camorra faction. It was not enough for him to see a group of Camorristas led away in cuffs, off to serve double-digit prison terms. He needed to see them all brought to an end. He wanted to achieve what had eluded every detective, Italian and American, who

417

had ever stepped in against the strength of the organization and looked to bring its churning engines to a
halt. But as he sat there, inside the secluded serenity of a
small and empty church, Lo Manto began to feel as if he
had ventured on a fool's quest. The doubts that so often
haunt even the most dedicated had slowly crept in and
started to gnaw at his steel-centered confidence.

He folded his hands on his lap and stared across the
aisle at the statue of St. Jude, the patron saint of lost
causes and police officers. The specter of so many ruined
and damaged lives haunted his thoughts and actions, and
even a prayer to his favorite of all the saints seemed a
futile gesture. He needed more than a series of arrests to
put a dent in the Camorra, more than simply to cause a
disruption of their steady flow of cash and drugs. He had
to look beyond the scope of paid assassins who sought
the blood of innocents in return for a padded bank
account. He had to venture past the informants who
offered their knowledge, expecting his leniency as their
reward. He had to cause a massive tremor within the
Camorra hierarchy, a blow that would buckle the
criminal enterprise and cause it to gasp for air. In order
for that to happen, Lo Manto had to accomplish the one
deed that had eluded him in all his years as a detective.

He needed to bring down the don.

Lo Manto lifted himself out of the pew, genuflected in
front of the main altar, and walked with quiet steps
toward the statue of St. Jude. He looked up at the sad
bearded face with the cold distant eyes, made the sign of

the cross, and whispered a silent prayer. He then reached into his pants pocket and pulled out a five-dollar bill. He folded the bill and slid it into the thin slot in the donation box that was fixed into the wall directly under the statue. He leaned over to his right, toward four rows of votive candles, half of them unlit, and pressed two buttons that turned on the soft glow bulb in each. He gave one final glance up at St. Jude, bowed his head, and slowly walked up the aisle leading out of the church.

The time for prayer was now at an end.

Felipe stood on the top deck of the Circle Line boat, both hands grasping the railing, a smile as wide as the Hudson River below him on his face. Lo Manto held the envelope Silvestri had given the boy, its lip torn open, glancing down at the four names written out on the folded sheet it contained. Jennifer had her back to the choppy water and her face to the sun, hands in her pockets, her hair held back by a blue scrunchie. "I was only kidding when I mentioned the boat ride to you," she said to Lo Manto. "I wasn't expecting it to turn into an open invitation."

"I thought my friend would like it," Lo Manto said, nodding at Felipe. "And I owe him a favor for what he did for me the other night."

"Is this a favor I should know about?" Jennifer asked. "Or maybe you can give me a little something on your friend here? Given that we are still partners, at least until your plane leaves New York."

"I already told you my name," Felipe said to her. "Other than that there isn't much left to tell."

"How about I ask the questions?" Jennifer said to Felipe. "And you just work your best to come up with the right answers."

Felipe turned away from the railing and started to walk toward the door leading to the concession stands. "How about I go get some candy bars and a soda first?" he said.

"Pay for anything you put your fingers on," Lo Manto said to him. "We get tossed from here, we have to swim back to the city."

The boy disappeared through the opening as Lo Manto stepped closer to Jennifer. He folded the paper along with the envelope and slid both into his back pocket. "It'll do us all a little good to get out of the city for a while," he said to her. "The river water gives us a chance to clear our heads and take in some fresh air."

"Didn't take you for the kind that liked to hang out with kids," Jennifer said, a little bit of a tease to her words. "You don't come off as the patient type to me."

"Felipe's a kid only on the outside," Lo Manto said. "Inside, he's older than you and me put together. He's seen a lot for a boy his age. But he's never been on the Circle Line and I thought it was time."

"My friends and me used to sneak rides on these when we were kids," Jennifer said, her stance softening a bit. "Usually on Wednesdays, when we had half days because the kids from public school would come over for religious instruction."

"I came here with my seventh-grade class one time," Lo Manto said. "We were a hard-to-control bunch—mix of Italian, Irish, Hispanic, and Eastern Europeans all roped together and handed over to one brother. I guess he figured the trip would be a bonding experience and maybe, with enough prayers and a little luck, even help calm us down a bit."

"Did he catch any luck?" she asked.

"Not even a five-minute break," Lo Manto said, smiling at the long-forgotten memory. "On the way up, we rifled through the concession stand like red ants on a piece of fruit. Then we jumped on the next boat heading back, leaving the poor guy stranded on the island, just him and three of the kids too afraid to make the move."

"That must have scored you at least a week of detention," Jennifer said.

"Try a month—and enough homework to keep us off the streets for about four weekends," Lo Manto said. "Not to mention the grief we had to get from our folks at home. Still, in spite of that, it sure as hell was worth the effort."

Jennifer stepped up to the railing, gripped the hard red wood with her right hand, the sea water spraying cool mist across her face and hair. She tilted her head to one side and gazed over at Lo Manto, the warm sun giving a yellow glow to his hard features. "How about this next move?" she asked. "You think that's going to be worth the effort?"

"If it doesn't happen here and now, then it will happen on some other street in some other city," Lo Manto said. "Fighting them is what I do. It's all that I do, until they put a stop to me."

"It sounds like they're looking to make your last stop on your old streets," Jennifer said. "You've been plenty good against them in the past. So now they figure the best way to put an end to all that is to come at you harder and heavier. I don't know much about what you have planned to balance that out, but I hope it's at least as solid as what we heard they have ready to go."

"We won't know that until it's over," Lo Manto said. "And most times it's luck, not the plan, that gets you through."

"Where does that kid in there fit in?" Jennifer asked.

"He doesn't," Lo Manto said firmly. "And he shouldn't. I want him kept out of the action end. He's been through enough shit in his life. There's no call for him to have to wade through mine."

"Same go for me?" Jennifer asked, moving closer to Lo Manto, his dark eyes staring down at her, his thick dark hair flowing in the warm southern breeze. "You going to try and keep me out as well?"

"You were asked to keep an eye on an Italian cop during his visit to New York," Lo Manto said. "You've done that, above and beyond. And for all that, you have my respect and my heart. But nobody, not Captain Fernandez and not me, asked you to give up your life. Not at the start of this and for sure not at the end."

"Do I get to vote?" she asked. She was slightly taken aback by both the force and the passion of his words, the first true indication that he thought of her as more than a police partner. "Or is this a decision that's only yours to make?"

"Only if your vote comes down the same as mine," Lo Manto said. "That's the case, then we have ourselves a landslide election."

"I have my orders, Detective," Jennifer said, pushing herself clear of the railing. "I expect to do what I've done from my first day on the job, and that's follow them as best as I can. You can like it or you can bitch about it. Either way's fine by me."

Lo Manto took her hands in his, his touch warm and soft. He gazed into her eyes and smiled. He leaned his head against her shoulder, his hair brushing the side of her face, and then kissed her gently on the lips. She moved her hands away from his and wrapped them around his neck. She held him close to her, not wanting to let go, not wanting to ever lose him, not wanting this moment to ever end. They stood there under the warm summer sun, their kisses lit with passion, their arms wrapped tightly around each other.

"I've seen a lot of people I care about die doing what I do," he whispered. "Many of them died because of me, the position I put them in, the choices I left them. That's not going to happen on this one. I won't let it. The Camorra is in this fight to bring me down. They have no quarrel with you. But if I let you come into this standing by my side, they'll take you out just as soon as they would me. And I can't let that happen."

"That's the case, then you better damn well be on your best game, Detective," Jennifer said. "I'm not all that eager to be toe-tagged in the Bronx, either."

Lo Manto turned away and looked out at the harsh waves of a cold river, the scenic tree-lined landscape, the occasional house breaking into the formation. He still wasn't used to working side by side with a partner let alone one he had fallen in love with, and he was never comfortable sharing his game plan with anyone. While other cops saw a partner as an added measure of security, one more gun to cover their exposed backs, Lo Manto saw partners as major impediments to the task at hand. They limited his flexibility, weakened his ability to alter his thinking on the fly, and forced him to stick much closer to a prearranged timetable. It was no longer enough for his plan to succeed or fail on its merits and his skills. He needed Jennifer to move and react as fast as the moment demanded, which meant she had to see not only what was around her but what wasn't. She had to know not just who was shooting, but why the shots were coming down at her from a certain position. She also had to know, instinctively, what would follow. Her ability to do so would determine whether she would come out of the shoot-out dead or alive.

"You do what I say as I say it and when," Lo Manto said to her, his eyes still on the river. "Every step of the way. If you're not okay with that, I need to know now, not when we're out there ducking shells."

Jennifer thought for a moment before she nodded. "You're the one who knows how they think," she said. "Not me. I'll let you have this one. But if I see or hear anything stupid about your plan, I'm not going to be shy about letting you know."

Lo Manto turned to her and smiled. "We won't have a problem," he said. "My plans are never stupid. Just dangerous."

"I'm not afraid of danger," Jennifer said.

"I am," Lo Manto said. He eased himself away from the railing, heading toward the candy shop in search of Felipe.

Pete Rossi walked on the water side of the West Side pier, his head down, listening to Gaspaldi give him the final run-down on the plan to rid themselves of Giancarlo Lo Manto. "There's no way the badge walks from this," Gaspaldi said, wrapping up. "Even if one, even two of the shooters are off their mark, it won't matter. There's going to be more bullets coming off their guns than we saw in *Saving Private Ryan*. He'll have no way to go but down. His family might as well start making funeral plans now."

"It's not a done deal until he's dead," Rossi said, his voice not bothering to hide the harsh sentiment behind each word. He had never felt comfortable around Gaspaldi, thought him too eager to go for the hard play rather than a smarter, more strategic option. Rossi also didn't like the fact that a pimp had risen as high as Gaspaldi had managed to do within the tight inner structure of the Camorra. It might have gone down well in the years his father was building his crime base, taking only the most ruthless and devious along with him, but not for an organized crime operation that was now three-quarters focused on the legitimate world. On top of which, he didn't like Gaspaldi and never turned to him for advice or counsel. He found the man crude, rude, and untrustworthy and didn't make any attempt to mask those feelings. Rossi lacked his father's ability to compartmentalize the men who worked for him, allowing each to flourish within his own category, wanting nothing more from them than what was expected. If they failed in the chosen task, they would be killed. Don Nicola Rossi was a great crime boss because he was able to deal with even the most complicated issues in the most direct manner. But what made him a legend as a don made him questionable as a father.

"He will be dead, Mr. Rossi," Gaspaldi said. "He may have walked from other jackpots in other years, but not this one. I'll stake everything I got on it."

"Believe me," Rossi told him, "that is exactly what you will be doing."

Rossi stood with his back to the low tide that beat against the sides of the empty pier, facing the traffic running both ways on the West Side Highway, the lower end of De Witt Clinton Park just visible beyond it. He had spent many a Sunday morning walking with his father on the cobblestone streets, a large pretzel coated with salt and yellow mustard in his right hand, the don's two silent bodyguards a short distance away. The piers were active in those years, still a steady and lucrative source of Camorra income, most of the money derived from stolen cargo from the hulls of packed ships and high-end cuts of workers' wages. Don Nicola was in an open competition with Tough Tony Anastasia's Pistol Piers farther downtown as to who could generate the most money each week. His father ruled these streets as if he were a king entitled to them by birthright, deciding who worked and who would be prevented from shape-up, who paid the weekly ransom and who would be allowed to keep a larger chunk of his salary or his haul. Rossi would see the looks on the faces of the hard-living men when they stood in his father's presence. It was a fretful glance filled with the residue of fear.

That was an element of his father's life Pete Rossi had always known about and, on many different levels, respected. The part that he didn't know and was now causing him grief involved his relationship with a woman he had been told only hours earlier was his mother. Even if she had executed an inappropriate means of escape, a don as powerful as Nicola Rossi would not have allowed it. He would have dragged her back and forced her to remain under a Camorra roof until the day of her death. It would have been her mission to raise the son. That in and of itself was troubling, knowing his real mother was alive and living in Naples.

But to know that his blood enemy, Giancarlo Lo Manto, was his blood brother shook Pete Rossi down to the very core of his being. It had rocked him more than any betrayal he had ever encountered, caused him more pain than any bullet that could be aimed in his direction. And it ultimately would do more harm to him as a sitting don than any charge that could ever be dreamt up by the various federal task forces breathing down hard on his organization.

For the first time in his entire life, Pete Rossi was at a loss as to which way to turn. The plan devised by Gaspaldi was as close to a slam-dunk assassination as any ever presented to him in his years as family boss. It would all but guarantee the death of his sole nemesis, a cop he respected and despised and one he swore to destroy. It would send a message to all the other police officers, on both sides of the Atlantic, cops neither as dedicated nor as driven as Lo Manto, that to interfere in Camorra business would only result in a brutal end. It would bring a suitable peace to his crime family and allow their on-going quest for power to continue unabated. It was the perfect move made at a perfect time, one that any crime boss would green-light without the slightest hesitation. Rossi understood that now was not the time for reflection, nor did it call for an examination of a life led. It was a time for action. A moment designed for him to step up and show his enemies the extent to which he would strive to maintain the iron grip on his crime family. Pete Rossi could not afford to take the time to think and react like a civilian. He needed to be a don and proceed with the most precious order given to someone in his position.

The ability to order another man's death.

"We're all locked in," Gaspaldi said. "The money's been collected and handed out. Other than your final say-so, we got everything we need."

Rossi turned his gaze away from the highway and looked back at Gaspaldi. "It's a go," he said, his words low and clipped.

"When?" Gaspaldi asked.

"Today," Don Pete Rossi said. "This ends today."

22

Lo Manto and Felipe walked down the slopes of Strawberry Fields in Central Park, each one munching on a street-vendor hot dog. "How far from here was he killed?" Felipe asked. "I mean, I know it was in front of his house, but where is that from here?"

Lo Manto turned and pointed to the Gothic building on the far corner, just visible through the heavy branches. "Lennon lived in the Dakota," he told the boy. "Him, his wife, and his kid. The guy waited and shot him just in front of the place in plain sight of anyone to see."

"For no reason," Felipe said, shoving the last of the hot dog into a corner of his mouth. "So I read, anyway."

"Most people get shot for no reason," Lo Manto said. "Famous or not."

"Shouldn't we be heading back up to the Bronx?" Felipe asked as they walked deeper into the mouth of the park.

"Why the rush?" Lo Manto asked. "You got a date

and forgot to tell me about it?"

"Don't I wish," Felipe said. "Every time I look at a girl she looks the other way as fast as she can. I guess they don't see the romance in going out with a homeless kid."

"I wouldn't worry too much about it," Lo Manto said. "You just haven't met the right girl yet. Once you do, she won't care where you live or how much money you have in your pocket or what kind of car you drive. She'll only care about you. That's when you'll know it's special."

"That what happened to you?" Felipe asked.

"Not yet," Lo Manto said. "But I'm not as good-looking as you and I lack your natural charm. Girls can look right through me, spot the cop in a heartbeat, and most of the time that's not a place they want to go."

"I never thought about dating a cop," Felipe said, stepping aside to let two young Rollerbladers zoom past.

"Why would you?" Lo Manto asked. "Why would anyone? It's a heavy suitcase to lug, even on the best of days."

"What about that partner of yours?" Felipe asked. "Jennifer. She definitely has the sounds for your kind of music. You can see it in her eyes. And I know you feel the same, you just haven't brought home the onions to talk to her about it."

Lo Manto stopped and looked down at Felipe. "Two seconds ago you said you didn't know anything about girls," he said to the boy. "Now all of a sudden you're Dr. Phil. Which is it?"

"I said girls didn't give me a second spin," Felipe said. "That doesn't mean I don't know anything about them. And what I do know is that you and the other end of your team have a soft place for one another. But I think she needs you to take a breath and make with that big first move. Which I would think is like rolling a natural, what with you being Italian."

"It's complicated," Lo Manto said. "Let's leave it at that. Unless you have some other deep insights on the subject."

"No," Felipe said. "My deck is clear, said all it is I have to say. The rest I leave to experts like you."

They walked over toward a bench that looked out at the softball fields. "Let's sit for a minute," Lo Manto said. "We need to talk. Been wanting to do it for a while, just haven't been able to make time."

"This about women?" Felipe asked, flopping down, swinging his legs in the open space under the bench.

"Let that go for a while, would you please?" Lo Manto said, sitting next to the boy.

"And if it's about me stealing, you can save your chat," Felipe said. "I've been thinking about going easy on that. It's a nasty habit and I plead guilty to it. It's going to take me a little time to break clean. But I'm working on it."

Lo Manto stared at the boy, shook his head and smiled. "You have a lot to work on and none of it is going to be easy," he said. "You started out with a sour hand, no folks, no family, no home. Most kids in your place, same situations, same setups, are out there mugging for money and snorting drugs to forget why. I don't want you to end up one of them."

"I don't know what's going to happen," Felipe said in a low voice. "I don't see myself going that way, but I can't swear it to you for sure. Sometimes it's the street that decides, not the kid living on it."

"That only happens if you let it, Felipe," Lo Manto said. "And no one could stop that but you. This is one you're going to have to face alone, just like everything else you've had to deal with. But you'll do it. You got the heart for it and the brains. Plus the cash that friend of yours told you to sit on for a couple of years. You can climb out of the hole and make a good life for yourself. You deserve to have that, get a taste of what that's like. I'd hate to see you miss out on it."

"Does that mean I'm not going to have you around to hound and check up on me?" Felipe asked. "You saying good-bye with this?"

"One way or the other, in coffin or coach, I have to go back to Italy," Lo Manto said. "And that leaves you where I found you. Jennifer will check on you now and then, but it won't be the same and it shouldn't. I don't want you to use any excuses, Felipe. I don't want to hear about how tough you have it and what other choices did you have that led you down a crooked path. That's all bullshit and you know it and I know it."

"What are you getting all steamed about?" Felipe asked. "Have I let you down since we teamed up?"

433

"It's not about letting me down," Lo Manto said. "I don't count in this one. It's about not letting yourself down, about being true and honest to who you really are. There's only one person that gets hurt if you screw up, Felipe. And that's going to be you. If I'm still alive, I would hate to hear it happen. And if I'm dead it won't matter. You've come this far on your own. You can go the rest of the way."

They sat in silence for several moments, content to watch the passersby, rummies mingling with harried young mothers pushing packed strollers along the walking path.

"Why did you pick me?" Felipe asked. "It's not like you needed me to get you through the day. You know more people in my neighborhood than I do. And I haven't done all that much to earn the twenty a day you're putting in my pocket."

"You can never have enough friends," Lo Manto said. "And there's only so many people you can trust. With you, I figured I had both bases covered."

"You work out a way yet for us to bring this crew down?" Felipe asked. "Or you just going to wait until they start shooting to figure up a plan?"

"There is no *us* on this," Lo Manto said. "You don't come anywhere near the gunplay. The next couple of days, I worked it with a friend of mine that you could stay at his place. He's old, he's blind, and he's got a mean dog. That should keep you in your place. He doesn't like to talk much, but when he does, he expects

434

you to listen."

"Do I get a say?" Felipe said.

"Not a word," Lo Manto said. "It's one part of my plan that I would hate to see changed. No give to it at all."

"When do I have to go?" Felipe said. He sat back against the hard wood of the bench, trying not to show any emotion, glancing down at the gauze still taped across his damaged palm. He knew that after this moment, he might never see Lo Manto again. At least not alive. He had tried not to get close to anyone, realizing life on the street didn't allow for such emotions. It was always the safer bet to keep most people at a distance and friendships to a minimum. It was too much of a risk to do otherwise. And he had tried not to like the cop from Naples, to treat what they had between them as a strict business deal and not take it any further. Felipe had learned that survival on the street required an ability to bury any emotion. It helped to keep him strong and focused and not fall prey to vulnerability or despair. He knew that to be homeless in any city, especially in one as harsh as New York, meant it was best to stay invisible. It made it so much easier to stay alive. Lo Manto changed all that. From their first moment together, Felipe knew he could no longer hide in plain sight.

"There's a car waiting for you on the other side of the park," Lo Manto said. "The driver will take you to my friend's office. You'll be comfortable there and safe."

"Where's this friend of yours live?" Felipe asked. "I mean is it a neighborhood I'm going to know?"

"He lives in Harlem," Lo Manto said. He stood and began to walk down the path leading to the East Side exit of the park. "It's just like the East Bronx. Only with better music. But that's only if he lets you hear any of it."

"Why don't you just lock me in a holding cell?" Felipe asked. "It sounds like I'd have a lot more laughs there than with this pal of yours. And I won't get mauled by any dog either."

Lo Manto pulled a pack of gum from his jacket pocket and offered a piece to Felipe. The boy slid two out and put them in his front pants pocket. "Any clown can end up in jail," Lo Manto said. "It's the easiest thing in the world to have happen. My idea is to keep you *out*. I hope I'm around to see how well I did."

"I'll make it work with your friend," Felipe said. "You got enough on your plate. There's no need for you to waste any more time worrying over me."

"You're my friend, Felipe," Lo Manto said. "And worrying about a friend is never a waste of time. Just do me one favor?"

"What?"

"Try not to piss off the dog," Lo Manto said.

Felipe smiled. "I can't promise," he said. "But I'll do my best. In return, how about you throw a favor my way?"

"What is it?" Lo Manto asked.

"Try not to get killed while I'm gone," Felipe said.

Lo Manto nodded. "I can't promise," he said to the boy. "But I'll do *my* best."

Jennifer sat in the kitchen of her father's house, sipping from a large mug of hot coffee, a radio tuned to WCBS-FM playing softly at her back. Sal Fabini was working the stove, making their favorite breakfast of two eggs, sunny side up, coated with roasted peppers and fresh mozzarella and placed on top of two thick slices of toasted Italian bread. In a second pan, he had half a dozen slices of fresh cut bacon sizzling over a low flame. He kept the serving plates in the oven, the temperature at 250 degrees, white oven mitt on the countertop within easy reach.

The smell of the food mixing with the fresh coffee and the low-volume voices of the Four Tops helped remind Jennifer of the happiest times she had spent with her father. It was when he allowed himself to just be her dad and not a famous cop working a hard-to-crack case or an abusive husband coming off a heavy binge and yet another brutal fight with her mother. On those rare occasions, he would sit across from her and smile when she broke the bread the right way and folded it over the top of the egg, using her fork to crack through to the yolk. They saved their conversation for the two cups of coffee and small slivers of Entenmann's Danish ring that would serve as the topper to their morning feast. It was during those quiet early hours, her mother either still asleep or running errands, that Sal Fabini took the time to catch up with her life. She filled him in on her school-work and her friends, few of whom he had ever met. She talked about her after-school sporting events and the plays she either wrote or acted in, none of which he ever found the time to attend. She told him about her teachers, who always asked about the detective they had read about but never seen. And she tapped him into the neighborhood gossip, keeping out the parts that involved his romantic affairs with some of the local married women.

"You're going to make a great cop someday," he would tease her as they stood side by side along the kitchen counter, Sal washing the dishes and Jennifer drying and stacking them away. "You remember every detail. Even the stuff most people leave out because they don't think it's important. More often than not, what went down, the key parts to every story, criminal or not, turn on those very basic elements."

"I don't want to be a cop, Dad," Jennifer would say. "One in the family is more than plenty."

"That's only if you listen to what your mother tells you," Sal said with a dismissive wave. "She never cared much for the badge or the person behind it. But you can't fight what's in your blood, and, like it or not, police blue is what you got running in your veins."

"I'm pretty good in English and my teachers all say I write pretty well," Jennifer said. "Maybe I could grow up and teach. That might be fun."

"You get off at three in the afternoon and have

nothing to do in the summers," Sal said. "What kind of way is that to live? Your cousin Theresa's a teacher in the Bronx. She's been razor-slashed twice in four years, all for trying to drum home some math lessons to a band of kids who only care about the numbers they take in from their daily drug sales."

"There are other things I could do besides teach, Dad," she said. "Being a cop isn't the only job in the world, you know."

"You could do plenty of other things," Sal Fabini said. "Dozens of different jobs you could tackle and there isn't a one of them that you wouldn't be good at. But a cop is the only job where you would be great. And that's almost impossible to pass up."

"We'll see what we'll see," Jennifer would say, leaving her father alone in the kitchen, heading out to spend a day with her friends.

"That's right," Sal would call after her, his voice calm and confident. "We'll see what we'll see."

Sal sat down and passed her one of the two hot plates filled with the eggs, bread, and bacon. He reached behind him and grabbed two large glasses of orange juice and nudged one to her side of the table. They ate and drank in silence for a few minutes, the warm food and cool drink going down smooth. "Coffee's fresh," he said to her, finishing off the last of his eggs. "I made it about two minutes before I put the food on."

"I'll get it," Jennifer said. She pushed her chair back

and brought her cup over toward the Mr. Coffee, the glass pot filled to the brim. She tossed what was left of hers in the sink and poured in the rich, black liquid that she knew he spiked with Italian Stock 84. "You want a cup?" she asked.

"I'll hold to it later," he said. "I like to save it for when I read my morning papers."

Jennifer walked back to her seat. "Thanks for making breakfast," she said to her dad, knowing how much he enjoyed being complimented on his cooking abilities. "This was one of your best yet. You were really on top of your game."

"I've changed it a bit since you were a kid," he said, with an appreciative nod. "I started adding oregano and basil to the mix."

"Whatever you're doing, don't stop," she said, giving him a slight smile. "It's good enough to give Emeril a run for his money."

"You don't usually come by during the week," he said, glancing at her over the rim of his juice glass. "In fact, if I think about it hard enough, I would have to say this is a first. Am I right?"

"You can put down your cop antenna, Dad," Jennifer said. "There's no mystery to it or plot behind it. I just came by to see how you were doing and grab a bite."

"This Italian cop they paired you with," Sal said, pushing aside his cleared plate and empty juice glass, "it working out okay?"

Jennifer looked across at her father and nodded. She

knew without being told that Sal had already been given as much information as could be gathered from his still-solid sources within the department and any attempts to dodge his questions would be futile. "He's the best partner I've ever worked with," she said. "Good on the street, great when our back is at the wall. He goes his own way more than I'd like to see, but that's all part of what makes him click, so I cut him some slack."

"From what I hear, he's going to need you to cover his back more than you'll need him to watch yours," Sal said, his voice taking on its more familiar cop tones. "Do you think the two of you alone are going to be good enough for whatever it is that's coming down?"

"Tell me what you think," Jennifer said, playing the game, tossing it right back at her father.

"I don't know the man," Sal said with a shrug. "Word on him matches what you say, he's a solid badge, runs on skill not fumes. He might need to be better than that, though, given the rumbles about what's about to meet him head on. Same goes for you."

"He's got a plan in place," Jennifer said. "I just don't know what it is and what part I play in it."

"I guess he hasn't learned the English word for *partner* yet," Sal said. He gave his only daughter a hard look, more the look of a detective than a father. He needed to get a sense of whether she was ready to step into what was sure to be high-end action. Sal had gotten enough feedback about Jennifer to know she was a solid street cop with well-tuned instincts. What couldn't be known yet was whether she had either the stomach or the knack for the quick kill, the ability to wipe the shooter's slates clean and still walk away from it a whole cop. "Or he just may not want you to be in with him on this business he's gearing up to face."

"It's hard to figure," Jennifer said. "He's not the kind that likes to share much of what he's thinking. A lot like you, Dad."

Sal Fabini smiled and pushed his chair back, ready for his first cup of coffee of the day. "He's good-looking, too, from what I hear," he said, his back to his daughter.

"What's that have to do with the price of tomatoes?" Jennifer asked.

"Not a thing," Sal said, turning to glance her way. "To me, anyway. How you feel about it might be a whole different story."

"Let's keep the talk to the work," she said. "And his looks, good or not, are not going to help him bring down the crew he's up against."

Sal sat down, a large cup of coffee resting on the placemat between his elbows, a wide smile on his face. "That answers that question," he said. "Which means you've already made your decision about which way you go on this and you made it before you walked in the door this morning."

"I can't let him do it alone, Dad," she said. "He thinks he can and he won't ask for any help. But I'd like to be there when it happens. It matters to me."

"You're making this personal," Sal Fabini said.

"That's the fastest way for a cop to get jammed up."

"You made every case you worked personal," Jennifer said, leaning the front of her body against the side of the Formica table. "It made you a shitty husband to Mom and not the best father to me. But it made you the best cop on the street. Making it personal *kept* you from getting jammed up."

"You came here for something, Jenny," Sal said. "And it wasn't just for my eggs and bacon. It's time for you to put it out there. What do you need?"

"Another gun," Jennifer said. "And somebody I trust holding it."

"You asking me to back you up?" Sal said. He sat straight back in his chair, his dark eyes alive, the aging muscles on his forearms showing signs of life. "Put myself out on the streets again?"

"There's going to be more gunmen in this than he can handle," Jennifer said. "I don't know that for fact, just feeling. And I also don't know when or how the attempt is going to come down. But what I do know is that he shouldn't be in this alone."

"Why come to me?" Sal asked. "You've been on the job long enough to have some pals willing to lend a hand, even to a situation that would put them in the line of fire. And the odds are better than good they'd be a whole lot better at it at their age than I would be at mine."

"You're my father," Jennifer said. She reached a hand across the table and rested it on his right arm. "And the best cop I've ever known."

443

"Even better than this Italian sidekick of yours?" he asked.

Jennifer smiled. "Yes, Dad," she said. "You're even better than Lo Manto. Just do me a small favor, if you don't mind, okay?"

"I know," Sal said. "Never tell him you said so. Don't worry. It stays between us, no matter how this situation turns out."

"That a yes?" Jennifer asked, watching her father push his chair back and walk to a small coatrack just off the kitchen entrance. "You helping me on this?"

"You tell me when and where," Sal said. He put on a blue blazer, opened the top drawer of a side cabinet, and pulled out two strap-holstered .38 Specials. "If I'm not here, call me on the cell. Don't leave any messages. You don't get me, keep trying until you hear my voice."

"Where are you going?" Jennifer asked, watching her father walk toward the screen door that led into the garage.

"The range," he said. "Been a while since I worked these guns. Be nice to see if I can still hit at what I aim, even if it's only a paper target."

Jennifer stood next to the kitchen table, leaning against a counter, staring across the room at her father. "Thanks for this, Dad," she said. "I owe you one."

"How about you do the dishes then," Sal Fabini said, heading out the kitchen door, a few feet from his parked Mercury Grand Marquis. "This way we can call it even."

23

Carlo Bertz rested the high-powered rifle on the white towel he had spread near the base of the roof. He sliced open a paper bag and pulled out a thick slab of Muenster cheese and a hard roll, leaned back against the curved black tar edge, and snapped open a blood-ed switchblade. He cut into the cheese and jabbed a long slice into his mouth, chewing slowly as if he were giving each bite some thought. He pulled a cold twenty-four-ounce bottle of Poland Spring from his jacket pocket and clicked the top up, washing down the cheese with several long gulps. Bertz looked down at the rifle and then up at the alarm clock he kept by his side. It ticked away loudly, the large white hand closing in on eleven-fifteen in the morning, the sun bringing with it all the power and heat of an August day. Bertz cut off a fresh piece of cheese, held it in his right hand, and closed his eyes, drowning in the noise and clatter that rose up from the long, narrow street. He was in the middle of the block, on the roof of a six-story tenement, one shot away

from the elevated subway running up and down White
Plains Road.

Forty-five minutes removed from his next kill.

Elmo Stalli walked along the backyards leading down
the hill from the large medical center that bordered the
Bronx River Parkway. He kept his head down, focused
on the work that waited as he made his way toward the
narrow building on East 234th Street. He had both his
hands curled inside the pockets of a long and thin gray
raincoat, fingers wrapped around the barrels of .38
Specials. On the inside of his coat, hanging on a leather
strap around his neck, he carried a double-pump shotgun. Stalli walked through the tight back alley of a local
bank and into the basement of the small row house that
bordered it. He found a folded garden chair resting next
to a battered boiler. He opened it and placed it facing
the small, cracked window that offered a view of the
curb and a row of parked cars. He sat down and rested
the shotgun on his lap, the guns still in his pockets. He
pulled a small CD player from his shirt and pressed Play,
the mellow sounds of a remastered Enrico Caruso
version of *Tarantella napoletana* by Rossini soon filling the
dank room. It was his favorite song.

The perfect song for a murder.

Mifo slid the gearshift into neutral and gently eased the
eight-cylinder 2003 Ford Mustang into an open slot
between a brown Chevy sedan and a Volvo station

wagon. He left the motor running, humming low, the supercharged, finely tuned engine clicking as softly as a row of piano keys. He was on the south end of East 234th Street, facing the middle of White Plains Road, the number two line rumbling above him, bringing carloads of tired passengers to and from the city. Mifo gazed out at the street traffic, quiet for a late summer morning in the middle of a nine-day heat wave. He checked the gauges on the car and tapped his right foot on the gas pedal, watching each white line flip forward. He reached into the front pocket of his leather jacket and pulled out a thin cigar and a butane lighter. He lit the cigar, laid his head back against the leather rest, and kept his eyes on the street. He checked his wristwatch and smiled.

It was almost time for someone to die.

John Rummy stood in the middle of the large Italian deli, checking out the shelves crammed with pastas of all shapes and sizes. He took a deep breath, overwhelmed by the vast and varied aromas, and walked slowly down each of the long aisles, all of them filled with foods whose names he could never pronounce. He stopped in front of the olive bar, over two dozen trays filled to the brim with products from each region of Italy. He picked up a large plastic container, scooped out the thick, green Sicilian olives that had caught his eye, and then snapped a lid over them. He went to the register, waited as the pretty young woman with a head full of brown curly hair and a wide grin weighed the olives and put them in a brown paper bag. He handed her a ten-dollar bill, waited for his change, and walked quietly out of the deli, out into the heavy blanket heat of the East Bronx. At the far corner of East 234th Street, Rummy turned a sharp right and stepped into a small entryway, his back wedged against a polished wooden and glass front door. He popped the lid on the container filled with olives, grabbed two, and put them in his mouth. He rested the small bag between his feet and felt for the two black nine-millimeters hanging down against his chest, locked into two thin shoulder holsters. He spit out the olive pits and rubbed the tired from his eyes. He could never sleep well the night before a job, too anxious to get it done, playing it out over and over in his mind. It was only after the job was done that Rummy was ever able to relax, the adrenaline rush of the hit long since dissipated.

The target's life brought to an end.

Gregory Flash Randell stood on the elevated platform of the southbound IRT number two subway line and glanced down at the street activity below. He leaned on the iron railing, munching on the back end of a ham and Swiss hero, a brown leather duffel bag by his feet. He was dressed light, thin black T-shirt, black jeans, and Nike sneakers. He knew there were four other shooters around, each one working out of his designated post, ready to take down the cop from Naples, none of them expecting him to be on the scene. That, he figured, gave him his first edge in the battle that would soon send a wave of bullets flowing down the streets beneath the station. He also was willing to wager that old man Silvestri had tipped off Lo Manto about the hit site and the cop would come into the situation expecting to be drawn on. Which meant he was primed for four gunmen and would never consider the possibility of a fifth. Randell had lain low and silent since his meet with Rossi, keeping his focus on all the elements he needed working in his favor. He didn't know any of the names of the other shooters, but was confident enough to believe that the fatal bullet that would bring an end to Lo Manto's life would be fired from his rifle.

One more notch on a killer's belt.

Giancarlo Lo Manto parked his unmarked sedan on the northwest corner of East 235th Street and walked into a small pizzeria. He stepped up to the counter and nodded at the chubby bald man behind it. "Which one is the freshest?" he asked, pointing down at the wide array of pies, each resting in its own silver tray.

"The Sicilian," the chubby man said, reaching for the still-steaming pizza to his right, crust dark and thick. "Came out just before you came in."

"I'll take a slice of that with a root beer, extra ice," Lo Manto said. He reached into his pocket and pulled out a five-dollar bill and left it on the counter. He waited while the chubby man clipped off a large piece and scooped it onto a white paper plate. He grabbed a plastic cup, jabbed it under a thin ice dispenser, watched it fill up to the top, and then shoved it under the root beer tap. He slid the cup onto the counter, leaving a thin line of white foam in its wake. "If there's any change, it's yours to keep," Lo Manto said.

He sat facing the street traffic, munching on his pizza and drinking his soda on a day he expected to die. He had been in a hundred dustups throughout his police career, both in New York and Naples, and in none of those had he ever gone up against either the skill level or the heavy firepower he knew was waiting for him two streets to the south. He had the inside information on the general layout of the hit, expecting the first move to come as he made his way up White Plains Road. It was Lo Manto's idea to leak his destination to the four shooters by way of a confidential informant who owed Gaspaldi both a favor and bundle of money he would never be able to pay. Lo Manto felt he stood a better chance fighting them out in the open, on a clear street, in the middle of the day, than having them come at him one fast gun at a time, from areas beyond his control, increasing the odds that one of them was bound eventually to succeed.

He had also kept his plans away from both Jennifer and Felipe, looking to shield them from any danger, not wanting to see either hurt. This was his fight and Lo Manto always liked the odds better when he walked into one on his own, free of the additional burden of having to give background cover fire. He had grown to respect his reluctant New York partner in their short time together, valuing her natural police instincts and her fearlessness under the hard gaze of a shooter's scope. She was a first-rate detective and one of the best he ever had working by his side. And there was one additional factor in play that drove Lo Manto to keep Jennifer Fabini as far from harm's way as possible. One he had never encountered before in his years as a detective.

He was in love with her. Those shared moments aboard the Circle Line only helped to prove what his heart told him was true.

He had not dared bring up the subject, afraid of what she would think and how she would react. In his many years on the force, he had never once dated a member of any police department, well aware of how much the negative complications of such a situation outweighed the physical pleasures. Besides, Jennifer had let her feelings on the subject be known to him and they echoed his own unspoken concerns, so there seemed little point in pursuing the matter to even a point of discussion. But as he downed the last drops of his root beer, two circular pieces of ice melting on his tongue, Lo Manto knew he had fallen for a woman unlike any he had ever met in his life. He slowly shook his head and drummed his fingers on the red-coated table and smiled. The tough cop with the killer body and the spend-the-night eyes had stolen his heart. That alone was worth the trip to New York City and a showdown with a band of Camorra gunmen.

Giancarlo Lo Manto had found love on his way to a fight to the death.

Lo Manto walked past Fran's Beauty Salon, his head down, his ears tuned to every sound. He wore his thin leather jacket large and loose, hiding the two .38 Specials in his waist and the nine-millimeter jammed inside the back of his tight jeans. He moved with a quiet sense of purpose, casually checking the street traffic and the thin rows of pedestrians moving past. Lo Manto needed to sense that first bullet, feel its rush as it was fired, knowing that to do otherwise would hasten his demise.

The blue and white city bus skidded to a slow stop at the corner of East 233rd Street, one block south of where he was walking, two elderly women stepping off, their arms weighed down with paper bags and purses. The overhead sun was strong and hot, drawing thin lines of heat from the cracked pavement and split-tar road. The hum and cackle of air conditioners could be heard up and down White Plains Road, dripping water leaking down from the back of their motors, drying the instant it touched the hot cement below.

Lo Manto saw the shooter from the corner of his left eye. He was out in the street, across from him, partially hidden by a double-parked Deer Park water truck. He kept to his pace, waiting for the man to pull his gun, aware of all that was around him, the sounds of the day disappearing into the distance. In these moments, the scant seconds before the shooting began, all was reduced to silence. In the past, Lo Manto had always likened it to being in the middle of a silent movie, the action nothing more than a series of blurs and freeze-frames, all of it played out in a slow-motion frenzy.

John Rummy stepped away from the white Deer Park truck and pulled out one of his weapons. He planted his feet and took aim, standing in the middle of a busy intersection. He fired two shots at Lo Manto, the first smashing through the side window of a parked VW Beetle, the second pinging off the bottom end of a fire hydrant. Lo Manto pulled a .38 from his waist and crouched down behind a large blue mailbox. He glanced up and down the street, Rummy heading his way, treading through the crowded thoroughfare as if it were an empty wooded area and he was out alone on a hunt. Rummy rapid-fired as he moved, shots bouncing one after another off the tops and sides of the mailbox. Lo Manto kept his back braced against the now riddled box, waving pedestrians away from the area, knowing he needed to move clear before Rummy got any closer. He didn't figure him to be the main shooter, only the lead scout whose job it was to bring the cop out into the open, primed for the primary to take him down.

Lo Manto waited for the last volley to clear and then made his move. He ran from the mailbox toward a parked Chevy Impala nosed in tight on the far corner of East 234th Street. Rummy emptied one of his guns firing at Lo Manto, bullets cascading around the fleeing cop, shattering glass, setting off car alarms, whizzing past him at all angles, one near-miss taking out the rear tire of a parked van. Lo Manto jumped over the front end of the Impala, rolled to the ground, came up on one knee and fired three shots at the advancing hit man, none finding a mark. Rummy kept walking toward him, oblivious to all the activity around him, a middle-aged Terminator assigned one duty and determined to see it through to the end.

Lo Manto saw the second shooter, Elmo Stalli, come out of a vestibule in the middle of the street, walking up toward him, guns loaded and ready. He knew Stalli would try to get him into a crossfire match with Rummy, banking on there being enough firepower aimed his way that there was little else for the cop to do but catch a few bullets and die. He also figured the third gunman to be working from one of the nearby rooftops, high scope aimed down. The street above and below was clear, police sirens wailing in the distance, the two shooters closing in, guy on the roof taking aim, the fourth assassin still out there, hidden. Lo Manto looked across his shoulder at Rummy and then turned to glance at the approaching Stalli, who had yet to let off a shot. He needed to take out one of them and had to go by instinct on which was the deadlier shooter. Gaspaldi had penciled in Rummy to be the stalk horse. It was either a ploy by the old pimp to make Lo Manto think the shooter wasn't up to the top job or a sign that Stalli was indeed as good as all the indicators signaled. There really could only be one way for him to find out.

Lo Manto moved away from the Impala and ran toward Elmo Stalli.

Carlo Bertz watched the action taking place below with amusement, like seeing a video game brought to life and played out in real time. He slid a long, thin bullet into the rifle chamber and clicked it in place with one quick wrist snap. He brought the glass end of the black scope up to his right eye, shut his left, and pointed it down, squaring in on Lo Manto as he ran toward Stalli, firing off four rounds in his direction. The cop whirled, tossed aside one of his guns, and fired several shots at Rummy with the second, moving in a slow, rhythmic ballet, bullets careening off parked cars, past screaming bystanders, and through storefront windows. Bertz placed the index finger of his right hand on the trigger and zeroed in on his target.

He froze when he heard the woman's voice. "One of your bullets leaves your rifle," she said, "and three of mine will find a home somewhere in your back."

"The cop will be dead before I will," Bertz said. "I'll see to that."

"That's going to have to be enough to last you for all eternity," Jennifer Fabini said. "If that's what works for you, then take the shot."

Bertz moved his finger along the edge of the trigger, his eye still at the scope, Lo Manto well within the kill range, the shot sure to penetrate center mass. He lowered his left hand from the end of the rifle, resting the weapon on the edge of the roof, still holding aim. He reached into the front flap of his jacket pocket, trying to grab for the butt end of the nine-millimeter wedged to the right side of his rib cage. He moved his eye away from the rifle scope and peered down at the action. There was still plenty of time to kill both the woman behind him and the target six stories down. Carlo Bertz just hated to put a bullet into anyone without a fee. He dropped the rifle and turned to face Jennifer Fabini, the sun at her back and square on his face.

Lo Manto was in the middle of the street, ducking and dodging bullets, a gun in each hand, both arms extended. John Rummy was closing in on him from his right, Elmo Stalli rushed down from his left, moving in and out of a series of parked cars. Combined the trio had fired over forty rounds and not one slug had yet to find its way to flesh, fitting the pattern of most high-end multiple-person shootouts. Lo Manto knew that hitting any target on the run, with background noises and movements added to the mix, was often a matter of pure luck rather than skill. There was no chance to take a steady aim, to focus the shot, to bring any form of control to the situation. A firefight was nothing short of organized chaos played out across an urban landscape. The odds of a spent bullet finding its prey always worked out against the shooter.

Rummy was firing like a man on his last breath.

spraying a stream of gunfire toward Lo Manto, each bullet inching its way closer to his body. Stalli worked a much more patient game, firing off a single round as he moved from one car to the next, making his way to where he was now within solid striking distance. Lo Manto cast aside the second .38 Special and was down to the shells in his nine-millimeter, shooting his way from the center of the street into the gated entrance of a basement apartment, a row of tin garbage cans as a shield.

"Cover my back," Stalli shouted toward Rummy, still hunkered down behind the front end of a Buick Regal. "I'm going in to waste the bastard."

"He's cornered and good," Rummy shouted back. "He can't move in any deeper. We either close in on him or wait and see if he makes a fresh run."

"You get his attention and keep it," Stalli said, lowering his voice, gesturing with his hands. "I'll move on him from the right."

The garbage can landed between Rummy and Stalli with a hard thud. Rummy flinched and fired off two shots, more from instinct than need. Stalli stumbled backward and fell to the ground, eyes blinded by the sharp overhead sun. Lo Manto ran from the entrance of the basement apartment and jumped on the front hood of a Chevy Caprice, firing his nine-millimeter at Rummy, landing two bullets in the shooter's right leg. To his left, Stalli shook off the daze and lifted his gun hand to aim it at Lo Manto's back. The first shot missed.

The second landed with a sound as soft as a bursting bubble.

The bullet tore through Lo Manto's leather jacket, catching him at the top of his left shoulder, its force tossing him against the side of a thin, dying tree, down to one knee. He pointed the nine-millimeter at Stalli and fired the last three rounds in the clip. He heard the shooter give out a sharp grunt and knew that at least one had found its mark.

Lo Manto lay against the tree, blood running down the length of his arm, cascading onto the dry dirt foundation. He closed his eyes for a few seconds, knowing the two gunmen would soon be on him, ready to pounce and finish him off. Lo Manto took a deep breath, opened his eyes, and saw the shadow creep up from behind. He lifted his head, expecting to see one of the hitters, bleeding and ready to do what they had been paid to accomplish. Instead, he looked into the eyes of his greatest enemy.

"How bad are you hit?" Pete Rossi asked.

Mifo shifted the gears on the car and eased it out of its parking slot. He had sat through all the action and now figured it would be his best time to move against the wounded cop from Naples. He had a clear and open path down the street and across the intersection. Once there, he would veer the charged and heated Mustang to the left, jump the curb, and ram right into Lo Manto, leaning against a tree halfway down the street. He calculated the speed to run up to at least sixty miles per hour by point of impact. If that wasn't enough to kill him, it was more than enough to leave him damaged and unconscious, primed for the sniper's hits from the rooftop. Once he had made contact with Lo Manto, he would slice the car off the curb at the first open driveway, take it down the steep hill, and head for the Major Deegan Expressway and freedom. His plan was nothing if not foolproof.

Mifo shifted from first to second gear, closing in on the intersection. He gave the gas a harder push and jumped the speed to thirty as he crossed out onto White Plains Road. The lights were red on the two main stops, East 233rd Street and East 238th, which meant no traffic would be moving in either direction. He shifted into third and prepared to release the clutch.

He heard the UPS truck before he saw it.

It was coming down at him full speed, pistons burning, engine creaking, a streak of white smoke rushing out of the tailpipe. It crashed against the side of the Mustang with such violent force that it sent the car hurtling into a steel subway beam. The double crash brought the speeding car to a blinding halt, the front end folded like a child's discarded music box, brown smoke and low flames billowing from the exposed motor. Mifo sat behind the wheel, squeezed breathless by an inflated air bag, his right eye cut and bleeding, his nose broken. There was a thick shard of glass wedged into the right side of his neck. His pained head hung to the left, resting against a panel of crushed metal. His body was cold and began to twitch violently. His eyes were opened wide and filled with a mixture of tears and blood oozing out from seared vessels.

The man behind the wheel of the brown UPS truck stepped down from the driver's seat and walked over to Mifo's smoldering Mustang. He peered down through the smoke, ignored the wail of the sirens and the squealing tires coming at him from all sides, and locked eyes with the dying assassin. "It'll be over for you in a few minutes," Sal Fabini assured him. "But you've probably been on the other end of enough of these to know that on your own."

"That was no accident," Mifo said. "And you're no UPS man. I've been on the other end of enough of these to know that, too."

"I would have preferred to shoot it out with you," Sal said. "But it's not the way you like to do business. So I figured I'd come at you in a way that would be familiar."

"How much did it cost them?" Mifo asked. "How much did they pay you to take me out?"

"Not a penny," Sal said. "Tell you the truth, I'm out of pocket on this deal. I got the UPS truck from a friend but he didn't know what I was going to do with it. From the looks of the damage, I'd say I'm facing a six-grand tab at the very minimum. But then again, it's going to be all on you."

"What the hell are you talking about?" Mifo spit out blood now running down the sides of his mouth, mixing with bubbly white foam.

"You ran a stop sign back at the corner," Sal Fabini said with a nod of his head. "Last time I checked, that's against the law."

He stared at Mifo for a few quiet minutes, watching as the life ebbed out of the killer's body. Then Sal Fabini turned and walked, heading toward the subway stairs and the ride that would eventually lead back to his home.

The last job of his police career was at an end.

Elmo Stalli and John Rummy were now both on their feet, four car lengths away from Lo Manto, Pete Rossi still by his side. Stalli aimed a .38 Special directly at the cop and was primed to pull the trigger. Rossi looked at Lo Manto and then over his shoulder at Rummy. "You have any ammo left?" he asked the cop.

"I'm empty," Lo Manto said. "And if it's all the same, I'd rather you take me out than leave it to one of your shooters. We both have earned the right to make that demand."

Pete Rossi smiled down at the bleeding detective and then pulled a nine-millimeter from his waist, pointed it away from Lo Manto, and fired two shots across the trunk of a battered car at a surprised Elmo Stalli. The first clipped the shooter in the ribs. The second left a small hole in the center of his right cheek and sent him falling flat to the ground, jammed between the bumpers of two parked cars, dead. Rossi turned and veered toward Rummy, crouching down, looking for the shooter who had now ducked inside a tenement vestibule. "Get behind one of the cars," he said to Lo Manto. "And stay low."

"What the hell are you doing?" Lo Manto asked.

"Shut up and do what I tell you," Rossi said. "Before I really do put another bullet in you."

Lo Manto pushed away from the thin tree and crawled toward the street, a short distance from the shooting, dragging his damaged right arm, leaving behind a thick blood trail. He rested his back against the curved edge of a wide rim and glanced up, watching Rossi and Rummy circle each other as if they were two gunslingers settling an Old West vendetta. The very fact they had their guns drawn indicated that none of the shooters knew Rossi on sight. The negotiations, the deal itself, and the cash payouts would have been handled outside his line of vision, probably by Gaspaldi the pimp. That all fit neatly together and made sense.

Pete Rossi's presence did not.

Lo Manto peered over at him, watching him stride close enough to Rummy to take the hitter, his instincts dictating which way he turned, his movements slow and in control, like a gray cat walking after midnight. Rummy may have been the one in the battle paid to kill. Pete Rossi was the one who had been taught the bloody art by the masters of the trade.

Lo Manto sat back against the car, checked out the police action about half a mile away, smoke billowing from a crushed car and a stalled UPS truck, and knew the uniforms would be on them in a few minutes, unless Captain Fernandez could hold them back and let the drama play itself out. There were still two shooters out there to be handled besides Rummy, plus Rossi, and at this point, anyone else with a gun ready to join the fray. And he was out of bullets. For the first time in his police life, Lo Manto had lost control of the plan of action.

"I figured you could use this," Felipe said.

The boy had scurried next to him, moving low from one car to the next, a loaded .38 in his right hand. Lo Manto turned, took the gun from the boy, and stared at him with hard eyes. "You can never have enough guns or bullets in a fight like this," Felipe said.

"This is a cop's gun," Lo Manto said, gripping the .38, finger fast to the trigger.

"That's why I'm giving it to you," Felipe said. "You're a cop."

"I told you I wanted you to stay with Blind Moe," Lo Manto said. "What part of that was confusing to you?"

"And I did like you told me," Felipe said. "I never left him. He boogied out on me."

"He say why?"

"Told me that him and that foaming brown bear he likes to call a dog hadn't been on a subway in a while and were going to go for a ride," Felipe said. "And that I was free to do as I pleased. Stay in his office or maybe catch a train up to the Bronx and see how you were holding up."

"And the gun?"

"Technically, it's not theft," Felipe said. "Blind Moe left it on the kitchen table. A note next to it had your name written on it. What would you have done?"

The two shots came at them from the elevated subway station to their right. They both missed their mark and shattered glass. Lo Manto dove over to Felipe and shoved him under the chassis of a parked car. "You only move if this car catches fire," he said to the boy.

Lo Manto got to his knees and jumped over the front end of the car, ignoring the pain shooting down his gun arm. He stood alongside Rossi, both men, now united, squaring off against Rummy. "You going to take this guy out or just teasing?" he asked Rossi.

"I don't think I called for help," Rossi said, his eyes and gun trained on the shooter crouched down across from them. "And if I did, it wouldn't have been for you."

"Right now, I'm all you got," Lo Manto said. "So, let's finish this so we can get down to the real fight. The one between you and me. It's what we both want and have both waited a long time to see. Today's that day."

"Fine by me, cop," Rossi said.

Rossi turned away from Lo Manto and walked fearlessly toward the shooter. Rummy fired two shots at close range, one skinning Rossi's upper thigh, the flesh wound drawing blood and tearing through the crease of his pants. The other went wide, lost in the dry wind of a bloody summer morning. Rossi emptied his gun in Rummy's direction, bullets clipping the wood in the vestibule, sharp chunks flying in the air, small circles of dust clouding the area between them. One bullet caught the already wounded Rummy in the shoulder and its force sent him out into the open, his back to a glass-paneled door. The next three landed square in his chest, each bullet tearing through a great artery and ripping the last breaths from his body. John Rummy went crashing through the glass, chips and large slivers raining down to the ground. One large chunk tore into the dead man's back.

Rossi walked over to the gunman, blood gushing from every open wound, and pumped a final bullet into the man's forehead. He gazed down at him for several seconds, tossed out the empty clip, jammed in a fresh one and turned to face off with his brother, Lo Manto.

Jennifer was thrown against the steel door leading down the tenement stairwell. Carlo Bertz reached over, grabbed her by the hair, and tossed her to the ground. Her right hand was coated red with blood, the result of a quick exchange between her .38 Special and the roof-top shooter's hidden nine-millimeter. Jennifer's bullet had splintered the bone in Bertz's gun elbow and the blood from the wound dripped down on her jeans and the soft tar ground. "You have cost me money," Bertz said to her, his words inflamed by hate and frustration. "And that will cost you your life."

The gun was four feet to the right of Bertz, its dark barrel gleaming in the sunshine. Jennifer lay flat on her back, legs out, arms by her side. They were in the middle of the roof, both bleeding and sweating heavily, both knowing that one of them was seconds removed from death. They could hear the sirens coming at them from below, smelled the smoke, absorbed the heavy gunfire, each anxious to get into the bigger game being played out six stories away. Bertz nodded and turned for the fallen nine-millimeter. Jennifer jumped to her feet, ran toward Bertz, pushed him off stride, sending him to the ground. She ran to the edge of the roof and picked up the cocked and ready high-powered rifle. Gripping it with both hands, her trigger finger drenched with blood, she aimed it at Bertz. He kept his eyes on Jennifer, ignoring the rifle aimed at his chest. "That is not a child's weapon," he said to her in a deliberate tone. "The force from the trigger pull will be enough to send you over the roof. I suggest you put it down. I promise to make you a painless kill."

"I'll go over, but not before I see you go down," Jennifer said, her hand throbbing, a sharp, hot pain running from the open wound up the length of her arm, intense enough to make her eyes tear.

"It ends then as it should," Bertz said. "Each of us down to a final shot. In my way of life, it is the ultimate dream exit."

Bertz jumped for the gun, did a double roll along the tar roof and came up firing, his single blast grazing past Jennifer and looping off a thick row of black tiles, sending them hurtling to the ground. Jennifer didn't flinch, pressed down on the rifle trigger, and braced herself for the recoil. The shock of the pull sent her reeling, rifle dropping from her hands, her upper body leaning over the edge of the roof. She reached for an iron rail sticking out of the base, held it tight enough to break the skin on her hand, her eyes gazing up at a clear blue sky, the sounds of the gunfire below filling her ears. With a slow and steady effort, she pulled herself back to her feet, dazed and shaken. She looked across the roof and saw Carlo Bertz lying down flat on his side, his eyes and mouth open. There was a small hole just below his neck bone, blood flowing out of it as if from a small fountain, his right hand pressed against it. She walked toward him, the blood still running down her right hand, picked up her .38 Special, and headed toward the door leading off the roof. She glanced at Bertz one final time.

"It's nice when your dreams can come true," she said, disappearing into the small, dark hallway.

Gaspaldi stood in the foyer of a building on the corner of East 234th Street, watching as the action unfolded. The police had blocked off both ends of the street, their sharpshooters crouching behind the cover of their parked cars, one man, a captain, controlling and co-ordinating their every move. Gaspaldi had seen his master plan to bring down the cop from Naples blown to shreds, ignited by Lo Manto's strategic countermoves and the stunning and unexpected presence of Pete

Rossi. He put a match to the tobacco end of a French cigarette, took a deep inhale, and wondered which of the two men he should aim to kill first—the cop who wanted him dead or the don who had betrayed his cause. Three of his shooters were spread out across two streets, dead. The sniper shots came from the subway station, not the roof, which meant there was either a cop moving without orders or another hitter in play. Either way, it didn't much matter. Gaspaldi needed to do what he should have done from the very start.

It would be the pimp who would bring an end to the cop's run.

Gregory Flash Randell had reloaded his rifle and was staring down at Lo Manto. Pete Rossi was on the other end of a parked car, gun in hand, walking toward the badge. He didn't know why he was there and frankly, to Randell at least, the reasons didn't matter. If Rossi had done a flip, that was Camorra business and would be handled by them in their own way. But if Lo Manto took a fatal bullet, then someone in the crime family would still pay top dollar for his body and that was cash destined for Randell's pockets. He clicked the bullet into the chamber and aimed down at the street, the eye scope squaring in on Lo Manto's upper torso. Randell shifted the muscles in both his shoulders and took a deep breath, primed to take out one more life, this one the most lucrative shot of his long career.

The English bulldog sank his jaw into the lower half

of Randell's ankle and stabbed his teeth around white flesh and thick bone. The shock of the bite forced the shooter to snap his body back, the rifle falling to the ground, his pants leg drenched with blood, the dog holding on to the ankle as if he were locked to it. Randell looked up and saw an elderly black man walking with a cane, wraparound shades hiding his eyes. "I'm going to kill your dog, blind man," Randell shouted. "You won't see it, but you'll hear it. That I promise."

"He's just a puppy," Blind Moe Ravini said, walking closer, each step carefully measured. "He don't really mean much harm. Just looking to play some. Only reason he bit down was because you were doing something he didn't care for. I don't know what that would be, but I'm sure it was valid."

Randell started raining down fists on the dog's head, each glancing blow jarring the bulldog, loosening his grip on the hitter. He was throwing punches with both hands, the dog's growl turning to a whimper. He didn't even notice Blind Moe Ravini standing over the two of them. "I hate it when anyone gets violent with an animal," Blind Moe said in a hushed voice. "Goes against my very nature."

Randell looked up at Blind Moe, his free leg kicking at the dog's rib cage. "Like I give a shit," he yelled. "By the time I walk off this platform, there's going to be two black bastards laying here dead."

Blind Moe Ravini lifted his face to the warmth of the sun and took in a deep breath. "I guess then it's on me

469

to make sure you never get the chance to walk off this platform," he said.

Blind Moe snapped his cane against the hard ground. The bottom half of the walking stick broke in two, exposing a thin twelve-inch blade, serrated and sharp as the crease on a designer suit. Blind Moe took two steps forward and rammed the blade into Gregory Flash Randell's chest. He held it there, twisting it, listening to the gurgles coming out of the shooter's mouth, ignoring the cut and bleeding hands Randell had wrapped around the cane, trying with all the strength he had left to pull the blade free. The old bookie stood his ground, his thin fingers gently rotating the walking cane, each twist causing the blade to carve through more tissue. He felt Randell's body slump to the side, his hands letting loose their grip. He gave the blade one final twist and then yanked it free. With a flip of his wrist, he snapped it back in place, the blade once again safely hidden within the white shell of the walking cane.

"Let's go, Little Moe," Blind Moe said to his shaky English bulldog, weakened by the blows but not defeated. "Our train's coming into the station."

Lo Manto and Rossi stood five feet from each other, each with a gun in his right hand, both bleeding, sweat streaking their faces. "Looks like it's just you and me," Rossi said, glancing at the dead bodies around them.

"And about three dozen cops," Lo Manto said, nudging his head toward the corner half a street away.

"Just waiting to get a jump on both of us."

"They'll only move on your say-so," Rossi said. "Not like them to go up against one of their own. No matter what country he lives in."

"I don't know why you did what you did," Lo Manto said. "I'm sure you had your reasons. But I came here to end this between us and I'm not going back until I do."

"It's been a long fight," Rossi said, "and we both gave as good as we got. You're right that it should end now. Right here, where it started. Down to just you and me."

"This one is for my father," Lo Manto said, slowly raising his gun to waist level.

"For mine, too," Rossi said, the nine-millimeter held away from his body, his finger on the trigger.

"Lo Manto!" It was Felipe shouting from under the car, half his body on the sidewalk, his eyes staring out at Gaspaldi sneaking down on the cop and the gangster. The pimp fired off the six rounds in his gun, tossing his last set of dice on a final roll. Pete Rossi moved first, standing between Gaspaldi and Lo Manto, his nine-millimeter aimed at the man who for the last fifteen years had worked under his reign. The bullets caught Rossi in the center of his back, buckling his knees, dropping him forward into Lo Manto's arms. The cop from Naples reached out for his most bitter enemy, held him close to his chest, reached over one shoulder, and aimed his .38 at Gaspaldi. With his left hand, Lo Manto grabbed Rossi's gun arm and pointed the nine-millimeter at the pimp.

"Take him out," Rossi whispered to Lo Manto.

"We both will," Lo Manto said.

He squeezed down on the .38 Special at the same time that Rossi used his sapping strength to pull the trigger on his own gun. The bullets from both caught Gaspaldi in the chest, neck, arm, and face. He landed with a loud thud against the brown brick façade of a tenement building and crumpled to the steps next to it. Lo Manto tossed aside his gun, bent to his knee, and brought Rossi down with him, holding the wounded man in his arms.

"Why?" Lo Manto asked him in hushed tones. "Why did you do this?"

"It's what my mother would have wanted," Pete Rossi, the most powerful Camorra don in the world, answered.

24

Lo Manto sat on a soft plastic chair facing the hospital bed. His right arm was heavily bandaged and resting in a sling. It ached whenever he moved. He was dressed in jeans and a thin dark shirt, his handsome face marked with a bruise along his left eye and a long cut on his chin. He looked over at Pete Rossi, asleep on the bed, the sheet folded up to his waist. A series of small tubes and needles ran from clear liquid bags hanging on silver hooks into his hands and arms. His breath came in slow spurts, his chest and back wrapped in rows of gauze, old blood drying in circular patterns. His forehead was wet with cold sweat and his face flaunted a two-day growth. His wife and children were waiting outside the large private room on the third floor of the hospital wing, along with several armed bodyguards.

Lo Manto poured some cold water on a small hand towel and dabbed at Rossi's head. The don opened his eyes and smiled up at him. "I usually like my nurses in tight white outfits," he said, his words coming out slowly

473

and embedded with pain. "Not used to getting wiped down by a cop."

"This is a new place for me, too," Lo Manto said. "And I'm not very good at it."

"What's she like?" Rossi asked.

"Who?" Lo Manto asked.

"Our mother," Rossi said. "I don't even have a picture. Never even got a chance to see what she looked like."

Lo Manto put down the hand towel, resting it on a countertop behind him. He reached into his shirt pocket and handed Rossi a photo. "It's for you," he said. "It was taken about three, four weeks ago. I don't have a lot of photos of her. She hates having any taken."

Rossi lifted the picture and stared at it for several minutes. "That's one thing she had in common with the old don," he said. "He'd rather set his own leg on fire than stand in front of a camera."

"I wish she were here with us," Lo Manto said. "For you to meet and get to know. She's a good mother, stubborn, tough, demands to have it all her own way. Most of the time, she gets it."

"It had to be rough for her," Rossi said. "Knowing the truth and never saying a word about it. You need strength and courage to do what she did. I respect her for that."

"I wish she didn't have to be put in that position," Lo Manto said. "Wish she could have had a full life with her children. *All* her children."

"There's nobody to blame," Rossi said. "Her husband was who he was and my father was a crime boss. Neither one could go against that, even if they wanted to try."

"I'll keep an eye on your kids for you, if you like," Lo Manto said.

"That'd be nice," Rossi said. "Be good for them to know they have an uncle who cares. Even if he is a cop."

"Is there anything you need?" Lo Manto asked, sitting on the edge of the bed, gazing down at his brother. "Anything you want me to do?"

"Just one thing," Rossi said, his voice starting to slip away. "You can say no to it and I'd understand."

"What is it?" Lo Manto asked.

"Stay with me until I die," Rossi said.

Lo Manto moved in closer to the wounded man and reached for his hands, clutching them in his, their fingers locking. "That's the least I can do for my little brother," Lo Manto said, his voice breaking, eyes welling with tears.

Rossi stared at him and nodded. "You would have made a great don," he said.

"And you would have made a great cop," Lo Manto said.

Lo Manto held the hands tighter and watched Pete Rossi's final breaths rumble through his ruined chest, his eyes shut, his body at rest. He laid his head at the edge of the pillow and cried over the body of his only brother.

A brother he had only known as an enemy.

25

Lo Manto and Jennifer walked along the quiet grounds of Woodlawn Cemetery, rows of headstones on both sides of the path dotting the beautifully landscaped property in the East Bronx.

Jennifer walked with a slight limp, favoring her left leg. Her right hand was in a cast up to her elbow, the arms of her leather jacket fitting snugly around it. They had just left Pete Rossi's funeral, the only two detectives in a crowded field of Camorristas. "It's odd, isn't it?" Lo Manto said. "A few days ago I would have exchanged gunfire with anyone in that party. Instead, now we stood there together all with tears in our eyes. As if we were all one big family."

"He *was* family to you," she said. "It's just that neither of you had the time to figure it out."

"How did you figure it out?" Lo Manto asked.

"More a hunch than anything else," Jennifer said. "And I only went looking for a connection. I never counted on coming back home with what I did."

"Why'd you go to him and not me?" he asked.

"I wasn't sure how you'd react," she said. "More likely than not, you would have hauled in headfirst against him, looking for all sorts of answers to any number of questions. With him, it was just about letting him know he had a mother and who she was. That seemed the easier of the two ways to go."

"I'm glad you did," Lo Manto said in a low voice. "I came here looking for closure on my father's murder. I go back with a whole other kind of closure. One I never thought I'd ever have to find."

"What are you going to tell your mother when you see her?" Jennifer asked.

"Not much," Lo Manto said. "I think I'll sit in the garden with her, put my arm around her shoulders, and let her take it from there. She wants to talk about it or she wants to keep it quiet, it's all up to her. She's more than earned that right."

"Are you just about ready to leave?" Jennifer asked. They were walking past a row of large, imposing mausoleums, most built at the turn of the century.

"It's down to a few days," Lo Manto said. "Captain Fernandez cleared a lot of the hurdles for the shootings. Not that anybody's going to complain too much, not with us taking five prime-time shooters off the page."

"He kept the link between you and Rossi out of the papers," Jennifer said. "And the police reports."

"He's a good friend," Lo Manto said.

"You seem to have quite a few of them," she said. "They really came through big-time on this one."

"Your father didn't do too bad for himself, either," Lo Manto said. "I always heard he was one of the greats. It was nice to be able to see it firsthand."

"Do you have any plans?" Jennifer asked. "I don't mean for when you go back. More like for dinner tonight."

Lo Manto looked over at her and smiled. "No, not really," he said. "Though a nice Italian dinner might do us both a lot of good."

"I was thinking more like sushi," Jennifer said. "There's this place I like on the East Side, makes a wicked salmon skin hand roll. It'd be my treat."

Lo Manto stopped and stared at Jennifer, the sun at her back, her face bright, clear, and beautiful. "Our work together is finished," he said to her. "You don't have to baby-sit me anymore."

"I know," she said. "It has nothing to do with business. We're both off duty."

"Does that make it a date?" Lo Manto said.

Jennifer moved down a narrow path, past a row of headstones, all surrounded by a thick field of elm trees. "Let's get you past the tekka maki and spicy tuna roll first," she said. "Then we'll decide what we'll make it."

"It's your call, Detective," Lo Manto said. "I'll just be there as backup. You decide where it goes and how it ends."

*

478

Lo Manto stared down at Jennifer, asleep in the crook of his left arm. He gently moved aside several strands of her hair and ran his fingers along her face and neck, her skin soft and warm to the touch. He kissed her forehead and held her closer to him, at peace in the soothing comfort of her presence.

He leaned back, his head resting on the center of a thick pillow, and closed his eyes. Outside the apartment window, he could hear the city slowly come awake, early risers running for exercise, men in suits rushing for crowded buses, kids giggling as they made their way to the start of day camp. But inside, under the warm sheets of the four-poster bed, all seemed frozen in place and Lo Manto knew for the very first time in his life what it meant to be in love.

Jennifer had sat across from Lo Manto, ordering all the different types of sushi she thought he needed to at least try, laughing as she watched him struggle with chopsticks and bravely chew on anything she put on his plate, quick to wash it down with long gulps of cold beer. "In Naples, the only fish we eat raw are clams and mussels," he told her. "And even there, we're very careful."

"There was a beat cop in my precinct," Jennifer told him. "Needed to lose sixty pounds or risk having a stroke. He went on a sushi diet and worked out every day. Three months later, he lost all the weight, got himself a new wardrobe, and even had plugs put in his head. He's like a new man."

479

"I like my clothes," Lo Manto said to her, a smile spread across his face. "And I have my own hair, and my mother thinks I need to gain weight, not lose it. So why am I eating all this raw fish?"

"Because you love me," Jennifer said, reaching a hand across the table and taking one of his. "And you want to make me happy."

"And don't forget, you're also paying for the meal," Lo Manto said, softly rubbing her fingers.

They walked and talked deep into the night, letting the lights of the city serve as their guide. Lo Manto held her close to him, her head at rest on his still damaged shoulder, her words soothing, allowing him to release the grip he had learned to keep on his emotions, free at last to feel the power of a woman's love. He had never felt more comfortable and trusting in someone else's presence as he did when he held Jennifer Fabini in his arms. "I didn't know there would ever be anyone like you," he told her as they approached her apartment building. "I didn't think women like you existed, or, if they did, that I would ever get to meet one. I don't know what happens to us from here, but I know I always will want you in my life."

"I guess that means you're coming upstairs," she said.

"That was my best shot," he said.

"I'm okay with it," Jennifer said, smiling and reaching for her keys. "But I'd keep an eye out for Milo. I don't know how this is going to sit with him."

"I'll try not to wake him," Lo Manto said. "Then, in

the morning, over coffee and a saucer of milk, we'll have a heart-to-heart. Talk it out man to cat."

"Sounds like a plan," she said, opening the door to the foyer. "But I warn you, he's not too chatty in the morning."

"Good," Lo Manto said. "I like him already."

They fell in a heap onto her bed, shedding clothes as if they were on fire, releasing the grip they had both kept on their passion for so long, across so many empty and often violent nights, free at last to love and be loved. Afterward, they fell into a deep and exhausted sleep, arms gripped tightly around each other, breathing and moving as one, both having found the missing piece to the puzzle that was their lives.

And when they woke, both Jennifer Fabini and Giancarlo Lo Manto knew they would be in each other's life forever.

EPILOGUE

Lo Manto sat on a lounge chair near gate 44A at John F. Kennedy International Airport, waiting for a seven-forty night flight to Italy to begin boarding. His niece, Paula, sat next to him, her head buried in an Andrea Camilleri novel, a stuffed backpack jammed next to her feet. "Are you happy to be going home?" he asked her.

"It's been an interesting summer, *Zio*," she said. "But it will be nice to see the family again. Work with *Nonna* in her garden. Be with my friends."

"And school is just a few weeks away," he said. "That should keep you plenty busy."

"How much do you want me to tell my parents?" she asked. "About what happened?"

"Whatever makes you feel comfortable," he said. "And on your own time. It's not something you should be forced into doing."

"What do they know?"

"That you were never in any danger," Lo Manto said.

"That the man who took you didn't mean you any harm."

"What has *Nonna* been told?" she asked.

"Pretty much the same," Lo Manto said. "She just knows more than the others. It will be easier for her to put the pieces together."

"Has it changed, the way you feel about her?" Paula asked.

"Yes, it has," her uncle said. "It's made me love her even more."

"I guess you had no plans to say good-bye," Jennifer Fabini said. She stood above him, Felipe next to her, his arms filled with magazines and candy bars.

"I thought I did," Lo Manto said. He stood and reached out for her hand and held it, glancing at Felipe and his haul. "But I'm happy to see you all the same."

"I'm actually here on a police matter," she said, her warm eyes betraying the harsh tone of her words.

"Let's hear it," Lo Manto said.

Jennifer reached into the right rear pocket of her jeans and pulled out a boarding pass and a passport. "This ticket and passport is made out to Felipe," she said. "Both of them courtesy of the New York Police Department. It's good for a three-week visit, then he has to haul ass back here to start school."

Lo Manto nodded. "I don't suppose he has a place to stay?" he asked.

"He's got no home here," she said. "What are the odds he has one in Italy?"

"Did you pay for any of those magazines and candies?" he asked the boy. "And tell me the truth."

"No," Felipe said. "I lifted them when the lady cop was in the bathroom. She's not on me as much as you are."

"She doesn't know you as well," Lo Manto said, smiling. He pointed to the girl next to him. "This is my niece, Paula. They just called our flight. The two of you get on the plane and try not to steal anything on the way there. I'll just be a few minutes."

The two teens nodded at each other awkwardly and walked together toward the open gate of Flight 614 direct to Rome. Lo Manto and Jennifer stood close to each other, watching them hand their tickets and passports to an airline representative. "She might teach him how to speak Italian," she said. "He's a smart kid, he might pick up a lot in a few weeks."

"And he might teach her to steal and not get caught," Lo Manto said with a smile. "Life lessons learned on both ends."

"You going right back to work, or you going to take some time?" she asked, standing close enough to smell the rich Italian cologne he wore. It was the same as that worn by his brother, Pete Rossi.

"I have a month," he said. "I thought I'd spend a week of it with my mother, help her sort out whatever she wants to touch. Then, if my luck holds, I'll finally get a crack at that Capri vacation. Nothing but good food, great beaches, and a lot of sun."

"I've never been to Capri," Jennifer said, staring into

Lo Manto's eyes. "Is it as beautiful as everyone says?"

"It's the people on the island who make it beautiful," Lo Manto said, his right hand brushing against the side of Jennifer's arm. "You should see for yourself and then decide. You're not the type of woman who makes up her mind based on what everyone else says about a place or a person."

"I have three weeks' vacation due me," Jennifer said. "The captain said I could take them any time I want."

"Then you should take them," Lo Manto said. "Go someplace warm. A place with great food, a hot sun, and long white beaches. A place like Capri. You think you'll be able to find it okay? It's pretty far away."

"I'll find it," Jennifer said. "I'm a cop. It's what I do. Remember?"

"You're a great cop," Lo Manto said. He picked up his gray leather duffel bag and moved toward the check-in counter. "The best I've ever known."

"Have a safe flight, Gianni," she said, giving him a slight wave. "And try not to get shot for a while. It might do you some good."

"I'll see you on the beach, Detective," he said to her as he turned away. "I'll keep a chair waiting and the wine chilled."

Giancarlo Lo Manto handed a dark-haired woman in a blue starched suit his boarding pass and then quietly disappeared down the walkway of flight 614.

The cop from Naples was going back home.

**POCKET
BOOKS**

Also by Lorenzo Carcaterra
GANGSTER

Ever since his best-selling *Sleepers*, Lorenzo Carcaterra
has told tales of Italian-Americans. Now, in this huge
story, he travels from the days of godfathers and
goodfellas to our own world of suburban Sopranos.
Gangster is an epic, compassionate portrait of one man's
fight against his fate – and the narrative of a family, a city
and a century.

Born into violence and raised in the shadow of a
shocking secret, young Angelo Vestieri chose to flee both
his Italian past and his father, and build a new life in early
20th-century New York. Through his bloody rise from
soldier to mob boss he deals in further betrayals – in his
brutal business, in friendship and in love – while coming
to understand loyalty and the virtues of relationships.

As he grows older, Angelo takes Gabe, an abandoned
boy, under his wing, and teaches him everything he
knows. Finally, he will learn which is stronger – the love
he has for the boy he cherishes, or the need to be a gangster and live by the savage rules he helped to create.

PRICE £6.99
ISBN 0 7434 1602 3

POCKET BOOKS

Lorenzo Carcaterra

STREET BOYS

Naples, late September, 1943. The war in Europe is almost won. Italy is leaderless; Mussolini already arrested by anti-fascists. The city has been evacuated, but the German army is moving towards Naples to finish the job. Their chilling instructions are: if the city can't belong to Hitler, it will belong to no one.

No one but the children. Orphaned or hidden by parents, abandoned or lost, some as young as ten years old, the children of Naples resist. Aided by a lone Allied soldier, cut off from the regiment, and armed with just a handful of guns, unexploded bombs and their own ingenuity, the street boys are determined to take on the advancing enemy and save the city – or die trying.

PRICE £6.99
ISBN 0 7434 5027 2

**POCKET
BOOKS**

These Lorenzo Carcaterra titles are avilable from your bookshop
or can be ordered direct from the publisher.

0 7434 9574 8	**Paradise City**	£6.99
0 7434 5027 2	**Street Boys**	£6.99
0 7434 1602 3	**Gangster**	£6.99

Please send cheque or postal order for the value
of the book, **free postage and packing within
the UK**, to SIMON & SCHUSTER CASH SALES
PO Box 29, Douglas, Isle of Man, IM99 1BQ
Tel: 01624 677237, Fax: 01624 670923
E-mail: bookshop@enterprise.net
www.bookpost.co.uk

Please allow 14 days for delivery. Prices and availability subject
to change without notice.